THE SACRED SEAL

a novel

pat mcgauley

a shamrock book

The Sacred Seal

Published by PJM Publishing
2808 Fifth Avenue West
Hibbing, Minnesota 55746

Author's website: ***www.patmcgauley.com***

Library of Congress (EPCN) number (pending)
ISBN: 978-0-692-53627-8

First Edition: November 2015

Shamrock Books from PJM are published by Bang Printing in the USA.
Cover art design by Renee Anderson, Express Print One, Ltd, Hibbing, MN.

Dedication:

My treasures are my three children.

My prayers along with every word in this story go out to you and to your children.

Acknowledgements:

I've said it many times, but Lennon and McCartney coined the lyrics and put the words to music… *"we get by with a little help from our friends…"* Among my many blessings are those I call my friends. My new story, like all the others, needed other eyes and other voices in order to become the pages you are about to read. I am especially indebted to Rich Dinter and Jim Huber for the hours they spent reviewing 'The Seal' and for their insightful critique of the plot lines and the characters. As she has done many times before, Gail Nevalainen did the preliminary editing, and Steve Koskovich reviewed the final manuscript before I sent this story off to the publishers.

Also, I would be remiss if I didn't thank you, my readers. You have always been my inspiration; especially when the writing hours become weary and the rewrites become tedious. Enjoy this new Father Mickey Moran story along with me.

I recognize the badge of my office as a symbol of public faith, and I accept it as a public trust to be held as long as I am true to the ethics of the police service. I will continually strive to achive these objectives and ideals dedicating myself before God to my chosen profession of law enforcement. I will obey the rules and regulations of this department—the orders of my superior officers—and strive to maintain a spirit of teamwork and cooperation with my fellow officers.

City of Duluth 'Oath of Office'

Friday August 22, 2014

1/ HILLSIDE

Adam Trygg was apprehensive. Part of the young cop's uneasiness was rooted in being alone; another part was that of a rookie's green inexperience. What if something happened? Something like the incident that occured two weeks before when a young UMD student was stabbed on a busy Duluth corner just after the bar closings? That was also on a Friday night. What if? If anything like that happened again he'd have to figure out what to do, and how to go about doing it, without his veteran partner. Brenden Murphy had taken a day off to attend a relative's funeral in St. Paul; leaving Adam to patrol the volatile neighborhood by himself for the first time. Another part of his nervousness was the streets where he was assigned to 'protect and serve', as the police code of conduct mandated.

Murphy. How fortunate Adam had been to have Murf as his mentor these past several months. Murphy knew the Hillside area better than anybody on the force. Adam smiled as he turned off Lake Street and headed toward Mesaba Avenue: what a guy he thought to himself! Not only had Adam learned the ropes from Murphy, he learned more about life in general than he had from anybody, but possibly, his own father—a droll man, so unlike Murf that any comparisons were impossible. The Irish cop was a worldly man with a sense of humor that laughed at life, and at being a cop as well. His easy humor and colorful stories could make a long shift pass like freeway traffic. And, Murf had seen parts of the world that Adam could only dream about; stories that made him feel green with envy. Adam had never been further from Minnesota than Chicago.

Only last week Murf shared what he had learned about the 'lost boys' of Darfur, in northern Africa, from one of the children who had escaped the Moslem raiders that pillaged their village. Murf had met the young man at a cultural symposium held at Macalaster College the previous spring. Adam had never heard of the lost boys before. "In the murderous plundering the boy (Asrat was his name) witnessed his father's beheading and the rape of both his mother and sister," Murf told him. Asrat's three-hundred mile trek to a refugee camp in Kenya was harrowing, and Murf told Adam the boy's startling story with every graphic detail imaginable. The day before, Murf talked about the Mount Vesuvius volcano and the ruins of Pompeii where thousands of people had died in an avalanche of lava. He and his wife had visited the Campania region of southern Italy two summers ago and were planning a trip to Greece in the near future.

Adam reflected on the concept of 'lost boys' as he turned back to retrace his earlier route. Central Hillside was a volatile neighborhood with every variety of unfortunate imaginable. Recent years had witnessed an influx of lost youth from Chicago and the Twin Cities—kids with histories of gang activity and drugs. The violent lives they left behind became the hostility they brought along with them to Hillside. Lately heroin and meth were as easy to buy as a pack of cigarettes, and there were more guns on the street than a city the size of Duluth should ever have to deal with. And, wherever there were drugs and addicts and gangs there was a spike in burglary, robbery, and violence of every shape and color—prostitution was a willing companion of drugs. Underlying all of these activities were high unemployment, widespread poverty, and every social malaise that characterized inner city life.

But, Murf knew the denizens of Hillside and had a compassionate way of relating to them. There had always been a mutual respect between Murf and the troubled kids, the derelects, and the'down and outers'— but that was changing dramatically as the neighborhood deteriorated. An unfounded racial-profiling complaint against Murf, months ago, had left him bitter and withdrawn for days. "I'm getting too damn old for this shit," he confided to Adam. "In three years I can hang it all up. Yep, that'll give me my twenty-five and I can hang it up with a little pension. Then it's gonna be all yours."

Young Adam Trygg had been fortunate so far this Friday afternoon. With six hours in and six to go his shift had so fare been relatively uneventful: a fender-bender on First and Superior Streets at 4:12 took nearly an hour of his time; a domestic episode at 5:22 in the Lakeview Apartment building took another hour to resolve; a drunk and disorderly at Rascal's Bar on Superior Street at 7:40 meant a trip to the downtown jail; and two minor traffic citations between the bar incident and now…his dashboard clock winked 10:38. The uneventful block of time he now experienced was disquieting…a part of him wanted something to happen—but, not something serious. He was alone after all and felt vulnerable. Adam remembered Murf's caution: 'be wary of the lull before a storm'.

Deprived of his partner's sage advice and good humor, Adam found himself slipping into conversations with himself, even humming a tune that he heard on the radio while driving to work days before. The lyrics of Willie's classic, *'Mama don't let your babies grow up to be cowboys…'* was a melody that he couldn't seem to shake. Why was that? For the past two days he couldn't get the song out of his mind. He laughed at himself, his terrible singing was a way of relaxing and letting go of the stress of expectation. *'Let them be doctors and lawyers and such…'*

Lawyers. Adam's father was a successful attorney—Trygg and Associates— in St. Paul. Adam's two younger brothers had joined the firm but he had chosen the army (and a stint in Iraq) followed by a Criminal Justice Bachelor's program at the U. in Minneapolis. If he'd followed his father's urgings he'd probably have income enough to do some of the things he found himself dreaming of doing. A smile creased his face at a reality he too often failed to acknowledge…Adam Trygg would do everything the same if he had it to do over again. He'd always wanted to be a cop and his ambitions were realized. Contentment was a blessing in his young life.

An oncoming car slowed as Adam's squad approached Lake Street. He might have ticketed the passing Buick for illegal window tinting but only watched as the taillights faded in his rearview mirror. Contrary to what many believed, the cops he worked with didn't go looking for people to cite for minor or marginal violations. The chief preached sound community relations as much as he did law enforecement.

Adam felt a nicotein tug as he passed the historic old Central High School and turned back up the hill. He'd only had three cigarettes in nearly nine hours but felt the craving now. "Damn it!" he said to himself, letting the urge dissipate for the moment. "You can wait another hour," he told himself. He thoughts wandered to his Susan…his wife of five years. Susan's birthday was on Sunday—the big 30! He'd teased her endlessly about 'going over the hill' at thirty.

Adam hoped the roses he had ordered for a Saturday delivery and the box of chocolates tucked in his locker at headquarters would be pleasing; even if it wasn't what she'd hoped for. He knew how much Susan had wanted a black leather purse she'd seen at Kohl's the previous weekend, but both agreed it was too expensive for their strained budget. They were saving every penny they possibly could to put down on a house of their own. Yet, he did have a surprise for Susan's special day that wasn't as much a gift for her as it was for himself. For months he'd promised his wife that he'd quit smoking. So, he had wrapped the *Chantix* box he'd purchased at *Walgreens* in a shoe box, taped on a big red bow, and included a note promising that he'd go the distance and endure the pain that would be coming because she, and their two year-old daughter Anna, meant the world to him. Of even greater concern…he and Susan had a son that was due to arrive in early January.

Stifling a yawn, he cruised down the hillside again and turned his squad east on Seventh Street. Crawling along the poorly lighted and seemingly quiet street, his eyes scanning the shadowed neighborhood for anything out of the ordinary. Murphy, with veteran instincts that Adam hoped would be his own some day, had trained him to always look beyond the obvious. Adam cut the headlights, pulled next to the curb atop a slight rise on West 7th Street, unbuckled his belt and stepped outside for some fresh lakeside air. He'd burn a quick one before heading back to headquarters to file his reports.

2/ TWO GIRLS

The evening had a chilly bite with winds off the big lake below the steep hill, stars glittered above the dark expanse like diamonds on black velvet. He pulled up his collar, lit a Marlboro, and…as he exhaled his first bitter billow he saw something move—something on the next block and off to the right near one of the few light posts still functioning. He took one last drag, flipped the cigarette toward a street curb, crushed it under his shoe, and slipped back behind the wheel. Slowly, with lights still off, he approached the corner where he'd seen what looked like two figures standing just off the buckled sidewalk pavement.

Coming to a stop, Adam rolled down the passenger window and leaned in the direction of two girls who looked to be in their mid or late-teens.

"Saw ya comin', Copper. Fer shame, you waz jus a'sneakin' down the street like an alley cat", said the taller of the two girls as she stepped toward the open passenger window. "Getting' bored are ya? Ain't ya made nuff busts t'night?" Her chopped-off words were dripping with a teen's provocative sarcasm.

Despite the Lake Superior chill the tall, shapely girl was scantily dressed in cut-off jeans that rode high on her slender thighs and she was wearing a yellow tank top that revealed her ample and braless bosom when she leaned immodestly in Adam's direction. Her smile and teeth were perfect, her lips glossed a deep red, and beneath her overdone makeup was an uncommon beauty. Her language and attitude, however, were an instant turnoff to Adam. Was she putting him on? Something wasn't right but he was at a loss about how to tell her to quit the charade—if that'what it was.

"Where's the Murf? If I'da known he wasn't wit ya, I'da been gone from here. I saw yer car up dere on tha' hill…" She pointed to where Adam had stopped for a cigarette. Adam believed her speech was too Afro-streety to be legitimate but wouldn't invite any sass.

Ignoring the girl's question about Murf, Adam said: "Kinda late for you and your friend to be hanging out don't you think?" Adam glanced over the girl's shoulder at the second teenager who had backed a few feet further from his idling squad. "Tell your friend to come over here for a minute."

"She ain't doin' nothin'. Ain't neither of us doin' nothin' but havin' a conversation. That against the law?"

The second girl didn't move, so Adam called in her direction a second time: "Say…you…I'd like you to come here for a sec."

When the second girl reached into her purse, Adam tensed: "Keep your hands where I can see them. And don't make me ask you a third time."

"Screw you!" she said. "Leave us alone. C'mon Lucy, let's split. He ain't gonna do nothin' cuz he knows he can't."

Adam was at an impass for the moment. What would Murf say…do? His partner usually took the window seat and had a way of handling matters like this with a veteran's ease. What would Murf do?

Lucy smiled, "She's right and you know it, don'cha? We ain't doin' nothin' but talkin'. No law sez we can't do that."

"You both know there's a curfew. Let me see some ID's. If you're old enough to be out after ten, I'll be moving on without another word. Okay?" Adam was certain that both girls were under eighteen. In a best-case scenario, he'd send them home with a warning and…

Then he saw something that sent an instant shiver down his spine. In the shadows behind the girls he saw the ember of a cigarette. There was a third person in a thicket of brush that he couldn't make out. "You girls by yourselves…or am I missing something?"

Lucy turned, called out over her shoulder: "Get the hell outta here, Jesse."

Adam was about to get out of his car when the girl with the purse took off running down the hill to her left. Whoever was hiding behind some bushes appeared to be a few steps ahead of her. Lucy leaned into the window blocking his view of the two fleeing figures; "Ya ain't gonna bother chasin'em are ya?"

Just then his radio chirped through nighttime static: *"...204 and all units, robbery in progress. Convenience store in Canal Park."* Adam knew the location well. He flipped on his siren, "Gotta run!" his voice was tight with apprehension. Peeling out from the curb, he sped toward Lake Street. "Oh, Jeeze!" he said. The memory of the recent stabbing incident flashed through his thoughts. He and Murf were the first responders that night…thank God for Murf! The veteran took charge immediately, kept the tense situation manageable, and expedited the young man's emergency trip to the nearby hospital; efficiently quelling the tension surrounding the scene. The victim was a college student-athlete. If Adam hadn't stopped to question the two girls he would probably be doing a loop through the Canal Park vicinity at this very moment. Typically he and Murf's last cruise of the afternoon shift passed through the popular tourist sector before returning to the station to file their reports.

3/ PURSUIT

Lights flashing, siren blarring, Adam sped over the I-35 bridge…adrenalin had taken over, heightening his every instinct. He saw another squad already parked near the filling station and could see the lights of a third car crossing Superior Street behind him. Officer Perry Blake pointed toward the *Red Lobster* restaurant to the right and shouted to Adam: "The perp is on foot. He ran toward the Irving (a retired iron ore vessel harbored nearby). Be careful, Adam. The guy's armed."

Adam was out of his car so quickly he nearly stumbled, he caught his balance and rushed toward Blake. "Should I pursue?" was the only thing he could think of asking.

"Wait for backup. Shelby's right behind you."

"Anybody hurt inside?" Adam gestured toward the store.

"No. The register guy is pretty shook-up but unharmed."

The third squad and officers Shelby and Thomas were already racing across the blacktopped lot with their sidearms drawn. Curious drivers began slowing and stopping to get a firsthand view of the chaos of cops and robbers and the scene was becoming dangerously congested. Blake was taking charge. "Adam, get those people and their damn cars outta here will ya? Jack, you and Marty come with me."

Adam was left by himself as the other three officers fanned out in different directions to pursue the vanished suspect. Implicit in Blake's command was *take charge*. Although Adam hadn't been in a situation like this before, his crowd management training came clearly to mind. He stepped into the growing traffic blockage and shouted his commands in authoritive voice: "Get moving! Get moving! There's a fugitive out there somewhere." He chose not to create a panic by mentioning the man was armed and dangerous. Adam waved his flashlight in sweeping gestures, shouting his orders over the city sounds around him, and getting everybody moving toward the downtown area across the interstate highway. In less than a minute he had cleared the immediate area. He stood in the middle of Canal Park Drive, the main entry to the park, with his flashlight in one hand and his Glock in the other. It was eerily quiet for a moment and strange to have unholstered his firearm. He flipped off the safety, one eye on the passing traffic and the other on the lamp-lit commercial area to his south. Adam wondered if he should join the others or stay put. Another what to do? Blake had said to monitor traffic—that's what he would do.

Suddenly he heard three shots fired in the direction of Grandma's Saloon two blocks away. Then…two more from a different firearm. Then, from out of nowhere's shadows, he spotted a car speeding toward him. Adam held his ground, waving his flashlight back and forth. The distance between him and the car was shrinking to less than a block. Realizing that if he didn't get out of the way quickly he would be run over— Adam leaped to the side at the last possible moment, nearly stumbling on the curb. On impulse he fired two rounds at the fleeing car's back tires. The car lurched but continued across the overpass at a dangerous speed. Adam raced to his parked squad car twenty yards away. Within seconds he was in pursuit and streaking up Lake Street when, from out of nowhere, he saw the SUV crossing the First Avenue intersection in front of him. He swerved but couldn't fully brake in time. His right front bumper hit the rear panel of the SUV, spinning both vehicles onto the sidewalk and taking out a parking meter. Adam froze for a what-to-do-now? moment, he didn't want to stop and explain anything to anybody as his squad was still drivable…and he didn't want to lose sight of the car he'd been chasing. In those few seconds, however, he realized that the fugitive's taillights had disappeared.

Shelby's squad was only seconds behind Adam, "Stay here," Shelby shouted, "we'll search the area. Did you get a make or model?…plate numbers? Anything?"

"Nothing much," Adam said. "Light colored…low-slung, fancy

wheels." Adam got out of his car as Shelby sped off up the hill. "You hurt, ma'am?" He stepped over to the rolled down window to find a distraught woman in her thirties sobbing profusely.

"Just woozie...I think," she said.

"I'm sorry about this, ma'am. Are you sure you're not injured?" She nodded without words and stepped out of her vehicle, nearly falling from the dizziness of her obvious shock. Adam stepped forward and caught her in his arms as she teetered. "You'd better sit down for a minute," taking her by the elbow and leading her to the passenger seat of his squad. "Everything's gonna be fine...just try to relax a minute. I'm officer Trygg." Looking up he saw that Officer Blake had arrived at the accident scene, "An ambulance is on the way," he announced.

With a senior officer present, Adam would tend to the woman sitting in his squad. "I've got to call my husband," she said through heavy sobs. "Will you please get my purse on the front seat?"

"You just sit, ma'am. I'll retrieve your purse in a minute." Adam offered the lady his cell phone. "We'll check you out before anything else, and hopefully, get you home in no time." He wrote the lady's name on his pocket-sized tablet; Janine Fitzgerald. Getting an assurance that she was unhurt, he managed to calm her down somewhat. She had stopped crying and was speaking coherently now. Mrs. Fitzgerald stood on steadier legs and walked a short distance from his squad. "I'm fine sir," she said with confidence as she returned Adam's cell phone. "Bob, that's my husband, is on his way. Shouldn't be more than fifteen minutes. He'll take me home. I don't need to go to the hospital."

Adam knew that nobody wanted to go the the hospital if they didn't absolutely have to; he cautioned the woman, "Let wait and see what the EMT's think ma'am. We want to be sure."

The woman sat back down. "I'm sure I had the green light, Officer. And I wasn't speeding or anything."

"It was all my fault, Missus Fitzgerald," Adam admitted. "I was chasing someone up the hill—someone that you missed by only a few seconds."

Blake, with his accident report form clipboard, joined them and handed the paperwork to Adam. He added his apology then added: "I suppose you can both see that the Tahoe can't be driven. I've called a tow truck. You can finish things up here, Adam, and I'll see you back at the station when you get in."

The ambulance arrived and twenty minutes later her husband pulled up beside the disabled Tahoe. The paramedics assured Adam that Mrs. Fitzgerald was okay enough to go home, and Adam was left to see that the mess of plastic and glass debris was cleared up. Just after eleven, Officer Blake called to report that the escapee's car had been located in a Woodland strip-mall's parking lot and had already been identified as a vehicle stolen days before.

Monday, August 25, 2014

4/ PARTNERS

On his drive to the downtown police headquarters the following Monday morning, Adam replayed the weekend in his thoughts. Susan's birthday was a big hit for the three Tryggs: his *Chantix* gift to her especially so. He was beginning his third day, but his smoking hadn't tapered off as much as he had hoped it might. Next Saturday was his D-Day—the day he would quit the reprehensible addiction forever!

Exiting the I-35 ramp, he eased his Toyota Corolla into the traffic on Superior Street and headed toward headquarters on West First. As he was about to turn off his radio the commentator on KDAL suggested "Having Monday off is a great way to hate Tuesdays." He laughed to himself…'Monday's ain't so bad, fella, it's a blessing to be alive and well and have a decent job to go to'. Today, a part of him was eager to learn if any suspects had been arrested in the Friday night robbery and shooting. He hadn't heard anything specific on the radio and the newspaper accounts on Friday nighjt's armed robbery had been vague.

"Hey, 'Crash'!" The welcome from Sergeant Charlie Cooney drew laughs from fellow officers. Adam puzzled at first then laughed himself as he realized the jest, "It's only a squad car. At least I wasn't injured," he rejoined. "That's the most important thing about it."

Murf came up to him, "Say, Partner, I'm gone for one stinkin' shift and look what you've gone and done. I really liked that car."

Adam grinned, "If you'd have been with me I'm sure none of this would have happened."

"You took the words right out of my mouth, son. Or should I call you 'Crash' along with your fan club?"

Both men laughed. Adam considered the truth in what his friend had suggested. The robbery might have occurred, but their response to the emergency could very well have been much different. When patrolling with Murf, the pair spent less time on the Hillside and more along Duluth's main drag of Superior Street and in Canal Park. Minutes and seconds mattered greatly in police work. Murf was staunch in his belief about being proactive where the money was being spent, and that wasn't Hillside.

The desk clerk handed Adam a folded slip of copy paper. "Phone message came in over the weekend. Some woman, said her name was Lucy, asked for you to get in touch with her. Sorry no phone number; only a name."

Adam looked at the slip. All it said was "*contact Lucy*".

Barney Miller sitting nearby asked, "You got something goin' on the side, 'Crash'?"

"I've already got the best, 'Fife'." Barney had the inevitable nickname 'Fife' from Andy Taylor's comical Deputy Barney of the Mayberry TV show, but this Barney was neither funny nor incompetent. Adam hoped that his new moniker wouldn't last through the week.

Murf asked him, "Who's this Lucy?" His tone was edgy; more serious than teasing.

"No idea Murf," he lied.

Cooney overheard the two men from his desk. "What's this about? Did I hear someone say Lucy?"

"Nothin', Sarge," Murphy said, giving his superior a wink. Changing the subject he asked Cooney: "Anything happening with the Canal Park robbery that we should know about before heading out?"

Adam stepped closer to Cooney's desk to hear his answer. "Nothing more than the stolen getaway car's been found," Cooney said. "You guys talk it up on the street. So far nobody's told us anything. The store guy said the perp was a medium height African American or Hispanic, wearing a nylon stocking over his head. Had latex gloves on. Didn't show a handgun but had something in his jacket pocket that might have been a gun."

"Obviously he was armed. Report says he fired at least three rounds at Blake," Murf said.

* * *

That night Murf was unusually quiet, not himself at all. Adam's attempts to engage him in conversation didn't accomplish much. Adam believed that the funeral he'd attended must have been someone close. Murf didn't want to talk about whatever was on his mind. That evening the two spent most of their shift in the college culture of Woodland neighborhood where the perp's car had been located, and where Murf believed they might pick up some vibes on the Friday incident. Adam's gut instinct was that the perp wasn't from the Woodland area but wouldn't argue with the senior officer. Twice Adam suggested that they swing through Hillside and twice Murf balked at the idea. "Day shift talked to everybody that knows anything about what's been happening. I checked their reports this afternoon and there's nothin' to follow up on."

Nobody knew Hillside like Murf and Adam was surprised that he didn't seem to want to do his own investigating on familiar turf. His veteran partner had always believed that the 'day guys' didn't know squat.

After work, Murf was anxious to split. "Gotta run, Adam. Take care of the shift reports for me and I'll owe you one."

* * *

On Tuesday night, Sergeant Cooney took Adam aside. "You'll be working with Symanski tonight. We're moving Phil from the east end to Hillside. Murf's been asked to do some special project day shifts until we find this bad ass and get him out of circulation."

"Did Murf ask for the switch or…?"

"Don't know. It came from above. Any problem?"

"Not at all. Symanski seems like a great guy."

"Okay. Done deal. Anything else?"

Adam was confused. Was it something he had done? The accident? Carelessly firing his handgun at a fleeing felon in a crowded area? The Lucy thing? If any of these or something else that didn't come to mind was the reason; why not tell him so? Yet, he didn't want any reprimands in his file. Maybe someone thought he simply wasn't up to par yet—that his involvement in the ongoing investigation was putting him in over his head. But, if that were so, why be partnered with a guy that wasn't much more experienced than he was? Adam reasoned that it had to have something to do with the accident on Lake Street on Friday night. Maybe a lawsuit from the woman's attorneys was coming down the road. Whatever, the change of partners was probably only a temporary one.

As Adam changed at his locker, the desk clerk came up to him. "That girl, Lucy, is persistent. Called again an hour ago. Wanted your phone number. Told her that wasn't possible. She cussed, told me: 'I'm a public citizen and have every right to know'. After a few minutes of my trying to explain confidentiality she finally let go of it. She was something else, Adam, told me 'don't let anybody know that I gave that cop my number. I have privacy rights too, ya know.'

"How would she know my name?"

"I don't think she does. All she said was 'the cop on Hillside last Friday. Murf's partner.' Here's her number anyhow."

Adam tucked the note in his jacket pocket, hung the jacket in his locker, and walked toward the door where Symanski was already waiting. The two men shook hands. "I'll drive" Symanski said as he dangled the keys in his slender index finger for Adam to see.

"Not a problem, Phil." He didn't acknowledge that Symanski had seniority and had every right to call the shots tonight. Maybe, his new partner would be pressing his seniority for lots of nights to come.

Phil Symanski was quiet, serious. His retired father had been one of the cops on the downtown beat years before; "I've got some big shoes to fill" he confided to Adam. "My dad was a distinguished officer; twenty-six years," he said with obvious pride. All that Adam knew was that Murf didn't think Phil Symanski would ever amount to much as a cop. Murf had strong views, both positive and negative, about every officer in the police department.

"My dad's gonna be pissed when he finds out I got dumped from day shifts to afternoons. So will Linda." Linda was the girl whose photo was taped inside Symanski's locker.

It was obvious to Adam that his new partner felt the change was a demotion of sorts. "My dad still has some clout around here so I might not be your sidekick very long."

Adam wouldn't be disappointed if that were so but didn't say as much. "I put in for a transfer to the West Duluth precinct months ago but that's not likely to happen for a long time," Adam confided. Adam lived in the western neighborhood of Riverside and had a half-hour drive to work every day. "I'll need more seniority. Any idea how much time a guy would need to get reassigned, Phil?"

Symanski shrugged, "No idea about that stuff. Say, where did you and Murf spend most of your time on afternoon shift? I'll probably try to keep us on the same routine as what you guys did before."

Symanski seemed determined to assert himself early on. "Mostly Hillside," Adam lied. He doubted if Symanski would call his bluff or talk to Murf about it later.

The shift went slowly, quietly, and coolly: several parking tickets, three seat-belt violations (Phil seemed to like writing tickets), two drunk and disorderly trips to the station's lockup, and a fender-bender on Mesabi Avenue. Add in four coffee stops and, for Adam, only two cigarettes in nearly eight hours.

5/ LUCY

After Susan had left to drop off their daughter, Anna, at day care and headed off to the gym for her Wednesday morning workout, Adam found the phone number in his jacket pocket.

The girl, Lucy, answered on the third ring. "Yep, this is Holly."

"Ooops, I'm sorry…I must have the wrong number," Adam said.

"Are you the cop?"

"Are you Lucy?"

"Yes, I'm Lucy."

"But you just…?"

Lucy ignored the question she anticipated was coming. "What's your name, handsome?" Then the girl laughed, "Just kidding. You're probably married."

"I am, and very happily." Adam's voice was edged with irritation and he came close to offing his phone. "What's this all about, anyway? And what's with the Holly thing?"

"You can know me as Holly…but not Murf. To him I'm Lucy, okay? But for now I need to keep this conversation between us—no further.

Agreed?"

"That depends. If it's a police matter I can't withhold anything."

"It is and it isn't. Part of it is personal."

"Tell me about the part that isn't personal first."

A long pause was followed by: "I'm being stalked. Brandy, that's my friend, she has seen someone too."

"Seen what? Be specific."

"We think it's a dark colored Buick with tinted glass—almost black, and probably illegal. Anyhow, almost every night…regardless of where we're hanging out; it's always a block or so away from where we are. Brandy thinks the plates are Minnesota…I don't think so. Whatever, we both know we're being watched."

"I can look into that and keep an eye out if that's what you're asking."

Another pause. "Do you guys have an unmarked car that fits that description?"

Adam didn't think so. "So…what's the diff? You girls selling drugs or…"

"I don't do drugs, officer," her tone sharpened. "Never have. Why do you guys think every kid in Hillside is a druggie?" The girl sighed, "So that's it, keep your eye out for that Buick". By the way, what's your name?"

"Just officer works fine for now."

"Okay. So, where's Murf been lately?"

Irritated by her question, Adam asked, "What makes you think he's anywhere? And…why is that any of your business?"

"You didn't answer my question."

"I not going to. Not unless you can tell me more about what you and this friend of yours are up to."

"Don't get so uptight. All I wanted was to alert you to someone who's up to no good, okay? My life is my business, your's is serving me and every other citizen of Duluth."

Adam wondered if he was actually talking to the same Afro-slang-sassy young woman he'd met on the street corner the previous week. This girl's language was precise—not cut and streety. "Be honest with me, Holly…are you really the girl that I talked to on Seventh that Friday night?"

"Yes. I'm Lucy on the street…but I'm not on the street right now."

Adam contemplated his next words, "Holly, what's the part of your story that you're not telling me? The part that a police officer can do something about…I mean beyond finding out who the person in the Buick is?"

"They might both be connected. I don't know. Maybe I've said enough already. Have a good day…Officer."

"Just a minute…I need to ask you about this guy who ran away with your friend the other night."

The phone went dead.

6/ 'JESSE' JAMES

The violent nature of Hillside reared its ugly head on the morning of Thursday, August 27th. The body of a young man identified as John James was discovered in a drainage ditch about fifty feet off of west Seventh Street. Two kids bicycling along a nearby sidewalk saw the body and reported it to their parents who went to the scene to see things for themselves before calling the police. It appeared as if the victim had been murdered execution style after being badly beaten with a blunt object.

James had a rap sheet that included several priors: drugs and paraphernalia, vandalism, a DUI, and probation violations. He'd done three months at NERC (a juvenile detention facility) and was someone on the cops watch list. Adam, and others, wondered if he was the recent perp wanted in the ongoing Canal Park robbery case. Whatever, the streets of Duluth would be somewhat safer with Mr. James' passing. The funeral service two days later was attended by a handful of people, none of whom were related to the young man. Murf and a priest from the detention facility were the only two adults at the cemetery for the burial.

For some strange—even disturbing reason—Adam hadn't seen Murf all week. Usually all the day guys and the afternoon guys mingled between shifts to share what had been going on and things to look for. Murf hadn't been among the minglers. Adam had wanted to find out what Murf knew about the girl Lucy and struggled with whether that was a good idea or if it was betrayal of the girl's confidence. Murf's absence made his decision that much more difficult.

That Thursday night Phil Symanski was unusually talkative. The James murder was the prevailing topic of conversation and both cops had different theories about who might have murdered the young man. Both agreed that drugs had something to do with it. "James was the perp in the Canal Park robbery," Symanski asserted with confidence. Then later, "It may be a gut feeling, but I'm rarely wrong," he added.

Adam disagreed with Phil's theory. "My gut feeling is that the two are totally unrelated. I'd bet that the James murder has a prostitution connection." In the back of his thoughts was a person driving a window-tinted Buick, but he hadn't said anything about his earlier conversation with Holly to his partner. Yet, whenever the two cops cruised through the streets of Hillside, Adam kept his eyes peeled for both the Buick and the mysterious girl with two contrasting identities.

* * *

The reclusive man seldom watched the local news on TV. Tonight, however, he was curious. He added a touch of whisky to his coffee and plopped himself in the worn recliner of the stuffy apartment he was renting from month to month. It was six o'clock and the national *ABC News* was concluding with another tragic west African ebola story. He waited through a series of commercials until the WDIO anchor's face appeared on the screen. "This just in. The body of a twenty-six year old man was discovered in a ditch off of West Seventh earlier this morning. The victim's name has not yet been released, but police say that the death is an apparent homicide. Other details will be forthcoming when available." From the headliner the news anchor went on to cover an escalating school board controversy.

It took a moment to register…then, the man screamed! "Oh my God, no…no! It can't be!" Then he began to cry. "I didn't mean…" His soulful wail could be heard through the thin walls of the cheap woodframed building.

Within moments, he heard a knock on the door…then a familiar voice: "John…John! Are you okay, John?"

It was Caroline. He recognized the fiftyish woman's voice. Caroline and her manager husband lived in the next appartment.

"No…I mean, yes…I'm fine." His mind raced as he headed to the door—he couldn't just let her stand outside his door without some explanation. A quick idea struck him. He dumped part of his coffee on the crotch of his pants, then opened the door. "Hi, Caroline…" he greeted with a pained expression. "Just a little accident I'm afraid…spilled my coffee; sorry to have alarmed you."

Caroline couldn't help but notice the accident, "Oh, my…did you burn yourself badly? Hot coffee can really…" She didn't finish the thought but added, "I have some aloe cream if you'd like…"

"Like I said, Caroline, it's nothing serious. The coffee wasn't that awfully hot. It startled me more than anything; but thanks anyway."

"You sure, John?"

"I'm sure," he said as he slowly began closing the door. "Thanks again. Sorry if I alarmed you." Caroline and her intentions were trouble he didn't need right now. He stood for a long moment after the door was locked fighting the urge to express his anguish once again. Insead, he only mumbled to himself: "Dear God, You know I didn't mean to kill the man. You must know! He was evil…so very evil. All I wanted to do was to punish him for what he was doing. That's all…You must believe me. You must!"

September 6, 2014

7/ MISSING PRIEST

Saturday night lights. The hilltop campus of the University of Minnesota, Duluth (UMD) was aglow beneath the towering light stands hovering like a yellow umbrella over Griggs Field. It was the Bulldogs season opening football game. The wind gusting off the lake gave the unseasonably mild evening a refreshing feel. In their pregame ceremony the university's marching band inspired rousing cheers from the maroon and gold clad student body. The atmosphere was perfectly choreographed for a college gridiron battle. Sitting among the more than five thousand fans were two priests wearing hooded Bulldog sweatshirts and cheering with the same ardor as the surrounding students. A third priest, who was supposed to join them before the opening kickoff, hadn't arrived yet. Calls to Father Bruno's cell phone were going unanswered.

"Try again, Mick...he's not answering his cell so maybe you can reach him at Brenner's House this time." Brenner was His Grace, Anthony Bremmer, the venerable bishop of the Duluth diocese. The bishop's church was The Cathedral of Our Lady of the Rosary. Unbeknownst to His Grace, however, the two priests irreverently referred to his church/residence as his 'House'. "What's with Bruno anyhow? You'd think he'd be calling us." An ardent Bulldogs football fan, Father Bruno Bocaccio worked for the Bishop in the Duluth diocesean offices on east 4th Street as the chief financial and budget administrator.

"Maybe he's still pouting over the player suspensions and doesn't want to give our boys the satisfaction of cheering them on. Just a thought, Mick." The thought came from Father Mario Morelli, Mickey Moran's closest friend.

"Ya think? That's overreacting just a tad I'd say."

"Bruno's as stubborn as spring in the Northland—these days nothing he might do would surprise me."

"Is it just me, or has Bruno been in the doldrums lately? At last week's 'Youth Aware' meeting he seemed to be in some distant place...kinda zonked I thought," Mickey said.

Mario gave his own memory of that meeting a moment's thought. "You know...come to think of it, I got the same impression. When I talked with him this afternoon he sounded okay; not excited, but okay. He told me that he'd been asked to do confessions at Saint Ben's this afternoon. Said he'd join us before kickoff."

"That's ten minutes from now. His confessions should have been done over with an hour ago. Must be something else going on," Mickey suggested. "Maybe his mom." Both knew that Bruno's mother was ill.

"I hope he's over the Robin Williams thing. That really struck him hard. Bruno loved the guy. How many times have we heard him get our attention with his half-baked imitation of Adrian Cronauer's *'Good Morning Vietnam'*?"

They both laughed. "I think he has DVD's of every movie Robin ever made," from Mario. "And watched them all a dozen times or more."

"That was tragic, though. Who'd have thought…? And the Seymore Hoffman O.D. last spring…Hollywood must be a stresspool."

"I like that. Where did you pick it up? *Stresspool*!"

"I'm quite clever. You should know that better than most."

*   *   *

Several UMD football players had made the mistake of being in 'the wrong place at the wrong time' the previous weekend. Duluth police officers raided an off-campus party and made several arrests. Among those cited were twenty-five football players, several were under-age and several were starting position players serving school-imposed suspensions.

Mickey found the number for the bishop's residence, punched his cell phone. "I just hope Bremmer doesn't pick it up. He'll be upset that neither one of us attended his ALS fundraiser this afternoon. He wanted to dump a bucket of ice water on me in the worst way. So, I'm in his doghouse again."

"So did I…want to dump I mean. Your cowardice underwhelms me at times."

"Shush!"

On the fourth ring a familiar voice: "Bishop's residence, this is Father Peter…"

"It's Mickey, Father. Mario and me are at the Bulldogs game…Bruno was supposed to join us and he hasn't shown up. Is he there by any chance?"

"Why wasn't I invited?" he teased. Peter wasn't into sports. "Who's playing? Are the good guys winning?"

"The Dogs, of course…say, any idea where the big fellow is?"

"Nope. He was scheduled for confessions at Ben's. Didn't say where he was going afterwards. Have you tried his cell?"

"A few times. Either it's off or he isn't answering. Anyhow, if you see or hear from him ask him to call one of us."

"By 'us' you mean you're with Mario?"

"No, Father. It's me and my girlfriend."

Father Peter found no humor in Mickey's answer. "Say hello to Mario. The bishop missed you two guys at the event this afternoon. He'll be talking to you both about your social priorities."

"God bless, Father," Mickey said as he tucked his phone in the back pocket of his jeans.

Mickey met Mario's eyes, "I don't have a good feeling about this, Amigo. It's not like Bruno to blow off a football game."

"Especially when he has the rare opportunity to sit beside the 'Wonder Boy' himself", Mario teased, knowing how the reference always incited a tooth-ache-like response from Mickey.

"Cut the crap, Amigo."

"Sorry. It just slipped out. A football game just sets my '*id*' into hyperactivity."

"Freud is passé if you haven't already heard. Psychology is a real science now days."

The substance behind Mario's 'Wonder Boy' reference was not without warrant. Father Michael 'Mickey' Moran had become a celebrity of sorts around the diocese and the community at large. Two years before, on a sabbatical to southwestern Florida, Mickey had been instrumental in the revitalization of the impoverished Hispanic community of TriPalms. His efforts in forging a joint commitment of contractors and financiers resulted in a series of renovations that transformed the village and earned him national attention and local acclaim as the 'miracle priest'.

That wasn't all. On Easter Sunday of this year, the esteemed priest disclosed that he was a 'father' in the truest sense of the word. Against his bishop's advise, Mickey informed his congregation that he had a son—a fourteen year-old boy living with his mother in Naples, Florida.

"Say…watch it!" Mario exclaimed, "You almost dumped your coffee in my lap."

In his excitement, Mickey had jumped from his seat as the Bulldog's quarterback hit his wide receiver with a touchdown pass putting the Dogs—who were stifling Concordia of St. Paul with their solid defense— went ahead by thirteen points with little more than another quarter left to play. "Did you see it, Mario? A perfectly thrown pass!"

"All I saw was a Styrofoam cup passing in front of my nose."

* * *

While the two priests watched the Bulldogs marching efficiently down the field, Father Bruno was stalking the streets of downtown Duluth. His cell phone was off, his eyes peeled, his focus steeled—truly, he was a man on a mission and a man in serious distress.

8/ THE CONFESSION

Saturday night lights below Duluth's hilltop campus were multi-colored neons enlivening the downtown streets. Yet Father Bruno Bocaccio's mission was leading him away from those lights and into alleyways and back streets. Bruno had hated shadows since being a child and shadows were everywhere. After parking his car near the *Essentia Health* building on a few blocks east of Lake Street, he'd been searching for a troubled man and had no clear idea what he would do if he found him. The priest's past several hours had been troubling beyond anything in his more than twenty years as a priest. Worse, he couldn't tell his friends at the ballgame anything about why he wasn't answering his phone...or, what was eating away at his insides. His recall of that afternoon's confessions at Saint Benjamins was as vivid as he walked the streets as it had been while it was happening. That troubling confession was like a tape endlessly replaying itself behind his bleary eyes.

* * *

That afternoon. Bruno checked his watch and noted that it was 4:50; only ten more minutes until the afternoon confessions would be over. He had agreed to fill in for a fellow priest at St. Benjamins. Being this was not his assigned parish, the few confessors he encountered were strangers to him. A man of deep empathy, Bruno disliked hearing confessions nearly as much as most confessors suffered through saying them. Mostly, it was the feeling of sorrow he felt for the person exposing his or her weaknesses and the darkness residing in their souls. Listening to another's vulnerability was as painful as it was exhausting.

The church's confessional had an open section for face-to-face interaction with the priest—a setting Bruno found most discomforting—and a private section that was screened, affording some measure of anonymity for both parties. Both were claustrophobic to him. This Saturday afternoon Bruno had heard only a handful of confessions; all of which had been conducted in the open compartment.

The elderly woman he'd met only moments before acknowledged that she went to confession every week. Her sins weren't really sins in the truest sense and she probably didn't need the sacrament of reconciliation (confession) more than once a year. Bruno imagined that her confession this afternoon was little different from the past many she had given. She had been angry with her husband several times, she had gossiped about her neighbor—a woman she had never liked—"not really gossiping" she had said "because I knew that Mrs. Anders stole last week's *Budgeteer* paper from the Johnson's driveway. Saw it myself but I shouldn't have said anything to anybody because that's hurting someone's reputation." Her greatest torment was that she had been over-changed at the grocery store, but upon realizing the mistake when she returned home, she had decided to keep the twenty-seven cents rather than return to the store and give the clerk back the store's money. She had never done "such a thing" before in all of her seventy-three years. Bruno suggested that if it bothered her that much she might consider returning the money on her next visit. "Maybe you could tell the clerk to give it to whomever needs a bit of change," Bruno offered. Despite the embarrassment she anticipated, she said she would do that. Bruno gave the woman a three '*Our Father's*' penance before absolving her.

Twenty minutes before the woman, a man in his late fifties or early sixties, who said his name was Ed, explained to Bruno that he had "impure thoughts about women", sometimes watched porn on his computer, stole a ream of copy paper from the office, and used "God's name in vain" much too often. Ed resolved to trash all his 'evil' websites, said he would return the copy paper on Monday, work on his "impure temptations" and think twice before 'taking God's name in vain'.

Barry, his first confessor, was probably in his teens and seemed very nervous. He masturbated daily…sometimes more, lied to his parents several times about things at school, and had smoked pot with some of his friends…twice. After his confession, Barry would say his five '*Our Fathers*' and five '*Hail Mary's*' and try not to "hang out with kids that might get him into more serious trouble". The boy's relief was palpable. Bruno's only suggestion was that Barry might consider hanging a crucifix in his bedroom where he found the greatest temptation to sin—something his own mother had done when Bruno was a teenager. He knew that the crucifix wouldn't subdue the lad's raging hormones, but it might make him think twice before succumbing.

Bruno yawned after checking his watch. He was tempted to open the confessional door and peer out into the sanctuary to see if there were other people waiting when the light above the private confessional blinked. He slid open the wooden plate between himself and the screen into the dark compartment beyond. Behind the screen was a man who's deep voice shook in trepidation…"Bless me Father…I have sinned…it's been years since I've been to confession."

Bruno tried to assure the man, "Bless you my son for coming…"

Before Bruno could complete his blessing the man blurted: "I killed a man!"

Bruno felt as if the man had hit him full force in the stomach. It took him a few seconds to muster his next words…Clearing his throat he asked: "You killed a man? I mean, actually murdered…"

"Yes. I murdered a man. A despicable human being that deserved to die and go to hell."

"Only God can…"

"I didn't mean that, the hell part, Father. Can I continue?"

Bruno felt a claustrophobic nausea rising from inside and found it difficult to even take his next breath. He managed to force out his next words. "You may continue, my son. Please..."

"I've probably committed every sin imaginable in my life. I've lied, stolen, cheated, cursed...divorced my wife and slept with many women. I'm not a good person at all but...but I need to get the murder thing off my mind...it's driving me mad."

"I understand," Bruno said—but he didn't. He couldn't. He'd never heard the word 'murder' in a confessional before.

The man's voice became subdued. "I just want God to forgive me. I truly do and I know that you can do that in His name. I used to be a good Catholic when I was growing up." He paused. "Maybe I can be again some day."

Bruno could feel beads of perspiration on his forehead, felt as if the oxygen had been sucked from the closeted air in his shrinking, claustrophobic space. His thoughts were swimming in deep water and he felt as if he was sinking into an undertow of no return. What should he say now? He let out a tortured breath, "please, continue, sir..." He'd inquire further about circumstances after the man had completed his confession.

"I asked you a question, Father. Will you do that? Forgive me of my sins? I think you owe me."

Owe me? Bruno, puzzeling over the man's strange disclosure, said: "Yes...I mean, I have the priestly power to forgive mortal sins but..."

He was cut off in mid-sentence. "Please say that prayer that you say to forgive sins. Please...can you do that right now?"

"Can we talk first, sir. I mean...can you explain the circumstances of your sins...I mean, of course, the murder. I feel as if..."

"Father...I implore you...can you say the forgiveness prayer? Like, right now. It's driving me half-crazy!"

Bruno was mind and judgement frozen. Nothing in his seminary years or priesthood had prepared him for anything like this. "I suppose I can," his words as doubtful as they were hopeful. If your are profoundly sorry and willing to..." He was going to say 'go to the police' but...but!

"Then, please do so," the man appealed. "I'll try to recite the *Act of Contrition* but I will probably need some help with some of the words." He began, *"Oh my God I am heartfully sorry..."*

Confused, Bruno bowed his head and closed his eyes, trying to do two things at the same time: both listen to the man's contrition and say his own prayer of absolution. *"God the father of mercies, through the death and resurrection of your Son, has reconcilied the world to Himself and sent the Holy Spirit..."*

The man across from him was mumbling his contrition prayer rather well. Bruno heard him saying *"...to do penance and amend my life..."* as he recited his absolution *"...through the ministry of the church, may God grant you pardon and peace..."*

When he finished with his final blessing and lifted his head he saw nothing but darkness behind the screen. The man was no longer in the confessional! Bruno's voice rose, "Are you still with me?"

Hearing no response, he stood, pushed open his own entry door and stepped into the sanctuary. Looking down the side aisle he saw the front door opening to daylight and a man fleeing the church. His eyes blurred from the change of lighting, Bruno nevertheless raced down the aisle of the sanctuary in pursuit. Huffing, he stepped outside the church and quickly looked in both directions...Nothing!

9/ HELP!

Bruno breathed deeply of the outside air to appease the nausea roiling inside. Not a person idled or passed on his side of the street. Two parked cars were at the curb but no one appered to be inside. A bicycle was chained to a pedestrian crossing sign. A *Ryder* truck passed in front of St. Benjamin's…a *Volkswagen* driven by a young woman passed in the opposite direction. Rushing down the steps and onto the sidewalk, Bruno called out to anyone who might hear, "Help!" Was that a stupid thing to say in his situation? What else could he do? He ran to the right towards the corner of the block where he could see activity in four directions. Light traffic. A mother pushing a stroller thirty yards away. Two old men conversing on the opposite corner.

"Oh my God…help me! What am I to do now?" Bruno stood as still as the lamppost nearby in absolute confusion and consternation. What had just happened? His head was pounding, his thoughts so convoluted he felt like a lost child. Everything of the past several minutes seemed surreal.

He turned back to the church. Entering the sanctuary he saw that two penitents were still kneeling in prayer. Near the back of the church and to his far right was the man he knew as Ed, and up closer to the altar was the older woman praying her rosary. He quietly approached the woman, his light tap on her shoulder frightened her. "What, Father?" Her thin face lost whatever color it had…"Are you closing the church?"

"No…no," Bruno assured. "I've just heard a man's confession but he left the confessional rather abruptly and I was wondering if you saw him leave?" Bruno was hoping for any detail she might recall.

"I'm sorry, Father. I was praying my rosary." Her voice was tight with emotion. "Is something wrong?"

Something was very wrong but Bruno wouldn't get into that with the woman. "I just wanted to talk to the man…but…I take it you didn't get a look at him?"

"When I'm saying my prayers I keep my eyes closed, Father. That is unless I'm somewhere that I have to see where I'm going."

"I understand. God bless you." Bruno turned toward the back of the sanctuary to see that the lone man had crossed himself and was getting up to leave. He called, "Can you wait a minute, sir?" He shuffled down the side aisle toward the man he knew as Ed. "I need to have a few words with you if you have a minute."

"Sure, Father." Ed was wearing a tee shirt that advertised *Trek* bicycles and holding a biker's helmet under his arm. "I'm not going anywhere special right now."

"Good." Bruno was short of breath from the short run down the aisle and earlier scuttle outside the church. "Did you see the man that left the church a few minutes ago?"

"Kinda. I wasn't paying much attention, though. Why?"

"I need to talk to him and I don't have a name or anything. Was he someone you know?"

"I don't think so, Father. I mean, no, I don't."

"Can you possibly describe him for me? Anything you remember would be helpful." Ed sat back down. "I wasn't paying too much attention to him…but, I sure saw you running down the aisle after him. I wondered what was going on."

"Yes. I'm afraid I wasn't able to catch up with him. Getting back to the man…"

"Like you, he seemed in a hurry for sure. But you couldn't have been more than a minute…even less, behind him."

"Well, if you can help me with a description, maybe…"

"Like I said, Father. I wasn't paying much attention. But…"

Ed looked away. "Let me see…he was wearing one of those, we

used to call them trench coats. You know, beige colored, below the knees? That's one thing I noticed."

Bruno probed. "Was he tall, short, fat, thin…?"

"Hard to tell with that coat on, you know. Kinda out of season to be wearing that. Don't you think?"

Bruno nodded, sat down beside the man. "It's very important, Ed. Think hard."

A light came on…"Oh yeah. I should have mentioned this right away. He was putting on a floppy hat as he neared the back of the church over there." Ed pointed over his shoulder. "Yes, a floppy hat like you might wear fishing or golfing. You know what I mean, Father."

Bruno thought he did. "Could you see what color?"

"Kinda light, I think. But not white. Maybe it matched the trench coat. Can't be sure though. Like I said, I only got a glimpse."

"Anything else?"

"I'm afraid not. He might have had longish hair. Hard to tell, though. I think he had his coat collar up. Can't be sure. He was kinda crouched. I mean his shoulders looked hunched as he ran by. Like yours, Father. Kinda hunched."

Bruno was heavy and out of shape. Apparently, he was hunch-backed as well.

Ed shrugged. "I'm sorry, Father. That's about all I can remember." Then, something occurred to Ed: "I haven't seen you here before, Father. Are you from Duluth? If so, I could contact you if I see someone that might be the guy you're looking for. I bike all over the neighborhood, you know. I'm retired."

Bruno found a ballpoint pen in his shirt pocket and a gas station receipt in his trousers. He wrote down his cell phone number on the back of the paper and gave it to Ed. "That would be most helpful," he offered his hand. "God bless…"

Bruno remained sitting in the pew after Ed left the church. A man wearing a trench coat and a floppy hat. Conspicuous attire when he thought about it. Was the outfit something he wore often? Or, was it part of some kind of disguise? Was the man on foot? He might come up with a hundred questions if he put his mind to it, but just sitting here wasn't going to do him any good. It was a few minutes after five and Bruno was hungry. He had another hour before he was supposed to meet the guys at the football game. As passionate as Bruno was about college football, at this moment he was obsessed with something far more important. He'd start looking. About twenty minutes had elapsed since the confessional incident—enough time for someone to get quite a ways away if he wanted to. Or not too far? Did he have a car? If so, a search would be futile…if not…? Where might the man be going? Downtown Duluth was only a couple of miles from the church. Two college campuses even closer. His best guess was downtown.

10/ FLOPPY HAT

Bruno wandered from the underbelly of dark corridors to lit up and spirited Superior Street. Now he entered a stream of traffic and headlights amalgamating with the multi-colored neons; now there were fewer shadows along with an eclectic hodgepodge of people milling about.

Walking by himself through Duluth's business district, Bruno's eyes scanned every passing figure, always on high alert for someone wearing a floppy hat and a trench coat. In order to rest his aching feet he entered Carmody's Irish Pub and ordered a *Guinness* on tap at the long, polished oak bar. Looking from face to face, Bruno saw nothing more than a handful of patrons enjoying the early Saturday evening on the town. He finished his brew in three swallows, paid, and stepped out onto the sidewalk and the fresh breeze wafting the late summer evening. His obsession unabated, he would continue walking west and poke his head inside the bars he encountered. Bruno skipped going upstairs of the Holiday Center and checking Sneakers Sports Bar—thinking it wasn't likely he'd find the person he was looking for among the younger crowd he imagined there. He poked his head inside Quinlan's Saloon, looked around and went back outside. In the past hour he'd checked five taverns on the main street; now he turned up the hill to West First Street. Rosco's Pioneer Bar had a small crowd of blue- collar folks, so he spent a few minutes with his second beer of the evening.

"Lookin' for a fella wearing a floppy hat…he left his umbrella at Quinlan's…thought he might have stopped here." Bruno fabricated a reason for his inquiry. The bartender shrugged, "Don't' think I seen nobody like that. Most of the folks here are regulars so's I'd notice a stranger."

So many taverns…so little time. He checked his watch, 7:25…he'd been walking the hillside streets for over two hours and his feet were screaming, sending angry messages to slow down and take a breather. For the umpteenth time that evening he vowed to lose some weight. To the north was the notorious Central Hillside neighborhood, and to his south the trendy Canal Park area. Walking the steep decline from First Street brought additional aches up his legs and into his lower back. Worse than the body aches was the throbbing in his head; a warning of something he would admit to only himself. Although a huge, even intimidating man, Father Bruno Bocaccio was as meek as a child yet possessed of a network of phobias…fears of the unfamiliar, fears of shadows, fears of being alone in unfamiliar places. Moments ago he felt a tug at his elbow and almost bolted when a missing-toothed woman, with her life's possessions in a black plastic bag, wanted a cigarette. He found a five dollar bill, "I don't smoke…take this instead," he said.

"God bless you," the old woman said.

"And you as well."

The priest had stopped briefly at the *Union Gospel Mission of East First* before heading down to Superior Street. While there he chatted with Willie Plank, a native of the Duluth streets for too many years. Bruno knew the down-and-outer well. Willie had been drinking and was, as he expected, of little help: "I'll keep my eyes peeled," he promised the priest. "If'n I see anybody tha'fits tha description you gave me, I promise I'll let you know, Father."

Bruno knew the promise was as flimsy as the man's handshake and would be quickly forgotten. He gave Willie a five anyhow and suggested that he get something to eat—knowing well that the alcoholic would find a liquor store before he would walk another agonizing block. Bruno checked his wallet and counted twenty-seven dollars—he'd need to be careful from now on. He hadn't eaten since leaving the church hours before, yet his stomach wasn't nearly as achy as his legs and feet.

Where would his quarry have gone after confession? The million- dollar question! If he had gone home, wherever in a city of ninety thousand people that might be, Bruno's search was pointless. Why did he cling to the notion that the man would be somewhere on these streets? Or, that someone might connect the hat with the man. Maybe he was looking in all the wrong places. He found a curbside bench, sat down, removed his shoes and massaged his malodorous feet. Still resolved, he'd give his futile mission another hour. Bruno checked his phone: Four messages from his priest friends at the football game. He was tempted to let them know that he wasn't going to show up, but didn't have a convenient lie to cover what he was up to. He dismissed the thought and replaced it with something that had been lacking from the start. A plan! A purpose without a plan was like a BLT without bacon. The thought of his favorite sandwich spurred his stomach to instant rebellion.

The reason for these wasted, unproductive hours were mired in the simple muck of being capriciously unsystematic. Think. Be creative. "Put yourself in the other man's shoes", he uttered under his breath. With his refocus, it occurred to him that there were two places that he had been avoiding, two places that he was morally abhorrent to. "Gotta do it," he said aloud and to himself.

Bruno almost stumbled on the two entry steps at the downtown casino. Inside, the Fond Du Luth Casino was a blur of flashing lights, pinging and ringing slots, along with the rancid cigarette smoke stinging his lungs. He wandered about the aisles of intent gamers searching faces, still without a clue of what the man actually looked like. While sitting in the confessional Bruno hadn't been wearing his glasses and the man's head was contritely bowed throughout the short minutes of the encounter. He had such scant information to work with that the faces his eyes darted to and from and back again would tell him nothing. It was a floppy hat and, he assumed, a timeworn beige trench coat that he was focused on. Jake Reed was the shift manager of the casino and the one person who might be able to provide some help by allowing the priest access to the overhead loft where the floor below was constantly monitored. Reed was having coffee in a back booth of the small restaurant with two buxom young women. He reconsidered making his request then dismissed it. Reed's hand was resting on the knee of a deeply cleavaged blond woman nestled next to him. Reed's wife, Janette, would be on them both with a fury he dared not imagine if she had the opportunity of Bruno's eyes at that moment. He'd leave Reed alone.

Back on the smoke clouded floor he found some loose change in his pocket and dropped a quarter, then another into 'Aladdin's Carpet'—an unoccupied slot machine…for his fifty cents he got a brief shot of pings and flashing lights, but no credits. Why did people gamble, he wondered at a question with an easy answer. The lure of fast and easy money was almost instinctive, addictive, something deeply imbedded in the psyche of some unfortunates—to others it was simply frivolous recreation. Whatever the justification, Bruno despised gambling, except, of course, for a small wager on a football game. Or, his church's bingo games and fund-raising raffles. Hypocrisy? Maybe? His tortured lungs and eardrums brought him back to the street after ten minutes of futile wandering through the narrow aisles.

11/ MORE BAR-HOPPING

At the corner of Lake and Superior Streets, Bruno contemplated making one last stop. To his west were several 'up-scale' bars, none of which held any promise. If his intentions were to visit another bar it would be the one he loathed the most. Earlier, he had parked his car several blocks to his east and the last place he wanted to check was several blocks to his south. It would make more sense to retrace his steps, get his car, then drive across I-35 into Canal Park—he quickly abandoned the idea of walking any further from his car than he already was. In a moment where common sense prevailed, he hailed a cab. Four dollars saved him a ton of pain. He gave the cabbie a five and got a grimace in return. What the cabbie expected he wouldn't know, because the yellow Ford was leaving the curb before the back door was completely closed. "Peace, Brother" he called to the taillights turning sharply back down the hill.

As much as he despised the place, he had a hunch…and Bruno rarely denied a hunch. It was after nine when he found a place to park in a motel lot across Canal Street from the *Saratoga Club*. The Saratoga was a 'Gentlemen's Club'—a.k.a. the local strip joint. If any foreign ships were docked in the bush harbor nearby, the place would be full of sailors and the women they were hoping to find. The thought froze him; could the man have been a sailor? Duluth was an international port with traffic from around the globe. In an afterthought he considered the voice…no, the voice was genuine Midwestern. But…it was deep, almost throaty…could it have been disguised somehow? Bruno didn't even know if the murder had occurred in Duluth. It might have been in Hibbing or Hobokken—he had no idea. Nor did he know if it was something recent. Or something buried in the distant past? Truly, Bruno was playing with a shortcarded deck.

He took a long minute to consider, then reconsider, going inside. Would someone recognize him? If so…that could be very awkward. He'd left his clerical collar in the car, but still wore the blacks. "Quit outthinking yourself Bruno", he mumbled. "The odds are pretty thin that someone would know who I am." The end result might be worth the risk.

Sure enough! Above the cacophony of hard rock music a giggle came from a circular booth behind where he was trying to stick to the wall like a life-sized decal off to the left side of the entry door. He turned his head and met the stare of Buddy Cleary. "What on earth…?" were the first words out of Buddy's mouth. "Father?" came next. The priest forced a smile, "It's not what you might be thinking, Bud." His face flushed and his tongue felt suddenly swollen. "I've been…I've been…looking all over town for someone who needs some serious help. I thought that maybe…?"

Whether his excuse was believable or not he might never know. "Buy you a beer or somthin'? Take a load off yer feet, Father. You look like you've had a rough night."

Bruno was convinced that Cleary must have thought the priest was somewhat inebriated but said nothing more than 'a rough night' as a passing comment. He was thankful for small blessings. "Why not," his agreement came in weak voice. Although his stomach rumbled for food, he'd have a third beer and find a burger place later. He pulled himself from the wall and took an empty chair, then turned it so his back was turned toward the stage where a topless dancer was straddling a pole. "As I was saying…there's this guy I met this afternoon…" He improvised a story that seemed plausible.

"A hat and a coat? That what yer lookin' for…?" The question came from a red-nosed man wearing a matching red wool plaid shirt, a purple Vikings cap, and leaning over his elbows and a half-eaten basket of fries next to Buddy.

"Have some," the third man, in a jeans jacket and mismatched blue denims, offered after removing his grease-stained fingers from the basket. Also on the round table was a second order of fries smothered in ketchup. Bruno's stomach raged and he was about to accept the offer when he noticed a fly crawling out from under the mound of crisped potatoes. "Thanks", he said, tucking his poised hand back under the table.

Within minutes Bruno realized the men in the booth were going to be of little help. "Guy might be in one of them motels across the street," Buddy offered. "You might ask the person at the desk."

"Yeah," from the third fellow who's name Bruno had forgotten, "Most folks are willing to help out a priest if they can. Leastwise, I'd think so. I would…every time."

Bruno considered the suggestion, then dismissed it. For some reason he had profiled the man he was looking for with different brush strokes. The man he wanted to find was unlikely to have the money to afford a luxury motel. As illfounded as his stereotype might be, he couldn't shake it loose from his mind's foggy picture. It was nearing ten and he hadn't checked in with any of the Bishop's staff since earlier that afternoon. They would be wondering where he was…so would Mickey and Mario. The football game would be over by now. He rose from the table, shook hands with his new friends, and headed for his illegally parked car in the motel lot across the busy street.

12/ MICKEY'S STORY

UMD had won the football game; defeating a stubborn Cobblers team. Bruno never showed; his empty seat was a bothersome reminder that their friend must have something important going on. What that might be neither had a clue. After declining Mario's invitation to join him for a pizza and beer, Father Mickey Moran admitted he was spent—totally wiped out! He hadn't been sleeping well and had too many things racing through his thoughts. His life was in turmoil and he wasn't sure what he might do about it. As he steered his Civic off Mesabi Avenue and onto I-35, Mickey headed back toward his parish residence in the far western neighborhood of Benton Park. A song by *Three Dog Night* ('Joy to the World') distracted Mickey. He usually enjoyed the melody and found the lyrics funky but not tonight. He turned off the radio and wondered about joy in his world. It was almost pathetic how he was beating himself up these days.

His Saturday morning had started as most…but the face looking back at him in the steam-framed mirror above the bathroom vanity did not offer a kind reflection. There were lines where lines shouldn't be on the face of a contented thirty-three year old man. "Are you frowning or…is this the way others are seeing you?" he remembered asking himself as he stroked his razor down his cheek. He had paused to give himself another critical look. The trace of wrinkles beside his eyes were as real as the shower curtain backdropping his image. And his deepset eyes, had they become a duller green, a green without the sparkle he seemed to remember from the good times?

Now in the eighth year of his priesthood, Saint Gerard's was his third assigned parish, and Mickey's first as a pastor in the sprawling diocese of Duluth. Only the year before he had convinced his bishop to support some much-needed renovations—improvements needed to support what appeared to be a growing and vital congregation. Only the year before…Father Mickey Moran was a local celebrity of sorts. His youthful charm and wit made his Sunday sermons an attraction that many felt worth the extra driving to get to. That was changing. In addition, his weekly radio progam on KDAL was blessed with a growing audience with willing sponsors—many outside of the Catholic community.

Earlier this year Mickey's glow began to fade. The beloved pastor learned that he was a *father* in the fullest sense of the word—Mickey had fathered a son. After graduating from high school, he had had a brief sexual encounter with a girl…not just any girl, Mary Reagan was undoubtedly the prettiest girl in school, and she had harbored a crush on Mickey since junior high. Afterward, both went their separate ways—Mary to the state university in Winona and Mickey to the College of Saint Thomas and then the Saint Paul Seminary. The years passed without the pair of one-episode 'lovers' ever having had any opportunity to meet again. Mary made certain of that. In the spring of 2000, Michael Reagan was born. Mary and her son Michael moved to southwest Florida, as far from her hometown of Hibbing in northeastern Minnesota as she could be. She raised her son without ever honestly disclosing who the boy's biological father actually was. All that changed when Mary and Mickey met after all those years—fourteen of them.

Mickey's first crisis was deciding whether he wanted to continue being a priest or begin a new role as a husband and dad. If that wasn't complicated enough, he struggled mightily with reconciling his true feelings for Mary, and for a boy he had come to love in the short span of recent months. Mary made his decision easier by making it clear that, despite her lingering love for Mickey, she would never marry him. Yet, he punished himself, with enduring doubts about their mutual understanding.

Mickey was never very good at putting issues to rest, nor at following the thoughtful advice of others: when all was said and done he believed that if he had created a problem it was his responsibility to resolve it. And so, disregarding the advice of his closest friend Mario, Mickey surprised (no, actually shocked!) his congregation on Easter Sunday morning with an admission that began with: "On this miraculous morning your pastor asks each of you to forgive…and to abundantly rejoice with him as well."

After the initial shock of a priest having fathered a child, and Mickey's sincere appeal for understanding, everything seemed to return to a new 'normalcy'. Even the ice of ultra-conservative Bishop Bremmer gradually thawed. But, that normalcy did not last—could not last. Role-playing became increasingly complicated: being the father of a fourteen year-old son and the pastor of a large congregation were incongruous—made even more so when considering that each role had to be played on stages that were separated by two thousand miles.

This past summer, Mickey's son Michael had spent a wonderful two weeks in early July with his grandparents in Hibbing and with Mickey in Duluth. Great times! Wonderful memories! Fishing, biking along the Munger Trail, white-water rafting on the Saint Louis River near Cloquet and virtually anything else Michael wanted to do. Both enjoyed too much ice cream and consumed too many burgers in those precious days; but regrets did not accompany the indulgences.

Now, two months later, subtle changes were creeping into their relationship; things complicated by time and distance and the simple aspects of living one's life. If mutli-tasking was requisite for a parish priest, mega-muti-taxing was a gift reserved for few. There was a time when he could shuffle, juggle, and strum 'Old Susanna' on his guitar at the same time. Yet Mickey was reluctant to admit to himself that he was becoming overwhelmed. The emotional overload was taxing; denial of his failings could only sink his ship. Attendance at Saint Gerard's weekend masses had been ebbing. His popular 'twitters' as well as his, once consuming email activity, were ebbing. Mickey could only blame himself for the many noticeable declines, but he felt a growing impotence about reversing the drift.

His homilies, once lively and inspired, were becoming punchless—even mundane. He wasn't putting as much effort into pastoral duties and getting even less satisfaction from them.

In June, the bishop of the Duluth Diocese and the bishop of the Venice Diocese in Florida had arrived at what seemed to be a workable solution to Mickey's unusual circumstance. On one weekend each month, Mickey was given an assignment at one of the Catholic churches in Naples or nearby Bonita Springs. This, it was believed by all parties, would enable him to keep a viable connection with his son Michael, without compromising his role as pastor of Saint Gerard's in Duluth. The cost of traveling to Florida, and other expenses incurred by his leaves, would be Mickey's responsibility. Fortunately, Mickey's sister Meghan and her family lived in Naples. And, Mickey's widowed mother (Sadie Moran) was blessed with considerable wealth.

Everything seemed too good to be true for the young priest. But, the seemingly ideal 'arrangement' was taking its toll by summer's end. Catching the late flight from Duluth to Ft. Myers on Thursday evening, and returning late on Sunday for his one-weekend-a-month, drained him of precious energy and strained his relationship with his Saint Gerard's parish. Michael had school on Fridays, Mickey had two masses on Sunday, and Saturday's were not entirely he and Michael's to do as they pleased. Sharing anything required sacrifice; sharing a child required structure and compromise—traits that stressed Mickey's winsome spirit. Being the father of his son was one thing; being the dad he wanted to be quite another—one was a given the other earned. Everything became even more complicated when Mary and her longtime boyfriend (Tom Blanchard) were wed in mid-August. Naturally, the ceremony was scheduled on a weekend when Mickey was back in Minnesota. When viewing wedding photos Michael had sent him and reading a line from the note his son had enclosed: *'I have never been happier...'* the unintended heartache nearly brought Mickey to tears.

Trying to reconcile his two dads was a strain on Michael as well. Tom was a likable man and a '24/7' dad who truly loved Michael—Mickey was the boy's father and a man who had been absent from Micheal's life from the time he was born until only a few short months ago. The father and son had an ocean of empty spaces to fill and hadn't had enough time to fill them. All three—or four—of them did their best to balance things; mostly it worked reasonably well.

Marriage to a man that she didn't really love was a sacrifice Mary had made for her son's benefit. Her feelings for Mickey were deeply-rooted and would always be strong. Naturally she found it difficult and discomforting when Mickey was in Naples. For the sake of Michael and Tom, both Mary and Mickey did their best to repress their honest feelings.

Mickey in the middle!

He smiled to himself as 'Malcomb in the Middle' came to mind, then turned off of Grand Avenue and into Benton Park's minimal business district. After mass tomorrow he had a 'First Communion' class for his eleven little angels, followed that evening by a scheduled meeting with the St. Gerard's parish council, and on Monday he'd be visiting with his bishop among other commitments across west Duluth. With so many balls in the air, Mickey needed a sense of stability, order, tranquility. Perhaps a leave of absence from his home diocese could be arranged: an'emergency leave'? He'd run the long-shot idea by his bishop when they met.

13/ BRUNO'S STORY

Although a remarkably bright man, Bruno struggled at times with common sense matters—a *Mensa* with so much on his mind that the trifling mundane was often elusive. Yet, when he set his mind to something he was ploddingly determined, even driven! He got these traits from his father, a man he struggled to love. Passionate by nature, Bruno was prone to behaving irrationally. Tonight was one of those times. The stir inside him was something he hadn't experienced in years...not since recovering from *the accident* years before. If resolve was in his task of the moment, obsession owned his heart. Part of him realized that locating the person he was searching for was little more than a fool's mission; the greater part of him believed that if it was God's will, he would find success.

* * *

Growing up as an only child of affluent parents in the comfortable Minneapolis suburb of Edina, was a challenge for Bruno Bocaccio. One wouldn't think that a bright boy with every material blessing he could possibly want would be unhappy or depressed. Bruno was both. For eighteen years his father, an obsessive-compulsive and hightly successful broker with a prestigious Twin Cities firm, had dictated the terms of his, and Bruno's mother's, lives in precise detail. Compliance was mandatory! 'B. P.' as Bernard Peter Bocaccio was known by his colleagues, ran his brokerage house with an iron fist and an intolerance for failure. He ran his home in much the same way. Martha was a dutiful wife with puppet strings. Bruno's every activity—be it athletics or academics— was scrutinized for perfection and too often he didn't come up to par. So, Bruno quit playing golf, gave up on baseball, and was dropped from the esteemed high school debate team in his junior year of high school: the latter by deliberately grandstanding in the regional tournament—without factual argumentation—during his final rebuttal.

What disturbed his father more than any of his son's antics was Bruno's refusal to try out for the academy's football team. Bruno had imposing size and the strength of an ox...but the softhearted nature of a contented bovine. B.P., a full four inches shorter than his son, and thirty pounds lighter, had been a college football standout at the U.

However, there was one area where Bruno excelled: academics. He could almost sleepwalk through every course in the college-prep curriculum. Upon graduation from the prestigious Minnehaha Academy, for the first time in memory, Bruno Bocaccio could breathe the inspiring air of freedom-

the feeling of emancipation that he'd longed for since he was old enough to write his name.

Bernard Bocaccio had arranged an elaborate graduation party for his son and invited business associates, local politicos, and other people of significant social standing to his mansion. Martha, his wife of twenty-four years, had little to do with the occasion's planning—hers had always been a role of quiet subservience—and B.P. wanted everything catered by licensed professionals. Martha's role was greeting guests and staying out of the way. It was during this party that Bruno would enjoy his long-awaited 'coming out' and when he and his father would have their inevitable falling out.

At that Saturday afternoon's graduation party an associate in B.P.'s accounting firm cornered the young graduate: "So…your father tells me that you're heading off to Princeton this fall", Leo Greene said as he offered a handshake and toothy smile. "Must make your dad proud that you're going to an Ivy League school."

Bruno placed his large hand on Mr. Greene's shoulder. "That's what he thinks. I haven't decided what I'm going to do yet…but I'm leaning towards taking some time off. You know, do some traveling, see how the 'other half' lives. I think the Academy life and growing up in Edina has warped my sense of reality, you know…all the rich people and their affluenza-suffering progeny can't help but give a person a false perception of reality. Do you get what I mean?"

Greene was more than mildly shocked with disbelief: "What does your dad say about that? I can't imagine…"

"I don't really know and care less. We haven't talked about it—which isn't unusual because we rarely talk about anything. But I'm sure he will be thoroughly pissed."

Greene flinched uncomfortably, loosened his silk tie: "Well…good luck with that, son."

Only minutes later, Bruno's father caught his elbow, "Having a good time?"

"Oh yeah, great bunch…your friends, I mean. Probably ten million dollars in corporate salaries gathered just in our living room…maybe twice that in the tent on the back lawn."

Bernard frowned, "Let's the two of us retire to my office for a few minutes. I just had a talk with Leo…Mr. Greene. Kinda disturbing. No, it was goddamned upsetting!"

To say that their conversation that afternoon didn't go well would be like suggesting that Gettysberg was a skirmish. The two men almost came to blows that would have cost B.P. a tidy sum in broken heirlooms that had adorned the financier's office for years when the father's temper exploded. "You ungrateful bastard!" he shouted. "After all I've done…" Bernard's grip on his son's sports jacket tore the shoulder seam…but, the much larger son was able to fend off his irate father without breaking a sweat. His muscled arms, and powerful hand, held those of his father pinned to his ribcage. "I plan to leave home next week. I've already told mom. Enjoy your party, I'm going out for a beer and a joint."

Bruno left his Edina home the next Tuesday with $1400 cash (from graduation gifts) and a duffle bag with two pair of jeans, two t-shirts, socks, and underwear. His mother 'borrowed' him her BMW. "Your dad will be furious…but…you go with my complete support and my prayers as well," she said. "If you ever need anything, Brew (his nickname), you know I'm just a phone call away."

His original plan was to head east to Madison, but he changed his mind at the intersection of I-694 and Highway 36. Rather than continue easterly into Wisconsin, he headed north instead. In less than three hours he found himself in Canal Park, the trendy Duluth tourist hub. The day was Minnesota June perfect and the breeze off Lake Superior as refreshing as his feeling of freedom. For two hours Bruno watched people and the passings of enormous ore boats, along with a variety of pleasure craft riding the rolling waves of the great lake. He couldn't help smiling often, he hadn't felt this good in years; maybe never before in his eighteen years.

By week's end, Bruno found a job at the McDonald's located on Haynes Road, not far from the Miller Hill Mall north of the city. By the end of August he was enrolled as a business administration major at UMD (University of Minnesota-Duluth). In three months, he had yet to talk with his father and only on rare occasion with his conspiratory mother. She told him to keep the car (Bernard had bought her another one), and upon learning of his enrollment, sent him a check for tuition and books for the first semester. By December, Bruno realized that more schooling wasn't in the cards for him—just more studies of stuff he already knew and wasn't really interested in. By that time he had met a girl, too. Linda Jandor was a sophomore pre-nursing student at nearby Saint Scholastica College. Linda's father owned *Reston*, a lucrative trucking business and, within three months, Bruno was a *Reston* employee, licenced, and making his first run—a trip to LaCrosse, in western Wisconsin. By the following June he was hauling appliances and furniture as far east as Cleveland. Bruno loved the open road.

Then the accident! The tragedy that would change his life in ways he never imagined.

Travling east on I-90, just past mile marker 112, Bruno hit a patch of black ice and lost control of his fully loaded *Peterbuilt* semi. The last thing he would remember was seeing his trailer jackknifing and the world spinning. Thrown against his steering wheel and then tossed like a rag doll against the passenger door he was knocked unconscious. A clipboard in his cabin came loose and cut an artery above his wrist, the side of his head was badly cut, and his clavicle along with three ribs were broken.

Running parallel to the interstate was a side road and several small homes. It was after one in the morning and an insomniac man was in his kitchen having a bowl of cereal. From his window he saw the eighteen-wheeler roll off the highway and into the snow-packed ditch. Grabbing his jacket and cell phone, then slipping into his Sorrell boots, John Belak raced to the truck. He found the driver unconscious and badly bleeding from his head and arm. John didn't know what to do. He tore off the sleeve of his pajama top and wrapped the arm wound as tightly as he could. His 911 call brought the Wisconsin Highway patrol to the location, and several minutes later, an ambulance from Black River Falls. By the time he was in placed in the ER unit at the local hospital, Bruno had recovered his consciousness but was still in shock. Four days later, upon his release, Bruno had his *calling*.

Bruno would later tell his Seminary friends, "It was like Paul on the road to Damascus. I was struck by the Holy Spirit and came to my senses for the first time in my life." From that moment, to this day, he would claim that a miracle happened on Highway 94: "I was given another shot at life and this time I was going to get it right." The accident occurred in November of 1988, Bruno was nearly twenty years-old at the time. In 1990 he enrolled in the Saint Paul Seminary, in 2008—the twentieth anniversary of his accident, Bruno was appointed to the position of financial director for the Diocese of Duluth and one of Bishop Anthony Bremmer's key associates.

14/ HANDS OFF

Wednesday, September 3rd, was Adam Trygg's first anniversary with the Duluth police force. Charlie Cooney, the shift sergeant was the first to offer his congratulations and present him with a collar pin. Phil Symanski offered him an expensive cigar, "Don't know if I dare," Adam said. "I know I'd inhale and then I'd be right back on the nicotine. But, thanks…let me think about it." Rather than put the stogie in his shirt pocket he put it in his locker under the baseball cap he'd worn to work.

As the partners were about to file out the door, Adam stopped abruptly near Cooney's desk. He spotted a file with the name John James. Below the name was a red sticker that read *'Preliminary Autopsy Report',* and the Medical Examiners scribbled signature. "Phil, check this out." Adam picked up the folder, opened it, and rifled through the four pages quickly. Highlighted in yellow on the second page he read: *'severe bodily injuries resulting from a beating with a blunt instrument (such as a baseball bat). The cause of death, however, was a single gunshot wound to the head delivered at close range. Preliminary indications suggest the bullet wound occurred some time after the victim's bodily trauma. (Appears as if the murder was execution style). Ballistics reports pending and other forensic data forthcoming.'*

"He was beaten up pretty badly and apparently left for dead," Phil observed as they returned the file and began walking out to their squad car. "Perp must've went back and found him still alive and finished the job. That's my guess."

"There must have been some real hatred going on—did you see any of the photos…?"

"Hey, what the hell you two guys doing? Do you see your name anywhere on that file? Keep your hands off things on my desk. Got it?" Cooney was more than mildly pissed at the junior officers.

"Sorry, Sarge…just thought…"

"Get your butt outta here Symanski; you too, Trygg."

Once outside, Adam said, "Jeeze, I've never seen Cooney blow his top like that before."

"For sure…hell, Adam, the murder happened in our territory

didn't it? So, what's the big deal if we see the coroner's report?"

"No idea. Do you think we should go back and ask Cooney what's got his ass in a bundle? There must be some good reason…" Adam's question hung between them, their squad car, and the door they had just exited. Cooney was standing there watching them. "You two have a problem with getting on the job this afternoon?"

"No, sir!" from two voices in perfect harmony.

While patrolling, the two officers talked about their rebuff. "I thought you and Cooney were pretty tight, Phil. Didn't he and your dad work together a few years back?"

"I guess so. He worked with all the old-timers. I don't know if they got along very well though. Cooney's always had an attitude. Somehow we get the impression that all of us cops are on the same page about things. Cooney's on his own page—always has been. At least that's what my dad says."

That night, Adam came very close to smoking the cigar he'd been given. If he had done so, he knew that it wouldn't take long and he'd be buying cigarettes again. Then, the suffering he'd endured would all be for naught.

* * *

The following day Adam found an envelope taped to his locker. Inside was a 'Congratulations' card and a $100 gift certificate for *Fitgers*, a fine dining establishment overlooking Lake Superior. The note said, '*Take your lovely wife out on the town, Linda and I will babysit Anna'*. The card was signed *Phil*. Adam was dumbfounded. What an unexpected surprise from his partner. Funny how one thoughtful deed can totally change one person's first impression of another. Symanski, who now inhabited the same doghouse as he did, must be an okay guy after all. Maybe he'd ask Susan if she'd be up to having a double date night with Phil and his girlfriend, Linda, one day soon. He couldn't remember the last time he and his wife had gone out to dinner.

15/ ADAM'S STORY

Adam grew up in South Saint Paul where the third generation of Tryggs had lived. His family was close-knit. He had two younger brothers, next to him was Noah, the third brother was Seth—both were junior attorneys in their father's firm. He had an older sister named Eve, lots of cousins, and grandparents on both sides. While in high school Adam played hockey—and played the game well. He was an all-conference center on a state tournament team. After graduation, he was a walk-on candidate for the UMD hockey Bulldogs. He didn't quite make it on a veteran team with several four-star recruits and a handful of returning skaters, several from Canadian youth programs. Disappointed over his failure to make the hockey squad, he finished his first year; then dropped out and joined the Army. After two Iraq stints he was discharged, and took a mechanical drafting position at *Cirrus*, the popular small airplane manufacturer located in Duluth. He enjoyed his work and banked some money, but seemed always to be restless, and searching. After breaking up with a steady girlfriend, he decided to register for the law enforcement program at Hibbing Community College. He was twenty-six at the time.

Adam met Susan Rolfzen while in his first year at Hibbing Community College in 2007. Susan was a sophomore in the nursing program and working parttime at the Walgreens Pharmacy in town. He told her on their first date that from the time he first saw her at class registrations in August, he knew she was going to be the one for him. Susan laughed at his admission. "I'll bet you say that to all the girls you date. How could you believe that if all you were going on was my looks?"

"I guess your looks were a window to your soul," he said. "Sounds corney but how else can I explain my feelings? I just knew in my…in my gut, I guess." Adam knew 'heart' would have been the better word choice and told her so.

On their first date the two of them just walked through Bennett Park and talked about school, future plans, music and family. "That's what it's all about—I mean what life's all about. My family is the greatest blessing in my life…I mean, not just my parents and sibs…but the whole Trygg clan down in South Saint Paul."

"What else, Adam?"

"My folks have a carved wooden sign on their deck. It says, '*Faith, Family, Friends*'…I guess that says it all."

Susan agreed. "It does, Adam. If you have the three of those you've got all you could ever hope for."

The two of them finished their evening date at Sammy's Pizza. Both liked the same combination— pepperoni and green olive. And, both chose Sprite to drink. Coincidence? Or, was it some kind of serendipity? When returning to Susan's house in Ryan Addition, Adam said, "I'd like to save a first kiss for a second date…can you agree to both?"

Susan agreed to both. She told her mom who was waiting up for her,

"If everything Adam said tonight is true…and I have no reason not to believe him; then maybe, just maybe, I've met my soul mate."

Her mother was skeptical of the soul mate concept. "I'm happy you had a good time but…but he's not from here…so we don't know much about him or his family."

Susan had expected her mother's response. "Well, anyhow, I gave Adam a hug and thanked him for a wonderful time. I told him how much I enjoyed getting to know him a *bit*."

A *bit* became a lot over the next three years. Adam and Susan were married in the Blessed Sacrament Catholic Church in October of 2010. Their daughter Anna arrived in March of 2012.

* * *

"I'd like to crack this thing, Adam." Symanski said in reference to the recent homicide. "I still think the James murder is tied to the Canal Park robbery. Too much coincidence."

Adam didn't see any coincidence in the two crimes and told him so. The two of them had gone throught the same argument before. "It's too much of a stretch to think that an armed robbery and the murder of a pimp are connected," Adam insisted. "Even if, and I can't by any logic, connect the two. Where does that take us in terms of resolving either crime?"

In one rebuttal that irked Adam, Phil had said: "Where was Murphy on both nights? Have you or anybody else ever checked that out?"

Adam thought his partner was grasping at straws, "Okay, you don't care much for Murf...let's just leave it at that."

In the back of his thoughts Adam believed that the location of the murder victim's body near Hillside's west Seventh had something to do with Lucy and her friend, Brandy. He had considered contacting Holly, or Lucy— or both?—again, but hadn't found the right opportunity. He hadn't seen the Buick the girl had described and he didn't want to give her any false impressions. If she wanted to know about anything relevant to the investigation, she could certainly contact him.

Coincidence. At the end of his shift, the desk officer handed him a note. "Some woman called for you; wants you to get back to her. ASAP, she said. Even if it's late."

16/ PHIL'S STORY

When Phil Symanski was in the fifth grade at Woodland Elementary he broke one of Miss Anderson's strictest rules; he was caught chewing gum in class. The teacher made an example of the youngster by making him sit on a stool in front of his classmates with his gum stuck on his nose. Everyone in class laughed and later poked fun at 'Gumnose'. Later he told his father about the incident. "Remember every kid that teased you and get them back," he scolded. The 'gumnose' experience had scarred his psyche for years afterwards. To the bullies, he was a wuss and was badgered and taunted at every occasion. Phil became an angry and withdrawn adolecent. One way to get his justifiable retribution, he was often reminded, was to become a cop like his father.

* * *

While growing to adulthood, Phil was a loner with few aquaintences and no true male friends. In the days that followed his reassignment, Phil got to know his new partner better than anybody his age. His gift of a dinner certificate to Fitgers was his way of trying to fill his friendship void and expand his relationship with Adam beyond the job they shared. The gift was his girlfriend Linda's idea. "You're too dependent on me all the time," she nagged. "I wish you'd make some friends."

"That was something as special as it was unexpected," Adam had said of his gift. Since that afternoon, he made more of an effort to get to know his new partner. He shared his story of growing up in South St. Paul, the army hitches, college, and Susan. Phil's story came out in bits and pieces; some of it fabricatioin and some of it factual. "I felt that the best way for me to help people was in public service…that's how I view law enforcement," he told Adam. Adam agreed, keeping his doubt to himself.

One night Phil said, "I guess my family and yours are a lot different. We've got some skeletons in our closet that I never talk about," he acknowledged with a pained expression. "My dad is twice divorced. I've got an older step-brother, by my dad's first wife. She moved out west and had his name changed back to her maiden name—his name is Tom Jordaine.

Really pissed my dad off when he heard about it. Tom and me are not very close—I hardly ever see him." He seemed embarrassed about his past and never spoke again about his sibling.

One afternoon Adam probed with a question about his mother. "Lost track of her," Phil admitted after giving the simple question much thought. "Ironically, she moved out to Colorado, too. Denver, I think. "

"Do you ever see her?"

"Hell no!" Then he laughed, "Dad said she was a tramp, slept with half of the Duluth police force. Dad raised me from when I was eleven."

Adam let it go at that. The admission might have been why Phil harbored such bad feelings about guys like Murphy and Cooney who might have been her paramours. A few silent, stewing minutes later he asked Phil, "What's her name, I mean your mom's…if you don't mind my asking?"

Phil maneuvered the squad car through the Superior Street traffic and then up the steep Lake Street hill. "Sarah," was all he said. In a conversation about family the following day, Phil surprised him by revealing, "I got a call from my mom the other day. Now she's in Boulder, that's outside of Denver. She's always liked to ski."

Later, Phil asked: "Do you ski, Adam?"

Adam didn't. "I played hockey in high school, South Saint Paul."

"Were you any good? I mean, did you score some goals?"

Adam laughed to himself, Phil wasn't much of a sports fan. "A few." In fact, he might have said that he was one of the highest goal scorers in the competitive Twin Cities area—and was an 'all-state' honorable mention his senior year.

"I played some baseball as a kid but wasn't much good," Phil said. I was a pretty good skier though." Phil still skied as often as he could and had a season pass at Spirit Mountain; on occasion he drove up to Biwabik and skied Giant's Ridge along with Linda who was a very good skier. Another pastime that Phil enjoyed was road-tripping on his Harley-Davidson 500. "Dad's got one just like mine. The two of us have been out to Sturgis three or four times. He's got some money invested in a small Harley shop out on east London Road."

When the two talked about family, Phil seemed remotely dark. Aside from a father that he seemed to idolize, he tended to belittle the concept of marriage; saying things like, "I don't really trust Linda," and "I'll never get married," and "Why run the risk of ending up in divorce court and losing everything you worked your ass off to accomplish?" But, in what seemed to Adam to be a contradiction, Phil would often comment on how neat it was that Adam would soon have a new son, or what a neat lady Susan was. "Must be nice to have a family to go home to every night."

It oftened seemed to Adam that Phil Symanski was, to use the lyrics from a classic Kris Kristofferson song, '*...a walking contradiction, partly truth and partly fiction...* 'Yet, the two unlikely men were gradually becoming the best of friends.

17/ LUCY'S STORY

Holly Goeden got her first name because of the day she was born. Her mother thought it would be clever to name her daughter 'Holly' because she was born on Christmas Eve day in 1997. Holly, of course, was too young to protest what she later believed to be 'a stupid Christmas berry name'. As a pre-teen her few school friends knew her simply as Goeden. As a teenager she made new friends who knew her as 'Loosey'—Loosey Goosey! None of her new friends, however, knew that her surname was Goeden. Last names were rarely shared in her crowd.

Holly Marie Goeden's birth certificate was in her mother's surname—not her absent father's name. Her father lived in Wisconsin, about ninety miles from the Goeden's duplex apartment in an area known as Gary— once a thriving community at the western edge of the long narrow city of Duluth. Holly's father lived with another woman, much younger than himself, but was never completely estranged from her. He never forgot a birthday and always spent too much money on the Christmas gifts he usually delivered in his rare visits to the Goeden household. If visits were rare, and phone calls erratic (usually every two months or so) the father and daughter had a strange bond and enjoyed any time spent together. He was very disappointed when she dropped out of Denfeld High School in the tenth grade and was insistent on her at least getting a GED. Her mother didn't really care what she did...never really had. Sarah Goeden's goal in life was getting a man and, over the years, Holly had usehered in a parade of losers.

After quitting school Holly took a waitress job at Bingo's Diner, a blue-collar breakfast and lunch café on Central Avenue in west Duluth. It was there that she met 'Margo' (not a real name) who was a dancer at the Saratoga Club in Canal Park. "You're a looker," Margo had said of Lucy. "When you're eighteen I could fix you up with a dancer job. We make some pretty good cash. Easy money, mostly tax free, too."

Later she met Jesse Jones, a pimp, then Brandy Larsen. Brandy and Lucy became fast friends; friends who could share everything with rare candor. From then until now Lucy's life had been in a downward spiral. From age sixteen she began living two very diverse lives.

* * *

"Glad you called, Mr. Adam Trygg."

"Where did you get my last name?" Adam wanted to know.

"Let's just say that I have my ways."

It was late and Adam was driving to his Riverside home. He wanted to keep the conversation brief and how she might have discovered his name seemed irrelevant. "I wish you wouldn't call the police station. People talk, you know."

"Give me your cell phone number, then."

"No way." Adam slowed, he was driving over the speed limit. "What's this about, Lucy…or Holly?"

"This is a Lucy call, Adam."

Adam was uncomfortable with her using his name. "Just call me Copper…like you did that night I first met you."

"Okay, Copper. If 'n thaz wha ya likes betta. I gonna be jus street Lucy fer ya. Dat hooker Lucy."

"Cut it out. I'm on my way home. I've got less than ten minutes, so let's get to whatever's on your mind. Okay?"

"Okay. How are you guys doing on the James murder? Any suspects? Or, isn't that any of my friggin' business?"

Adam's first response might have been 'none of your friggin' business'; instead he said: "Nothing yet." Adam would be careful not to divulge anything about the ongoing investigation. Yet that investigation seemed to be running into dead ends. "We've talked to a hundred people so far. Nobody saw anything, nobody knows anything, nobody seems to want to talk about anything related to it. But that's par for the course in Hillside. Why? You got some information?" He felt his back stiffen in anticipation.

"I know you have a positive ID on the guy who was murdered, but what about the kinda stuff he was into? That's gotta be important. You know; the motive thing. Papers haven't said much of anything about who or why or what for."

Adam would go out on a limb. "You probably know the guy's name was John James—called Jesse by most. He's had a checkered past. Came up here about five years ago from Detroit…or Chicago. Family there didn't seen to care if he was alive or dead."

"I know all that, Adam. Everyone on Hillside knows him. Among other things—like drugs and all the shit that goes on up there—he was also a pimp. My pimp, and Brandy's as well, to be honest about it. A bad apple."

Adam's mind slid into reverse…back to that August night of weeks before. The guy in the bushes. The guy that took off down the hill just moments before the Canal Park robbery call came in. "That was John James with you and your girlfriend?" Then it occurred to him…"sure, a nickname, and obvious nickname…Jesse. Jesse James!"

"You're an Einstein. Yep. One and the same. Our notorious pimp. Or, like he calls himself—'manager.'"

Adam would probe. "So, do you have some information? Like I said, we're in the dark."

Lucy paused for the longest moment. "The killer or killers could have been almost anybody—man or woman. Jesse was despised by everybody. Hypothetically, it could have been me or Brandy or five other girls he handled. Brandy was closest to him; they had a 'thing' going for a while. Have you talked with her or any of the other girls who have been arrested for prostitution? You must have a list of some kind in your department."

The police had such a list and had talked with several women with prior citations. Nothing! "Okay. Where are you going with this? I'm running out of time, Lucy."

"Remember what I told you about my being followed by someone?"

"Yeah, the Buick with the tinted windows. I haven't forgotten, nor have I seen any cars that meet that description."

"Well, Adam, I have a theory. Interested?"

"Yes…but make it quick. I'm almost home."

"There's a connection. I can feel it in my bones. The guy who's been stalking me could actually be stalking Brandy…or Jesse. Understand what I'm saying? Believe me, there is a connection of some kind. Do your homework, Adam. Brandy said once that there's a crooked cop or two that know more than you realize."

Adam considered Lucy's 'theory'. Could be? But, cops covering up seemed utterly off base to him. "Okay. I'll be extra vigilant for your Buick. See if you can get Brandy to contact me; would you do that?"

Lucy wouldn't tell him that she had been trying to reach Brandy without success since the murder went down weeks ago. For now, that didn't seem of any importance. "Yeah…okay, talk to you later."

As he approached west 85th at Grand Avenue, Adam closed with: "Keep me posted." He wanted to add, 'Now you've got an opportunity to clean up your act'. He didn't. He would, however, talk to some social workers he knew—some very good ones. For reasons that he couldn't understand, he wanted to help the girl with two names. Lucy (or Holly) was smart and had a good heart—but she had made a boatload of very bad decisions.

Adam had one last question on the tip of his tongue before he exited on 85th, but the line was dead. He wanted to get names from Holly; names of some of the girls she knew. Girls that Jesse would have known? Too late, maybe the next time they talked.

Would that help? He wondered to himself. Holly had told him that the girls use several names—"it's kinda like a game with us.

I've got three driver's licenses; so do most of the others. Two or three of the girls go to UMD part time. They live off campus and stay under your radar. One of them has two kids and two jobs—college is expensive." Holly knew that Brandy had taken college credits across the bridge at Superior State College. Brandy had mentioned a sociology professor's class more than once. Both girls had often talked about getting out their rut and going to college. "One of these days I'm be one of the few lucky ones that put all of this crap behind and and make a life for myself."

Adam thought of Mario at UMD and his many connections in the academic community faculties. Maybe that was something he could help Adam with. He made a mental note to introduce Holly to his friend one of these days. Maybe Mario could do her some good.

September 18, 2014

18/ FLIGHT TO FT. MYERS

Thursday afternoon found Father Michael Moran watching the flight board in the Duluth International airport. His flight to Ft. Myers was 'on time' and would be boarding soon. Scanning the morning *Star-Tribune* sports page, as was his morning ritual, he found the box score he was looking for buried well into the section. His Minnesota Twins, still mired at the bottom of the standings, had won yesterdays game by a 2-1 score over Arizona at Target Field. Phil Hughes pitched another masterful game and rookie Danny Santana had three of the Twins four hits. Maybe next year he lamented? Maybe a new manager? Maybe some of the promising young players the Twins like to keep buried in the minors? There were too many maybes for too much optimism.

Putting the paper aside, he watched the people coming and going in the airport corridors. He enjoyed 'people watching' and imagining their life stories. Across from where he was sitting was an interesting couple. The well-dressed man with big ears and a sharp chin looked to be in his sixties. His attractive and shapely wife was at least twenty years younger. Her wedding diamond was the size of a dime. What imaginings crop into one's mind when contemplating another person—what capricious judgements does one make? Mickey hated the fact that he was often too judgemental and well off base. He generally used clothes and grooming as his first tools of assessment...and skin color couldn't be avoided. Was he prejudiced? He hated to admit that sometimes he was (a sad indictment of a stranger he would readily admit) yet he was always outspoken about his hatred of any kind of discrimination. Human contradictions!

The couple across from him seemed rather easy for his amateur stereotyping. The wealthy man, with a pallid completion had probably been divorced a time or two, before finding his 'trophy wife' in the lovely blonde at his side. The lovely blonde girl had likely found her 'sugar daddy' in her Florida traveling companion. She was richly tanned and probably enjoyed every material happiness that wealth could provide. Or, was it happiness? Did a bank account measure a 'happiness quotient'? Neither looked very happy at the moment. In fact, both seemed absorbed in deep thoughts of their own. Sad thoughts. Maybe the husband's age was becoming a problem for her. Every one has heard that 'money can't buy happiness'; or, Mickey wondered...could it? He knew many rich and happily married couples. His weekend homily began taking shape in his mind. A perfect subject for the congregation at the new and elegant Saint Williams Church in Naples might be something on the obligations of wealth. Naples expressed it's affluency to the extreme.

Mickey remembered a quote he had picked up somewhere,

'Money is only good for the good it can do.' He hoped he'd remember the thought for his next homily on stewardship. Sitting by himself to Mickey's right was a man in his fifties wearing a 'Vietnam Vet' cap. His hair was worn in a ponytail, his neck tattooed with an eagle. A part of Mickey wanted to get up and walk over; then thank him for his service to country. An expectant mother with two little kids distracted him. The kids were under five and hyper. He hoped his seat was not next to theirs. Thinking more deeply on the veteran and what stories he might have of the unpopular war, he noticed a small smile crease the man's ruddy face. What was his thought? Of course, Mickey would never know. But, he had a thought of his own—a prideful one. Earlier that summer he had done something good that he'd kept mostly to himself. He'd committed to the *Wounded Warriors* project. Like most things Mickey had done lately he wondered if his honest intent was what his monthly twenty-dollar check would accomplish in helping a paraplegic veteran and members of his family…or if it had more to do with his own feelings of a noble deed done. Or, on another negative note, was he being too hard on himself for being foolishly self-centered? It was a good thing to do in both regards…wasn't it? Too much thinking and analyzing was giving Mickey a headache.

Ironically, the interesting couple he'd been watching had seats next to his in row twelve. As he often did, he introduced himself simply as Mickey Moran. His dress—jeans and athletic shoes and a light jacket—was casual enough to have any occupation.

"Mark Walters, Mickey. And, this is my daughter, Lisa."

Ooops, Mickey had once again badly misjudged a couple he had previously given a mental definition. "Nice to meet you both." He noticed that Lisa had tears in her eyes and considered, then dismissed, making an inquiry. Lisa, however, noticed that Mickey had noticed. She dabbed at her tears. "A sad week for us," she said.

"I'm sorry, Lisa," Mickey said; wondering if Lisa was expecting him to further inquire. Instead, he frowned without commenting.

"My gramma's funeral was yesterday." She reached across and gave her father's hand a squeeze. "Dad's had a tougher time with the saying 'good-byes' than I have. They were so very…" she couldn't finish the words that Mickey could imagine anyhow.

Mickey learned that Mark Walters lived in Hibbing. His daughter had talked him into coming down to Bonita Springs for a visit. "Do him some good to get away from the house and enjoy his grandkids," she said.

Mickey agreed. He learned that Lisa had a son in college (making his age assumption several years off-target) and a daughter in high school. He learned that her father, Mark, was a retired geologist from *Hibtac*—a large taconite operation north of Hibbing.

The three-hour flight passed quickly as the threesome talked about people they knew in Hibbing and life in Florida. Mark had known Mickey's father, Amos, quite well and offered his condolences on Amos' recent passing. "A good man. But not a very good golfer." Both laughed at the reality. Lisa knew Mickey's sister, Meghan. "Not very well. She must have been in junior high when I graduated."

As the airliner passed over the Gulf with Saint Pete off to the east, Mark admitted: "I might just settle somewhere down here. I don't think I can handle another winter like we've just had. It was brutal."

*   *   *

As he deplaned at the Ft. Myers terminal, Mickey said goodbye to the Walters' and promised to be in touch with them at some time down the road. As he walked away he wondered if he really intended to be 'in touch' with his new friends at some future date. He had said that same thing too often and always faulted himself for the transparent innuendo. 'Get off it!' he told himself. Passing through the busy corridore, he found his cell inside a pocket on his wrinkled jacket. As promised, he called his sister. "Just got in, Meg."

"I'm still at least ten minutes away…Matthew's game went extra innings." Matthew was Meg's fifteen year-old son and a promising third baseman in the Community School baseball program. Meg was Meg Williams. She and husband Kenny had relocated from Hibbing to Naples the previous fall.

"No rush. I'm starved. I'm going to get a burger or something. See you outside in a few minutes."

September 25, 2014

19/ NAPLES

Mickey's life had been slipping from bad to worse. He'd talked at length with his closest friend, Mario Morelli, but no one else. As was always the case, Mario's wisdom was uplifting but otherworldly at the same time. *'Stop telling God how big your storm is, instead tell the storm how big your God is.'* The concept was profound, but…but what? Mickey found himself talking to himself again. He wondered, should he unload some of his junk on his sister Meghan as well? In the recent past the siblings had experienced a checkered relationship but, to her credit, his sister had a good head…and she was family. Some things he had been comfortable in sharing, others even Mario didn't know about. One thing was becoming increasingly clear to him—this one-weekend-a-month experiment was grinding him down. Maybe his in-and-out visits were putting an undue strain on Meg and Kenny as well. Maybe? Yet, his niece and nephew loved seeing him, maybe even more than his own son seemed to.

Michael had been thriving since the tense disclosure when Mickey and Mary revealed the boy's long-undisclosed lineage months before, and enthusiastically supported his mother's recent marriage to a man named Tom Blanchard. Now Michael's family was complete—he had the dad he'd always hoped for. For some strange and very selfish reason, Mickey had hoped that his son's world wouldn't be as rosy as it seemed to be. To his mind, the new chemistry was troubling and he punished himself with guilt over his jealousy. Mickey wanted to believe that Mary still had strong feelings for him, and if he could ever summon the courage, he'd confess to lingering feelings for her. But…was it love? Or…was it something very different? He had no way of knowing. Why couldn't it be 'out of sight, out of mind'?

Rather than grab a quick burger, Mickey settled for a candy bar and a Diet Pepsi. As he contemplated the next few days, the poetic lyrics from the grunge band Nazareth back in the nineties came to mind…

'Love hurts, love scars

Love wounds and marks.

Any heart not tough

Not strong enough,

To take a lot of pain

Take a lot of pain,

Love is like a cloud

Takes a lot of rain…'

Little did Mickey know that those lamentable lyrics would stay with him and replay themselves well into his weekend.

* * *

Brother and sister hugged before Mickey tossed his carry-on into the back seat of Meg's Honda CRV. "So what plans do you and Michael have for the weekend?" from Meg.

"None, really. When we talked on Tuesday he told me…his exact words: 'We'll just play it by ear'. So that means I'll have to come up with something again—like I always seem to do. Any ideas?"

Meg shook her head, "What's with you? You make it sound like a chore for heaven's sake. Ideas? Well, Matt has been begging me for a sleep-over with some kids on his baseball team and would like Michael to come. I told him that Friday night works for me, but not Saturday."

Mickey didn't ask why, but noticed Meg's jaw tighten. She'd tell him why 'not Saturday' without his asking. "Saturday night is going to be my night—mine and Kenny's. That's going to happen!"

Mickey let a few long moments pass without comment. "Was that an exclamation mark statement?"

"An emphatic exclamation mark!"

"Okay. What's going on Meg? I can tell you're already upset about something…is it my visit? Is it something about mom? The two of you talk every day." Mickey chose not to ask the obvious—is it you and Kenny? "Com'on, Sis, let it out."

"Kenny's never home. Never! He's got a project up in Bradenton and another in Winterhaven. Last week he was home a grand total of one day and two nights. And, while he was home, it was like he and his damnable blueprints were having a love affair with one another."

Kenny Williams was an architect. He worked for and with an old Moran family friend named Larry Wheeler. Larry's development firm was swamped with diverse projects as the Florida economy was as hot as the Naples summers. Kenny was designing two high-end gated communities and working on a 'request for proposal' for an upscale shopping center.

Mickey tried to lighten the conversation as Meg cruised at eight-five down I-75; his flip question "Were the two nights you had pretty good?" was asked in levity.

Meg looked at him and scowled. "What kind of question is that? And coming from a priest..."

"Just a simple question, Meg. Are you giving it some connotation that wasn't intended?"

"I know what you meant...and no. Kenny fell asleep on the couch watching some stupid movie."

"What movie?"

"What difference does that make?"

"Just askin', sis."

After a long minute, Meg laughed—more at herself than at her brother's question. Reaching over with her right hand she gave Mickey's leg a pinch. "Sorry, Bro...I've been all wound up these past few weeks".

Mickey's smile matched his sisters. "I know of what you speak...

I've been wound up myself; for different reasons, of course." He didn't elaborate and Meghan didn't inquire.

* * *

The trip from Ft. Myers to the Williams' home in Naples took forty minutes. Both siblings had lots of things going on in their heads but not much to say about any of them. Mickey was wondering if he would see Mary on this trip. On his last trip he hadn't seen her at all. Truth be told, he looked forward to seeing his former 'girlfriend' more than he should. That bothered him greatly...but...what could he do about feelings? To his way of thinking, feelings didn't need any justification because they just happened. Or, was he lying to himself? Whatever, God knew...Mickey didn't.

When Meg reached for the radio knob on the dashboard, Mickey broke the long period of silent stewing. "How are the kids doing? Are they getting better settled into the Florida lifestyle?" When the Williams' moved from Hibbing to Naples the previous fall, it was a traumatic change for his niece and nephew: for all of them, but mostly for the kids.

Meg took a moment to answer. "When we spent most of August back home I didn't think I'd be able to get them to come back to Florida. No, they miss Minnesota. Big time!" She did not add that she did, too. She dared not admit that she was very tempted to take the kids one of these days and move back. Things between Kenny and her were that strained.

"That's too bad, but you knew it wouldn't be easy from the get-go. At their ages a major relocation is hard to handle. I miss them. Their 'Nana' misses them—terribly!" Nana was Sadie Moran. Sadie still refused to visit Florida. The Naples home where the Williams' lived was once the winter home of Sadie and her late husband, Amos. Amos had passed away just after the first of the year. 'Too many memories' Sadie had said...again and again.

"The kids are anxious to see their uncle. You know that you are their favorite uncle; hands down!" She smiled for only the second time since leaving the airport.

"Thanks, Meg, you can't imagine how much I needed that assurance." Mickey, of course, was their only uncle.

20/ THE SEAL

Father Bruno Boccacio's torment would not bury itself under the requisites of his administrative job. His week had brought few smiles, one was an email from his friend Mickey that read: *'There are three kinds of people, those who can count and those who can't'.* For the past several weeks he continued his clandestine search for a man wearing a floppy hat and trench coat. Always to no avail. Questions from fellow priests about where he was going at night, and what he was up to when gone, went unanswered or evaded altogether. But, it was killing him to keep everything inside. Yet, what could he say? The seal of confession was entrenched in Roman Catholic cannon law, and every priest knew its restraints as well as they knew the *Our Father.* And, they knew the consequence for violating the seal was excommunication from the Catholic Church. Bruno had come to know that reality better than most. Since his confessional experience he had done more research on the subject than he had done for his seminary thesis. Still, he remained confused by what he was learning. He knew that the seal is absolute in every possible regard: a priest was forbidden to discuss any aspect of what was learned from the penitent during the course of the Sacrament of Penance. *Any aspect!*

In September of this year (2014) a case testing the seal had finally been submitted to the Supreme Court. Many priests, Bruno more than most, had been following a case in Louisiana for the past few years. A girl and her family had sued the Diocese of Baton Rouge and the priest who had heard their daughter's confession. The case was particularly challenging because the confession and the law were in conflict. The girl confessed to being abused by a parishioner who had since died. It appeared from her testimony that the priest did not do anything of consequence to help her. In the initial trial the girl waived her own right of confidentiality and testified in a deposition that the priest did no more than give her counsel…to deal with matters in her own way. Failure to report the abuse of a minor conflicted with the Louisiana statutes compelling disclosure.

The trial court allowed the claims against the priest and the Baton Rouge diocese to go forward. The appeals court concluded that the defendants (the priest and the diocese) could not be mandated to report what was revealed in confession and dismissed the claims. The Louisiana Supreme Court reversed the appeals court, and the diocese had since appealed to the U.S. Supreme Court.

Bruno's dilemma, however, was unique in that he wasn't certain if the penitent had actually, or sacramentally, been absolved of his sins. The man's *Act of Contrition* was certainly valid as Bruno had heard much of it as he prayed himself. But, as was his manner when saying his prayer of absolution, his head was bowed and his thoughts were burdened by what he had just heard. When he finally lifted his gaze to make a sign of the cross, he realized the small screen door had been partially closed. Confused, he knocked on the thin divider to get the man's attention and whispered loud enough to be heard: "Are you there?". He knocked again and asked his question in louder voice…but no response. It was then that he stepped into the sanctuary, pulled the compartment's curtain aside to find it empty. Upon that discovery, his eyes scanned the sanctuary to see if the man was still in the church. It was at that precise moment that he saw the man fleeing out the front entrance of the church. That fleeting glimpse had replayed itself behind his eyes so many times that it was like etchings in granite.

Was his absolution faulty? Had there been true contrition? Had Bruno completed enough of his prayer of absolution? If either case were so, or even if they were not, could he seek the counsel of another priest? If there had been some tangible impediment to absolution, that impediment would render a grave injustice to his God, to his Catholic Church, and the penitent himself. Bruno reasoned that the impediment would lead the man to believe that he had received absolution when he actually hadn't. Bruno's conundrum was suffered daily, even hourly. He knew that the seal was absolute, and that he was dutybound not to discuss anything about the penitent, nor anything about the sin that had been committed. Questions, without the means of finding answers, were compelling him to locate the long vanished man. If, or when, he found him he might be able to derive some justification, or even get permission, to reveal the sin without revealing the sinner. Bruno's quandary was so stressful that he couldn't eat, couldn't sleep, couldn't concentrate…he'd lost weight, and with it energy. And, always embedded in his thoughts was his serious, and undisclosed to anyone, health issue.

If emotional torment, and the pain that was its companion, brought any measure of growth, Bruno might be satisfied. But, he suffered alone and without any redeeming qualities. Worse than even these excruciating afflictions, however, was a job that compelled the priest to rouse a sufficient measure of concentration to perform his duties as the diocean financial manager during these critical times: Father Bocaccio was responsible for the parish assessments in the annual United Catholice Appeal project. Bruno's perfomance was becoming a concern to Bishop Bremmer in their weekly meetings. On more than one occasion he was reminded of delinquent reports. "What's wrong, Father?" Bremmer asked in their last conversation. "Do you need some help?" Bruno assured his bishop that he would have everything up to speed by the month's end.

If, in fact, Bruno could confess his stress, and the reason for it, whom might he talk to? Certainly not the bishop. His two closest priest friends were Mario and Mickey. Perhaps he might engage them in some philosophical wrangling—both enjoyed argumentation more than almost anything else. Unfortunately, he hadn't seen either priest since that Saturday night nearly a month ago. Nor had Bruno attended any UMD's football games since…and, his beloved 'Dogs' remained undefeated in their first six games. As with nearly everything else, Bruno wasn't interested.

October 20, 2014

21/ TRANSFER

For the first time in weeks Adam was approached by Brenden Murphy. "Hey partner; where you been keeping yourself?" Murf was dressed casually in a blue pin-striped shirt, and navy blazer; his khaki slacks were rumpled and loafers scuffed.

Adam puzzled. "I'm here every day, Murf. Where have you been?"

"Some special assignments. Working odd hours."

"I had no idea." Adam extended a hand to his old friend.

Murf thought better than a handshake and gave Adam one of his bear hugs. "I've got some good news for you. Sarge said I could pass it on to you being we're old friends."

Everything about this suddenly 'old buddies' thing didn't set well. "Good news is always welcome, especially coming from Sarge Cooney."

Murf tugged at Adam's elbow, moving the two of them away from the lockers and toward a corner of the conjested room. "I pulled some strings for ya, kiddo. Got you that transfer you've been hoping for. Starting a week or ten days from now you'll be day-shiftin' at the West Duluth department. What say you about that?"

"You've gotta be kidding, Murf." Adam couldn't contain his surprise, gave Murf another hug—not quite as bearlike as Murf's had been. "How'd you manage to do that? I thought it would take years…and a day shift to boot! God, Susan will be even happier than I am; especially with the baby coming soon. Being home at night…Jeeze we can finally live like a normal family. Thanks a ton! I'll have to thank Sarge, too."

Murf put a finger to his lips, "Just keep it between the two of us for now. Okay? Don't want Symanski or any of the other guys wondering what happened. You must know that this will ruffle some feathers."

Adam puzzled again. This conversation was beyond strange. If it came from Sarge why all the secrecy? And, why hadn't a vacancy been posted? Adam checked the bulletin board daily. "Will Sarge let Phil know or should I?"

"I doubt Cooney will do it. At least not for now. If there are any questions he'll deal with them as they come up. Just don't worry."

Without any further explanation, Murf gripped Adam's shoulder, winked, and walked down the corridor toward Sarge Cooney's office.

Dumbfounded, Adam shook his head, walked toward his locker where Symanski was sitting on the bench with a styrofoam cup of cream-saturated coffee. Phil was on his cell when he saw Adam approach. He finished his conversation and gave Adam a smile. "Just saw you talking with your old partner...what's that about? I thought you two were on the outs and then I saw this big Murphy hug."

Adam conjured a quick lie. "He just wanted me to let Susan know that he was thinking of her. Asked about when the baby is due. Small talk, not much else."

Phil frowned, "Kinda weird don't you think? From out of the blue?"

"Yeah, I thought so too.

Adam knew that Symanski didn't care much for Murphy. More than a few times he confided that his father, a former cop, had never trusted him. The senior Symanski wasn't a trusting kinda guy, Phil had admitted. But when a cop has a time-share in Miami, and a big house on London Road things just don't add up. Apparently Murf's wife was a high maintenance lady too, and drove a Mercedes convertible. "Cops don't live like that, Adam," Phil had said a number of times.

*　　　　*　　　　*

Adam hadn't seen or heard from Lucy since their phone conversation some time ago. That fact was just fine with him. He wondered if the murder of her pimp friend had made her rethink her lifestyle…if so, that would be a welcome change. The John 'Jesse' James case was getting colder by the week; likewise the Canal Park armed robbery episode. Regardless of Lucy's apparent disappearance, Adam continued to keep his eye peeled for that dark-colored Buick with the tinted windows as he and Symanski patrolled Hillside every afternoon.

The first six hours of this evening's shift were as quiet as the two officers patrolling the Hillside neighborhood. Adam was consumed with the prospects of his new start in life, but keeping his good fortune secret was eating away at his insides. Several times he was tempted to call home and tell Susan to wait up for him. What might have been going through Symanski's mind this afternoon remained as mysterious as his new, but secreted, assignment.

Symanski wasn't into sports so Adam always struggled to come up with something to talk about that wasn't police related. Adam was an avid Wild fan and the Minnesota NHL hockey team was off to a good start before beginning a slide toward mediocrity. But Phil didn't follow the game. Politics was another subject that Phil avoided: "They're all incompetent, sleezy, bastards—the ones that are in office now and the ones who want to take their jobs." He held lawyers in low regard too, and virtually anybody who made lots of money from investing other people's money: "Legitimate money comes from hard work not from using someone else's money to make your own," he'd asserted more than once. Phil, Adam was learning, seemed like a classic cynic. When Phil referred to everybody in Hillside were 'low-lifes', Adam took exception. "Don't ever say that in front of Murf, he'd kick your ass!"

"Screw Murphy."

Adam and Susan had double-dated with Phil and his girlfriend Linda the weekend before. It hadn't been a fun time. Linda was a pharmacist and seemed to Susan like a control freak. Linda went so far as to tell Phil what he would *like* from the menu: "Don't order shrimp, dear, you always order shrimp. You'd much rather have the garlic sirloin." And, "I ordered you a red wine like we're all having, dear. You can have a gin tonic anytime." Of course, Phil had steak with his Merlot.

"What are you and Linda planning for the weekend?" Adam broke the long silence.

"Don't know what *her* plans are," Phil said. "Linda hasn't said anything about the weekend yet."

Adam swallowed his 'I might have guessed!'

*　　　　*　　　　*

Saturday would be Adam's last afternoon shift at the downtown DPD and he hated to keep his news from Phil. Over their weeks together, Adam had come to appreciate his partner and respect his police work. Phil knew the law by it's code and technical applications. Unlike Murf, Symanski gave a deserved priority to Hillside. Unlike Murf, he wasn't full of BS or dirty jokes. But, nobody Adam knew was quite like Murf.

By late Friday Adam couldn't contain his 'secret' any longer. The two were parked on the corner of the two firsts—Avenue and Street—and sipping the last of their thermosed coffee. "Gotta tell you something, Phil, but you have to promise not to tell a soul until it gets out officially from Sarge."

Phil met his eyes, "Shoot. You've got my word."

"I'm getting that transfer I signed up for months ago. West Duluth."

"Bullshit! That's not possible. There must be five guys with seniority that want outta here. Who told you that?"

"Murf. He got it from Sarge on Monday."

"Murphy? That must be some kinda sick joke, Adam. You've gotta know things don't work that way—never have."

"I checked with Sarge. He confirmed it. Like Murf, he told me not to say a word to anybody. If there is any flack when it becomes public information he said that he'd douse it."

Phil Symanski could only shake his head. "I still can't believe it, Adam. Why the secrecy?"

"Puzzles me, too. I don't get what's going on any more than you. But, to say the least, I'm happy as hell about it. Susan's ecstatic."

"I'm sure you both are. But, I've gotta be honest with you. Shit is going to hit the fan when word gets out. Someone will have a lot of explaining to do. Not you necessarily, but someone. Do you have the slightest clue…I mean someone with influence had to pull some strings."

"Funny you should say that, 'pull some strings'. Murf told me that he had pulled some strings. Why, I don't know. We got along pretty well when we had afternoons together."

"But you told me that it's been a while since you've even seen him. Matter of fact, you told me that you were convinced that he was angry with you for some reason."

"I thought so. But…" Adam swallowed the last of his coffee. "I'll be honest…I still think he's got something against me. My first thought was that he wanted me out of the downtown PD. But why? I've racked my brains to figure out why Murf has been avoiding me."

"Do you think he thought you botched the Canal Park thing?"

"That's about all I can think of. He must think I'm too green for the Hillside assignment."

Phil was quiet for a long time. Something wasn't right. He

would betray his friend's confidence and talk to his dad about what had happened. His dad still had some tight connections with the DPD. "Don't think I'm not happy for ya, buddy." He swallowed hard. "I'm gonna miss working with ya, Adam," was all he could say.

Adam thought he saw a tear forming in the corner of his friend's eye.

22/ SWAMP BUGGIES

When Mickey arrived at Meghan's house it was already after nine; the kids were finishing their homework. Mickey gave them both a hug, sat on the sofa with one on each side, and asked them about school and life happenings for a few brief minutes. He still hadn't made arrangements for the weekend and it was getting close to Michael's bedtime as well. "Sad to say guys, but you'll have to excuse me for a minute…I've gotta make a call."

"Say hi to Michael for me," Katie said. "Tell him he was being a showoff in school today."

"What's that about?"

"Oh, we had a program this afternoon. Some musician—he played a guitar and sang some corny songs that nobody knew. Michael was one of the MC's. Anyhow, when he introduced the guy he said, "Here's Johnny" kinda hammy—like that guy from Johnny Carson used to do. You know what I mean? Only a few of us had ever heard of the Carson late night show. So, I thought that was a stretch."

Matthew interrupted. "Well the guy's name was Johnny Gray, Katie. I would have done the same thing. And, the Carson guy was named Ed something. Ed…?"

"You would not! I mean, you're not that clever."

"What do you know!"

Mickey skirted the argument and slipped into the hallway to make his call. Kenny wouldn't get home until tomorrow night, and Meg was baking cookies or something that smelled great in the kitchen. He heard her call to the kids to say goodnight. "It's bedtime, I'll be up to tuck you in."Mickey hoped that Mary would answer his call before passing the phone to their son. Mary's voice always evoked memories; both bitter and sweet. Her lilt also seemed to give rise to the unresolved relationship questions that he—too often—allowed to torment him. His hopes were dashed after three rings…"Hi Mickey," it was Tom Blanchard. "How was your flight?"

A minute of small talk preceded Tom's call to Michael asking the boy to pick up the phone. "Oh, I almost forget," Tom said. "You might be pleased to know that Mary has talked me into taking religious instructions. I'm learning that the theology of Catholics and Lutherans are not much different at all. So, one day soon I'll be baptized again and we'll all be able to participate in mass together. And you, along with the three of us, can worship together on your weekends in Naples."

Part of Mickey was happy; a bigger part not so much. His congratulations lacked the enthusiasm that Tom had probably anticipated. "Good talking to you, Mickey. Michael's standing here…Mary said to mention that you're invited to join us for breakfast after your Sunday mass. Hope that works for you, Mary's planning a kinda brunch."

Tom Blanchard was a nice man. Too nice! Too thoughtful! Too much of everything that a good husband should be. Whenever he saw Tom he felt a twinge of jealousy. It bothered him far more than appropriate that he still hadn't completely let go of his feelings for another man's wife. When he confessed them to Mario, as he often had, he felt some degree of forgiveness in his heart…but even Mario's cautions couldn't get him away from his covetous thoughts for very long.

"Hey…what's up for the weekend, Mickey." Although Michael had once asked if it was okay to call him 'Dad', he hadn't done so since that night of revelation; that fateful night when the three of them—mother, father, and son— had come to grips with the stark reality. Mickey could replay every word that was spoken by each of them that night, and had done so countless times. He and Mary told Michael that March night that Mickey was the father the boy had never known about. It was probably the most emotional evening in the lives of each of them.

"Thought you might have some ideas, Michael. Oh, by the way, I heard you did a nifty job at the school program this afternoon. Tell me about it."

They both laughed and came up with some ideas for things they might do the following day. "Something that may sound kinda weird but a kid at school says it's fun…" Michael's laugh was subdued, "They have swamp buggy races at this place off Rattlesnake road—I think that's east of Naples, but not too far from here. I've never seen them…have you?"

Mickey hadn't but thought they might be a fun thing to do. He'd pick up Michael sometime around mid-morning. "We can do a breakfast at the IHOP out that way and then find the swamps…okay?"

Their time together that day was a blast while it lasted. They had to leave early, before the main event, but had already seen enough mud-splashing, and wheel spinning to last them a lifetime. Michael had to get to the library before closing and Mickey was committed to afternoon confessions at St. Williams. Taking in a movie that evening would be up to Mary and Tom. Mickey replayed the day in his thoughts. As much fun as Michael seemed to be having, he wasn't altogether with it. At times the boy was more pensive than Mickey had noticed before. He had asked his son if he had something on his mind; if he wanted to go and find something else to do; if he hadn't slept well the night before; if school was going well—anything he could think of to get through the fog. "You seem a little off," Mickey said on the eight mile drive back to the Blanchard's house. "Do you want to talk with me about it?"

Michael declined, "No…I'm fine. Do you remember when buggy

twelve, Mickey— the purple and yellow one that got stuck in that huge pothole at the far end of the track?" Effectively, Michael went into recap mode; whatever he was bothering about remained buried under the mud of his thoughts.

Tom was washing the family's white Volvo SUV in the driveway when the two of them arrived. He put the hose down and opened the door for Michael: "Your mom baked brownies, *son*," he said. "Just came out of the oven a few minutes ago."

The word son burned like a flare in Mickey's psyche. Was it deliberate? Or, was that an every day reference? Whatever it was, it cut him like a razor.

Michael smiled and said, "Okay if I go inside, Mickey? I'll call you after supper." Mickey nodded, leaned toward the boy for a 'good-bye' hug, but Michael was already on the porch and the opportunity was lost. Mickey and Tom were left alone.

"Did you guys have a good time? I've never seen a swamp buggies race…except on TV a time or two. Always meant to…but…"

"We had a good time, Tom. But I won't be in any great hurry to see them again."

Tom had something on his mind and didn't quite know how to get it out. "Do you have a minute, Mickey? There's something I'd like to talk with you about—away from Michael and Mary."

*   *   *

When Mickey returned to his sister's house after confessions in the late afternoon, Kenny was home and Meg had put together all the fixings for a family barbeque. Mickey joined his brother-in-law at the patio grill and accepted the *Corona* Kenny offered.

"Meg mentioned that you and Michael were going to the swamp buggy races this afternoon…how'd that go?"

Mickey gave a brief description of the event. "A good-ole Southern redneck event. I enjoyed people watching more than the buggy racing. The crowd, and it was a big one, reminded me a little of the stock car races on summer weekends at the fairgrounds in Hibbing. I was just a kid when my dad first took me…" Mickey's memories gave him a strong dose of nostalgia. He and his dad did so many things together; bonding things…things he'd never have the time or opportunity to do with his son." With the nostalgia was an even greater dose of melancholy. Mickey finished his recount of the day and his beer at the same time.

Kenny was a sensitive man and saw something in Mickey's eyes that told him that the story he told was not the story he felt. He wouldn't probe.

Instead he commented on his task: "If I remember correctly, you like your burgers well done."

"I do," Mickey said absently. "Can I get you another *Corona* from the cooler, Ken?"

"Can't allow our guest to drink by himself," he smiled. "Sure."

Mickey went to the cooler thinking about Kenny's innocent reference to his presense there, '*our guest*!' That's what he was on his weekend-a-month program—a guest. And, with Michael it probably wasn't much different. Maybe Tom's 'just between the two of us for now' idea would be best for everybody. Mickey's back was to Kenny as his eyes misted at realities he couldn't deal with now.

"Maybe I've got to rethink some things," he said to himself.

Meg came out to the patio to check on Kenny's grillwork. "Oh, forgot to mention that Mary called while you were at confessions, Mickey. She said they were looking forward to seeing you for brunch tomorrow morning."

"Did she say anything else, sis?"

"Nope. I've gathered that Mary's not much of a conversationalist…at least not when it comes to me." There seemed to have been some unspoken tensions between the two women ever since Meg had moved her family to Naples nearly a year ago.

"Is everything lookin' good on your end, hon?" Meg gave Kenny a kiss on his cheek. "I'll be ready to serve things up in another five minutes or so."

"We're one beer away from being done…right Mick?"

Mickey missed the question as he was tangled in thoughts of profound disappointment. The evening went about as well as the swamp buggy races had. Confusing. Was he trying too hard to please or was everybody else tiring of him? Mickey and Michael didn't see each other the next day. Mickey declined the brunch invitation on Sunday morning after mass.

23/ WEST DULUTH

Adam felt like a misfit when he reported to the West Duluth Department half an hour before his duty time. The captain, Ned Seeley, was nice enough in welcoming him and Sergeant Ben Grubich gave him a thorough orientation. His parameters would be from the Denfeld High School area east to Fond du Lac in the far western reaches of the city. "We've been keeping an eye on the high school lately. Drugs mostly. And Central Avenue has its share of troubles," Grubich said. "Not quite like Hillside, but we've got our fair share of riff-raff."

Adam would patrol with a veteran named Carl Rodland. "He's been around for more years than I can remember, so he can show you the ropes better than most."

"Sounds good to me," Adam said.

"After a few weeks…we'll see what Carl has to say…if things pan out, you'll have your own squad car next month."

Carl Rodland was a heavy man, several chins merged with a neck as thick as his own thighs. And as gruff as a troll with a toothache. When shaking hands he noticed a Shriner's ring and a small eagle tattoo on his forearm; Rodland's smell was that of a bakery. "Suppose we'd better get out so I can show you the ropes; ain't that what the captain says I've gotta do today?" Adam felt like a nuisance the veteran was told to educate and endure. "Yer kinda like a surprise, Trygg." Adam would be Trygg to Rodland for some time to come. "Just dropped on us from outta nowhere. One of our best officers got bumped to the downtown headquarters to make room fer ya. We all hated to see him go."

Adam didn't know how to respond to that. "I was as surprised as anybody, sir." He would be respectful until told otherwise. "Just happened last week."

"I know. Murf filled me in."

"Oh, you know Murphy?" Adam forced a smile. "We patrolled together for nearly a year."

"Yeah, your first year. You just had an anniversary didn't you?"

"I did." Just a single year's seniority prior to his new assignment was something that would bother lots of people on the force.

"Murf and me came in about the same time. We've kept in touch over the years."

While patrolling the Raleigh Street neighborhood in west Duluth, Adam saw a dark-colored Buick with heavily tinted windows parked near a duplex. He wanted to say something about Lucy's description of the car that had been watching her. But...did he want to open that can of worms on his first day? No! Listen and learn, he reminded himself as they approached the Buick. He hadn't heard from the girl named Holly in quite some time and maybe it was best to just let things ride. He did, however, make a mental note of the address.

"He's illegal," Rodman said as he gestured toward the car and slowed.

"Much too much tinting. If he were driving I'd give him a 'fix-it' ticket."

Adam suggested, "We could write one up and slip it under his wiper."

"Not worth the bother, son." Carl accelerated past the car. "Trouble comes looking for you...not the other way aroung. Let's take Grand Avenue out to Fond du Lac. There's a coffee shop in Gary that's got pie to die for."

Adam memorized the license plate and would run an ID later. He should have written it down—one wrong number or letter would make the search more difficult.

*　　　*　　　*

The afternoon brought a brushing of snow and the stiff northerly winds that accompanied the snow whipped up little drifts along the curbsides and low areas. So far, the late fall had been a lamb awaiting the lion that was sure to follow. For the remainder of the shift Adam had the Buick in the back of his mind. He had Lucy's phone number scribbled on a note pad in the glove box of his car. On his drive home he tried her number and left a message: "Haven't forgotten about your 'issue'. Don't call me. I'll be in touch later."

After leaving the message he wondered if it had been a wise thing to do. He was probably better off forgetting about the prostitute; yet Adam had a cop's nagging curiosity.

His cell rang. "Gotta minute?"

"I told you not to call me."

"Just say 'wrong number' if you can't talk."

"I'm almost home. I've got a quick question; that's all. Do you know anybody on the eight hundred block of Raleigh Street?"

"Not that I can think of. Why?"

"Nothing." As he pulled off Grand and onto 85th, Adam said: "I'll keep in touch, okay?" Then he cut off.

The John 'Jesse' James case was going nowhere. Adam was convinced that Loosey Goosey knew more than she was willing to disclose. Maybe he shouldn't have hung up on her. Among other things, he'd forgotten to ask the girl what she'd been up to these past few weeks. Since the murder he hadn't seen much of the double-identity girl he'd come to enjoy in a brotherly way. Why did he seem bothered by that?

24/ MOTHER AND SON

October in northeastern Minnesota can be very nasty or quite pleasant. In that regard it was much like any other month—unpredictable! This fall it made a magnificent and camera-worthy presentation. Mild temperatures and resplendent color kept most minds off of the inevitable deep freeze that was winter. In the fall Mickey's father had always taken his wife for a hike up on Beauty Mountain, south of Hibbing. But, Amos Moran had passed, and his widow had no desire to make the trek without her husband. Sadie

Moran was too often lost in her marriage memories and reluctant to strike a new life for herself. She had turned down every invitation to join Meghan and Kenny and her grandchildren in Naples. Why? Simply and succinctly, because the home on Banyan Boulevard, where the Williams now resided, had been the winter retreat of Amos and Sadie Moran for many years. When Kenny took a job in Naples months earlier, it made simple sense to live in the Moran home…Sadie had insisted upon it!

Sadie Moran, still lovely at seventy-two, might never get over her loss. She and Amos were 'soul mates', if ever that expression possessed any grains of wisdom and truth— and the pair were inseparable. His passing was all too sudden and Sadie had taken it badly. Amos, she would admit to everybody, just didn't take care of himself the way he should have. What she wouldn't admit was that she had failed to be more perceptive and assertive. So, when Mickey called her on this late October Friday evening she had to relive old and painful memories of a lost time. "No…no. That's out of the question. But I'm delighted you're going to come up tomorrow and visit. It's been weeks and you don't call enough," she scolded. Mickey would never deny his negligence; Meg called their mother almost daily and often talked with her for an hour. "I'll put a pot roast in the crock pot and make your favorite cherry pie."

"I won't take no for an answer, Mom. It's supposed to be a gorgeous day and perfect for a hike. The leaves should be golden and the fresh air will do us both some good."

Sadie stewed. "That would be too hard, Michael." Sadie nearly always called her son by his given name as she didn't think 'Mickey' sounded very priestly. "You must understand that. Beauty Mountain and your dad…" She didn't finish the thought.

"What if I won't come if you won't promise to at least take a drive up the road to the lake? Then we can just turn the car around and come home."

"Michael, don't do that to your mother. Besides, this 'if you won't then I won't' is childish and beneath you. It might even be sinful; you should have learned 'honor thy father and mother' better than most. Regardless of her adamance, Mickey was almost certain that he would be able to use his charm and change her mind. "See you tomorrow, Mom."

While driving north on Highway 73, Mickey watched the leaves fluttering across the asphalt pavement. The maples and oaks were shedding their color and most were nearly naked already. The brushstrokes of God's exquisite palate had vanished. Somehow, this season's changings had escaped his notice until now and he regretted his myopic disregard. Maybe a walk along the road circling Carey Lake would be a more reasonable outdoors alternative. He'd present that option to his mother.

* * *

Mickey needed to talk to someone about his recent Florida visit, but his mother was not his first choice for anything confidential. Sadie's world had already been rocked to it's fragile essence and her family sensitivity would be provoked. On Sunday afternoon he would be watching the Viking's football game at Mario's place on the UMD campus. Maybe the two of them would find an opportunity to talk about 'things' afterwards. Well-grounded and candid, Mario knew him even better than his mother and wasn't about to pull any punches. And, Mickey needed someone to right his lost and rapidly sinking ship before it began taking on too much water. He would, therefore, paint a rosy picture for his mother—even if it wasn't as honest as it should be—'*mea culpa*', he mumbled to himself.

For the past two weeks his brief conversation with Tom Blanchard had been eating away at him. That, along with a cluster of fifty other 'issues', were going to give him an ulcer if he didn't do something about them soon. His next monthly trip to Naples was just over a week away.

The permission that Tom asked for should not have been a big surprise, nor should it have been a big disappointment. It was just that his proposal was coming much too soon. After all, Tom and Mary had only been husband and wife for a little over three months. And, Mickey hadn't found an opportunity to talk to Mary about the proposal—the two of them hadn't said a word to one another since Mickey skipped the Sunday brunch with the Blanchards. He had wrestled with the idea of calling Mary at NCH, the hospital in Naples where she worked, to discuss her feelings about Tom's adoption request. After all, her feelings were just as important as his…or Tom's…or Michael's. What hurt him the most was the heart-wrenching notion that his son seemed to be drifting away. On his last visit, the two of them had only had a few hours together, and that wasn't nearly enough to nurture the bond he so wanted to have with Michael.

The travel-visit-return 'grind', as much as he hated to call it a grind, was not accomplishing what Mickey had hoped and prayed for. He had to be honest with himself about that reality despite the pain it was causing. 'Accept the things you cannot change', he reminded himself almost daily. In recent days and weeks, however, everything seemed to be suffering: his ministry, his relationships with friends and family, and his self-perception more than anything. At times he even believed that he might have made a colossal mistake by not breaking away from his beloved Church and allowing himself to become a husband and father. Despite Mary's refusal to consider it…he still clung to the belief that he could have made it happen if he had persevered. But, he hadn't. Was it a lack of courage or a divine intervention? He might never know. She loved him still—of that he was certain. But, what difference did that make? Now he was paying the price of his choice; wondering if Mary was paying the same price.

25/ PRAYERS

On the early evening drive from Hibbing to Duluth, Mickey replayed the visit with his mother in his thoughts. It had been a pleasant day in most respects; they had enjoyed a wonderful walk and found some unexpected color in the birch and aspen forest surrounding Carey Lake, they'd shared a delicious dinner together, and spent hours conversing and reminiscing. He wasn't disappointed. As he drove east on highway 37, then south on 53, he tried to pray. Try as he might to focus, Mickey found his thoughts wandering all over the place and back again to his visit. His lack of appropriate concentration was as troubling as his punchless homilies were becoming. Often some transient idea would inspire him while on a road trip and away from the everyday, mundane routines that shaped his life. But, that wasn't happening now. While passing the Anchor Lake rest area, he found himself in spontaneous prayer: *Dear Father I'm becoming a mess and I know that You can see it. I'm blocking Your love and getting too absorbed in my self. It's been me, me, me! I'm sorry—truly sorry. On this lovely evening I ask you again...help me with my decisions, big and small. Help me be a good son to my mother, a good brother to Meghan. Help me to be a good priest to my parishioners. Help me to be a good friend to Mario tomorrow. Help me to be a good father to Michael every day of my life."* He paused from his prayer, and taking a deep breath, he continued: *"Michael is Your greatest gift to me...as important as the gift of my priesthood. Help me do justice to both, because I don't think I'm doing very well with either. I ask you these things in the name of Jesus, Your Son, and my Lord. Amen."*

Mickey should have felt better...but didn't. Although blessed in so many ways the emptiness inside would not go away. As an afterthought, he added a footnote to his prayer: *"Bless my mom, dear Lord. I think that she has something heavy on her mind...something she wouldn't share with me but something that only you could know.*

Help her find happiness again." Sadie, like her son, did have things on her mind…things she believed were best left unsaid. The Morans had always been good at keeping their pain to themselves. Meghan wasn't happy. More honestly, she was very unhappy. Maybe it was some arcane Moran malady… Mickey's grandfather had once told him that the family was star-crossed.

*   *   *

Mickey's Sunday mass homily departed from an explanation of the Gospel reading. He felt a need to preach about the power of prayer. *"When you talk to God just lay it out there…whatever is on your mind. If you're angry about something, or somebody, feel free to let Him know it. We might think that He knows everything—and, maybe He does—but, regardless, He needs to hear it from each of us. That gives our issues a legitmacy in His eyes. When things aren't going well we're quick to ask God for help and if things don't go as we like we…well, I'll let each of you finish the sentence in your own way. As hard as it may seem at the time, we should thank Him for not letting that thing go as we thought it should. He's pretty clever that way…and it makes Him feel good that you took that moment to say 'thanks'—thanks for the disappointment and pain—I guess I needed that!"*

When Mickey walked from the lecturn to the altar he smiled to himself. *"God, why can't I take my own advice?"*

For the first time in a while he was seeing something that had been missing for too long: His congregation was listening to what he said…and maybe, just maybe…even thinking about making some changes in their prayer lives. Another positive, Mickey had kept his inspired homily within his twelve-minute time frame.

26/ RALEIGH STREET

Adam would never admit that he had forgotten the license plate number on the Buick he had spotted on Raleigh Street. For the next week, whenever in the Central Neighborhood, his eyes were focused more on cars than on people. Feeling more accepted by his partner in their third week together, Adam had shared Holly's story about the mysterious Buick and the girl's alleged stalking story. After a few quiet moments while cruising Central Avenue, Adam asked Carl Rodland: "Tell me more about Raleigh Street. I've heard it has quite an interesting history."

"You've got that right, Adam. My uncle, Martin, he lived there back in the forties and fifties, anyhow he could tell you some stories."

Adam waited for some stories. But, it took a few turns and a run down a trash-strewn alley before Carl continued. "It might have been the toughest neighborhood in all of Duluth." He offered a wide smile and continued, "You ever heard about Willie the cop? Legend has it that the Raleigh Street Gang pinned Willie's badge to his ass and used his cuffs to tie him to a light post. Willie had boasted that he was going to tame Raleigh Street." Rodland laughed heartily as he elaborated the story. "I guess it's true enough, least some of the 'old timers' still tell the story. Happened just up ahead at the corner of 57th and Raleigh."

"It's not one of those so-called 'urban legends' then?"

Carl grinned widely and winked, "It is and it isn't."

Through their first shifts together Rodland had seemed surly and, all too often for Adam's sake, reminded the new cop in town that he was starting out on his left foot. "Lots of feathers got ruffled," he had said more than once. "Guy's wanna know who's butt you kissed downtown—what crooked politicos got you hooked up here?"

On their third shift together Rodland assured him, "I told the guys you're okay—just a regular cop. Kinda green, I said, but asks lots of questions. They seemed okay with that. They like the idea that you live here on the west end. Riverside, ain't it?"

Adam nodded. He let Carl know that he appreciated the veteran's glowing endorsement and told him that he was looking forward to meeting some of the guys. "I almost feel like a leper when I come to work."

"That'll change," Rodland assured. "Friday night after work most of the guys go over to the Kom On Inn, know where that is over on Grand?"

Adam did. "Across from the zoo?"

"Yep. Anyhow, stop in and join us if you want."

Adam was driving that day, so he made a pass by the duplex he and Susan rented on Cato Street in Riverside. "That's where I'm living these days. Lots of history here in Riverside, too. Down on the St. Louis River used to be a huge shipyards—built ships for the Second World War."

"Yep…my dad worked there…and my grampa, too," Rodland said. "Those days everybody had a job…not like now." Carl had an attitude about the underclass and government handouts. "My dad would roll over in his grave if he knew what things were like today." Rodland was much more talkative when he wasn't driving the squad.

Their last swing of the shift was a slow run around Denfeld. Adam parked for a few minutes just off of Grand so they could watch as the high school kids were crossing the busy street. Most were weighted down with over-stuffed backpacks. "Notice something, Adam…not a lot of happy faces. Didn't used to be that way. I never had much homework…never took home more than a book or two…and that was only if we had a test the next day. Now they're packing a library on their backs. I swear, they're all gonna be stoop-shouldered one day."

Adam laughed. "Another thing you notice is how many of them have cell phones. The other day at a restaurant I saw two young people—I guessed they might have been on a date—anyhow, they were texting each other rather than talking. What a concept." Adam chuckled, "It has an upside I guess. If one of them writes something, maybe a wrong idea or an offensive word, they can delete it before sending sending it on. We never had that opportunity. My dad used to say, 'a word is like a bullet...once it's fired you can't get it back'."

From Denfeld, they swung down Central one last time on their way back to headquarters. Rodland smiled like the teacher who knew it all. "Let me fill you in on something...there used to be lots of bars down here. With bars came almost everything you might imagine. Some of the bar brawls that happened here on Central are legendary. Only thing they didn't have down here back then was drugs. At least my uncle Martin didn't know about them. Lots of pretty good athletes came out of here, too. Mostly they played for Denfeld back in the day when football was for men only. Uncle Marty was one of 'em. Nobody ever messed with Marty Rodland."

*   *   *

Adam had no more than departed the police station when his cell phone vibrated in his pocket. Probably Susan with a list of groceries for him to pick up on his way home; but just as he said 'hello sweetheart' he heard a giggle—it wasn't Susan.

"Hello . . .?"

"It's me." Adam recognized the voice.

"What's happening?"

"I saw that you just left the station," Holly said. "I heard that you got a transfer."

"Are you stalking me Lucy? And who told you about a

transfer?"

"No to the first question and...none of your business to the second—at least not for now."

"Do you have something for me?" Adam's impatience was evident and he wanted the girl to know. "I'm pressed for time Lucy...or Holly? Is this relevant to anything?"

"Not really. Just want to keep in touch...that's all."

Adam softened, "You keeping your nose clean, Lucy? I don't have to tell you that it's a crazy, dangerous world out there. Especially Hillside."

" Yes, I'm behaving myself. And, don't call me Lucy anymore. You call me Lucy and I'll talk like Lucy: "Loosey Goosey ain't been a'hookin' if'n thaz wha'cha mean."

"Cut it out. I much prefer talking to Holly."

The line went quiet for a long minute. "I talked to my dad last night. He told me that he's got a new girlfriend. Her name's Jenny. Anyhow, she lives on Raleigh Street. Remember when you asked me if I knew anybody on Raleigh?"

Adam did. "And...I suppose you're going to tell me she drives that window-tinted Buick?"

"Not quite. My dad does. I asked him. Then I asked if he's been following me. He denied it but I think he was lying."

"Does your dad live on Raleigh?"

"No, he's got a place out in Fond du Lac...at least that's where he said he was living these days. He's kinda like a rolling stone, you know..."

Adam finished the cliché, "...gathers no moss."

"That's dad."

"Anything else?"

Another long pause, she picked up the thread: "We've gotta talk. Soon." Another pause. "I've been scared as hell since Jesse got whacked. Brandy's scared, too. Even more than me. She's left town to live with her parents…I talked with her last night. She's never coming back—at least that's what she says."

"I hope that's true. I hope the same for you, Holly. You're young and smart and good-looking as well. You can have a life—a damn good life— if you choose to."

"Aren't you just full of compliments, Mister Adam Trygg. Do you charm Susan, too—tell her that she's smart and beautiful?"

"Every day." Then it struck him, Holly knew his name…and Susan's? "Where did you…?"

The line went dead.

27/ QUESTIONS

Sunday afternoons had become a wind-down time for Mickey and a few fellow priests who congregated at Mario's place on the UMD campus— 'Football Sundays' as the gatherings had come to be known. Everybody who came brought something along with them—beer, soda, or chips—while Mario collected five bucks from each of the guys and ordered pizzas. Hoping to have some time to visit privately with his dearest friend and mentor, Mickey arrived on campus early. The weight of the previous week's issues was heavy and he sensed there was still another ton waiting in the wings. Father Bruno's call the previous night troubled him: Tom Blanchard's call on Wednesday night troubled him even more.

Wednesday, after the Blanchard's dinner, was when Mickey always called his son. This time things reversed, Tom called Mickey just after six in the evening. "Have you thought it over enough or do you think you need to talk with Mary about it?" *'It'* was Tom's hoped for support of his proposed adoption of Michael. "It's been over a month, Mickey. And, to be honest, I'm anxious to get the ball rolling."

Mickey needed to get a better grip on his feelings and still remained reluctant to talk with Mary about '*it*'...if she was in agreement with her husband, it would be like thrusting a dagger in his heart. If she didn't—and, why would she go against Tom's wishes—what then? If he agreed, he would be closing a door he wasn't ready to close; not quite yet. Why? What was preventing him from doing what was best for Michael, and maybe for Mary as well? Why couldn't he just let go? Mickey knew that his wrong-thinking had to end—and end soon. He knew it in his head...but his heart seemed miles behind.

Mickey knew that Michael had always wanted a 'dad' and that Mickey wasn't a dad—couldn't be a dad! Not in his present circumstance. Maybe...maybe Michael loved Tom more than him? Maybe it was Michael, even more than Tom, who wanted the adoption to happen. What if it was Mary, more than either her husband or her son, who wanted Tom to be her son's legal parent? What if that was what the reality...? Were these and other questions the reason he wasn't ready to talk to Mary? Maybe it was a dark fear of the truth. Mickey's thoughts were touching nerves he didn't want touched. So many questions:

-Could Tom simply procede with an adoption regardless of whether

he had Mickey's legal support or not?

-What if the issue went to court?

-What if there was a vindictive side of Tom Blanchard?

-What if something happened to Tom?

-What if Tom and Mary were to get divorced?

-What if Michael didn't want to be adopted?

-What if Michael did? Would Michael hate him if he refused?

-And, what did Mary want? Was it more about Mary's feelings than it

was anything else? More than Michael's? More than Tom's?

After putting his phone away, Mickey realized what he had just said; "It's up to the three of you. I won't stand in the way." Was he relieved…or would he rue his concession for as long as he lived? That was the question that burned a hole in his heart.

* * *

"Mickey, my amigo!" Mario greeted. "Why so glum? You look like hell. Talk to me. You've got me and my profound insightfulness all to yourself until Bruno gets here, and it looks like it'll just be the three of us today."

"If he shows up," Mickey said. "He's been off on some other planet for weeks. Have you heard anything about what's up with him?"

"Nobody seems to…but, believe me, his remoteness hasn't gone unnoticed. It's like he's got the weight of the world on his two shoulders—not that he couldn't handle the weight."

"I saw him at Beamer's place last week," Mickey said. 'After saying he wanted to talk to me, Beamer came into the room. Bruno said 'It'll keep until Sunday' then he disappeared into his office. And…"

'Beamer' was a nickname for His Grace, Bishop Anthony Bremmer. Only Mario and Mickey ever uttered the moniker. "And…?" Mario said as he took Mickey's coat.

"And what?" Mickey asked.

"Finish what you started to say. Did you or didn't you get a chance to talk with Bruno?"

"I didn't."

Mario's eyes betrayed his confusion. "What were you doing at the bishop's place anyhow?"

"He had some bad news for 'your's truly' and wanted to tell me in person." Bremmer had told Mickey 'no more Florida vacations'. "That's what he called my visits with Michael, 'vacations'! At least not until sometime next year." Mickey took a Diet Pepsi from Mario's overstuffed fridge. "He told me that too many things have been slipping through the cracks at Saint Gerard's."

"What did he mean by that? What things?"

"Pretty much everything." Mickey plopped in Mario's Lazy Boy and continued: "Late reports, missed meetings, collections…pretty much all the things I'm supposed to be doing. Sad part was I really couldn't argue with anything he said. Truth be told, I think I've been slipping through the cracks along with everything else."

"That sounds dire." Mario took a place on the couch across from his friend, muted the Viking's pregame mumbo-jumbo. "Sounds like the stress mess to me, Mick. Why don't you tell me about it."

"Hard to explain, Mario. It's like my head just hasn't been in it. Is it possible to be burnt out at age thirty-seven? That's what I feel like…like I simply can't do the things that used to be so easy; so natural."

"The priest things…is that what you mean?"

"Yes and no. That's a big part of it. I mean, like I just said, things seem to be crumbling around me and I'm just not coping. Maybe what I need is a leave of absence; a few months off might get me back on track. I don't know."

"Maybe you should consider another profession. Like becoming an ornithologist or something." Mario suppressed a smile at his suggestion but Mickey wasn't looking his way anyhow. He waited for a response, "Are you listening to your counselor, Mick?"

"Yeah," he turned toward Mario with a quizzical expression, "What in God's name is an...what's the term you used?"

"Orinthologist. I read something about what they do in a *National Geographic* magazine."

"I have no clue whatsoever," Mickey admitted. "What makes you think...?"

"I remember you telling me how fascinated you were watching a pair of robins build a nest last spring. You were gaga over robins, and finches, and chickadees...and what else? Bluejays. Maybe you should be a birdman, that's what orinthologists do. You could protect bird habitats against the intrusions of money-hungry developers."

Mickey nodded, "Great advise, my friend. If I agreed with you we'd both be wrong." Mickey's laugh was phoney but Mario shared it with him. "That's good, Mick. I'll have to remember that," he said.

"Maybe I could become the reincarnation of a contemporary Saint Francis of Assissi. I'd like that," Mickey suggested.

Mario frowned, "Seriously, Mick, when did all this start...and what can I do to help you get your head on straight. You are the best priest in this diocese...even Beamer, if he were honest, would admit that."

Mickey knew that he was a good priest—just not so much lately. "This funk I'm in has been going on since after Michael's trip up here in July. What I thought would be a growing relationship with my son is on the ebb these days. And, I don't know what to do about it."

"I'm sorry to hear that, Mick. I wish I could help with that but I'm afraid I can't. That's something exclusively yours."

"I know that. But, that's only one piece to a thousand-piece puzzle. I don't quite know where to start with it all." Mickey stroked his stubbled chin, realizing for the first time that he had forgotten to shave that morning. He looked away and took a long swig from his can of Pepsi, "What can you do to help me out? Well, for one thing you could borrow my parish about seventeen grand—that's what the bishop says that our deficit for the annual Appeal amounts to. I've beaten my parishioners to death with pleas for stewardship…to no avail. It's looking like I'll have to run to Mom again. She's already paying for my flights to Florida."

Mickey's mouth went dry, his throat tightened, "I know that she can

afford to do it, and she never hassles me about it, but…still, it makes me feel awfully damn…"

"I hear ya. That's probably what Bruno wanted to talk to you about—the shortfall. I just hope he doesn't spoil our football afternoon with all the money stuff. Everybody knows the golden rule: 'no business talk allowed' on football Sunday.

Mickey had a feeling that Bruno, like himself, had some serious matters on his mind. His friend had sent him a strange text message that morning: *Need to talk after the game. I'd be more comfortable in Mario's chapel on campus. See you this afternoon. Brew.*

* * *

Bruno had changed his mind five times before actually getting in his car and driving to the UMD campus to join the guys. The *sacredl seal*, and his priesthood vow, were pushing him to the edge of a cliff, and if he didn't unload some of the tension, he would jump. Suicide as an option was still on his table. It was that bad— and it was getting worse by the day. He'd researched everything he could think of from *Canon Law* to practical Catholicism to no avail. He was stuck with a confession he couldn't confess. There was a lost sheep somewhere out there and he couldn't find him; couldn't bring him back to the flock.

Several weeks ago Father Bruno had seen the story on TV and read about it in the next day's newspaper. A young man by the name of Jones had been murdered in Hillside. He was certain that the murderer—the man in the floppy hat—had confessed that very crime to him. The police didn't have much of anything to go on. Bruno had something…and, by the vow of his priesthood, he couldn't tell anybody.

His text message to Mickey that morning was pure desperation. Of all the priests Bruno knew…he had chosen Mickey for the guidance and trust that might afford him some measure of peace. Maybe, after talking with Mickey, he'd be able to inform the bishop. Maybe?

28/ THE PARADOX

Mario answered his doorbell, then yielded to Father Bruno's welcoming hug. Usually his ribs would ache for hours afterwards, but not this afternoon. "Where's all the gusto, my friend? I can still breathe."

Bruno forced a laugh. "You want a bone-crusher, do you? Well com'on my fellow Italiano, I'd be more than happy to indulge."

Mario stepped away from the dare and playfully stretched out his arms to fend off the huge man. Mickey got up from the sofa where he was perusing the sports pages of the morning paper. "Let me at'em, Mario. I can take the full Bruno crush without being a wuss about it."

Mickey stepped between his fellow priests. "Love ya, Brew," he said as he stepped confidently into Bruno's warm embrace. "We'll catch up later…okay?" he whispered in the burly man's ear.

Fathers Galloway and McCarthy joined the men early in the first quarter of the Vikings game, and left after only one beer and more than their fair share of the pizza Mario had provided. Even worse, neither priest left the expected five-dollar bill. By halftime, the ho-hummer of a pro football match-up, had provided nothing more than a single field goal. The Tampa Bay scoreboard looked more like a baseball game than an NFL game.

Mickey had been watching Bruno across the room more than the big-screen TV in Mario's living room. Bruno, usually boisterous, had hardly spoken a word all afternoon. An astute football conneseur, Bruno had rare strategic insights and the capacity to analyze the complex blocking techniques of both the offensive and defensive linemen. Most viewers were riveted on the quarterback, running backs and receivers.

"Mario, I've gotta talk with Mickey for a few minutes. It's important. And…I think I'd like if the two of us can go over to the chapel; that's if it's okay with you."

"What…and leave me here all by myself!"

"That way you'll be in good company," Mickey chided.

In the small chapel the two men knelt in prayer for a few minutes. When Mickey looked across he saw that Bruno was losing his battle against tears.

"Will you hear my confession, Father?" His reference was to *Father*, not the familiar Mickey.

Without saying so, Mickey nodded turned the chair behind him in order to face Bruno. He offered his colleague a traditional blessing: *"In the name of the Father, the Son, and the Holy Spirit…"*

It took Bruno a long and unpleasant minute to begin. "Can I ask you a few questions before I get into my sins? I'm really struggling with something…something that's been killing me…literally killing me!"

"Absolutely, Brew! Anything at all."

"Has the *sacred seal* ever been a problem for you?"

Mickey puzzled for a moment. "The *seal* of the confessional?" He asked; giving the matter a long thought. "Not really…at least nothing that comes to mind. Jeeze…what can I say to that? If I were to fully answer that question then I'd be violating the *seal* itself…wouldn't I?"

"Would you? That's the question." Bruno's eyes betrayed a deep emotion. I mean, if you didn't give me any names nor any specifics of any kind…then what?"

"Bruno, you're a helluva lot smarter than I am about those kinds of things. You mean…say, if someone confessed to me that they had robbed a bank could I tell you: 'I know someone who robbed a bank'? And, supposing I didn't give you any names or places or times—like if it was without the slightest incriminating detail?" He scratched his head. "I think I'd say no I couldn't…no, I'm quite sure that I couldn't do that. Certainly, I'd tell the penitent that he or she should go to the police: if the penitent did or didn't would be none of my business. I'd be through with it. If the police came to me and asked if I knew anything I'd simply say 'no'—or 'I cannot say'."

"But that's not the truth, Mickey? You *do* know!"

Mickey contemplated: "What if…let's say that I told the penitent that his sins were forgiven if—and only if—he went to the police?" Mickey tried to answer his own question. "I guess that I would be denying absolution…wouldn't I? I couldn't do that either."

"How about if you didn't know if the penitent's confession was valid?

Say…something like…say he left the confessional before the priest had completed his 'Prayer of Absolutioin'?"

Mickey knew Bruno's dilemma without being told in so many words. "Okay…enough of the hypothetical. If you were to tell me that you have heard a confession in which someone had committed a serious crime, in that case I think you would be violating the *seal.* That's my take anyhow. I suppose that I'd have to run it by the bishop…but that would be walking on thin ice, too." Mickey forced a smile. "On complicated things like what you're asking; I think my theology is kinda weak."

"So we have a paradox, don't we."

"A 'Catch 22'…damned if you do and damned if you don't."

"Something like that," Bruno said as he wrenched his heavy hands. "Damned if you do…I mean *damned* in the most literal sense."

Mickey met Bruno's eyes, "I can't hear your confession if you are, in any possible way, stretching an interpretation of the *sacred seal.* I'm sorry, Bruno. I can't let you risk excommunication from our Church."

"Thank you, Mickey. I think you understand my dilemma. Forgive me for burdening you with my questions…will you do that for me?"

"Of course I will, you know that without asking." Mickey considered a dilemma of his own. Should he simply say 'I forgive you, Bruno' or recite the 'Prayer of Absolution'? What was Bruno actually asking him to do? Did his friend consider this conversation to be his confession? Before he could decide, Bruno rose from his kneeler and dabbed his handkerchief at his reddened eyes.

"Why don't you go back and rescue Mario from himself, Mickey. I'm thinking that I'll stay on here for a few minutes and say some prayers. Okay?"

Mickey gave his friend a hug. "See you in a few, Brew." Mickey hoped his parting comment would lighten his departure. "I'm a poet who doesn't know it."

Bruno's forced smile came with no words of accompaniment.

29/ LETTING GO

November slipped in quietly and passed swiftly. Frigid temperatures and brisk northerly winds made most Minnesotan's happy to be done with her aggravations. Winter was peeking around the corner as if she were planning to jump out and surprise everyone. But, winter's blast was never a surprise to the natives of northern Minnesota.

The Moran family had an unusual Thanksgiving. Meg was in Hibbing to spend a 'few days' with mom—leaving Kenny and the kids behind in Naples. Kenny was "in the middle of a big project" and the kids "couldn't miss school" Sadie was assured. Mickey drove up from Duluth. The day was snowy and cold outside— and chilly inside as well.

Tension came in the door with Mickey. "You look great, Mom…love the new hair cut. I havent' seen you with short hair in years." He went on to compliment her outfit, "Super looking dress, too." Sadie was wearing a stylish burnt-orange two piece combo with a pearl necklace that Amos had given her years before."

After giving his mother a kiss on the cheek, he turned to Meghan, "You look great, too, Sis." He appraised his sister's outfit with a frown, "Aren't those slacks a bit tight? I mean, not much left to one's imagination."

"They are yoga tights, for your information. Everybody wears them these days…they are both casual and comfortable—just for your information."

"I am duly informed, Meg. Is it okay if I don't think they are appropriate?"

Meghan didn't offer her cheek for a kiss. Instead she turned into the living room and gestured for her mother and brother to follow: "Let's the three of us catch up on things before dinner. Mom, take a break…you've been in the kitchen enough already."

Sadie and Meg sat near one another on the long sectional while

Mickey chose his father's old recliner across from them. The living room was large and tastefully furnished; with the drapes pulled back it was also bright and amiable. After talk of the gathering snowstorm beyond the picture window, their conversation became more personal and less cordial. Meghan's discomforting issues followed them into the dining room; interrupted only by the saying of Grace and fixing their plates with heaped servings of Sadie's wonderful servings.

"It's wearing me out!" Meg confessed in a voice strained by emotion; tainting Mickey's apitite for turkey with all the trimmings. "The routine, I mean." She was explaining things to Mickey that Sadie already knew. "I felt that I needed a break from it all."

Meghan Moran Williams had experienced these issues before, and Mickey's counsel had left her both angry and confused. Her personality was such that her very stress became a palpable disability. Everything had to go her way without offering any middle ground for compromise. "Maybe I was meant to be single," she blurted. "I mean, that way I could get a challenging job and grow professionally. I'm not growing, Mickey. I'm as stagnant as the pond behind our house. Kenny thinks it's more important to stay at home and be a mom to the kids. Says his income is more than enough to pay the kids' school tuitions and enjoy a comfortable lifestyle as well. 'Comfortable' he says. Comfortable for him, maybe. He's got his perfect job—and sometimes I swear he loves it more than he does me."

Mickey considered a confrontation but dismissed it. He'd let his sister vent and get all her cards on the table. Strangely, Sadie hadn't said a word pro or con. At times she nodded her understanding of Meghan's feelings; at others her face was impossible to read. Mickey wondered: Did his mother support her troubled daughter?

"What say you, Mom?" Mickey cleared his throat, put down his fork, while leaning over his elbows on the table. "You've been conspicuously silent through Meg's marital rantings."

That was it! Meghan burst out her anger. "Rantings? Is that what you call my best attempt at sharing my feelings? I'm upset, damn it, and you're making it sound like I'm a looney or something. For God's sake, Mickey, get off your high horse and listen for a change."

"I've heard your song before," Mickey said. "The poor, neglected, misunderstood, overburdened, and taken-for-granted housewife. I wish you'd take some time now and then to count your blessings. There are not many women who have the luxury of life that you enjoy."

Meg pushed away from the table, "I'm going upstairs to my room. Let me know when my brother's gone, mom. Happy Thanksgiving Father Moran! And...Merry Christmas as well."

Sadie glared. "Sit down, young lady!" Then she looked at Mickey. "Is something bothering you son? I've never heard you talk to your sister that way. I don't think Meghan is looking for sympathy...she just wants us to understand that she's going through a difficult time right now."

Mickey met Meg's angry stare. "Maybe I spoke too sharply, Sis. If so, I'm sorry." He swallowed the truths he had on his tongue. Stress seemed to run in the family these days. But, he wasn't going to lay his own issues on an already cluttered table.

Before leaving in the late afternoon, Mickey informed his sister, "The bishop has me grounded for a while. With the Advent season and Christmas a month away, he wants me to stay put. No more Florida trips until further notice. So, I'm a little wound up myself these days."

"Does Michael know?"

"He does. We talked last night. Says he feels bad about it. But..." Mickey let the 'but' hang between them. "I'd better get on the road. Might take a me a bit longer with the snow and all."

"But...but what?"

"Nothing," he leaned in toward Meg for a goodbye hug and called for their mother who was wrapping foil over the half of the cherry pie that Mickey hadn't devoured. "Just a minute, Mick. I'm sending along some leftovers with you. Why do I always buy the biggest turkey in the bin?" she called from the kitchen. "Be sure to give some to Mario...and give him our love as well."

When he his kissed his mother's forehead, Mickey thanked her. "As always, Mom, we didn't get much time to talk. Sorry about that."

Sadie might have said: "What else is new?"

*   *   *

Minutes later, while driving east on Highway 37 toward the south 53 cutoff to Duluth, Mickey swallowed through a lump in his throat the size of a golf ball. The special day had offered more disappointment than joy. For the past several miles he had been reminiscing about Thanksgivings shared with family over the years. While growing up, Thanksgiving Day had been one of the most enjoyable on the family calendar: the Morans always had so much to be thankful for back then. It seemed apparent to him, that the bonds had loosened. Memories were like old photographs faded with age: Grampa Pack the grizzled old local cop, Gramma Maddie the lovely elementary school teacher...Dad, sitting at the end of the table and slicing the turkey. Saying their grace with reverence. Memories are golden. But the perfect treasures of that day were buried now, and as tragic as that truth might be, Mickey could only smile upon what once had been.

Mickey had noticed something back at the house that bothered him—no, it spoke to him in a profound way. The portrait of mom and dad that had graced the mahogany bookcase for so many years had been moved to another location…or stuffed in a closet somewhere. Whatever, it was conspicuously missing. In its place was some contemporary art piece that splashed a myriad of colors across the living room's wall; it bothered him to distraction. The portrait, he later discovered, had been relocated to the den where Amos had spent so many hours with his legal work and his *New York Times* crossword puzzles. What did that say? Sadie rarely spent time in the den. He had wanted to ask his mom, but didn't think it was any of his business. But there was something else even more disturbing. In the nearly four hours of his visit, Sadie had not mentioned her late husband once. He had been racking his brain for nearly half an hour and couldn't recall a single spoken word about his father. Strange. Very strange!

Maybe Sadie was letting go…finally. Maybe that was the healthiest thing for her to do. At the end of the bereavement cycle of denial, anger, and depression was something psychologists believed was acceptance or—in the terminology of today: *closure*. Mickey believed the notion was no more than a stupid spin on an emotion too deep to fully comprehend. To the priest, closure never really happened. Closure was some ideal that people used to justify themselves or their bad decisions. Yet, letting go was something altogether different—something less complete. 'Letting go' didn't have the finality of closing something forever. It meant getting on with other things…getting on with life. Yes, Mickey mused to himself…getting on with life made so much sense at the moment. How would it feel tomorrow? The next day and the ones after that? Perhaps— just maybe?— he was ready to let go of the one thing that meant the most to him, but he had never actually possessed. He still hadn't heard anything more about the adoption from Tom Blanchard. He still hadn't had the conversation with Mary— the conversation that might give him *closure*. In truth, he still had nothing more than questions he couldn't answer.

Mickey couldn't help thinking of the contradiction that he had become. A line from an old Kris Kristofferson ballad came to mind: '*He's a walking contradiction partly truth and partly fiction taking every wrong direction on that lonely way back home.'* How many wrong directions had he already taken…how many lie ahead?

Mickey took the Proctor cutoff into west Duluth. He'd give his newly installed *bluetooth* system a go. He told 'Miss Annonymous'—who had tabs on all of his friends— that he wanted the 'call' option, then said "Mario" and magically the ring: "Happy Thanksgiving, Amigo."

PART TWO

"He who covers his sins will not prosper, but whoever confesses and forsakes them will have mercy."
Proverbs 28:13

30/ 'MURF'

Adam Trygg's afternoon phone call to his wife was his third that day. Susan was getting close to 'her time' and her mother had driven down from Aurora to be with her for a few days. "This little bugger just won't cooperate with me, Adam. I thought I was getting labor pains about an hour ago but it was just another false alarm."

"Are you okay? I mean, do you need me for anything?"

"Mom's here and I'm fine. Why do you ask?"

"Well, hon…some of the guys from the station are going out for a beer after work. I thought I could make a little public relations attempt; maybe it would let the other cops know I'm one of them. Rodman thinks it's a good idea for me to meet the guys in a different setting."

"You go right ahead. Don't leave your cell in the glovebox like you usually do…okay? I've got a feeling that it could be any time."

"I'll be one with my phone, Hon. Promise."

"Have a good time but be careful. You don't do well after a few beers. And, don't be too late.

*   *   *

When Adam entered the bar his eyes had trouble adjusting from the late afternoon sun outside and the dark interior of the tavern. He took a minute to survey the place for his partner who had left the station a few minutes ahead of him. As he scanned the dozen or so faces along the bar, he thought he saw someone familiar on a stool near the end. And, he was certain that the man he saw had seen him as well. "Hey, Adam…over here." Carl Rodman's thick voice came from the booth to his left. Adam turned, paused, walked over to where his partner was sitting: "…I'll be just a minute, Carl, I think I see someone at the bar that I want to say hello to."

When he looked back to where Murf had been sitting, the space was empty. Adam thought of rushing to the exit sign at the back door and see if his old friend was in the alleyway where many patrons parked their cars. After all, he still hadn't properly thanked Murf for whatever strings he had pulled downtown to get him the transfer. Instead of checking the back door he wandered over to the vacant space at the bar. "Say, excuse me, but was that Brendon Murphy sitting here next to you just a minute ago?" he asked a man dressed in a shirt and tie. The man's eyes narrowed as he gave Adam's uniform a thorough look. "No idea who the guy was. Why? Is he wanted for something?"

"Just thought it was an old friend of mine…that's all."

"I've never seen him before," the guy said. "Expect he might be back though. Said he was going to take a leak."

Adam smiled, "Okay," he said. Then he turned to the man to his left: "That guy who just left say who he was?"

The sturdy-looking man wearing a floppy hat and a plaid shirt had longish hair and the beginnings of a dark beard. Looking Adam over from head to holster, he shook his head and shrugged before turning back to the man he had been conversing with before Adam arrived. The strange look that crossed the man's face seemed to say one of two things: either he didn't like cops…or he feared them. Whatever? Adam turned away and was about to head back to the booth where Carl Rodland and the other cops were sitting.

"Sorry, Bud. Wait a few minutes and see if he comes back," from the first guy. "If he does, do you want me tell him that you're looking for him?'

Adam stood perplexed for a long minute before saying he would be sitting over in the booth along the far wall. "Thanks, yes, that would be fine. My name's Adam if he asks. I'll keep a lookout for him, too."

The man with the tie that he had been talking to looked familiar but Adam couldn't place him. And, the man who looked like Murf was taking a long time in the men's room. As Adam joined Rodland and Petrich in the booth the well-dressed fellow walked toward the back door where the lavs and back exit door were located. "Kinda strange," Rodland said as he noticed Adams gaze toward the back of the bar. "Looks to me like that guy from the commission drinks here with us common folks."

"The guy who's leaving? What commission?" Adam asked.

"The police commission. He's a political hack named Bentley. A big Republican with lots of bucks. He's in the dry cleaning business, owns a chain of stores from here to the Cities. I think he's got a cycle shop as well."

"Probably launders money," Petrich said. The three men laughed.

* * *

After getting two year-old Anna to bed, Susan decided to lie down early and try to get some much-needed rest. She hadn't been sleeping well for some time—a combination of feeling bloated and anxious. Neither she nor Adam knew the gender of the new baby they were expecting to join their family at any time. Both hoped that little Anna would have a brother. They had decided that a son would be Andrew Thomas and, if they had another girl, she would be Angela Marie. Susan's suitcase was packed and she would be ready for the trip to St. Mary's on a minute's notice.

Adam got home before seven and, after greeting his mother-in-law and giving Anna a big hug, headed to the bedroom where Susan was resting. Adam found his wife wide awake and smiling that perfect smile that always made him feel special. "Love you, Suz…how are you doing? Sitting beside her on the bed, he began rubbing her belly and sharing his wife's impatience: "This one's taking his sweet time isn't he?"

Susan gave him a poke in the ribs, "You always call our little peanut 'he' or 'him', I know you want a son but just won't ever admit it. Will you be terribly disappointed if…? Just then, Adam's cell phone rang.

"Who could that be?" he mumbled. "Nobody calls this late in

the evening." He might have added that few people had his cell number.

"It's not even eight, Adam," Susan said.

With a pained expression, Adam was about to say 'hello'…

"Might be your parents, Adam?" Susan started to sit up. "They didn't call yesterday and they've got to be as anxious as we are."

Adam's caller ID read Symanski: "Phil…how the he…heck are you, buddy." He turned to Susan, "It's Phil Symanski, Hon. I'll go into the kitchen and let you two get some rest."

The former partners small-talked for a few minutes before Phil expressed the reason for his call. His father had been doing some poking around; talking it up with some people he knew.

"My dad says that an AFSME union guy, someone who's on top of things going on around town, told him not to mess with Brendon Murphy. 'He's trouble' is what this guy Flarehty said. When my old man pressed him to elaborate, he got put off, like defensive, you know. Flarehty told my dad that 'Murf' is connected'; whatever that means. When he asked about your unexpected transfer Flarehty said 'whatever Murf wants Murf gets'."

Adam was perplexed. "Where are you going with this, Phil? And what's with your dad? Sounds to me like your dad's messing with things that aren't his to mess with." Adam knew how much his friend respected his father, and wished he hadn't said what he just had.

Immediately on the defensive himself, Phil said: "My dad's got lots of experience, Adam. 'Moxie', he calls it. Anyhow, he knows how much we'd like to crack the James murder case. I think it's great that he's doing some sleuthing." Phil's voice suddenly became more of a whisper, "Anyhow, Adam, Dad went even one step further...talked with Cooney."

"About Murf?" Adam knew that Cooney and Murf were pretty tight. "Why did he talk with Cooney?"

"Cooney's the guy to see about any grievances." Phil did not add that his father was trying to start some fires under Murphy. "My dad simply asked Cooney why the west Duluth position wasn't posted so any guy with seniority could put in for it? Cooney told him to talk with Flarehty at the union; said he was as surprised as anybody when your transfer came down."

Adam processed the information. Was Murphy the 'Jeckle and Hyde' that both Phil and his father wanted people to believe? He wasn't naïve enough to think there weren't any bad cops on the force, but he'd never have guessed that Murf might be one of them. "For the life of me, Phil, I can't understand any of this." He considered mentioning that he thought he had seen Murphy, and a police commissioner, at a west end bar earlier that evening— he dismissed the thought. Instead, he asked Phil Symanski: "Have you heard any rumblings in the locker room? I mean, guys that are pissed at me? Pissed about how the transfer thing went down?"

"My new partner, Phillips...that tall, skinny guy that chews—carries that pop can around wherever he goes...anyhow, he told me that most of the guys were happy for you. I guess you were pretty well-liked."

Adam smiled to himself. That afternoon at the bar he found good vibes from his new group of colleagues as well. "I'm glad about that. Anyhow, I think we'd both be better off if we just keep out of this Murphy business. I mean, all that we'd be doing is opening a big can of worms, Phil. Probably not a bad idea to suggest the same to your dad."

Adam asked about Phil's girfriend, Linda: then confirmed that it could be any time now for Susan. "She's more than ready…so am I. You'll be one of the first I call with the news, Phil." After a few more minutes, Adam said his good-bye and promised to keep in touch. "Thanks for calling, Phil."

Before Adam could walk to the bedroom to check on Susan his cell phone rang again. The caller ID was blank and he considered not answering.

Despite being a 'public servant' he was off-duty…reluctantly, he said "Hello…"

"We've gotta talk. The restaurant where I work, next Saturday afternoon…about five."

At the same time Adam heard Susan's pained call from the bedroom. He cut the call and immediately rushed to his wife. Susan was standing by the end table holding her stomach and offered him a wan smile. "It's finally my time, Hon."

Adam saw that Susan's nightgown was wet and she was standing in a small puddle at her feet. "Grab a towel in the bathroom and tell mom and Anna. I'll get dressed and be ready in a minute."

31/ HAPPY NEWS…SAD NEWS

On Friday, December 5th, Adam and Susan Trygg had the son they had hoped for. Andrew Thomas Trygg came into the world at the exact same weight as his father had some twenty-nine years before: Anna's new brother was seven pounds and ten ounces. Adam's parents drove up from South Saint Paul that same day and the Trygg's—three cars of relatives and close family friends—celebrated the new arrival until late that night at the downtown Raddison Hotel. The following two days were equally hectic for all. Adam found himself running from Riverside to St. Mary's Hospital and back again several times. In the excitement of everything he forgot the meeting with Lucy that he had suggested.

On Sunday afternoon Susan was back home and concentrating on giving Anna, nearly three, far more attention than her new brother was getting from everyone. Anna was disappointed that her mom hadn't asked the hospital to give her a little girl and she needed to have her sense of importance pumped up. As Adam was reading Anna 'Charolette's Web' his phone vibrated. He checked the caller ID and put his cell back in his pocket. Later, after Susan had nursed the baby and fallen asleep herself, Adam returned the call.

"Congratulations Adam…oh…you're forgiven for standing me up on Saturday. I get it. Okay?"

"Make it quick, Holly. I'm totally wiped out." When he thought about her comment he was irritated. "How do you know any of this? Are you stalking me or something?"

"Not really…but, I'm sure I've told you before that I'm connected to lots of different networks. Anyhow, I'll give you a rain check on the broken date. You'll be rushing home after work tomorrow so how about we meet at six in the morning? Same place."

"I'll try…that's all I can say."

His phone went dead.

*　　　　*　　　　*

With Christmas only two weeks away, Mickey spent Saturday afternoon shopping at the Miller Mall. That evening he would join Mario for a Catholic Youth seminar at the Newman Center on the UMD campus.

After mass the following morning he made the call to his son that he'd forgotten to do the busy night before. On Thursday night, when he posed the question 'What would you like for Christmas?' to Michael, his son's candid response was 'money'. "I've got everything else I need and Tom's getting me an *Iphone* of my own…so I'm all set," Michael said. With little insight on possible gifts for his son (Michael had told him: 'please no clothes, or books, or video games') Mickey wandered from Penneys on one end of the mall to Old Navy at the other end he found nothing that might be of interest to Michael. Maybe he'd find something to give himself from Santa Claus? The busy *Barnes and Nobel* store was as good a place as any to find something he'd enjoy reading. As Mickey was examining a book by a Hibbing author he heard good things about, his cell phone rang.

"Where are you? I'v tried the rectory, called Mario…" It was the bishop's unmistakable voice.

Bremmer sounded almost out of breath. Mickey said, "I'm Christmas shopping, Your Grace. Up at the mall. Trying to find the perfect gift for my boss."

Bremmer never seemed to get Mickey's subtle humor. "Can you come to my place right now? Something's happened, something very important, we've got to talk about as soon as possible."

"Am I in trouble, Your Grace?"

"You're always in trouble, Mickey." His reference came as a surprise; Bishop Bremmer detested the nickname 'Mickey' and almost always called him either Father Michael or Father Moran.

"I'm on my way."

Mickey purchased a copy of *To Bless or To Blame* for Mario and an *Itunes* card for his son before rushing out of the mall. Michael liked music. He'd find something else for his son to go with the card later. In twenty minutes he was knocking on the Bishop's front door. Father Peter greeted him, "The Bishop is expecting you, Father. Come with me, please."

Bremmer looked wrung out. His face was pallid and his jaw slack. Without so much as a hello he led Mickey into the office located to the back of his large diocean residence. "Sit down, Father. Some bad, some very bad news, I'm afraid.

The bishop's communicating style was usually blunt and direct; then followed by whatever elaboration the matter required. "It's Father Bruno!"

"His mother passed?"

Almost annoyed by the question, the bishop said…"Worse, much worse, I'm afraid."

Bremmer's initial pronouncement was fleshed out with a back-story of sketchy details leading to the 'much worse'. He acknowledged that Mrs. Bocaccio had passed two days before. Both men, and most of the priests in the diocese, knew Bruno's story: his attachment to his mother and his estrangement from an arrogant and aloof father. That summer Ruth Bocaccio was given her terminal lung cancer diagnosis and since had been receiving care from a local hospice program. Bruno kept that matter mostly to himself, much as he did most personal things. "Two weeks ago Mrs. Boccacio's disease got really bad," the bishop said. "I told Bruno to go down and spend as much time as he needed with his mother. He left last weekend…I hadn't heard a word about anything until an hour ago."

Mickey's throat was dry with pent emotion. "I'd imagine Bruno has taken his mother's death pretty hard. When did she pass?"

"On Thursday afternoon. Her funeral's been scheduled down in the Cities on Monday."

Mickey assumed that the Bishop would encourage he and Mario and to attend the funeral out of respect for Bruno. "If it's okay, Your Grace, I'll head down tomorrow morning after mass and give Bruno any assistance he might need to get through this difficult time. I'm sure Mario will want to go along as well."

Bremmer's eyes began to tear.

Mickey found it hard to believe that his stoical bishop had such depth of emotion in his veins. After a suffering moment, the bishop said: "That, I'm afraid, won't be necessary. Bruno is dead!"

Mickey's heartbreak was sudden and intense. "Oh my God…it can't be…" He began to sob uncontrollably…Bremmer did as well.

Shaking his head in disbelief, Mickey said, "Heart attack?" Bruno had always been fifty and more pounds overweight and spent most of his hours sitting at his desk. "He couldn't take the loss…and his heart…"

Bremmer stood, "Join me in prayer, Father." Bremmer took Mickey's hands in his own. *"Eternal rest grant onto your child, Bruno, Oh Lord..."*

He swallowed hard before continuing through his tears, dabbed at his running nose with his shirtsleeve. *"May your perpetual light shine upon him and may his soul, along with the soul of his mother, rest in your eternal peace."* Then Bremmer added a few meaningful words to the familiar prayer, *"He loved you, Jesus, more than anything. Please ask our beloved God to forgive him for what he's done to himself. Amen."*

Mickey released his hands from the bishop's tight grip, "Don't tell me, please, Your Grace…"

"I guess he couldn't take the loss. As we all know, they were very close, she had always been his harbor." Bremmer cleared his throat of emotion, "I should have done something, Father. Bruno has been down in the dumps for weeks…I could see it but…I didn't take the time to ask him if there was anything I could do." Bremmer's self-deprication continued; "I get myself so wound up in the big things that I'm supposed to do that I lose sight of the little things…the loving things. I don't realize that the well-being of my associates is so much more important than anything else I'm supposed to be doing. And, I've never been very good at dealing with people's personal issues, Mickey. I'm pretty good at running the business things and terribly poor at…" he lost his voice for a moment. "I guess people have always been the tools that I use to get those necessary things accomplished. It takes something like this to remind me how trivial church business matters really are. My God…" Bremmer swallowed hard before uttering "how I have failed…" under his breath.

His bishop was so broken down by the weight of his claim of ownership that he was talking and sobbing through his profession of guilt. Mickey stepped toward His Grace and placed his hands firmly on the smaller man's shoulders, then squeezed gently: "We all get our priorities out of whack…" What other comfort could he offer?

Releasing from the hug and drying his tears, Bremmer stepped away and pulled closed the heavy drapes on the south window of his office, returned to his desk, and flipped on his desk lamp, before sitting down again. Clearing his throat he said, "I suppose you wonder why you're the first person I've called?"

Mickey nodded without words as he took a chair across from his

bishop. The room was too dark for him to clearly see the bishop's face, he sensed that His Grace probably wanted it that way after his admission of failed responsibility. In the back of Mickey's thoughts were the last few words of the bishop's prayer: *'Please ask God to forgive him for what he's done…'* "Can I ask you a question, Your Grace?" Without waiting for permission he continued, "What did Bruno do? I mean, why the appeal for God's forgiveness? That good man would have gone straight to heaven."

"What did Bruno do?" Bremmer repeated the question in an almost dramatic tone. "Mickey…he took his own life!"

Mickey felt his stomach turn, for a moment he thought he would heave…"Oh, my God…no! Not Bruno."

"I'm afraid so," Bremmer said.

Stunned, Mickey was at a complete loss for something to say. He wanted to know the how? The where? The when?...all of the irrelevant details; but, under these tragic circumstances, he was reluctant to ask the bishop.

Behind the soft glow of his lamp, but still darkly shadowed, Bremmer answered the questions Mickey hadn't asked. "Apparently last night. He hung himself from rafters in the family's garage. One of the groundsmen on the Bocaccio estate found him early this morning."

Mickey shook his head in sorry disbelief at what the bishop had just revealed. "Father Mario will be devastated, Your Grace. I'm going to be seeing him in an hour or two...can I share this with him or would you rather...?"

"Everybody will be devastated. Father. I'll let the staff know first, everybody here loved the man...then I'll send an email to all the priests. I'm thinking we'll get everybody together early next week...some kind of memorial...I just don't know what to do yet. The messenger said that Mister Boccacio hasn't made any formal arrangements yet...it's gotta be a difficult situation right now— first a wife then his only child. He's probably feeling as guilty as I am. They weren't at all close, and..." Bremmer let his thought hang between them.

Nothing was said for a long minute, "...But, yes...in answer to your question: I'd appreciate if you'd explain the sitation to Father Mario. I plan to talk to him myself later this afternoon."

Mickey stood, anticipating that the bishop was about to dismiss him.

"Just a minute. There's one more thing. The reason I called you before anybody else. Here...this is for you." He handed Mickey the sealed envelope with his name scribbled across the front. Mickey recognized the handwriting—it was Bruno's.

"This was hand-delivered by someone that worked for Mr.

Bocaccio just before I called you. The man said that it was found tucked under Bruno's belt. I was tempted to open it myself…but I couldn't do it."

Mickey's astonishment dried his throat, making his mouth feel like it was lined in sandpaper. "What…? For me?" he uttered, not quite knowing what he should do…what it might be that Bruno wanted him to know?

Bishop Bremmer made his decision easy. "Don't read it now. It might be a suicide note. I trust your good judgment on this. In fact, I think I'd suggest that you read it later tonight…after the youth seminar on the campus. If it's something that you believe I ought to be made aware of…then you might…" He abandoned the obvious thought.

32/ A FRIEND IN FULL

Mickey fell asleep at his desk. Tears stained the soft white page of the note that was pinned below the forearm upon which his head had fallen.

Mickey,

I am returning to my God in who's judgement I deeply fear. But, as we discussed weeks ago, I will not violate the sacred seal of the confessional. I have been on the verge of going to the police with my story but from the edge of the world where I find myself now I could not.

My last wish is for a great favor from an even greater friend. There is a very troubled man somewhere out there. This penitent has been my torment for weeks now. I've looked everywhere for him to no avail. He needs God's love more than I do. I have no name and no more than a hastily provided description from another stranger: 'A man with a floppy hat and wearing a trench coat'. He may not even live in Duluth. Alas!

I can no longer cope with things as they are any longer. I beg your forgiveness and our Gods even more. Pray always for my soul.

Forever

Your brother in Christ, Bruno

Mickey had wept through several readings of Bruno's last words. *A great friend!* "Bruno!... Bruno!...Bruno!..." he wailed into the empty room. "You are mistaken my friend...it was me who failed you! I let you drift away from me without the human compassion—the empathy you so deserved. Why? Why? Why? Why hadn't I understood the depths of your torment." Mickey's conscience was punishing him with a grief so deep he found the weight to be almost unbearable. His brief conversation with Bruno in the chapel left him cold with regret. Why hadn't he followed up their talk with so much as a phone call? Why hadn't he done a thousand things? Into what chasms of human love and compassion was he slipping? Worse...what could he possibly do now? Bruno's last wish was to follow a lead that must have driven his friend half crazy. Now Bruno had passed the baton to his '*great friend*'.

Hours later, Mickey found himself awake and sprawled on his bed in the clothes he had been wearing the previous night. His head was still pounding with a guilt that must have drained him of vitality and walked him to his bed. The desk lamp was still on, the note still laid on the bedstand where he must have left it. It was 7:40...morning mass was at 8:00. Mickey raced to the shower, was out and dried in three minutes, and dressed in five. He'd shave later...if at all. Familiarity with every word and ritual of the holy mass served him well. His homily was the briefest ever: "I have lost a dear friend and I am too deflated to say anything more than please, each of you pray along with me for Father Bruno Boccacio's departed soul." Together Mickey, his altar server, and some fourteen befuddled parishioners said three '*Our Father's*' and three '*Hail*

Mary's'.

Back in the rectory he called Mario—the one person in whom he had an unequivocal trust, and whose gifted insights he sought on almost everything that troubled him. Mario's distress was palpable: "I'll never get over this, Mickey. I keep condemning myself for not doing something when I could see that Bruno was carrying a great burden. We both could see that—everybody should have seen that. And what did we do…?" The answer hung between them like the body in the Bocaccio's garage.

Mario recalled that Sunday afternoon when the two of them last saw Bruno. It was the Vikings game on TV at Mario's. Bruno was not his usual boisterous self—not even a shadow of his former self. Mario remembered those last minutes vividly: "We talked about it after the game. We both knew something was wrong. In fact I asked him how he was feeling at the door as he was leaving…he said that his mom was sick and we both let him go with that flimsy excuse. I can't erase my mind's last picture of Bruno. It's sad beyond my comprehension."

"But we already knew about his mom's cancer, Mario. He had talked about it several times. What we didn't get a handle on was how much her illness was affecting him. We really missed the boat."

"C'mom Mick. We knew how tight the two of them were. She was the world to him…she, more than anybody, supported his becoming a priest."

"You're right about that. Just as we've known how much he despised his father. I wonder if his dad had as much to do with Bruno's decision as the loss of his mother did? Whatever…it was something…something what? Painful to the point of being almost unbearable."

Mario agreed. "A combination of things, I'm sure. Things we'll never be able to understand."

Mickey wasn't ready to divulge the contents of the note that had been passed along to him. Not even to his most cherished friend...not yet. He didn't have a clue of what he should do next...not yet. One thing was certain, Bruno's note was a confession of sorts, and he felt the grip of the sacramental seal weighing on him now. He would not go to the police. Neither would he confide in His Grace the bishop. Like Bruno, he would keep a secret locked inside and suffer the loneliness his friend must have carried with him for the last miles of his life.

Mario was puzzled, disturbed, and on the verge of asking something that would be a betrayal of confidence. The bishop had told him the previous afternoon that Bruno had left what must have been his final note for Mickey. Perhaps...a suicide note that might explain Bruno's state of mind. Mario felt himself being left in a confounding darkness.

The conversation ended with empty feelings on both ends of the strained conversation.

* * *

John Belak was another man on the edge. His unemployment money would run out at the end of the month and he doubted that he would qualify for another extension. He hadn't been looking for work because he didn't want to work. A much bigger worry than a job, or an income, was hearing a knock on his door and a police officer wanting to talk to him. He'd spent the week following the murder with his old girlfriend in Wisconsin before returning to Duluth and his new girlfriend living on Raleigh Street. He worried about his daughter, too. He'd curtailed his cruising Hillside after the murder and spent most of his time keeping out of sight in his far western Duluth apartment.

He saw Godfrey's approach through the parted curtains of his livingroom window. He stiffened at the tentative knock on his door. Godfrey was his neighbor Caroline's husband, and the landlord of the Fond du Lac apartments where John had been renting. His monthly payment was due—overdue…again! The two men had never gotten along. Godfrey thought his wife was getting 'too cozy' with the good-looking guy next door and his tolerance level was strained to its absolute limit.

He let the landlord in without any greeting. "Yeah, yeah…I know. Just gimme a minute," he said. Belak left the room and found the hidden coffee can, with his stash of cash, in the back of the cupboard under his kitchen sink. He withdrew three fifties and two twenties—leaving him with seventeen dollars and some change. He returned to the living room;" here's half of what I owe ya. I'll get the other $210 by the weekend, okay?"

Godfrey grumbled, "Sunday at the latest. I saw ya tuck some money in yer back pocket so I know ya got more than yer givin' me, Belak.

John's smile was twisted. "You saw shit, Godfrey. Just scratchin' my butt. By the way, when you gonna do the painting that you promised the last time we talked? This place is a dump. And the carpet stinks. I got a list of things that ain't the way they otta be."

"Whadda ya want fer yer four-twenty? I do the touchup painting in da spring…shampoo da carpets then, too—not never before." He laughed, "You prob'ly won't be here when dat time comes around."

Godfrey was a red headed stump of a man and John would give him his due before leaving the rat trap behind him; maybe a broken nose or bruise a couple of ribs. Whatever, he'd find something worthy of a jerk: something to remember his soon-to-be former tenant by. "One never knows, does he Godfrey?" John smirked…"are we done now?"

Godfrey huffed, "Remember, ya got til Sunday. And can'ya be on time next month so's I don halfta come knockin again. Okay? I can evict ya for all the crap you give me you know."

John stepped closer, "If you could you would. But, you can't and you're blowing smoke is all. See ya," he began closing the door." As Godfrey stepped away, John said "... Give my best to Caroline."

Ten minutes later John was driving his Buick past the Benton Park exit on Grand Avenue when he spotted a squad car behind him. He tensed immediately. Signalling a right turn, he pulled off the avenue and into a neighborhood the locals called Smithville. The cop continued past. John heaved a sigh of relief.

* * *

Adam was talking hockey with Rodland as the two drove east on Grand. Rodland, like Adam, was a big Wild fan and a former high school player as well. When Adam turned his head, and looked past his partner, he thought he saw the Buick he'd been looking for these past weeks. It was already too late to make the turn so he said nothing. If that was the car he'd been looking for he'd check out Smithville later. He made a mental note to make a pass by on his drive home after the shift. One of these day's he'd confide what he knew about the James murder case with Rodland.

33/ COFFEE TALK

Even in her waitress outfit, she looked radiant— and she knew it! Her makeup was always perfectly done, her naturally blond hair clean and fresh. She stepped behind the small café and into the alley for a quick cigarette before returning to the counter. She had come in early and asked the boss, a dumpy man named Boles who had a belly that hung in a wide lump over his belt, if she could have a longer morning break. The diner wasn't busy at the moment and he had no objections. She washed her hands, filled a decanter with coffee, found two cups and took a place in the back booth. It was nine-thirty. Looking up from her seat in the vinyl-cushioned booth, Lucy smiled as Adam approached. "How's the new dad?"

Adam didn't answer right away. "I don't have a lot of time, Lucy. You said you've got something important to tell me."

She smiled, flashing her perfect teeth. "You never do. It's always slam bam thank you ma'am when it comes to talking with me. Relax, Adam. Enjoy your coffee…here…" she poured from the copper-colored coffee decanter. "You act like I'm trying to hit on you."

"Okay, I'm relaxed so…" his smile wasn't as sincere as he wanted it to be. "You staying off the streets, Lucy…or should I say Holly? I think I prefer the way Holly talks."

"Waz I loosey-goosey talkin', Adam?"

"You were."

"Off the streets?" She pondered Adam's question. "Yes and no. Things aren't always what they might seem to be—I hope you know that. Anyhow, I'm not hustling like I did before—that's a chapter of life that I've written 'The End' to. So, for a change we don't have to go there this time. Lately…how should I put it? I've got some regular Johns; just a few."

Adam shook his head dismissively, shifted his weight from a lump in the vinyl cushion, and sipped at this tepid coffee. Holly interpreted the body English as indifferent—even rude. "Cut out the squirming or whatever, will you please?" She leaned over the tabletop and made eye contact. "Let me tell you something about us girls, I don't think you've picked up enough street smarts yet to really understand, Adam. We're in the pleasure business and that's the one and only way we should be regarded by you, the public, the pope or the president…everybody! Okay?" Holly's eyes were wide with an undercurrent of emotion. "The bottom line, just so you get it Adam, is that prostitution is a victimless crime. Don't you learn that in school? Anyhow, just think about it. Lonely guy finds willing girl. Nobody's hurt. For years marijuana was illegal and people got busted for using it. Then it evolved to where smoking pot has become largely ignored by the authorities; something you're well aware of being a cop. Now it's legal in several places and by the time I have kids of my own it will probably be legal across the country. Go figger."

Adam demurred. He'd avoid an argument he'd only lose. "So, you're still hooking? Is that where you're going with this cultural expose?"

"Quit it, Adam, and don't use that word. 'Hooker' pisses me off, big time."

Adam sat back in the booth, "Okay. We can let it go at that."

Holly had more to say: "My current Johns are all respectable men. Albert is 70, widowed, and sick with lonliness. Sometimes we just come here and have coffee, sometimes we do more, at least we try to do more. He's a perfect gentleman in every way. And, he's rich. A night with Albert puts two hundred easy dollars in my purse—tax-free dollars. As much money as I make waiting on these tables in a week. Matter of fact, it was Albert I'd been with that night we first met. Remember? That night up on Seventh? Where me and Brandy were standing?" She giggled, "and where our agent was hiding out of sight behind some bushes?" Well, let me tell you that Jesse was hanging around mainly because of Brandy, not me. Brandy's kinda wild and does tricks for almost anybody—Jesse included. I wouldn't ever do that. Anyhow, I'd give Jesse a little split of what I did on the street, but mostly he didn't know most of my guys. At least not the important ones." She refilled both cups. "I've kept most of what I do to myself. Tonight I'll see Freddy, not his real name—he's married. His wife is a stressed-out attorney who's always too tired, know what I mean? He's discrete. See this necklace, Adam?"

Adam nodded, "Pretty. Is that a real diamond?"

"You'betcha…yes it is. Probably cost quite a bit. Freddy gave it to me as a friendship gift. No strings attached. Not bad, huh?

Freddy was another guy that Jessie didn't know about. Never will." Holly went on about her 'new' life.

Adam checked his watch and drew a frown from across the table: "Holly, believe me, I'm not judging any of those men— or you— for God's sake. But you know the dangers…and, I've told you before that you've got too much potential to go and waste it doing what you're doing."

"Waste it? You should know by now that I'm not stupid, Adam. I'm what you might call an entrepreneur. I've been saving for college for the past two years. I'm going to be someone some day— you just wait and see."

"I'd love to see that happen." Adam checked his watch again, declined another refill. His impatience couldn't be disguised. Susan's mother had returned to Aurora that morning and he'd left her alone with Anna and a fussing Andrew.

"What's your problem? I mean…you look like you have indigestion or something. Is it me? Am I boring, or immature, or too damn naïve to understand my self or what I do with my life. Does my lifestyle repulse you so much that you'd like to blow outta here?"

Adam smiled, "I'm sorry. And, no, I rather like you. Honestly, I do."

Holly chuckled but wouldn't get into Adam's lukewarm admission. "Thanks for owning up to that, Adam. I kinda thought so but it was good to hear it." Holly leaned over her elbows. "All right. Here's the scoop. It's my dad that's been following me. I'm sure of it. I checked out Raleigh Street last week…felt like a sleuth doing so, you know. I saw the Buick with the tinted windows. I know it's my dad's because—despite all the tinting—I could see the hat he always wears on the passenger seat. So mystery solved."

"I sense there's more, Lucy."

Lucy avoided his eyes, her teeth sunk into her lower lip.

"I hesitate to tell you what I'm thinking...but...I have this weird suspicion. This theory. Now, say my dad's the one who's been watching me—and, like I said, I'm almost positive that he has. So, he probably knows full well what I've been doing. He's very protective of me despite being mostly out of my life. I wouldn't put it past him to do something about it—like ..." She let her thought drop.

"Like go after your...should I say you're manager, or agent?"

"Jesse was a pimp; plain and simple. A rotten person inside and out. Nobody feels bad that he's gone. But...getting back to my theory...my dad would never kill anybody. Never—not in a million years. He'd beat the crap out of him...but that would be enough for him. He's got a temper for sure and he's not someone to mess around with. He was an MP in the Marines." She paused in thought, "I'm positive that someone else did the dirty deed. But he may know some things that could help you. I'm guessing he's spent lots of time up on Hillside."

Adam pondered her theory. At some level it made sense. He wondered if 'suspicion' was grounds enough to bring Lucy's father in for some serious questioning. So far nobody in Hillside was saying anything and the murder was getting colder by the day. It would be encouraging to 'a person of interest' in custody to mollify the press folks."

"Does your dad have any firearms? Like a .22, let's say?"

"I doubt it. He can take care of himself without one. Why?"

Adam wondered if he should have mentioned a specific firearm. He had better keep some details of the John James murder to himself. "Just askin'. Anything else, Holly? I've gotta get going."

Holly looked over her shoulder and saw Boles point toward the wall clock behind the counter. "There you have it, Adam. I've gotta get going myself. Get back behind the counter and make the customers happy." She brushed Adam's folded hands with hers, "Was it worth your time?"

Adam reached across the table and took her hands. "It was, Holly.

You are worth the time. I hope you know that."

"Be careful, Adam. You're getting kinda mushy."

Adam laughed. "You ought to know better. But, I do like you."

"Are you a Catholic, Adam?"

"Where did that come from? But, yes…why do you ask?"

"Because I'm thinking of going to confession. If I do…I'd probably have to say good-bye to Albert and Freddy. I think I can do that. I've checked into student loan programs on my computer and, with the money I've saved…maybe in the fall I could start taking some classes."

"That would be great. I've got a priest friend at UMD. I think he'd help you out in any way he could. Just let me know."

As Adam stood he said, "Anything else, Holly?"

She gave him a strange look, one he'd not seen before. "Have you been in touch with Murphy much lately?"

"Why?"

"Just asking. See ya around. The boss is getting antsy." As she stood to go a thought crossed her mind. "One last thing. If I see my dad in the next few days I'll try to find out if he knows anything. I'll keep you posted."

34/ STELLA'S KITCHEN

The diner where Holly worked was within walking distance from where her mother lived in the Benton Park neighborhood. She walked into a stiff northern wind, and by the time she reached her mother's house her face felt raw, and her gloveless fingers tingled with early frostbite. Holly's thoughts were rife with dreams of a new life since her conversation with Adam earlier that morning. Her dreams, she realized, would be just that until she mustered the compulsion to do something about them. Adam's casual 'I like you…' had sunk deeply into her fragile psyche. People didn't say that unless they meant it. And, her new friend seemed to have lofty hopes for her…*if*- if only! And, *if* was the longest and most challenging two-letter word in the dictionary. Had she really been as serious about college as she claimed to be? And, what about going to confession?

Kicking snow from off her Uggs—a gift from Albert—Holly called for her mom as she stepped inside the foyer, "You home, ma?"

She heard Stella Goeden's shrill voice from the kitchen as she was slippin out of her boots: "Ya, hon. Just takin' some brownies out of the oven. Coffee pot's on if ya ain't up to yer eyeballs with the stuff already."

Holly walked through the messy living room of the narrow duplex apartment where she grew up. Magazines, DVD's, dirty dishware, and yesterday's clothes were strewn from one wall to the other. Having grown up poor and living in an unkempt house had made her determined to do so much better with her life. Her own apartment in Norton Park was always orderly and clean.

Stella was at the counter with a baking sheet in one hand and her stained Minny Mouse coffee mug in the other. Stella's mug was as old as Holly—and was a Christmas gift from a girlfriend of hers who'd been to Disney World. "How ya been, hon? Ain't seen ya in days."

Holly poured herself a cup of coffee and found a chair at the table. "Car wouldn't start after work so I called a friend to come and jump it. He couldn't get there until five or so. Said he'd drop it off at your place when he got it started." It was four fifteen so she'd hang around until she got her car back. The kitchen was toasty warm and smelled of fresh baking, a pleasant reprieve form the greasy odors of the diner that lingered in her hair, her clothing—even her skin. Stirring in a spoon of sugar, Holly said, "Say, who's that young priest at Saint Gerard's—the one that everybody at the café talks about. It's Mickey something…?"

Stella looked toward her daughter, "Ya, Mickey somethin'. I guess he's got a kid somewhere and he's still a priest. Go figger. I ain't been to church since…God, I think it was on Easter…maybe four, five years back. His last name starts with M, it think. Or N? Why ya askin' me? You can prob'ly look it up in the phone book if ya wanna."

Holly rarely went to mass and hadn't been to confession in more than two years. "Just asking, ma."

"What? Stella couldn't contain her laugh. You gonna go an tell me yer gettin' some religion? Jus like yer father does from time to time?"

"He does? That surprises me. John doesn't strike me…" Holly didn't finish her thought. "How's dad doing? I haven't heard from him for some time."

"Oh, he's probly got two, three women on a string. That man's libido ain't never satisfied."

Holly had often wondered what her father ever saw in Stella. John was handsome and sociable—a talker, not much of a doer. Stella was everything opposite. Stella placed a plate of brownies on the table and sat opposite her daughter. Holly noticed how heavy she'd gotten and that she seemed to be breathing deeply. "You okay, ma? You seem out of breath."

Stella lit up a cigarette, blew the smoke off to the side. “Ya, just old an fat, tha’s all. These damnable smokes, gonna quit onea these days.”

“How often have I heard that?”

“Don’t nag yer ma. I ain’t expectin’ ta live til I’m ninety. I think ya know that when my dad died he waz only fifty-two. Anyhow, lets us talk about somthin’ else. Wha you been upta? Got a boyfriend? Ya otta. You been a lucky gal, got yer dad’s good looks an all.”

Holly was antsy and didn’t quite know why. “Not even looking for a guy, Ma.” She put a brownie on a used napkin and took a bite. “Not bad. Maybe I’ll take a few along with me. That okay?” At five o’clock she got up and paced across the kitchen linoleum. If she was going to make some serious changes in her life, maybe this was as good a time as any to make a start. “Can I borrow your car for a few minutes, ma? Just thought of something I need to pick up at the IGA.”

“Cancha do that when yer car comes?”

“No, I’m going to be rushed. I’ve got to get home, shower and change, and meet some girlfriends downtown at seven,” she lied. “Just be a few minutes.”

“Keys are where I always hang’em on the hook by the closet door,” Stella said as she finished her third brownie. “Don’t be too long.” Stella waddled into the living room and clicked the remote to a rerun of *Ellen*.

31/ THE MAGI

The weeks and days before Christmas had been somber ones for a priest needing an uplift of some kind. Now, already the twentieth of December, Mickey realized that the following Sunday would be the fourth and final Sunday of the Advent season—Christmas Day would be arriving on the next Thursday. Mickey had spent his morning helping the church ladies with the assembly of the traditional crèche scene—a chore that most of the women had been doing for years.

"Are you sure that we should put out the camels this year? I wonder if the whole scene isn't getting too cluttered." Mickey said teasingly.

Lorraine Bunt, a smallish woman with squinting eyes, was the first to take the bait, "My gosh, Father, we always have the camels standing behind the Magi. Always!"

"But wouldn't the wise men have let them graze in the pasture after all that travel?"

Ardis Miller, a woman of seventy, was holding one of the kings, not sure where Lorraine wanted to place it. "I think I agree with Lorraine, Father. We've always had the camels and the sheep…the parishioners seem to like it that way."

"Which of the kings have you got there, Ardis? His name, I mean."

Ardis shrugged, "No idea, Father. We always put him to the right of Joseph. The kneeling one is placed closest to Mary and the other one just standing by his camel."

"Which camel is his?"

"The tallest one, I think," said Ardis.

Millie Foster, the youngest in the group, strongly objected. "No. It's the one that's down on one knee. The tall camel goes over by the shepherds."

Mickey was enjoying the consternation he had incited. "The Bible says that King Melchior was the first to offer his gift. You've got King Balthazar closest to the manger, Millie."

Millie frowned toward Lorraine, "He's always been there,

Father. Are we wrong?"

Lorraine, the roundest of the four portly ladies, shrugged. "Nobody ever said anything before. And, Father…you didn't say anything last year about any of this. Matter-a-fact, you said it all looked lovely."

"Ahaa, I did. But…this year I'm expecting the Bishop to stop by. He's a scholar, you know. He's really into Biblical details." Each woman looked at the other in bald confusion. Mickey added to their dilemma: "What's this guy's name? The third king? And what's that he's holding?"

"No idea, Father," Lorainne confessed. "Is it all that important?"

"Heaven sakes, Lorraine, the Bishop might be coming! Yes, I'd say it's very important," Millie insisted.

Margaret Beach intervened, "Ladies, please. Let's have Father Mickey tell us where things ought to be. He's the priest."

All seemed relieved. "If nothing else we'll have the three kings placed where they should be," said Margaret. "By the way, Father, what is the third king's name? I can't for the life of me remember."

Mickey frowned, "I thought you all knew that—you've been doing this for years, Lorraine?" Lorraine shrugged her 'don't know', Ardis and Millie shook their heads along with their leader.

"Is that important, Father?" from Margaret.

"I think so. He's the one who gave the baby Jesus the gift of myrrh." Mickey knew that the third king was alleged to be Caspar but had no memory of which king offered what gift. He would prolong his tease. "According to Scripture—Matthew's Gospel—I believe, it was Caspar who offered the gift of myrrh."

All nodded in agreement. Mickey waited for the question he anticipated but it didn't come. "I'm sure you all know what myrrh is…

Don't you?"

Lorraine spoke for the group. "Perfume of some kind. From where they came from—some far away land, I think it was out east. Am I right?" At least the other three woman seemed to agree with Lorraine.

"Kinda like a sweet smelling ointment? Well done! Was the perfume for Mary or her child?"

"Baby Jesus," all four nodded. Margaret, however, seemed offended by Mickey's question. "You know better than to ask that, Father. Mary wouldn't wear perfume."

"Would her baby, Margaret?" from Lorraine.

"Can I make some small correction, ladies?" Mickey scratched his head in apparent deep thought.

The circle of smiling women assured that Mickey could make any correction he wanted, "Myrrh is indeed a scented oil…but…" He paused like a maestro ready to strike down his baton at the drum section. The 'but' hung for a long moment. "Myrrh is an embalming fluid…symbolic of death."

Looks of revulsion spread around the crèche scene. Mickey had created enough stress. He dared not risk the women walking out and leaving him with the project to complete by himself. "Would you mind terribly if I left everything up to you four ladies?"

Lorainne spoke for the group. "Would it be okay if we did the same arrangement as last year…and the year before? I mean, we'll put the one Ardis is holding next to the crib."

"Manger," Margaret was quick to correct her friend. Now the three were divided. "Manger is the barn they were in…wasn't it father?"

"That's the crèche," I think.

"Don't you know, Father?"

"I'm not sure about any of this. Maybe you had it all right before I said something about arranging the camels."

Lorraine was aghast, "You been funnin' us, Father?"

"Just spreading the Christmas spirit of joy, Lorraine. I've enjoyed helping you this morning."

None of the women knew quite how to take his idea of enjoyment. Apparently Lorraine wasn't in the least amused by Mickey's behavior. "You gave us all headaches, if that's your idea of the Christmas spirit, Father. I for one was almost ready to call it quits."

Mickey reached into his jacket pocket and withdrew four envelopes. Each contained a lovely card and a twenty-dollar bill. "My joy is in you fine women and all that you do for Saint Gerard's. Merry Christmas." He bent over and gave Lorraine a hug…then each of the others in turn. "God bless you all."

*　　　*　　　*

When Mickey turned on the sanctuary lights before hearing confessions that afternoon, he noticed that there were more penitents than expected. He had hosted a Communal Penance earlier in the week with Mario and Father Lucas assisting. Many Catholics found attendance at the Christmas and Easter celebrations as a sufficient acknowledgement of their faith. Many of these found the sacrament of reconciliation as an annual obligation. Were he to have counted the heads already in church they would have numbered close to twenty. One young lady toward the back of the sanctuary did catch his attention. Mickey couldn't remember ever seeing her at a Saint Gerard's Sunday mass where gray heads were most prevalent.

35/ THE LIST

The lovely young woman sitting across from him in the open, yet private, confessional, had many serious matters to confess. Mickey assured her that 'Jesus came to call all sinners to Himself' and that He must love her very much to bring her to the church this bitter afternoon. After listening to her lengthy, and detailed confession he smiled, "All of this is forgiven, my dear. You can leave here and begin life anew." He asked if she had a rosary…she didn't. "Let me give you mine," he withdrew it from his pocket. He helped her through an 'Act of Contrition' and suggested that she pray the rosary. After his prayer of absolution, he asked: "If I stop by the diner for coffee one morning will you join me?"

The penitent was at a loss for words. "Ummm, I suppose that would be okay with me, Father. It's not very fancy, I mean, there's lots of bad language there. I usually have a break around nine-thirty."

* * *

For supper that evening, Mickey chose a *Jack's* frozen pizza, passing over an array of frozen *Stouffer's* dinners in his freezer. That morning's *Duluth News Tribune* was spread across the tabletop—Mickey liked to read and eat at the same time. The front-page stories, like most bannered stories, were rife with gruesome news. The murder of two cops in Brooklyn was the latest in a series of 'police officer' tragedies—this one being an apparent retalliation for the killing of a black street hustler. He pulled out the sports section for something lighter, more positive. Sports were a man's diversion from workplace stress and every day routine. The UMD men's hockey team had won their game the night before and were on a roll—as were the Gopher hoopsters. The Timberwolves remained a hapless disappointment and the Wild were beginning a slide into mediocrity. He made a mental note to watch some of the Wild game on TV that evening—after his scheduled seven o'clock parish council meeting.

He found his calendar buried under the paper, slid it out to check if he had the right day and meeting time…he did. Lately he had been forgetting things more often than usual. Looking over the next week's schedule he had penciled in hospital visits, nursing home visits, Confirmation and Holy Communion classes, along with the names of parishioners that had scheduled appointments to see him. Mark and Nora Monson (marriage counseling), Janice Lundeen (unspecified), Arthur Hall (religious instructions), Adam and Susan Trygg (Baptism arrangements). Mickey smiled, on his calendar was a smiley face on Sunday afternoon: 'Mario's' Go Vikes!

The vibration in his shirt pocket startled him. Checking quickly, 'Blanchards' blinked on his screen. Was it Tom…or Michael?—Mary hardly ever called? Although he had given Tom a green light to proceded with the adoption of his son, he still had a bitter taste about it. Let go of it, he reminded himself every time the thought came to mind…it was probably an inevitable development anyhow, and something out of his control. These days almost everything seemed out of his control. "Hello."

It was Mary. "Merry Christmas, Mickey. We got your card; it was lovely…but your note was kinda brief this year. 'God bless you all …' I'd think you'd have more to say than that."

"Sorry, Mary. I guess that my heart isn't in the right place these days, but I shouldn't use that as an excuse. I've been doing too much of that lately—making excuses for bad behavior."

Mary puzzled, "I don't get it."

Mickey explained the loss of his dear friend…and the tragic circumstances. "So, we're all still kinda reeling about it. Anyhow…I suppose you're going to ask me about Tom's plan…" he didn't get a chance to complete his question.

"That wasn't why I called. My dad had a heart attack on

Thursday night. He's in critical care at St. Mary's. Mom says it's very serious...she doesn't expect him to pull through this one. He's had stents put in twice before. She's never been this scared." Mary began to sob, softly at first. "I'm planning to fly up to Duluth in the morning. Michael's on Christmas break from school, Tom can't get away until mid-week..."

"Will Michael be coming up with you?"

A painful pause, "Not with me...he wants to wait and come up with Tom instead...that's if it's necessary."

Mickey's throat tightened, "Why, Mary? He's off from school..."

"I don't know. I don't push that issue, Mickey. When it comes to you and Tom I walk on egg shells."

Mickey wouldn't press her on that subject. "I'll get over to the hospital..." he was going to say tonight but it would have to be late. And, he had mass in the morning. Yet, he knew Mary would expect him to do something. He looked at the smiley face adorning the box for December 21st and swallowed hard. Mario's party was the one social event he had on his calendar for the week—and he'd promised...but, an opportunity to see Mary—without Tom—hadn't happened since last spring.

"Could you possibly pick me up at the airport, Mickey? My flight arrives at 11:45 tomorrow morning."

"I'll be there."

Some parting small talk ended with a painful barb. "I was going to ask my sister to come," Mary said. "She's at the hospital with mom now. But, Tom said I should ask you instead."

Mickey swallowed bitterly, wanting in the worst way to tell Mary that her footnote wasn't necessary—all he said was: "Tomorrow then."

*   *   *

"Are you all nervous and all sweaty about next Sunday, Mick? I'm really hyped, but that's not really news is it?" Sunday was the annual 'news in review' event. "I hope you've given due diligence to your list." The list that Mario reminded him of was an annual end-of-the year get-together, or contest, of sorts. Each invitee was asked to prepare a list of the top ten 'newsworthy' events—sports included—of the previous year. 2014, Mickey believed, didn't present him with much of a challenge. If he was hit-and-miss with a lot of things; watching the news (and reading daily newspapers) was an integral part of his daily diet. Considering what the other invited priests might bring to the table, a lively debate was expected. "I've given this a lot of thought," Mickey lied. "I've listed one through ten in perfect order—as I always do. So you might consider not starting with me and ruining the afternoon. When I present…our colleagues will throw in the towel for sure."

" Not likely to happen, Mick. But, I honestly hope you do better this year than you usually do. It's almost embarrassing for me to listen to you babbling about the trite and irrelevant every year. Don't you ever tire of peer criticism?"

"I'm sorry I dissapoint you, Mario. Maybe I should listen more closely to your every word whenever we discuss the news—you're so sagely insightful."

"And you, my friend, have just expressed an insightful observation. Like I've always told you, listen to Mario and learn. A wise man once said, knowledge is knowing a tomato is a fruit; wisdom is not putting it in a fruit salad."

Mickey suppressed the laugh that he knew Mario expected. "Then why do you always serve slices of tomato with pineapple rings and blueberries?" Mario laughed at the clever retort.

"Let me assure you, I have given much deeper thought to my list this year." Mickey said. He told Mario that he might be a few minutes late. "Sorry, but something has come up. I've got to make a hospital visit late Sunday morning—support for a Hibbing family I've known for years." He was careful to omit the essentials of who, what, and why. Some things were best left unsaid—even with his closest friend.

Mickey left a half-eaten pizza at the kitchen table, but took his bottle of Diet Sprite with him, as he wandered from his small kitchen to his even smaller office. He was trying to remember where he had put his events list. If it was on the top of his desk he might never find it—the accumulation of paperwork on top of books, on top of manila file folders, on top of legal pads, was a mountain he might never be able to conquer. Had he typed it on the computer and saved it? Not likely. He seemed to remember writing it down on an index card—no, that was an idea for a future homily. He saw the corner of a legal pad peeking from under a half opened, half finished novel he had been reading. Slipping it out he hoped… 'Damn'—followed by a quick apology to the empty room. The tablet page was blank. When having search difficulties, Mickey—like many Catholics—called upon an expert. *"Saint Anthony...sorry about the 'damn' but I could use some help in finding my list. I'm sure you know the one I'm talking about. Thanks."*

As he started to rummage through the pile with new resolve he carelessly brushed against the soda can resting precariously off to the side of his desk near the landline telephone. As it began to tip toward the legal pad he had just put down…Mickey lunged, grabbed…he had it, then lost it. The phone and the Wallace Stegner novel, and the legal pad, along with a few layers of paper all were given a sticky Sprite shower. Frantically, Mickey tried to minimize the damage, sending several 'damns' toward Saint Anthony as he swabbed handfuls of *Kleenex* tissues over and under and around the damage area. The effort was in vain…the recovery effort a failure. The phone would be fine, the book he could replace, the paperwork…maybe it would be best to trash the soggy paper without sorting it and saving the important stuff…but, he reasoned, if it was important it wouldn't be buried off to the side of his desk—would it? When he picked up the legal pad that was responsible for initiating the carnage, a light went on in the back of his mind. Ahaaa! He remembered writing his list on the cardboard backing of the pad. Turning it over he had his 'voila!'…his scrawled list of events had been rescued—albeit, blurred and sticky to the touch. *"Saint Anthony why didn't you just tell me to turn the tablet over and spare me this mess? It's your fault, you know. But, I'm sorry for all the cussing; it was totally uncalled for. Thanks again."*

36/ MARY

After going to mass and receiving Holy Communion, Holly Goeden felt better about herself than she had in years. Father Mickey's homily seemed to speak volumes to her. He spoke with great affection about Joseph's faith and trust in God's will as he led his congregation to the time and place of the morning's Gospel's story. "Nazareth was a small town—maybe two or three hundred people at most—when Joseph was told that his betrothed Mary, was with child and that he was not the father. What would Joseph think? What would all the townsfolk think? It must have seemed much too impossible for him, or anyone else, to believe the miracle story that Mary had shared with her betrothed husband. Joseph, being a kind man, was nevertheless, determined to spare her any shame. Maybe he'd just leave town without notice, or maybe he would marry and quietly divorce his new wife. How could this humble man understand that his future bride was pregnant but had never had relations with a man? How could anybody? Yet, miraculously, he did. And, in doing God's will, this simple carpenter— who we know so little about—was willing to become the foster father of Jesus." Mickey's emotions seemed to be deeply rooted in this story of a man's unyielding faith.

After the mass, Holly greeted Father Mickey in the vestibule and thanked him, "Your faith rubs off, Father. I think I'm already a better person for having met you. I mean that!" Mickey smiled at the young woman's sincere compliment, "Maybe Jesus led you to me because he wanted you to find Him."

"Food for thought, Father." Holly could see that several others were waiting to greet the priest so she excused herself, "See you next Sunday, Father. Or…maybe sooner? Remember my coffee invitation."

"I haven't forgotten, God bless…" Mickey said before taking the hand of Lorraine Blunt's husband, Edward. "You sure had the ladies going yesterday, Father. My wife got home and got on the computer and found out everything she could about the crèche scene. She knows all of the wise men's names now, and knows the gifts they brought with them."

It was moments like these that enriched him. He could tell during his homily that he had his congregation with him…much like it had been during the good times. He thanked God for blessing him with a wonderful start to his Sunday and prayed that he'd be able to keep it all going.

* * *

On the drive from Benton Park to the airport, Mickey rolled thoughts behind his eyes like old films from his high school days. The one clip that needed rewinding was a kegger beer party only days after graduation—his one and only intimate time with Mary Reagan. Their son, kept secret from him until only months before, was the miracle of their short-lived union. As much as he loved Michael, their long-distance relationship had created a myriad of problems that went well beyond the two of them. Maybe he had to let go…allow Michael to have the normal family that the boy had been deprived of for so long. It was becoming increasingly obvious that his son had adopted Tom as his dad, as much as it was the other way around. It would be foolish, even irrational, for him to interfere with a constructive flow of matters best allowed to evolve in a natural way. As much as Mickey had resolved himself to support the formal adoption that Tom had proposed, he found himself doubting. "Why can't I make a decision and stick with it," he spoke to himself and the steering wheel he was gripping. Only Mary's feelings on the matter were still hanging in limbo. She was the mother and the one person who meant the most to Michael. The circumstance of her father, Liam Reagan's serious heart issue, might not be the best time for he and Mary to come to terms with their son's future…but?

The Duluth International terminal building was quiet in the late morning. Mickey noted that the United flight from Ft. Myers was on time and should arrive within the next few minutes. His stomach was queasy, the onset of a headache was like a snare drumbeat in the back of his head.

Mary Reagan looked much as she had as the prettiest girl in the Hibbing High School class of 1998. Slender, pony-tailed, perfectly featured in every way; she even walked with a subtle and unpretentious elegance. Mickey stood from his cushioned seat near the baggage claim area and stepped toward her embrace. "Thanks so much, Mickey. I'm sure Sundays are hectic for you and coming here must have caused you to change some of your plans."

Mickey met her deep green eyes, "Any time…any place. You know that."

"I just talked with mom. She's waiting for me at the hospital. It seems that dad is doing better—much better, in fact. We all thought we might lose him this time; he's had two previous episodes, but this was the scariest."

"That's good to hear. Maybe you've got a few minutes to grab a quick lunch on the way to St.Marys…?"

"Love to. I'm starved. A bag of peanuts for breakfast just doesn't cut it." Both laughed. "It would give us an opportunity to talk…catch up on things."

The commercial strip that was the Miller Trunk Road, and/or US 53, ran between the airport and the hospital. Mary spotted a Perkins restaurant just beyond the sprawling Miller Hill Mall at the same time that Mickey did. Agreement was instant.

Mickey hated small talk but that's how most conversations started—and, sadly continued for much too long. Mary was enjoying nursing—she always had—and Michael was getting straight A's in school, Tom was always busy. Life was good and Mary seemed happy. Mickey would break the ice still covering the still waters between them. "Then you're happy, Mary?" His observation was more question than assertion of fact.

Mary looked away for a moment, obviously wanting to choose her words carefully. "I guess so, yes…life is good. And you, Mickey?"

"Life is good, for sure. I get some curve balls now and then, but I haven't struck out…not yet anyhow. I guess that mostly it's life in the slow lane."

Mary frowned, "That's not a ringing endorsement of how things are with you. I can tell something's on your mind. What is it?" She paused, biting her full lower lip. "Or…just tell me if it's none of my business."

"Do you have any idea how I feel when I see you? The things that go through my mind? Not just the memories of youth…but hopes and dreams and questions without answers. It's a virtual cacophony!" Mickey looked absently out the window at the drab winter landscape—the hundred shades of gray that was this Minnesota winter. "Sometimes I don't think that I've properly…maybe completely is a better word? Anyhow, put my life back in order since that night with you and our son."

Mary smiled almost knowingly. "You must, Mickey. I have…I guess I had to. When I married Tom I let go of you—once and for all—I had to do that. Maybe I did it for our son…maybe for myself, maybe for both of us—for all three or four of us." She tried to laugh, failed. "You asked whether I was happy—that's where we started wasn't it? Well, I sometimes think that happy is an ideal illusion that slips in and out of our lives but only resides for a brief visit. I think that what really keeps us plugging along is 'contentment' …so let me use that mundane choice of words. I guess I've become a genuine pragmatist."

Mickey gave a long thought to her own dismal sentiment before offering one of his own. "Commitment is another uninspiring word, and probably a close relative of contentment," his sober expression said as much as his words did.

There was another 'c' word that wanted to escape Mickey's mouth but he swallowed it. For him, there might never be '*closure*'.

Any deeper conversation became lost when the waitress delivered their breakfast orders. Even what should have been easy small talk was lost before they arrived at the front entry of Saint Mary's hospital forty minutes later. Their 'good-byes' were brief and left both with a chill to match the early afternoon.

37/ JOHN BELAK

Still feeling the spiritual uplift from her Sunday morning, Holly made a long-delayed call to her dad. "I'm free this afternoon, what say you?"

John Belak smiled to himself, "Any time, any place, Holly."

"Where are you now?'

"Up at Black Bear." Black Bear was a popular casino west of Duluth and not far from John's Fond du Lac apartment. "How about yourself?"

"Not far from there...how about a late breakfast or an early lunch up there. Don't blow all your money; I'm expecting you to treat me this time."

"You're on, honey. Half an hour?"

* * *

Even at mid-morning on Sunday, the casino was too busy for any relaxed conversation. "We need to talk, dad...and I'm thinking this isn't the place to do it."

John had a thought, "I know someone who works here...talked to him earlier this morning. I'll bet he can find us a place with some privacy. Just a minute." John must have known the man well, he had the number in his directory. "Trevor, can you do me a favor?"

Two minutes later a tall, ruggedly handsome man met them near the casino entry door. His crisp white shirt was open at the neck where an Ojibwe necklace—a single bear claw—could be seen. "You can use my place...just call in a food order." Trevor Windsong had his own suite on the second floor. John introduced Trevor to his daughter, "I think I've mentioned Holly to you before," he said.

Trevor smiled, offered his large hand, "My pleasure, Holly." His eyes locked with Holly's for a brief moment. He gave John a key ring, "Number 202. Enjoy yourselves." As he walked away, Holly asked her father. "Who is he...I mean, how do you know him?"

"Like me, Trevor's been battling his demons for a few years. We first met at an AA meeting. He was quite an athlete a few years back, any sport you can think of naming. Now he's one of the better golfers around these parts. I don't know what his position is here, but he does quite well. Folks like him, trust him."

"What demons? Holly asked.

"Gambling, booze…he's been clean. I guess he's found the Lord through it all; like most of us do at some point. If we don't…well, that's another story. Trevor's quite religious these days. That priest in Benton Park is an old and dear friend of his."

* * *

The three-room suite was clean and fresh. On the kitchen table was a bowl with apples, red grapes, and bananas; on the counter a half-filled coffee pot with its lingering aroma. John pulled out a chair for his daughter, made a call to the restaurant—both wanted cakes and bacon and juice. In ten minutes the cart arrived and the table neatly set.

"So, to what do I owe the pleasure?" John's face wore a curious expression. "Need some money?"

"Screw you, dad. I could probably borrow you some money. You look like you could use it. Maybe buy some razor blades."

"Touché!" John winced. "So where do you get your money, Holly? Is it that filthy street money?"

"Jeeze, all pleasantries aside—you want to cut-to-the-chase, don't you?" Holly offered an enigmatic smile; "maybe you could tell me some things about this street money and the people spending it. I know you've been watching me…don't deny it, dad. Prowling around Hillside like a pervert in that old, window-tinted Buick…"

John nodded without answering.

"I told the cops about it, you know," Holly admitted. "I'm sure that they've been looking for you. At least there's one cop, a friend of mine, that's looking for a guy that drives a car just like yours."

John's face lost color, his eyes watered. "I'm not surprised. I've been laying low as they say." His voice was tight, his demeanor guarded. "What are they looking for, Holly?"

Holly frowned, her father looked almost frightened by the mention of cops. Maybe her theory about the recent Hillside murder had some measure of truth. "You tell me, Dad. What are the cops looking for?"

The water in John's eyes became streaks down his cheeks, "God knows I didn't mean to do it." His voice heaved, "I only wanted to beat the bastard up, the scum…I'd never…you know me well enough…I'd never…"

"Well, I guess you did. Jesse's dead and buried—you busted him up pretty badly I'm told." Holly wouldn't mention that Jesse's casket had to be closed. "So, now what are you going to do, dad? You can't lie low for the rest of your life. Life on the run is worse than the slammer."

John got up from the table, began to pace across the kitchen. "I know that, Holly. I'm scared…I'm scared as hell. I did go to a priest. I tried to confess but I don't know if I actually did. I mean I panicked, got up and ran like the devil was chasin' me outta the church. Maybe he was. Anyhow, I've been on the run since. I hardly go anywhere these days. Over to Raleigh Street and see a lady friend, stop by a bar down by the zoo now and then…I can't live like this, Holly. Other day, I saw a group of cops at the bar and I almost crapped in my pants."

Holly wondered if John had seen Father Mickey. "Did you see Father Moran at Saint Gerards?"

"No. I went downtown. There was this priest I knew from years ago. I guess I might have saved his life back then—when I was living in Wisconsin. At the time this priest was a truck driver…his rig went off the highway, I saw it happen from my kitchen window. I was living in a little house off the Interstate—you weren't even born yet. Anyhow, I was first on the scene. I got the guy's name later—Bruno Bocaccio. A few years later I learned that he became a priest. I thought that maybe…maybe he could help me. He once said that I saved his life and that he owed me. I don't know if I actually did…but, I thought that Father Bruno was the one I should see. As I expected, he didn't recognize me. How could he after all this time? And, I used the screened booth—that way we're both kinda shadowed." Belak allowed the memory to replay itself in the back of his mind. "Anyhow, like I said, I lost it in the confessional. I was tempted to tell him who I was but couldn't. I think he wanted to help…but, I lost it and ran."

John wrung his thick hands, "Just as I was thinking of finding Father Bruno and finishing my confession; I read in the paper that he died somewhere down in the Cities. It broke my heart…" Choked up he didn't finish his thought.

Holly stood, "Come here, Dad." She gave her father a hug. "Maybe I can help. I know a cop—a good cop. I'd trust him. Maybe there is some way that he can help. I don't know how…but you've gotta do the right thing. You killed a man, a low-life…but…"

"I know what I did, Hon. It's been eating me alive for weeks." He walked to the window, looked out over the casino's parking lot, rubbed at his eyes with the sleeve of his shirt. "Okay. I'll have to take my medicine." Turning, he forced a laugh, "Your dad is flat-assed broke right now. Maybe prison is the best place for me to spend the rest of my days. Gotta be better than running scared and scrounging for money. Besides, they'll probably take better care of me better than I could ever do for myself."

"Don't talk that way."

Then, Holly had another idea. "Maybe you ought to see another priest before you go to the police. I could recommend a good one."

"You friends with cops and priests these days, Holly? Maybe I've been seriously misjudging you."

Both enjoyed a laugh at the moment.

38/ MARIO'S PARTY

Christmas came and went more quickly that any in Mickey's memory. The evening before, and day of, were largely uneventful, 'A Christmas to forget' was how he would later describe the day. On a positive note, Tom Blanchard had sent him a very pleasant email; thanking him for his support and promising nothing would change in Mickey's relationship with his son. 'Maybe the three of us could hang out sometime—golf, fish, go to a Twins spring training game or watch the local affiliate, the Fort Myers Miracle team, play.' Tom had said. The bishop had already told Mickey that he could resume his monthly visits to Florida in January. Mary's father, he learned, had recovered nicely and returned home the week before Christmas.

On another page of the day, Meghan had called and told him that all of the Williams' had enjoyed a pleasant Christmas and thanked him for the lovely card. His niece and nephew liked the itunes cards he'd sent. Mickey and his mother spent the holiday afternoon in Hibbing. Sadie's ham and scalloped potato dinner was followed with cherry pie, and after that, the two of them had butter-drenched popcorn while watching an old DVD—*Doctor Zhivago*— in Sadie's living room. The movie, he remembered, had been Amos' favorite and Sadie teared-up throughout the tragic romance.

The Sunday afternoon following Christmas was Mario's traditional 'year in review' party. Mickey had his list of 'most significant events' on a folded recipe card in his shirt pocket. Mario had told him earlier that he expected several fellow priests, many of whom had never participated before, to join them for the afternoon. "I'm torn between watching the Packers and Lions game and Vikings and Bears," he had confided to his friends. The cheese-heads were playing for the NFC North championship, the Vikes and Bears for last place in the division. All were committed to keeping the event on an upbeat tone and not dwell on their recently lost friend. On that matter, no one disagreed.

Mario muted the TV at halftime and produced his neatly typed list of the 'top five news stories of 2014': "I think this discussion is going to go quickly this afternoon," Mario said. "I can't imagine anyone having the slightest dispute with my list."

When Mario read off his number one story, the Ebola crisis, Mickey stood in immediate protest: "You're crazy, Mario! How can you possibly consider that over the ISIS incursions in the Middle East, the beheadings and massacre of thousands of Christians, the threat they pose to our national security." Father Beckers, usually meek and confused disagreed with Mickey. But, the intellectual Father Huber gave Mickey vociferous support: "That's on the top of my list, too, Mickey. Let's have a straw vote and get on with Mario's already compromised list."

Beckers grumbled, "I vote with Mario." Fathers Holgate, and Grant stuck with Beckers...Saccoman and Jackola gave Mickey their nod. Father Grant shook his head in dissent, "Don't any of you guys have the Ferguson riots as the major story? That's my choice and I'm gonna stick with it!"

"It's my number Two," Mickey announced from the middle of the room where he was hoping to steal Mario's thunder. "And the Malaysian air crash was the top story for weeks. That's my number three."

Mario stepped into Mickey's face, "Please take a seat, Father Moran. You are clearly out of order here." He gave Mickey a light shove backwards...Mickey dropped the paper he was holding and pushed back. Their mock fight amused the priests. Saccoman, the 'Corleone of the diocese', stepped between the two men: *"...smettere di combattere..."* he shouted in his thickest Italian accent.

Both stopped their scuffle immediately, Mickey barked: "what in God's name was that, *amico*?" Then, leaning away from Mario, he went nose to nose with the sturdy Italian priest. "Did you insult me in Italian? If so, I want an immediate and sincere apology!" Rather than respond, Saccoman lifted Mickey off his feet and returned him to his chair to the amusement of all. "If you cuss first and call me your 'friend' in the same breath, please try to use your best Italian accent imitation, Father. That was pretty lame."

The priests went from politics—the Republican sweep of off-year elections, and Obama's use of executive action on immigration, to the Ukraine crisis—to sports. Derek Jeter's retirement, Germany's win of soccer's World Cup, and the Minnesota Twins' dismal season; and their off-season activity. The men were evenly split on the acquisition of Torii Hunter and spending too much money for a questionable starting pitcher in Ervin Santana.

The *Pizza Hut* delivery man, balancing the five large boxes, arrived as the third quarter of the Packers game ended. Mario immediately wrapped up the discussion with a final announcement: "I'll entertain a motion to accept my list as the official list of the Dioces of Duluth…and submit it to His Grace in the morning." Nobody responded. Instead, every hand in the room grabbed for one of the pizzas spread across the table, or pulled a can of beer or soda from the cooler. Father Dorsher, who had arrived late and been unusually quiet during the debates, called for his fellow priests to join him in saying an appropriate grace. He bowed his head and began: *"In the name of the Father, and of the Son…"* He footnoted the prayer with an extemporaneous oration on reconciliation: "We are all asked to bury our disagreements and find peace in discord. I, for one, would like to have Mario concede to Father Moran and shake his hand in good faith." All were amused. Father Zdon, noted for his voracious appetite, nudged his fellow priest away from the table: "Nobody's listening, Father. If you're not eating, please finish your prayers away from the table so I can get at the pepperoni pizza box."

January 11, 2015

39/ BAPTISM

After Sunday's 10:00 mass, Mickey baptized his first baby of the new year. Andrew Thomas Trygg, a reluctant participant in the brief ceremony, voiced his protest of the occasion in cries heard throughout the Benton Park neighborhood. Susan was beside herself over her new son's reluctance to join the Saint Gerard's community. Adam, holding a Baptismal candle and his wife's baby bag, was of little help.

"I think the water's too cold," suggested Andrew's sister, Anna. It wasn't until the boy was passed from Susan to his godfather that Andrew went silent. Phil Symanski winked at Adam, "This little guy knows a good cop when he sees one."

Afterwards, Father Mickey joined the Tryggs along with Phil and Susan's friend, Lori, for a brunch at Adam and Susan's apartment in nearby Riverside. Lori Burns, a classmate of Susan's, had been asked to be the godmother.

"So you and Phillip were partners in the downtown Hillside neighborhood," Mickey said to Adam. "Back when I was assistant pastor at Saint James parish, I used to do some 'streetwork', I'd guess you might call it, in a somewhat quieter Hillside. Me, along with a man by the name of Father Polich…do either of you know him?"

Both cops knew the name and the work he'd done over the years. "Frank Polich? He's been a saint, kinda like an urban legend," Adam said. "Lots of kids would be in big trouble if he hadn't been there for them."

"Mostly runaways as I remember, Father," Phil chimed in. "We don't see him as much these days, but I believe he's still working with kids up at the juvenile facility."

Frank Polich was actually a former priest. His apparent falling out with the church was something nobody fully understood. Word had it that he simply felt that he could serve the Lord much better on his own terms, rather than through the structured bureaucracy that was the Church. Frank was a close friend of Mario's. "We need more people like him," Mickey said.

* * *

Later that afternoon, Mickey had an appointment with the young woman he'd met only weeks before. Holly Goeden wanted the priest to meet her father, a 'fallen away' Catholic she claimed, who was "…in a bad place."

The football guys would have their get-together at Mario's at noon—the Packers and Cowboys had a playoff game—and afterwards Mickey would stop by St. Luke's Hospital to visit a former alter-server who had been in a snowmobile accident the day before.

At six-thirty, Mickey answered the doorbell and invited the two visitors into his small living room. "This is my dad, John Belak," Holly introduced. "He lives in Fond du Lac—not the reservation, but near the river a few miles west of here."

The situation was as awkward as Mickey had imagined it might be. A relative stranger was introducing him to another stranger. Although he had learned a part of Holly's life, he didn't know much of anything beyond their confessional conversation. John Belak was a man he couldn't remember ever seeing before. When the three of them were seated, Mickey commented, "I've seen you at mass, Holly. Keep it up, Saint Gerard's might be the best kept secret in town." Holly nodded and Mickey turned to John who was fidgeting with his large hands and surveying the room. "And, John, we've got lots of empty pews here for new members."

John chuckled, "I've not been inside your church, Father…but, I've driven by it several times. I remember that sign you had in the church parking lot—what ever happened to it?"

Mickey shook his head and offered a wide smile, "I got in some trouble with the bishop over it, John. The bishop and I have a very different sense of humor."

Holly was confused, "What sign?"

John, still giggling, said, "The sign said something like, *'Church parking only...violators will be baptized.*"

Holly laughed out loud, "I think that's pretty clever."

"Mention that to the bishop sometime," Mickey rejoined.

Small talk between relative strangers rarely lasts beyond the weather and, possibly with other men, sports. So far, January hadn't been much to talk about and neither visitor had watched the Packer's game that afternoon. After an awkward minute, Holly said: "Go ahead, dad...let go of it."

'*It'* was something that weighed a ton and darkened the room. John Belak had murdered the man in the unsolved Hillside case. "I tried to confess it to a priest downtown, Father Bruno—you might have known him, a big man...? I read that he passed away a short time ago."

Mickey swallowed hard, nodded, and let the man continue. John described how he had followed the James guy for weeks. "He was responsible for corrupting lots of young girls—Holly included. I just wanted to send a message, you know...I used an aluminum baseball bat on him, Father." Belak began to weep, "I didn't mean to kill him, Father. You've got to believe me. When I saw on TV that I had murdered the man, I called the diocese office and asked for Father Bruno." John cleared his throat of phlegm. "He once told me that he owed me his life and I was determined to collect on his promise." John explained the truck accident of years before. Mickey, and most fellow priests, knew Bruno's story. "So when I was told that he was hearing confessions at that church up by the campus...well, I went there. I had good intentions, Father."

Mickey was putting pieces of John's confession together with his last conversation with Bruno. John Belak was the man that had so tormented Bruno as to push him toward the edge of sanity. John Belak was the elusive penitent—*the man of the seal*! Mickey looked to Holly, "Can we pause here, John? Holly, I think your father and I will need some privacy. I'd like to hear his confession in my office ...is that okay with you? You'll find coffee on the kitchen counter and soda in the fridge. Feel free to help yourself to anything you can find."

The two men left the room leaving Holly with a *Sports Illustrated* magazine and a worn *Saint Joseph's Bible* for reading material. In the small and littered office space Mickey listened, asked questions, and finally gave his absolution to a tearful John Belak. He did not mention the tragedy that was Father Bruno Boccacio's suicide. Maybe at another time—but, that didn't seem at all likely. What purpose would another burden on this troubled man possibly serve?

"I promise that I will go to the police, Father. Holly has a friend on the force...she's going to set up a meeting for the three of us...next week sometime, I think."

Mickey had to wonder *if*...*if* this wounded soul across from him had gone to the police after confessing what he'd done to Bruno...*if* only? Would Bruno be alive today? He fought back his emotion, "That would be the right thing to do, John. If you'd like, I'd be more than willing to join you when you visit with the police. Or...go with you to the police department."

Belak only nodded absently. "I don't want to keep this to myself any longer, Father. Maybe Holly can call her cop friend yet tonight; that's if it's not too late for him."

* * *

Holly told Adam how to find her father's address in Fond du Lac.

Adam arrived at Belak's dingy apartment just before seven-thirty. After introductions, the three of them talked for over an hour about the James murder.

"I had a good confession with Father Mickey," John told Adam. "So, he knows everthing. Now, you're the next step in getting my life back together."

Adam, unsure of what he should do, simply nodded. His mind was busily summoning details of case studies from his college criminal procedure classes, but instead of answers he seemed struck with the paralysis of a rookie's indecision. Certainly Holly's father had committed a serious crime. Assault and battery came to mind, leaving the scene…probably others offenses were also linked.

John interrupted his thoughts. "I lost my temper when this punk told me to f-off. When he saw the bat I had under my jacket he pushed me and tried to kick me in the…" he glanced at his daughter sitting across the room…"you both know where I'm talking about."

Adam nodded, then proceeded to ask several questions in order to clearly establish that John Belak had, indeed, been at the crime scene on the night of the James murder. He took copious notes on John's testimony, but was careful not to disclose any details about the body of forensic evidence the police had gathered.

Adam didn't know what to say or do about the confession: should he make an arrest on the spot? Or…or what? It was Murphy's case. Maybe he'd better talk to his mentor about what to do. "I'll follow up on things as best that I can Mr. Belak," he offered in a weak voice.

As much as it pained Adam to let Holly's father continue to carry his burden of guilt, he would need to talk to Father Mickey and…maybe, Murphy or Phil Symanski, the following day.

"Are you going to arrest me?" John asked.

Holly began to sob, "Adam…what can you do?"

Adam didn't have his badge or cuffs along with him. Worse yet, he hadn't read John Belak his Miranda rights? He stood, "I need your word that you won't leave town. I'll talk to my superiors tomorrow. Okay?"

40/ CONSPIRACY THEORY

Adam Trygg had a sleepless night. Of the people he should talk to, for reasons he couldn't quite understand, he chose to corroborate the Belak story with Father Mickey Moran before going to Murphy. Shortly before ten the following Monday morning, Adam visited the St. Gerard's rectory. "And, we meet again Father," Adam said at Mickey's door. "Sorry that I couldn't speak with you over the phone last night, but Andrew was fussing and Susan needed some help."

"Ahh, yes, the tribulations of a young father after another sleepless night. I'm sure you're giving Susan all the rest she needs these days." Mickey humored the young officer who looked nervous about what he had to say. "Come in…please…it's frigid out there. I'll get us both some coffee—black or with something? And, I'll see if we've got anything to go with it."

"Black, Father. Don't worry about anything to eat."

When both were seated comfortably on Mickey's well-worn sofa, and had dispensed with the small talk of remembering the recent baptism and how Adam's family was adjusting to new addition, Mickey steered their conversation. "You said that you've got a conundrum…that's the word you used, wasn't it, Adam? Anyhow I had to look up the word in my Webster's dictionary." Adam smiled for the first time as Mickey continued. "At first I thought you might be needing some advice on the 'natural method' of birth control." Mickey laughed at his weak stab at humor that was intended to relax his smartly uniformed guest. Adam, who was fidgeting with a Spiral notepad resting in his lap, got the joke. "Maybe another time," he rejoined.

Mickey freshened Adam's cup, "Okay, should I call you Adam or Officer Trygg this morning? I'm guessing that this is more of an official than a social visit."

"Father…just Adam, please. Now…here's what I'm confused about and need some help with." He explained his conversation with Holly Goeden and her father, John Belak, the night before. "I'm told that Mr. Belak made a confession…?"

"Yes, he did," Mickey felt a tinge of discomfort. "And I'm sure I don't have to tell you about the sacramental seal of confession, Adam?"

"Yes, of course…I'm not going to ask you to divulge anything relative to that…can I say, that 'specific' confession'?" Adam's eyes connected with Mickey's as he looked for some indication for him to continue with his line of questions. Finding nothing more than a puzzled expression, he went on. "I would hope, however, that you could answer 'yes' or 'no' to a few questions from the conversation that occured prior to the sacramental confession." Adam's eyes shifted from Mickey to his notepad where he had jotted down some questions.

Mickey relaxed the officer with an easy smile, "Go ahead and continue with your conundrum, Adam."

Adam's voice cracked, "Holly said that she and her dad had told you most of what happened the night of the James murder; that's before he made his confession…am I right about that?"

Mickey nodded.

So, I've reasoned that anything said in that conversation would not violate your vows…" Adam looked for some expression from the priest. " Is that an accurate assumption on my part?"

Mickey gave the question some thought. "That's a good question, a very good question in fact, Adam. The reason for John's desire to confess to me, however, was that he wanted to be sure that he would be absolved of his sins. You see, he wasn't certain that an earlier confession he'd made had been a valid one. Does that make any sense to you?"

"Yes, that's exactly what he told me, Father." Adam jotted something on his note pad, met Mickey's eyes again. "...it just doesn't add up, Father. The story John gave me didn't fit the facts of the homicide...and, believe me, I've been trying to get to the bottom of it for weeks. You see, this James guy didn't die from the beating he'd endured...the autopsy revealed that a gunshot to the head was what actually killed him. It appears most likely that the victim's death was an execution style murder. It is further believed that the gunshot wound might have occurred as much as an hour or more after the beating that James received. I saw the coroner's report only a day or two afterwards." Adam breathed in deeply before continuing.

"Now, when I called a friend of mine in the downtown department earlier this morning, I learned that the James file does not contain the medical examiner's report that I'd previously seen. Somehow it seems to have gone missing. I was put off with 'it might be in the state crime bureau's possession' and 'it's none of your concern anyhow'. I couldn't believe that my own department was stonewalling me. Is this making any sense to you, Father?"

"Sadly...nothing surprises me these days," Mickey shook his head. "Anyhow, are you telling me that it's your belief that John Belak didn't actually kill the man...?"

"Yes, but...but, that's gonna be hard to prove if the guys downtown have other ideas. John claims that he doesn't own, and never has, a firearm of any sort—the report said the firearm was a twenty-two caliber. He told me that, at the time of his encounter with James, he didn't believe that he had actually beaten the man to death…but, then he saw the news on TV saying the man had been murdered. 'He was semi-conscious and moaning when I left him,' John told. 'All I wanted to do was beat him up and send a message' he claimed. Then, John remembered telling James—after beating him up— that if he didn't leave his daughter, and the other girls alone, that he'd be back. And, I'm wondering if he could use a 'self-defense' argument. From his account of things it was James who initiated the altercation…if I can call it that."

Mickey nodded, Adam's account matched what John had told him, however he chose not to confirm any of the officer's contentions.

Adam leaned forward on the couch and continued. "The earliest news reports didn't contain any details about the murder. As a matter of fact, the details didn't come out for several days—by then the case was already getting pretty cold."

Mickey puzzled, "Is that a routine thing—withholding details of a homicide? Sounds fishy to me."

"I agree. At least not for that length of time. And the details that eventually did get released did not mention anything about a gunshot wound—which brings me back to the missing report. It's almost like the report has been covered up by somebody…somebody with quite a bit of influence I'd think. That seems to me like it would be someone at headquarters."

Mickey was digesting Adam's conspiracy theory, "There must be several people, besides yourself who saw the autopsy report—and, there's the medical examiner as well."

"It gets even stranger. The ME claims that his duplicate copy of the 'official report' makes no mention of a gunshot wound. I talked to him myself. Then, my friend—you met Phil Symanski at the Baptism—anyhow, he said that I might be upsetting some people downtown. Phil told me to keep my nose out of it for the time being. He agreed that something fishy is going down."

"What does John think about all this, Adam? I mean, he's gotta feel very relieved."

"Well, that's another part of the issue. I didn't tell him about the gunshot wound. My gut instinct was to keep it under my hat for now. If there's something going on behind the scenes…and John's name comes up—he might be in danger."

"How so?"

"Well, Father. Say John gets pulled over for the illegal window tinting on his car. Or, something else…the cop does a car search…and wow!…presto!…there's a .22 hidden in the trunk of John's car. Just so happens that the gun matches the ballistic test on the newly rediscovered ME files. Sh—, I mean, stuff like that happens."

Mickey nodded, "Sad to admit but I guess it does."

After a few more minutes Adam was checking his wristwatch. "Sorry if I've dumped on you, Father. Would it be okay if we keep this between us for the time being? I think I'm over my head and at a loss of who to confide in. Susan has her head full with the kids…and, even Phil seems a little distant lately."

Mickey assured his visitor that he could stop by anytime, "I'd rather see you in the flesh than talk with you on the phone. Please know that you're not alone in this, Adam. And…let me know if there's anything I can be of help with."

41/ LAYING LOW

Holly was perusing a dated *People* magazine while waiting for her dryer load to finish. Monday was her day off as well as her laundry, house keeping, and grocery-shopping day. The laundromat was only a short walk from her apartment, but the windchill on this January

Monday morning made taking her car the best option. Her Tracfone pinged for the second time in the past ten minutes. Probably her mother. Only a handful of people knew her Tracfone number. Holly would wait. Whenever Brandy texted her, which was very seldom, her first message was always *'10 minutes'*, nothing more or less. She checked the time, waited. The second message was equally brief: '*669'found me. Safe to call—asap.*'

669 was someone that none of the girls knew; but someone who knew each of the girls. *669* was the throaty voice that pulled Jesse's strings when Jesse was alive. *669* was a kingpin of sorts and someone to be feared. Jesse had once told Holly and Brandy that *669* was dangerous business, 'you don't never wanna cross him' he'd told them. If he asks you to do something or see someone—it's 'no questions asked'.

"What's up, sister?" Holly said.

"I'm runnin', Lucy. I got a call from you-know-who last night. He tol me to come back to Duluth. Tol me to check in with the bartender at the Saratoga. Said, don't mess with me—don't forget you belong to me."

"How did he get your cell number?"

"I donno. Does he have yers?"

"I don't think so. Does he have any idea where you are now?" Holly felt the creep of goose bums moving up her arms.

"He said he did. That's why I'm gettin' my ass outta here. I got a cousin who just got a place in Denver. I don wanna do that stuff no more, Lucy. I gotta split."

"I hear ya. Good luck."

"Reason I texted ya, Luce, is he's lookin' for you. He asked me, threatened me. Said if din't tell'em he'd make my life miserable. Good thing you got a different apartment after Jesse got killt. Lay low, Lucy— that's unless ya wanna get hooked up again…and I don think ya do."

Lucy feared that *669* would find her if she remained in Duluth. Some of Jesse's girls knew that she worked at a diner in west Duluth. "You know I ain't doing that stuff any more. I'll lay low for a while; take some time to figger something out."

"Does he know your *real* name, Lucy?"

"No. Nobody knows my real name—not even my regular Johns." On second thought she realized that Boles, her boss at the diner, had her name—so did her bank.

Brandy's voice garbled, "Low battery…maybe I'll let you know how things are goin' in a week or two. Say a prayer…"

"Don't Brandy. Don't call. Let me get in touch with you."

The buzz tone told her that Brandy was gone.

* * *

Lucy placed the laundry basket in the back seat of her Honda CRV and drove toward her apartment. From a block away she could see a strange car idling where she usually parked. That meant trouble. She took a sudden right turn back toward the laundromat, then onto Grand Avenue, and headed west. What to do?…where to go? On an impulse, she punched a number from her directory. No answer. Damn, Adam was working and his cell phone was probably turned off. She wouldn't be able to contact him until after four when his shift was over. Was it safe to go to her mother's place? Maybe not. Her father's place in Fond du Lac? A better choice. But, for the moment, maybe the safest place might be the priest's place in Benton Park. She pulled off of Grand and entered the quiet neighborhood of Riverside, parked her SUV in front the Trygg's duplex. She sat in her idling vehicle while a song on her radio played out. What to do kept running across her thoughts. Susan was probably busy with the kids—it wouldn't be proper to interrupt her. Should she call…or just drop in? Holly felt the stress moving up her spine. The fewer calls she made the better.

Nope. It didn't feel right. She made a U-turn, returned to Grand, and continued west to the 85th Street exit. At Saint Gerard's she parked in front of the rectory, turned off her engine, ran up to the door, rang the bell. An older woman who said her name was Millie came to the door and invited her inside. She learned that Father Mickey was visiting the *Garden House* assisted living home and wouldn't be back until the early afternoon. Likely, another two hours. Millie suggested that she wait, Holly did. "Still some of this morning's coffee in Father Moran's pot…let me microwave a cup for you. Make yourself comfortable," Millie said. "I'll just go about my Monday morning cleaning. Father never puts things away after himself—just one of his bad habits."

Holly wondered what that meant but didn't inquire. "I think I'll try some coffee. Don't bother about me."

Holly relaxed on the saggy beige sofa, picked up a Missionary magazine. In the small living room the old TV was tuned in on some game show, a rerun of Family Feud she guessed; the sound was muted. As she looked around the room she noticed some framed pictures…two were of Mickey and a boy about fifteen years-old, Holly guessed. She puzzled before remembering what her mother had told her about the priest. When Millie brought in the coffee, Holly asked. "What's the boy's name; the one in these pictures?"

"That's Michael. Isn't he just the handsomest young man? He's Father Mickey's son. Lives down in Florida." Holly set the cup on the end table next to the plate of cookies Millie had provided. "Store bought…I'm sorry. Father eats all the homemade ones in one sitting. That man is a sweetsaholic if ever there was one."

When Millie left the room, Holly pondered the photos. Mickey had what appeared to be a teenage son? What was that story?

42/ GUILT-TRIPPING

On his drive from the *Garden House* assisted living facility back to Saint Gerard's, Mickey tried to estimate the percentage of his waking hours spent behind the wheel of his Civic—maybe twenty-five percent, mostly back and forth across the long, narrow city. And, the time spent on his cell phone with calls and texts—another twenty-five percent. What activities consumed the other half of his waking hours he wondered to himself. Could he give his prayer time ten? Priestly responsibilites twenty? The two would combine for less than one third of his active life. He must be miscalculating…this was certainly not the way he'd imagined it would be when he began his first assignment as an assistant pastor at Saint James, a parish not too far from where he was now. But, back then, he'd spent much of his day with the children at the parochial school. Time well spent. The same was true at Saint Francis parish in Brainerd. What had changed? As he pondered that question his cell rang. The ring tone was Meghan's. He considered not answering. Lately, Meghan's calls had been gripe sessions that he found tedious and stressful. He caught the fifth ring…

"So, what's the complaint of the day, Sis?" He'd no more than said it when he wished he'd swallowed the thought.

"That's a helluva greeting, Mickey. You sure know how to push my angry buttons. I'm damn tempted to hang up on you."

"Sorry, Meg. My day's gotten off to a lousy start. I won't go into that but …what's on your mind this morning? Are you still up in Hibbing?" He might have added 'in abandonment of your family' but didn't.

"Mom's sick. I think that it's more than this flu crud that's going around. Vomiting, diarrhea, no appetite. Maybe you should come up. I can't talk her into seeing the doc. She's as bad as dad was about that and look where it got him. We saw he wasn't well and didn't do anything. I was down in Florida…but you…"

Meg had a way of guilting her brother. "But I what? You talked to mom every day and neither of you let me in on his failing health." Shifting the blame and reguilting his sister was about all he could do.

It was Monday and Mickey tried to recall his calendar for the day. Nothing too important came to mind. Yet, he didn't want to make the drive up to Hibbing for nothing—Meg was probably bored and exaggerating their mother's condition. And, snow was forecast for the afternoon and evening. The up and back meant nearly three hours on the road. Yet he didn't have an honest excuse. "Tell you what, Meg, I'll call her when I get back to my office. I'll try my powers of persuasion about seeing a doc." What else should he promise? "And, if she's still adament, I'll try to get up there tomorrow or Wednesday."

Meghan sighed loud enough to convey her unspoken disappointment. "I suppose. My always-too- busy brother."

Mickey's fuse was short. He'd just given the last rites to Edith Sampson, an elderly parishioner that he had been very fond of. His visits at *Garden House* were always depressing. He would give Meghan a dose of her own medicine. "So, how are Kenny and the kids getting along?" The 'without their mom' footnote wasn't necessary.

Meghan swallowed a caustic comeback, "Later!" was her one word signoff.

* * *

Mickey didn't recognize the car parked in front of the rectory just behind his housekeeper's Dodge Caravan. Usually Millie would call if he was out and there was something he should be made aware of, or if he had forgotten an appointment of some kind. He would readily admit to being forgetful; one fault that had put him in embarrassing situations more than once. He tried to think of what had been scribbled on his calendar for the day: *Garden House*, niece Katie's upcoming birthday (he'd sent a birthday card and another Itunes card last week), a Confirmation class that evening, and what else? As he walked past the car he noticed a pair of laundry baskets in the back seat with women's things neatly folded. He'd use his office door, recheck his calendar, and make a quick scan of telephone messages on his landline—the phone that was listed in the Duluth directory and Saint Gerard's bulletin. The calendar was just as he remembered it; no phone messages blinked on his phone, He wasn't much in demand these frigid post-Christmas days: the doldrums of these nondescript early January days.

As he hung his coat, he noticed that the coffee pot had been emptied. It was nearly noon and he'd skipped breakfast, but there were a few remaining cookies in the Tupperware container. He'd grab a handful while passing through the kitchen on his way from the office to the living room.

"Good morning, Father," from the attractive young woman who greeted him as he stepped into the living room. Mickey's surprise was expressed in a wide smile: "Holly!" He thought quickly of what she might have wanted…hopefully, she had taken his invitation to begin Confirmation preparations to heart. "To what do I owe the pleasure?"

"I've got some problems, Father. I'm scared."

Mickey told Holly to sit back down, "Is it something I can help you with?"

"I don't know…I just panicked and found myself coming here."

"A good decision, I'd say. That's my specialty, you know."

Holly forced a smile, "Maybe it was your God who steered me here."

"Mine and yours, Holly. He's even better with problems than I will ever be. So, what's happening?"

Holly explained; beginning with some of the things that she had already told the priest about in her earlier confession. "I knew that what I was doing was something that I couldn't just walk away from. There are always consequences. Serious consequences."

43/ SAFE HOUSE

It was mid-afternoon when Officer Carl Rodland suggested Adam pull into a Conoco gas station off of Central Avenue so he could fill the tank and take a quick coffee break. "I think I bought last time," Rodland said with a wink. He hadn't bought coffee in the six weeks the two had been together. Most places, however, never charged a police officer while on duty. If a clerk 'ahuumed', or worse yet, gave the 'that'll be two bucks' appeal, Adam would pay and the station was striken from the list of regular stops. That had only happened once or twice, but the list of coffee shops wasn't what it had been in the 'good ole days' when west Duluth was on better terms with the economy. While waiting for the tank to fill, Adam checked his cell for missed calls or messages. Susan rarely called while he was on duty, but she had this afternoon. Holly had texted '*need help*', and surprisingly, Father Mickey had texted him as well: *'we've got a situation here. Stop by after work if you've got a few minutes.'* Something was happening. He'd check with Carl Rodland and get his permission to place a quick call to his wife. Rodland hated cell phones in general, text messages in specific, and anything that distracted he and his partner.

Rodland nodded, resumed his conversation with an old-timer at the coffee bar; probably someone he knew from the Raleigh Street neighborhood. Adam called Susan first. "No, nothing's wrong, Adam." The baby was napping and Susan was ironing. "I've talked with Father Moran and he asked for some help with a *young woman you know*." She gave the last four words a special emphasis in a teasing way. "I told Father that it was fine with me. I told him you'd stop by after your shift. We can talk, the three of us, when you get home."

Adam was confused, "What's going on, Suz?"

"Father will tell you all about it. Okay? Ooops, Anna just spilled her milk all over the table. Gotta run...luv ya."

* * *

While waiting for Adam to arrive, Mickey stewed. He'd always had problems with boundries, but now he was really stretching them. His was supposed to be the business of saving souls...not criminal investigation or witness protection. Yet, he was hooked and he knew it. 'So much easier to get forgiveness than permission' he reminded himself.

Mickey did most of the explaining. "I know it's asking a lot, Adam. But Susan told me that she was more than willing..." He reviewed his earlier conversation with Adam's wife. "What a sweetheart she is. She said that you could move the sofabed into Anna's bedroom and the baby's crib would fit in your room. Oh, and she said that she'd love to have some extra help with the kids."

Adam wasn't as certain as Susan about the arrangements being planned. He shook his head, "But, Father, if this *669* guy is as dangerous as you and Holly think he is...well, I'd be putting my family in danger."

"We all realize that, Adam. Like I said, it's asking a lot. I could have Holly stay here for a while...but, I might be putting myself in another awkward situation." He wouldn't elaborate the contention. "Bottom line, the poor girl just doesn't have any friends." He looked from Adam back to Holly. "Or, maybe I should say, none that she can trust right now."

Holly, who had been mostly silent for the past twenty minutes, offered another perspective: "Father Mickey's parishioners are already coping, many rather poorly, with his Florida connection.

Staying here is not an option, Adam."

Adam knew that story. "I suppose that's true enough."

"I'm sure I could find a safe home for Holly with any number of people in my congregation. But, their wellbeing would be compromised just as yours would."

Adam finished Mickey's thought, "But I'm a cop, right? This badass, sorry Father, might think twice about messing with me."

Mickey allowed a long moment for Adam to process the risks and benefits. "Holly, why don't you tell Adam what you told me before he arrived?"

Holly swallowed, fought back tears, "He's located Brandy now. She hopes to get away before there's any trouble. If I don't give myself up, he might do something bad to her. He's one scary dude!"

"Yes, that…but the other thing?" Mickey said.

Holly's eyes locked with Adams for the first time, "It's just another theory of mine, Adam. But I think the police are, what's the word?…*complicit* in this prostitution business: at least one or two bad apples that are looking the other way. They could make busts every night if they wanted to. I think we've already had that conversation. Some of the soliciting going on is pretty conspicuous."

Adam shook his head in defense, "Nobody I know on the force is soft on anything illegal, Holly. That's the truth."

"I'm not accusing you or condemning the entire force. It only takes a couple of bad apples to spoil the whole barrel you know, and I'm sure you haven't met all the cops."

"Does your theory go any further? I mean, are there any cops that you have reason to be suspicious of?"

Mickey interjected, "She gave me a name, in confidence, but …go ahead, Holly. Tell Adam."

"I think your friend, Murphy. All the girls seem to like him. That's why I approached you that night. I knew Murphy wasn't on duty. I wanted to check out the newest cop on the block. I had seen you out patrolling with Murphy for months. You guys never spent much time on Hillside on your afternoon shifts. I always wondered why that was. And..." she paused for a few painful seconds, "and...once I saw Murf and Jesse talking. Murf was off duty at the time. I saw Jesse hand Murf an envelope of some kind. No idea what that was about."

Adam shook his head, "I think you've got it wrong there. Yes, I worked with Murphy...he's a good cop; taught me a lot." He didn't mention that it was Murphy who had arranged his transfer to west Duluth. "And the Hillside thing, Murf always felt it was best to concentrate our attention on the commercial stuff—Superior Street and Canal Park. It made sense, at least it kinda did..." Adam's expression changed from denial to doubt. Did Murphy want Adam out of Hillside after Jesse's murder? Did he think Adam was getting too close to something? Everything seemed to have changed once Holly had left the message for him to call her. Murf had noticeably cooled toward him. He kept his thoughts to himself.

Adam checked his watch, he'd been at the rectory for nearly forty-five minutes. "Does anybody know what kind of car you drive?" he asked Holly.

"It's registered in my name, any cop could find whatever information they want," she said. She didn't add, including your friend Murphy.

Adam rolled his eyes, "Stupid of me not to think of that."

Mickey smiled, "If it could help, Holly could leave her car in the garage out back; it's got a stall that's never used."

"What about Holly's job at the diner? Anyone can find her there." Adam said.

Holly warmed to the idea, "I can call Mr. Boles...tell him I've got a family emergency out of town. His daughter can fill in for me—he'd like that I think. That's not a problem, Adam."

"If I don't go along with this, Susan will be on my case. So I guess it's gotta be okay."

"That's not a good reason." Holly stood, glared at Adam. "If that's the way you…"

Adam stepped toward her, stretching out his arms, "I've got a terrible sense of humor, Holly…come here, give me a hug. I care about you—always have."

Holly's emotions burst, tears streaked her face, and she sobbed deeply, as she hugged Adam. "Thanks, I needed that."

"Let's go home. I'm starved and on Mondays Susan makes this fantastic stew with the beef roast we have left over from our Sunday meal. Her stew is to die for."

"Give me your keys before you go, Holly. I'll put away your car. Oh, and I've got Confirmation classes on Monday nights."

Holly smiled, "When we get through this Father, I promise I'll join your Confirmation group. Okay?"

Mickey caught Adam's elbow, "You haven't said anything about Holly' father. Have you talked with your superiors about it?"

Adam frowned, "No I haven't, Father. I guess I've talked myself out of going to Murphy for the time being. I might be putting my head in a noose but I'm not sure who to trust these days."

44/ MARIO

As he did with almost every problem in his unconventional ministry, Mickey shared his thoughts and concerns with his friend Mario. "Amigo, how was your Monday? Another kick back and watch movies on TV kinda day?"

"I wish! What's your problem, Mick? You never call me on a Monday. Counseling will cost you a small fortune. But, get it off your chest before I turn on the soaps.

"That's not much of a greeting. What's your problem Mario? I think you need some help; some serious help!"

"I asked first."

"That's a playground answer. Did I catch you at a bad time?"

"I never have a bad time…you, on the other hand…"

"Okay. Somehow I've put myself in the middle of something that you might be able to help me with."

"As always. Don't tell me that it concerns the bishop because I'm on pretty good terms with Beamer these days."

"Surprisingly, so am I—I think. No, this time it has to do with cops and extortion, possibly kidnapping, and harboring fugitives…the kinda stuff that you deal with all the time."

"You've just described my Monday, Mick. How about yours?"

Mickey explained the triangle of Adam Trygg, Holly Goeden, and himself. "So, I have a question. Are you still in touch with Father Frank?"

"Frank Polich? Not as much as I used to be. Why?"

"Does he still have his street ministry?"

"I'd expect so…but I've heard that he's been spending most of his time at NERCC these days." NERCC was the Northeastern Regional Corrections Center, a minimum security facility dealing with the rehab of juveniles. "But, he still prowls downtown, mostly connecting with runaways. You'd be surprised how many kids are living on the streets. He's a saint, Mick."

"Could the three of us— I mean you and I and Frank— get together one of these days? The sooner the better."

Mario didn't ask why. "I'd enjoy touching base with Frank.

What's on your agenda for tomorrow?"

Mario promised to get back to Mickey the next morning after mass.

* * *

Mickey walked from the rectory to the sacristy of Saint Gerard's in a light jacket. The winter of 2015 had been kinder than most, and this early February Tuesday morning was no exception with temperatures in the low twenties. So far there were only a few inches of snow cover; what was Mother Nature holding in store for northern Minnesota's March, he wondered? This morning's news featured another, in a series of punishing blizzards, in the northeast (Boston and New York) as it's first story. After morning mass he'd swing over to the Trygg home and pick up Holly for the meeting Mario had arranged for 10:30 that morning.

* * *

Susan was nursing the baby in the living room when Mickey arrived, Holly and Anna were playing with a miniature kitchen set on the living room carpet. *Dora the Explorer* blinked from the muted television. Mickey turned his head away from Susan, said hello to Anna. "Just a minute, Father," Holly said as Susan moved from the sofa to the nearby bedroom. "We'll join you in the kitchen in two minutes. Coffee's made, and I set out the last of our blueberry muffins on the counter for you."

Mickey poured himself a cup, found a napkin, and took a chair at the kitchen table. The morning *Tribune* was resting atop the microwave. He opened the newspaper to the sports page, and scanned a story on the Twins spring training optimism. The home team would be starting it's camp in two weeks down in sunny Ft. Myers. A wave of nostalgia swept into his thoughts; only two Februarys past he'd been down to Florida with friends and watched the veterans and prospects go through their preparations for the upcoming season: another season of disappointment for the Twins faithful.

When Holly entered the kitchen, Mickey appraised the outfit she was wearing. "Let me suggest something more conservative," he said. Holly was wearing skin-tight yoga pants, along with a red sweater that appeared to be a size too small. "We're going to a corrections facility, Holly, a den of hormonal retention and outrage—if you can understand the scene I'm depicting. We don't' want to inspire a riot."

"I'm wearing Susan's clothes, Father. Remember, I didn't pack anything for this…this relocation."

Susan had put Andrew down and joined the two in the kitchen. "I've got some jeans that will fit, Holly. And, I think one of Adam's sweatshirts will work."

45/ NERCC

The regional corrections facility was located in Saginaw, a small dot on any map of the North Star State; about ten miles northwest of Duluth. Mickey took Cody Street up and over the hill to I-35, then onto US 2, and exited at Munger-Shaw Road.

Holly hadn't offered much in the way of conversation, so Mickey turned on the car radio. Holly gave him a hard look and turned it off. "I still don't understand why I have to go along, Father."

"It's your story we're working on; don't forget that. At best this is a shot in the dark."

"I've been there before, NERCC I mean…visiting friends."

"You didn't tell me that."

"There's lots I haven't told you about."

"I'm sure there is. Does anything that I should know about before we get there come to mind?"

"I still don't know what we're hoping to accomplish. All you've said so far is that you want me to come along. Why?"

Mickey smiled, ignoring her question. "Did I mention that you look much more presentable in substitute outfit that Susan gave you to wear?"

"I look hideous, Father! This Vikings sweatshirt goes down to my knees…and purple isn't one of my colors."

"And obscene black yoga pants aren't one of my colors either."

Glancing at Holly's pony-tailed blonde profile, Mickey was reminded of the way Mary usually fixed her hair. Thinking of Mary he smiled to himself; he would resume his Florida visits the following week. He'd talked for twenty minutes with Michael the night before, and his son was looking forward to seeing him—it had been six weeks since Mickey's last visit.

Mickey and Holly were a few minutes early for their meeting, and after registering, found that the conference room was in use. Apparently, an intake counselor was explaining the institution's rules and responsibilities to a young Hispanic girl. The two of them wandered down the long hallway to kill some time. Even in her oversized Viking sweatshirt, Holly was drawing some stares from a group of boys on their way to a classroom.

"Hey, stranger." The tall, bearded man in baggy khakis and wearing his long hair in a ponytail nearly as long as Holly's, had a distinctly deep voice. "Long time no see, Mickey."

Mickey stepped into his hug. "It has been, Frank. Good to see you; you're looking good."

"Who's the young lady?"

Mickey introduced Holly. Frank took a long look, fingered his beard: "Haven't I seen you before?"

Holly smiled, "Hello Father Frank. Before today, I had no idea that Mickey knew you."

Mickey puzzled, "How do the two of you know each other?"

"Lucy used to visit us here. It was your friend Sarah…Sarah Bennett wasn't it? But…I don't remember your name being Holly." His expression was quizzical. "There must be a substory I'm not aware of."

Holly explained to Mickey. "Sarah was one of the girls…a runaway from the Cities. Frank found her…must be over a year or so ago by now. I heard that she had OD'd on heroin and almost died. Father Frank saved her." Holly and Sarah had been friends at the time."

"That's right. She's back home with her family in Saint Cloud; keeps in touch with me from time to time though," Frank said.

The conference room door opened and the counselor along with her new charge left the room. "Hi, Father," the heavyset woman greeted Frank.

Frank made introductions. The woman's name was Heather. "I've heard about you, Father," she told Mickey with a wide smile. "You're the priest with the son in Florida." Then she broke into a giggle, "The one that baptizes folks who park in your church lot."

After informing Frank about his short-lived parking sign and a few minutes of small talk, Mickey explained the reason for his visit. "I'm trying to put some puzzle pieces together, Frank. A police officer friend of mine has been working on a homicide down in Hillside; do you by any chance, remember a John James, went by Jesse most of the time? He did some time here at NERCC for drugs, vandalism…and, I think car theft."

Frank nodded, “And add running away from here more than once. Sadly, Jesse’s list of criminal activity is a long one. Tough luck kid. Came here from Gary, Indiana…broken home, dad in prison, mother an alcoholic…got into the wrong crowd. The inevitable stuff happened soon after he got here.” Frank swallowed hard, “I went to his funeral, a closed casket affair, took some kids that knew him from here along with me. Sadly, just a handful of people attended. Tragic story. I wrote his mother about the funeral…never heard back.”

“Did he have any enemies you know of?” Mickey queried. “From what I know—although it might be hard to prove—he was shot, execution style. Papers didn’t mention that; I think the *Trib* reported that he’d been beaten to death.”

“What do you mean…hard to prove?” Frank asked.

“It seems that the autopsy report has disappeared.”

“How can that be? Have you talked with the ME about it?”

“A friend of mine has. He, the ME I mean, now claims that this Jesse was beaten to death. But, my cop friend is certain that, for reasons he can’t understand, someone’s covering up the truth. He told me that he’d seen the original report shortly after it arrived at the downtown police station. Strangest thing.”

“I’d say so. I think I might be able to help, Mickey. I happen to know the ME…” He tugged at this beard, his eyes narrowed as something else crossed his thoughts. “And I know someone at the station. Matter of fact, he visted Jesse a few times when Jesse was here. Cop named Brendon Murphy, know him?”

Holly, who had been quiet for the past several minutes, flinched. Mickey, sitting across from her noticed but Frank hadn’t. “Murf, that’s what we knew him as up here. Anyhow, he used to visit with our kids from time to time. Not just the guys, but a few of the girls we’ve had here.”

Holly swallowed, "Did he visit Sarah?"

"Matter of fact, yes…I believe he did. We've got records of all the visitors—goes back a couple of years. I can ask the secretary, lady named Benson, to check that for you."

Mickey looked at Holly, "What do you think?"

Holly shook her head. "I don't need to know any of that, Father." She looked disturbed and Frank caught it. "I know Murf, Father Frank…and I'd rather you didn't call him for any information."

"Why is that, Holly?"

Mickey intervened, "For reasons I'm not clear about, she thinks Mr. Murphy is looking for her. Holly's been off the streets since the James murder. She's almost certain that Murphy is…how can I put this…that Murphy is connected to some of the prostitution downtown. Sounds kinda crazy, but I'm wondering if maybe she's got something there."

Now it was Father Frank that seemed visibly disturbed. He looked at Holly with narrowed eyes: "I find that hard to believe, Holly. All of us here have the best relationship with…"

Mickey met Frank's eyes, "I know what you might be thinking. It might sound off the wall, but I'd like to do some checking myself. My cop friend, a guy named Adam Trygg, worked with Murphy for several months. I think he'd like to keep this under the radar for now. Are you okay with that?"

"If you are, Mickey…Holly? I think you're both mistaken…but, of course I'll help you guys in any way I can."

"You've already been more helpful than you can know," Holly said with mild satisfaction. "I think we've made an important connection, Father. Oh, and will you be sure to give Sarah my best the next time you talk to her?"

Frank stood, "Sure thing." He smiled at Holly and offered her a hug, "I'm glad to hear that you're putting your life back together. Keep it up. I'll keep you in my prayers." A renowned hugger, Frank embraced Mickey as well. "Tell your friend Mario that he might consider inviting me to some of your football parties. I always have to get the local clergy news second hand."

Mickey promised he would.

46 / WHAT NEXT?

Neither Mickey or Holly were aware of a developing story out of Forest Lake, a suburb north of Saint Paul. Seventeen year-old Olivia Larson had been reported as missing three days ago. The girl was last seen walking home from a local convenience store. Surveilance cameras caught a distant, and indistinct, image of her entering a white van nearly a block away from the Super America store. The story would not have aroused much curiosity in west Duluth— Holly and Mickey would not have recognized the name of a girl both knew as 'Brandy'.

On the drive back to west Duluth both Mickey and Holly seemed immersed in thoughts of their own. Holly spoke first. "Now what? We're no better off than when we left this morning." She bit at her lower lip, "I'm worried Mickey, a corrupt cop can do almost anything and get away with it." It was the first time Holly had called him Mickey and it felt awkward off her tongue. "Can Frank be trusted not to tell Murphy that we suspect him…or that we think he's involved in some shady dealings?"

"Frank said he wouldn't…so, he won't. Period!"

"I lost my sense of trust a long time ago. I trust you and Adam, it doesn't go much further than that these days."

"We need a plan of some kind," Mickey mused mostly to himself. Holly only nodded and looked out the window at the bleak winter landscape. Her thoughts were consumed with running away; going some place where nobody knew her. Her father had a sister that lived somewhere in Texas—Galveston, she thought. But she hadn't seen her aunt Glenda in years; she didn't even know if she was still there.

"…Father. Mickey…"

"What was that? Sorry, I wasn't listening."

"I said that we'll have to talk with Adam. Maybe we can put our three heads together and come up with something."

"I guess I was thinking the same thing."

Holly nodded without speaking.

Driving down the steep hill past the Calvary Cemetery on Stebner Road, Mickey spoke mostly to himself, "I remember Adam saying that he's got a cop friend whose father is connected with some of the department insiders. Maybe that's a good place to start."

Now a self-absorbed Holly wasn't listening. "I wonder if I should see how Brandy's doing. Do you think it's safe to call? She's got a Tracfone that can't be traced. We've got this secret code of sorts between us."

Mickey wasn't listening either. He was trying to think of people he knew that had connections to the police and wasn't coming up with much of anything. His cell phone rang.

Mario was on the line. He was curious to find out how his meeting with Frank Polich went. "Hard to say, Mario. Gosh, the man is ageless. He looks the same as when I last saw him, and that's been a few years."

"He has a serenity about him doesn't he? Maybe that's what keeps him young and why he relates so well to troubled teenagers."

"Well, to be honest, he looked a little agitated this morning. We brought up a name that seemed a bit disturbing to him."

"Who's that?"

"A cop by the name of Murphy."

Mario mused for a moment. "Can't say that I recognize the name. You said 'we', Mickey. Were there more than just the two of you?"

"I brought Holly along." Mickey wondered if he'd shared Holly's story with Mario. "Have I mentioned her to you before?"

"I don't think so."

Mickey changed the topic. "Maybe you can help us out with something. Do you have any contacts with the Duluth police?"

Confused, Mario asked: "Is this Holly a cop, or is she in some kind of trouble that Frank could help with?"

"Neither, she's with me now." Mickey's mention would deflect further inquiries about his passenger. He asked again, "Anyhow, do you know anybody…?"

"I'm trying to think, Mick. I still don't have a handle on where you're coming from with this."

"I'll tell you more later…okay?"

"I guess so. One of my Newman Center kids has a brother-in-law with the department, but I can't think of the name right now. I can ask him later …but I'd like to be able to tell him what you are looking for."

"Are you free…let me see…?" Mickey tried to remember what he had on his calendar. "Are you free tonight, around seven? I've got to visit Saint Mary's hospital one of these days—a parishioner's daughter just had breast cancer surgery and I promised…"

"Then you'll be in the neighborhood."

"Yep. Can I stop by?"

"Let's meet for a late dinner. I'm craving pizza. Even if it has to be one of Luigi's."

After putting away his phone a thought struck Mickey. In some strange way this whole business might have some bizarre connection to his late friend Bruno. The thought was too vague to do much with.

* * *

Mickey dropped Holly off with Susan Trygg just after one in the afternoon. "I'll pick you up around five. Someone else I'd like you to meet. I'll treat you to pizza up by the UMD campus." Mickey wondered if he should ask Adam if he could join them, but kept the idea to himself for now. The more heads he could bring together the better. Someone connected with the downtown police department would be helpful. Maybe Adam could make a few suggestions. He'd get in touch with Adam later.

Back at the rectory, Mickey realized that he had forgotten about a seven o'clock meeting with an AA group in Esko, a rural community twenty miles west of Saint Gerard's. He rarely missed their meetings as three of his parishioners were active in the group, and he was the 'de facto' chaplain. He called Lester Reynolds, a Lutheran minister and close friend of his for years. Lester was free and willing to 'pinch hit' for the evening.

47/ PRAYER AND SUPERSTITION

Feeling mentally drained, and spiritually void, he felt a deep need for prayer and meditation in the quiet of his church. As was too often the case, he needed to get himself reconnected with his Lord. *Dearest Jesus, I'm trying to do too much by myself these days...and I'm not doing a very good job of anything. I love you and need you and I ask for Your Divine help in every aspect of my life: with every dimension of my priesthood, with my parishioners, with my family, with Michael, and Holly. I've been spreading myself too thin to do justice to anything I get myself into. You know that much better than*

I do." When Mickey prayed, his prayers were more like conversations, and he spent time after each of his issues to allow God to help him think it out. *"I've gotten myself involved in the problems of Your child, Holly. You led her to me in one of Your mysterious ways and I'm asking you to help me to help her. And, I thank you for Adam and Susan Trygg and their help as well."* After pondering the coming evening meeting he continued: *"Thank you for my friend Mario and for Reverend Lester. Be with my AA group tonight and with our group at Marios."* Mickey smiled to himself, *"And may the pizza we share tonight be much better than the last one we had at Luigis."*

After his 'prayer time', Mickey returned to the rectory and made a call to Adam. He explained the visit with Father Frank at NERCC and invited him to join the rather spur-of-the-moment meeting he had arranged with Mario. "We'll have coffee and bounce ideas off each other. Oh, lest I forget, do you know anybody on the downtown force that might be able to join us and offer some insights? The more heads the better."

Although reluctant, Adam said he'd be more than happy to help and would make a few calls. Mickey told him that he'd pick up both he and Holly around five. Adam told Mickey that what he and Mario were planning was 'kinda unusual'. "We'll have to make sure that we don't give anyone the impression that this is 'official' police business, Father."

"Just brainstorming, Adam. We'll be careful to keep it at that. Okay?"

Mickey then called Mario again, "Looks like I'll be bringing along some friends. "I'd like you to meet Holly." He gave Mario an abbreviated background on her situation; "and Adam Trygg." Mickey suggested they get together around seven. "Maybe you can get that private room at Luigi's. As an afterthought, he added: "You might call Father Frank and invite him to join us if he's free. We kinda left him hanging this morning and I feel kinda guilty about that."

"The more the merrier," Mario chided. "Anyone else? Mayor Ness? Congressman Nolan? I know some TV people at Channel 10?"

Mickey fumbled for something witty to rejoin with, "All of the above. And maybe our beloved Bishop Bremmer could come and say grace before we eat—I mean enjoy, one of Luigi's masterpieces."

Mickey ran the names across his mind; Mario, Holly, Adam, Frank if he could make it…and himself. Five, if Adam could find someone from the Duluth PD, the group would be six. Mickey was superstitious about even numbers. Looking up from his desk he focused on an alibaster elephant resting atop a bookshelf, "I know, superstition is foolish and irrational, but what harm is there to knock on wood?" He chuckled to himself as he rapped on the mahogany desktop.

48/ A RANSACKED APARTMENT

On the drive to Luigi's, Holly asked a favor: "Mickey, would you swing by my apartment so I can pick up some of my own clothes and girl stuff? It'll only be five minutes."

"Not a problem, I've got a stop to make as well before we meet Mario." Mickey said over his shoulder to Holly in the back seat. "But if you can pick up a few clothes and women's 'stuff' in five minutes you're the fastest female on the planet."

When Mickey came to a stop in front of the small, beige, stucco apartment building where Holly lived. Holly suggested that Adam go with her, "I'll grab a few things on hangers for Adam to bring along—that's if you don't mind women's dresses hanging in your car."

"If I said no, I'd be considered a sexist, wouldn't I? Go ahead the two of you, I'll give Mario a ring and tell him we'll be a few minutes late."

"What's the rose for?" Holly picked up the paper-wrapped flower from the seat beside her as she stepped out of the car.

"That would be for Lillian—a parishioner. I want to say hello and wish her a speedy recovery. She's recovering from a double mastectomy at Saint Mary's."

Holly smiled at the thoughfulness. "Let's go Adam."

* * *

Holly gasped when she opened the door to her apartment. From the hallway she could sense that something was wrong. "Adam…someone's been here. I can feel it." Adam was quick to put his arm in front of Holly to keep her from going into the room: "Sorry Holly, if your apartment has been compromised, this is a potential crime scene. We'd better not go inside." Adam pulled his cell phone from his trouser pocket and called the department. Marge Sampson at the desk told Adam she'd dispatch someone to check it out.

Holly began to cry, "This is what I've gotten all of you mixed up with. I'm sorry Adam…maybe it's best if I just get the hell out of Dodge before something more serious happens to me, or someone else. I don't think that whoever is trying to mess up my life will stop with this."

Adam took a few pictures from the doorway. From where he stood he could see through an opened door into Holly's bedroom beyond the small living room. He made a mental note that drawers had been pulled from a dresser and clothing scattered across the floor. "Let's wait and see what the cops find out. Susan can take you shopping tomorrow and help you get whatever it is that you need."

*　　　　　*　　　　　*

The group met at Luigi's Pizza Parlor, where Mario had arranged for the private room off the kitchen. Mario seemed to know everybody in the Kenwood neighborhood surrounding the campus—including Luigi Napoli. Although Luigi was a friend of his, and never charged him for the pizzas, Luigi's pizzas were usually either underdone or overbaked. The room near the kitchen ovens was uncomfortably warm when Mickey, Adam, and Holly arrived.

Adam had contacted Phil Symanski who couldn't make it—Adam had forgotten that Phil worked afternoon shifts. But his friend had suggested inviting his father to join them if it was just a get-together and not anything official. "After all, my dad's an insider. He knows both Sarge Cooney and Murphy…and lots of the politics going on in the department. He'd be happy to help if he can. I'll call him and tell him where you're meeting and what it's about."

Adam thought Phil's idea was a good one and thanked him. "We'll need all the help we can get. A veteran and an insider at the same time—sounds perfect to me."

*　　　　　*　　　　　*

Larry Symanski, Phil's father, was the last to arrive. He introduced himself to the others and informed the group that his son had already briefed him on the situation. The elder Symanski took a chair next to Adam and offered a weak handshake. As Adam was shuffling some papers on the table, the former cop stood, cleared his throat and made a sharp accusation: "From what I've been told, I'm already convinced that Murphy's the guy we should be focusing our attention on."

Mickey squirmed, wondering to himself where on earth this stranger was coming from. He bit his tongue and noticed shocked expressions around the table. The tall, thin man, with a long neck, and protruding ears hadn't even allowed Mickey to introduce everyone at the table before beginning any discussion of the matter at hand. "I don't think we want to start our meeting with any rash assumptions…Larry. I think we're better off listening to what Holly and the others have to say before going off in any directions."

Adam raised his hand for Mickey's attention, "I agree with you, Father. For openers, I'm Adam Trygg, west Duluth police department. Although we've never met, Mr. Symanski, I was a partner of your son's on the Hillside beat a short time ago."

Shrugging his shoulders, Adam could tell that Symanski was preoccupied with Holly sitting across the table from him.

Mario introduced himself, Mickey, and Father Frank. "Nice to meet

you, Holly—any friend of Mickey's is a friend of mine." Mario smiled across the table. "I've ordered pizzas for seven thirty…they may be terrible, but the price is right." He slipped a blank sheet of paper across the table, "If you'll all jot down a beverage of choice I'll pass it next door to the kitchen."

Mickey acknowledged Adam who stood up from his chair and got the discussion going; "First off, we've just been to Holly's apartment. We think it's been burglarized, or compromised in some way, since she left it three days ago?" He gestured to Holly sitting to Mario's right: "Are you willing to bring us all to speed on what's been going on these past few weeks? Maybe you can begin with when we first met and bringing us up to what happened tonight."

Holly cleared her throat, looked down at her clasped hands, then met Mickey's eyes. Mickey and Adam were the only two people she felt comfortable with. Her voice was tight, she deferred to Mickey sitting to her right: "If it's okay with him, I'd rather that Father Mickey explain things. Then, I'll try to answer any questions that you have as he goes along."

Mickey was at ease in leading a group. "If you'll help me

along, Adam…and Holly. Any one of you just stop me if you have any questions so we can all be aware of how each of us is processing the story."

Mickey walked the group through the past several weeks, beginning with the brutal death of John James on Hillside. He was careful not to divulge some elements of the story—including the information that John Belak had shared with him. He ended with the mystery surrounding the disappearance of a girl known as Brandy in Forest Lake. "Adam, will you share what you learned this afternoon?"

Adam stood, "A man I work with, names Carl Rodland, got word that a young woman by the name of Olivia Larsen is missing. Olivia is a friend of Holly's…we're very concerned about her safety." Adam would leave it at that. Holly nodded without adding anything to what Adam had disclosed.

Obviously agitated, Larry Symanski shook his head: "When Brendon Murphy's name comes up in this story I'd like to offer my two cents."

Twenty minutes later, the senior Symanski offered his two cents.

49/ FATHER AND SON

The meeting lasted nearly ninety minutes. Of the three large pizzas Mario ordered, only about half of the slices were eaten. It wasn't so much that nobody was hungry…the pizzas were undercooked and the crust doughy.

When Larry Symanski left Luigi's he called his son as he had promised he would. "I think I steered them all to Murphy," he said. "When I told the group about all the money Murf had been spending over the past few years, their suspicions seemed confirmed. Only this priest…Frank something, defended Murphy. 'He's a good man', he kept trying to convince the group. Your buddy Adam…nice guy, I suppose…but he kept whatever cards he had close to his vest. Either that or he's not as perceptive as you seem to think he is. Anyhow, he didn't add much of anything to what you've already told me."

"How about Holly?"

"She's a babe, ain't she? At times she seemed intimidated. One thing is for certain, I didn't like the way she looked at me. Suspiciously. The mess at her apartment was stressing her big time. I think she knows things that she shouldn't know. We'll see."

"Did you come up with any plans on what to do next?" Phil asked. "Like, who's gonna confront Murphy about all this?"

"I think they believe Adam is in the best position to do that. But I didn't get the impression they were in any hurry— or that your friend was up to the task. I could tell that he was unsure of himself like most rookies are."

Phil disagreed but kept it to himself. "Anything else, dad? I'm about to pinch a lady who can't seem to keep her car from wandering from one side of the street to the other. I haven't cited anybody in two hours."

"Then you better give her a ticket, son. I used to hand out more tickets than half the other cops put together."

"I know."

The elder Symanski was about to hang up: "Keep me posted on what Adam has to say about the meeting. He said he'd be in touch with you in the morning. Oh, and like I've always told you…and don't forget it: when you know something nobody else does; keep it that way."

*　　　*　　　*

On their drive back to Riverside, Mickey asked Adam how he

planned to approach Brandon Murphy.

"I don't know yet," Adam admitted. "The two of us haven't talked in quite a while."

"You mean that you haven't told him about your conversation with John Belak yet? The poor man must be in misery thinking that he's a murderer," Mickey said.

Holly assured Mickey that her father was staying close to home these days. "I've told him enough to give him some peace, but he's still waiting to be arrested on some serious charges. He's promised to lay low for now."

Holly had a question for Adam, "This name…Cooney, came up a few times; what do you know about him, Adam? I've heard the name more than once or twice before. Do you know if he and Murf are tight?"

Adam answered, "I'd imagine they are. Both have been on the force together for years: matter of fact…I think they were partners at one time. Then Cooney moved to the vice unit if I remember correctly…and a couple of years ago he took the Sergeant job. Nice enough guy…" Adam told her that it was Cooney that had blown his cork over the autopsy report that he and Phil had taken off of his desk a while back.

"I'm trying to remember where I've heard his name. I'll have to call Brandy and see if she can place the name."

Mickey hadn't said much. "I really didn't care much for Larry Symanski…much too overbearing; like he came in with an agenda."

Holly agreed, "I think I've seen him some place but I can't remember where. He's got shifty eyes…and thin lips. That kind of guy spooks me. I got the feeling he was undressing me with his eyes."

Mickey had noticed the ogles as well, but didn't affirm Holly's observation. "Obviously there's no love lost between Symanski and

Murphy. That's a story we should be more than curious about," Mickey added. "Maybe you should find out more about the father from his kid," he suggested to Adam.

Adam said he would. After a few quiet minutes, his thoughts shifted to Father Mario. "I was impressed with your priest friend, Father Mario. He's really smart...and connected."

"Street smart," Holly said, leaning over the front seat to be heard by the two men. "That's the best kind of smart. I think he and Frank could really be helpful. When Father Mario mentioned that he knew a few members of the police commission, it got me thinking."

"Symanski got kinda defensive when Mario offered to make some inquiries," Adam said. " He said that it's best to stay away from the politicos. Yet, I remember Phil saying his dad was tight with some of the commission members. Strange."

"Believe me," Mickey added, "Mario is a super sleuth. He's privy to more political stuff that goes on in this town than the three of us combined. I'll talk more to him tomorrow."

Adam's cell rang. "It's Brett Ward an officer from our west Duluth department," he mumbled. He listened for a long minute, "Will do," he said as he returned his smart phone to his jacket pocket. He felt Holly's squeeze on his shoulder. "It's my apartment isn't it?"

"It is. They've given it a once-over but want us to stop by if we can." The trio was just approaching the Central Avenue exit on I-35 when Adam told Mickey to take the off ramp, "The cops need to talk to Holly, Father."

* * *

Officer Ward met them at the door. "We've taken pictures and scanned for prints, but need to find out what's missing," he told the group. Holly's eyes scanned the living room. "My computer's gone," she said immediately. Looking toward her desk, she noticed that the top corner desk drawer was slightly open. She stepped toward her desk, "Can I touch things?" she asked the officer closest to her. He nodded. Holly rummaged through the three drawers. "I had an address book in the top drawer…it's gone."

Adam was quick to inquire, "Names and addresses you wouldn't want anybody to see?"

"I don't think so. There's not much on my computer either…I erase almost all of my emails once I've read them." Holly didn't mention that the names and phone numbers of a few of her men were in the address book. Nor did she say that Brandy's parent's name and phone number were listed as well.

Ward spoke, "You're not going to like what you see in the bedroom, Holly. Whoever was here was one sick sonuva…"

Nobody finished the word. Holly's face wrinkled, "Why do you say that, officer?

"The perp is a sicko…he urinated in your underwear drawer."

Holly teared, "Can you get rid of the dresser and everything in it for me. I don't ever want to see it again."

Ward nodded. He would get the underwear to the crime lab and have DNA tests done.

Holly asked the other officer who was wearing latex gloves to open the other two drawers for her. She noted that her clothing was ruffled but everything seemed to be where she last saw it. She looked into her closet and saw that nothing was missing. "My jewelry box," she said as she moved past Mickey and Adam to the bedside table. She opened the drawer and opened the lid…a sigh of relief escaped her lips: "It's still here," she said as she lifted the diamond necklace from the box. "I wonder why…?"

"Is everything there?" Adam asked.

"Seems to be. This is the only thing of any value," she said as she clutched the necklace to her breast. "Thank God."

A routine walk through the kitchen and bathroom didn't reveal much of anything. Adam could see the residue of print dusting powder on countertops but didn't comment. Within fifteen minutes they were ready to head back to Adam's house. Holly agreed to return the following afternoon to give her apartment a more thorough examination; officer Ward would join her.

50/ SECOND THOUGHTS

Adam didn't sleep well; his thoughts were consumed with being chosen to make some kind of approach to his former partner. Nobody had given him any suggestions about how to go about it. Father Frank Polich, who knew Murphy well, had offered to join Adam if he wanted, but Adam hadn't responded one way or the other. He liked the NERC priest well enough and found him to be sincere in wanting to be a buffer…but? Adam wished that he could figure out what the 'but' was about. Frank had been critical of any confrontation with Brenden Murphy; "He'd push back if his integrity was questioned and that would put a damper on our ability to go forward."

Adam could't discount the priest's insight…but, if anybody in the group was going to do it, it should be him. The following morning during a coffee break Adam called Phil Symanski. "Has your dad given you the scoop on our meeting last night?"

"Haven't had a chance to talk with him yet. What did you folks come up with?"

"Well, the consensus seemed to be that Murphy was our man."

"I'm not surprised. Isn't that what I've been telling you all along, Adam? Murf's on the inside of everything that goes on."

"Your dad was adamant about that very same thing."

"What did the others think?"

"Based mostly on what your dad told us about Murf…for the most part, I think they agreed with him." Adam didn't mention that Father Frank had issues with the former cop's assertions. "Unfortunately for me, I was the one chosen to come up with some way of taking the next step—that being some kind of confrontation, I guess."

"Anything I can do to help?"

"Nothing I can think of now."

Symanski offered, "Just let me know, okay? Anything else?"

Adam said he'd keep in touch.

For reasons he wasn't quite sure about, Adam asked Siri for the phone number of the Newman Center on the UMD campus. Father Mario had also been reluctant to share the elder Symanski's perspective. Mario caught the second ring as he was heading out the door.

"Father, Adam Trygg…from the meeting last night."

"Sure, Adam. What's up this morning?"

"Nothing much." Adam went on to explain his lingering doubts. "So, I'm still wrestling with how to go about approaching Officer Murphy—wondering if it's really such a good idea."

Mario listened without raising any questions. "I think you'd be wise not to rush to any judgements." He told Adam of the conversation he'd had with Father Frank after the others had left. "This matter of Murphy's alleged wealth and his wife's lavish spending…well that's awfully misleading. What didn't come out was the fact that Alice Murphy, his wife, is the daughter of Lucius Allan Mongomery."

"The investment guy? The one who went to prison for some

kind of pyramid or investment scam some years back?"

"One and the same. He left a trust for his two daughters, Alice and Audrey. Both got small fortunes that the banks couldn't touch. That, I'd say, explains a lot of the accusations flying around the room. Frank said that whenever he hears innuendos and suppositions he sees red flags. I agreed. Furthermore, he's heard this name Cooney come up before. He's going to get back to me later today—after he's done some checking of his files."

"Interesting," Adam said.

"There's more. I just got off the phone with Mickey. He says that Holly isn't so sure about Murphy either. She thinks that she should have corrected this Symnanski guy when he told us that Officer Murphy wasn't trusted by his fellow cops and that he always went light on kids who did drugs. She told Mickey that he told her more than once that he'd kick butt from here to Sunday if he ever heard that she was messing with narcotics. She said her prostitue friend, girl named Brandy, I think...said both of them, and other girls she knew, had some king of weird respect for him. "

"That's a surprise to me. She's never mentioned that to me before."

"Maybe there are some other things she hasn't told you, Adam: 'silent water runs deep', you know. I'd suggest you have a heart-to-heart with her before you reach any conclusions that you might regret later."

Adam agreed, "I'd like to speak further with Father Frank, too. Is he up at NERC most days?"

"Yes, I think so. Let me give you his cell number."

Adam thanked Mario and agreed not to do anything before following up on the priest's suggestions.

After work, he asked Susan if he could talk privately with Holly about some things. His wife and Holly had done some shopping that afternoon and Holly was trying on some slacks and tops. "Let me see if she's decent, Adam. Andrew is napping in our room and Anna is watching a Dora DVD on TV."

Susan gave her husband a nod, "She's decent. Wants to show off some of her new things, too."

Adam knocked and entered, "Holly, I picked up something today that I want to talk with you about, have you got a few minutes?"

Holly smiled, did a quick twirl; "Let me show you a few things first." Her new clothes were layed out on the top of the bed.

After a show-and-tell, Adam found a place to sit on the end of the bed and related his conversation with Mario.

Holly admitted she should have said more at the meeting the night before. "That Symanski guy was intimidating; lots of bad vibes from him. He kept giving me those 'white trash' looks. Murf isn't an evil man. If you talk to some of the kids on Hillside they will tell you the same. To think that he would piss in someone's drawer just doesn't work for me—no way!" She mentioned something that her friend Brandy had told her once. According to Holly a girl that Brandy knew was pregnant with a mixed race child and planning to get an abortion. "Murf talked her out of it and found an adoptive family for the baby. He did it without any fanfare or 'look what I did'. It worked out wonderfully for all of them." There were other stories as well.

"Your trying to make him out to be some kind of saint, Holly. I know better than that. I've spent hours with the guy and know some things that you don't know about my old friend, Murf."

"Such as?"

"I don't know that it's anything you need to know about."

"Oh, so it's Holly tells all and Adam tells nothing. That pisses me off." She turned her back to him and laid out a pair of sequined fashion jeans on the bed; matching it against a lacy white blouse she had purchased. "Are we done?" she said.

"Okay. Your beloved Murphy, the same guy you've bad-mouthed in the past, and don't forget that you were the first to point a finger on him, is suddenly some benevolent do-gooder. That may be true, but he's also got a dark side...for instance, I think he's a racist and a sexist. Do you have any stories about his helping out any of the Black or Hispanic kids on Hillside?" Adam didn't mention that Murphy also cheated on his wife more than once. "And, he's got a vulgar sense of humor—knows more off-color jokes than ten sailors. Furthermore, from what he's told me more than once, he thinks women have no place in law enforcement."

"Half the cops are probably racists and sexists. And...dirty jokes? I'll bet that you've told a few yourself, Adam Trygg. Women? So what if he's a sexist pig...he's only one of millions." Holly smiled, "Just sayin', Adam."

Adam was quick to dispute her contention about cops. "That racial accusation bothers me, Holly. These days too many people are playing the race card about cops and it's just not the case. Murphy is an exception...and, he doesn't go out of his way to profile minorities. It's just that so many of them are poor and get into trouble because...because of a lot of things. Working Hillside changes one's attitudes about race...broken homes, fathers in jail, mothers on drugs, all kinds of crap."

"Let's not argue. I just think that Murphy's no different than your or me or anybody else—he's got two sides...it's just that there's a good side that nobody wanted to talk about last night. And...and you took every little negative I told you about Murphy and ran with it last night."

Adam let it go at that.

Holly might have said some bad things about Cooney, but had chosen not to. She tried to remember a connection of some kind but couldn't. Adam was fidgeting with his hands and not making consistent eye contact, appearing to be anxious to leave the room. "Nobody said much about another cop you worked with downtown…this Cooney guy. Why's that?"

"What's to say about Cooney? Do you know something I don't? If you do, let me in on it."

Holly was quiet for a long stressful minute; then it came to her. "I've got to get in touch with Brandy about that. Her battery must be dead because I haven't been able to reach her on her Tracfone for the past three days." It had occurred to her that Cooney was once one of Brandy's guys but she wasn't certain. "I'll let you know if I remember something. Okay?"

When Adam returned to the kitchen where Susan was boiling noodles for yesterday's leftover spaghetti and meatball sauce, she told him that she heard his phone register a message. Adam checked the message, *"Let's talk. I'm a night owl if you're free tomorrow after work. Ask Mickey to come along if he's free. He'll tell you where I live."* The text was signed: *Frank.*

51/ A COONEY CONNECTION?

Mickey told Adam that he could join him on Wednesday night. "Father Frank lives downtown where he's always been the most comfortable. You've probably driven by the Yorkshire Apartment building a thousand times. It's pretty run down these days, but in it's day it was luxury living for affluent Duluthians. Back in the seventies, they began chopping the suites into small cubicles, and made it a high-density place for the less than affluent. Frank says he doesn't need more than a kitchen, bathroom, and a bed to sleep on. As you'll see, that's about all he's got."

Mickey had had a wonderful conversation—the best in some time—with his son Michael the day before, and he had finished his packing for Thursday's flight to Fort Myers. Michael had not only made the Saint Anne baseball team, but had two hits in his first game. His stepfather, Tom, and his cousin Matthew, had been helping him with his hitting and it was paying off. Also, Michael had maintained his straight A's in school. At one point his son had called him 'Dad'…Mickey's heart virtually melted. Later he wondered if the boy had made a slip or if he really meant it?

* * *

Father Frank's digs were even more dingy than Mickey had described them.

Sparsely furnished with threadbare furniture, the living room with a foldout couch, served as his bedroom. The kitchen was not much bigger than the phone booths that once occupied most of the downtown corners. The stained grey carpeting crept from corner to corner. After scrunching next to Adam on the sofa, Mickey suggested they get into the Cooney matter that Frank had checked into. "His daughter, Nancy Cooney, spent a few months at NERC in 2012; records indicated she was dealing meth. While she was here she had three visitors, her dad and mother…and John James. An interesting twist, wouldn't you say?"

Adam was taking notes, "I wasn't on the force back then, but do you think she was one of James' girls?"

"Hard to say," Frank said. "But you might talk to her if she's still around these parts. File says that our last follow-up indicated she was living in Eveleth…working at a convenience store or somthing. Leeme see," Frank checked his own notes…"That was seven months ago."

"Anything else on Cooney, Frank?" Mickey probed.

"Yes, matter-a-fact, he's in our registry twice in mid-August of last year. The log says he was visiting for an interrogation of one of our 'detainees' as we affectionately call our wards. *Interrogate*, of course, is pretty vague. The man he saw was named Munter, Richard Munter…he's the guy his daughter was living with back when she was in trouble. He came to us from Chisholm, I think. You've probably got a file on Munter downtown."

Adam made a note to check it.

* * *

On the drive back to Riverside, Mickey commented, "This puts a different slant on things dosen't it, Adam?

Adam didn't respond, looking out the side window at the passing

traffic and trying to find a way to reconcile the new information about his colleagues on the police force. "Well, it gives me a couple of things to check up on; the Cooney girl and her former boyfriend for sure. Didn't Frank say this Munter guy was in his forties?"

Mickey nodded as he turned down the Mesaba Avenue hill, "Yes, probably a good fifteen years older than Cooney's daughter. Probably a meth relationship…that stuff's the absolute worst."

Adam agreed but his mind was on something else. "I hate to admit that two of my fellow cops are suspects in a murder investigation. Part of me hopes that we're wrong on both counts."

"It's not out of the question that this Munter guy knew James," Mickey suggested. "If he thought James was abusing his girlfriend…would't that put him on the possible suspect list? Maybe you should be talking with Cooney rather than Murphy; see how this Munter guy fits in. How tight are Murphy and Cooney?"

"You're not the first person to ask that very question, I'd guess pretty tight, Father. They've worked together for years—I think they were partners some time ago. I'd have to think that if one of them knows something the other one does as well. As much as I dislike the guy, maybe I ought to talk with Larry Symanski, too…he's got some history with both of them. It's quite obvious that he has no love for Murphy though. I'd have to guess that he feels the same about Cooney."

Adam wondered to himself if he was getting himself into matters that were out of his league. He recalled that Susan had warned him to stick with his day-to-day policework and not get embroiled in a murder investigation that no longer any of his business. These days the only people he could actually trust were his wife, father Mickey, his friend Phil Symanski…and maybe, his new partner Carl Rodland. Could it be that his coupling with Rodland had been orchestrated from downtown headquarters? Who could he turn to now? Through jumbled thoughts, and a diminishing self-confidence, he tried to figure out where to go from here.

When he returned home he texted Phil Symanski: *'When you get five minutes give me a call. Some things you might help me get a handle on.'*

52/ MICKEY, MOM, AND MEGHAN

If Mickey needed more drama in his life it was just around the corner. As he waited for passenger boarding in the Delta Airlines gate, he got a call from his sister. Meghan was distraught: "Have you talked with mom in the past few days?"

Mickey hadn't and felt a pang of guilt over his negligence. As she had for months, Sadie Moran had paid for his flight and mailed him his tickets the week before. This time he hadn't even taken the time to call and thank her. Sometimes he felt like a little boy asking for an allowance; his mother's generosity had no bounds. Mickey's behavior was deplorable and he knew it better than anyone. "No…look, I'm about to board right now, Meg. We can talk when

I arrive—about three hours from now. Okay?"

He could hear Meg sigh, "I suppose. Why does everything always have to be on your schedule? You're a spoiled…" Mickey heard his connection click off. "What now?"

* * *

Upon his arrival at the RSW terminal in Fort Myers, Mickey called his mother to see if she could tell him anything about Meg's apparent crisis of the moment.

"She's upset with me…that's all. I told her that she wasn't welcome in my house for any long-term separation. She's being irresponsible and I told her that in no uncertain terms. You know how Meghan expects everybody to do her bidding. She tires me out sometimes."

"What do you mean by that, mom?"

Sadie took a minute to answer. "She asked me to tell Kenny that she needed to 'get away from things'—needed some space," she said. "I called her a coward and that really set her off. She said Kenny didn't understand her depression."

"Wasn't she just visiting you in Hibbing a week or so ago?"

"She was…and she wanted to stay longer. Even if it meant she'd miss Kenny's birthday." Kenny's birthday was yesterday.

Mickey cursed under his breath…he'd forgotten Kenny's birthday again this year. "I'm with you a hundred percent on this, mom. What's with Meg these days? She's too young for a mid-life crisis."

Sadie wouldn't remind Mickey that Meghan had gone through these bouts of anxiety—or whatever it was?—more than once before. "She's too self-centered for her own good. I told her that, too."

"Okay, mom. Thanks for the heads up. I'll try to be sensitive about all this." Before pocketing his cell, he asked: "Anything else I should know about?"

A long pause followed his question, "I think I'll let Meghan tell you. Give Michael a hug and kiss from Gramma...and Mattie and Katie, too."

Mickey almost forgot his thanks, "Oh, thanks for getting me the tickets again. I feel so..."

Sadie had already hung up. "Damn!"

Let Meghan tell me what, he wondered, as he stood too close to a smoker, who inhaled his second cigarette, outside the terminal. Three hours without his nicotine must have been misery for the guy. A Dodge van with four kids scrunched at the windows slowed at the curb. A tall woman wearing a workout outfit stepped out and circled behind the vehicle and rushed to embrace a business-suited man with a wide beard. The two kissed as their children clapped at the reunion. Obviously, this family had something special going on. Mickey could only grin at the kids, he wished he could magically produce ice cream cones for all of them. As he wandered a few feet down the wide pickup corridor his attitude was uplifted. The Florida sun was glorious and the breeze warmly refreshing. It had been nearly two months...two long and frigid northern Minnesota months!

53/ SISTER AND BROTHER

Mickey didn't recognize the metallic blue SUV that pulled to the curb where Mickey had taken a pause near a small, bald man in a FGCU sweatshirt who was talking to himself and picking at his nose. He saw the back hatch open on the Nissan Rogue, and expected the man to grab his bag and toss it into the open cargo space. But, the man only looked the other way. "Hey, bro!" The voice was familiar.

Meghan appeared from behind the vehicle, "Do you want a ride or are you just holding down the sidewalk?"

Mickey laughed, stepped forward and embraced his sister. "Yeah…I'll take a ride to wherever you're going in that new car of yours. You look great, Meg. I like the new do, the outfit, the fancy shades." Meg did look great. His sister was a pretty woman and the yellow top she wore gave her face a wholesome glow.

"You're not looking too shabby yourself. When did you last get a haircut…or is this some new look?"

Mickey ignored the question tossing his duffle bag in the back hatch and climbing into the new SUV while inhaling the new car smell. "I like it. Is it yours or Kenny's?"

"All mine. Kenny surprised me with it when I got back last weekend. Sometimes he spoils me."

Mickey wouldn't comment on the extravagance of Kenny's 'gift'; rather he followed his compliments with a tease that he knew would strike a nerve: "So, I heard that mom kicked you out."

"Funny!"

Mickey gave his sister a playful poke on her shoulder, "I talked to mom. What's going on?"

"With me or her?"

"Both of you, I guess."

Meghan merged into the traffic departing the terminal in the left lane that would take her to I-75 and south. "Well, I've been going through another one of my 'mini depressions'. Thank God for Kenny…he knows me and my moods and he's always there to pick me up when I slip and fall. Truth be told…I guess I just miss Hibbing sometimes. Go figger!"

Mickey finished her thought, "And you hate Florida sometimes."

"I do. The traffic…the snowbirds who don't know how to drive…and…"

Mickey finished her sentence again, "…and, you miss the subzero temps and the shrunken gray winter days of Minnesota. I think that's why we get all of the 'sunbirds' up North…everybody down here wants to wear parkas and shovel snow."

Meg laughed. "Question, Mickey…if you could get a transfer of some kind to here; would you take it? Close to us, and Michael?"

Mickey had considered that very question a thousand times. "You know, I can't answer that, Meg. I just don't know."

"What if mom were down here?"

"Well, that's not ever going to happen. Her whole life is wrapped up in Hibbing; her friends, her clubs, her church, doctors…everything that keeps her ticking."

Meg ramped onto the interstate heading south toward Naples. Nothing was said for a few minutes and the silence was comforting to both. "Just thinkin'" Meg said. "What else did mom have to say?"

Mickey would not say that their mother thought Meg's behavior was immature. "She did say something kinda strange, though. She said that you would fill me in on something else."

Meg regarded her brother, "Do you read the Hibbing obits very often?"

"Not too often, why?"

"Last month Alice Cleary passed away. Not too long ago it was Barbara Selvog. Mom's best friends for years."

"I heard about Barb…I sent a card to …what's her husband's name? Dad was a close friend of his."

"Edward."

Meg continued. "And the Dinters—Ralph and Marie—sold their

house and moved back to South Dakota where the family has had a farm for generations. It's like her cozy little world is coming apart at the seams." Meg noticed a tailgater in her rearview mirror and changed lanes. "And, dad, of course. It's been just over a year already. Seems like only…" Meg's voice cracked and she found a Kleenex in the purse tucked near her left foot on the carpeted floor-board. "I miss him so. He was my rock, too—not just yours. We were lucky, Mickey. Dad was so wise and kind and…spiritual. Did you know that he read the Bible from cover to cover twice?"

Mickey wasn't sure where Meg was going with her reminicence. Looking out at the palmlined landscape he swallowed his own lingering sorrow. He'd steer their conversation away from their beloved dad. "Things change for all of us, Meg. So what's been going on?"

Meghan tucked her tissue in a litterbag slung over the shifting box an arm's length away. "Mom did not 'kick me out'…you should know that. Do you remember that little saying that mom had on the fridge?"

Mickey shrugged, "which one? She had several."

"I've got it memorized and think of it often: *'life is like an onion, we peel off one layer at a time, and sometimes we weep'*."

Mickey remembered but said nothing.

"I think I was making her uncomfortable when I was there. At first I begged her to come down and visit us for a while. Of course, she wouldn't have any of that. Then I went a layer deeper. I told her about a condo near the beach and Saint Anne Church. I've seen it and it's darling. It wasn't easy, but I got her to look at some video of the place on my computer."

"Mom's not going to rent a condo down here…she'll never move

Meg. She's seventy-two for heaven's sake. And, you've told me she hasn't been feeling great lately. Older folks don't want drastic changes."

"Just let me continue. Then I played dirty. I called the kids and asked them to beg their Nana to come down and see them. 'Tell Nana how much you miss her'. I think that made her weaken a bit."

"Why didn't you tell me all this before now?" In a way, Mickey wouldn't mind the idea of Sadie living in Naples; or even renting a place there for the winter months. The year-around sun was good for one's health and Olde Naples had so much going on all the time.

As Meg took the Pine Ridge exit into the north Naples traffic, Mickey put down the visor against the afternoon sun hanging in the western sky. Checking the dash clock he realized that school would be letting out in just a few minutes. "I'm anxious to see the kids…and Michael. I promised him I'd call and check in with him around supper time."

54/ NAPLES

Michael sounded enthusiastic. "Mom said she'd let me see *American Sniper*; will you take me? And what do you say about breakfast at IHOP tomorrow morning? I've been doing some planning, Mickey."

Mickey was hoping for an 'I missed you dad', but settled for his son's thoughtful planning. It had been much too long for the two of them not to have seen each other. *Facetime* on their smartphones was a poor substitute for real time. "You're on, buddy. And, I promised to take you on an airboat ride in the Everglades whenever you're up for doing that."

Michael would be honest, "My friends told me that it's not all that great. I mean, this time of year there's not much to see…and it's awfully noisy. I heard that the alligators out at *Wooten's* are pretty cool though—even if they're domesticated just like the ones at the zoo; you know, I mean they're fed every day and just lounge around for people to stare at and take pictures. Oh, have you seen the *Geiko* commercial with people harassing the camels at a zoo somewhere?"

Mickey had...both laughed. "And the new one with the goat in the peanut butter factory?"

The conversation ended with both looking forward to the following day and the many options in store for them.

Kenny barbequed ribs on the Weber patio grill while Meg prepared salads in the kitchen. Matthew and Katie brought their favorite uncle up to date on their schoolwork and extra-curricular activities. Fifteen year-old, Mattie, was a gifted athlete and doing very well in baseball; pre-teen Katie was active in the school's drama club. Mattie was excited about the Twins new acquitions—especially the return of Torii Hunter (his favorite all-time Twin), and spring training in Fort Myers was only days away. Katie's club had recently seen a big-time stage production—*The Phantom of the Opera*— at the Barbara Mann playhouse, also in Fort Myers.

After dinner the kids retired to their rooms to do homework, and the adults lounged outside with a bottle of Pinot Noir wine on the mild February night. Meg had done a great job with her landscaping and she proudly identified the flowering Hibiscus shrubs, Bougainvillea, and a variety of colorful annuals that were surrounding the patio.

Just after nine Mickey excused himself for some alone time. He told his sister and Kenny that he needed some prayer time. "I've got to prepare a homily for mass on Sunday morning." On his monthly trips to Naples, Bishop Cordoba of the Venice diocese assigned him to a local parish—this time it was Saint Peter the Apostle in East Naples. "I'll be back in an hour or so."

The Gulf beach and Lowdermilk Park was only a walk of two blocks from where Meghan and Kenny lived. Mickey found a bench near a small pavilion overlooking the quiet water. The night was clear and the stars were splattered across the dark heavens, like diamonds on black velvet. He thanked God for the wonder of His creation and for his reunion with loved ones. As always, he prayed for his son and his mother, his friends back home, and asked forgiveness for the negligence in his prayer life of late. Although rare, when he was able to envelop himself in a spirit of peace, he could block out distractions or drift away from the time and place of his escape. What might have been an hour or more later, he found himself kneeling in the sandy soil; in total harmony with heaven and earth. *"Thank You for choosing me to be Yours Lord, for blessing my life in so many wonderful ways, and for the peace of this prayer time."*

He was startled by a voice behind him, then it rang familiar…"I thought you might be here," Meghan said above the melodic roll of the sea. "I hope you prayed for me along with everything else."

Mickey got to his feet, "I did. What time is it, Meg?"

"Nearly eleven. Let's go home." She took her brother's hand and the two of them walked back to the house without any words between them. It was a time when silence was golden; far better than any contrived conversation could be.

* * *

On Friday morning, Mickey got a call from Adam Trygg. "I envy you, Father, it's thirty below zero with who-knows-what for a wind chill up here." Adam went on to say that he had called Brenden Murphy the night before. "We're getting together for a beer after my shift this afternoon. There's a bar over near the zoo that we're both familiar with."

"What do you plan on saying? I mean, are you planning to confront him with the things we've been talking about?"

"Before calling Murf, I had a long conversation with this Larry guy, my former partner's dad. Anyhow, I told him about our suspicions about Cooney."

Mickey was dubious, "Was that a wise thing to do, Adam—aren't the two of them, I mean Murphy and Cooney— close friends?"

"They are. Symanski thinks that it could be that both of them are in cahoots. If one's got something on the other…or they've both got some dirty linen they want kept in the closet, he thinks that would lead to some kind of bond that neither would dare violate…that was the jist of his words. I'm paraphrasing of course, Father. What Symanski thinks may be true or it may be out in left field. I just feel better about telling what I've heard everybody saying to Murf—face to face, no holds barred!"

Mickey wasn't so sure if it was the right time to confront anybody. He wondered if Adam wasn't a lamb stepping into a lion's den. "Are you sure about this? I mean, it's an awfully ballsy thing to do."

"There's more. Holly hasn't been able to get in touch with her friend, Brandy. Worse yet, she doesn't even know what Brandy's *real* name is. Remember, the last time the two of them talked Brandy was in some kind of danger. She thinks something bad has happened. She wants me to see if Murphy knows anything about Brandy's whereabouts. I even talked with Father Frank. He's going to talk with some of the street kids that might know something about Brandy. He told me that he's built up a lot of trust with the Hillside kids, and if they think one of their friends is in some kind of trouble, they would tell him whatever they knew. Holly's been using my cell phone to make calls to her former friends as well. She doesn't even trust her Tracfone anymore."

"You've been busy, Adam, I'll say a prayer that all goes well. Keep me posted, okay?"

"Oh, there's one other thing I might mention. Holly's father told her that if someone doesn't do something pretty soon he's going down to headquarters to turn himself in for assaulting John James. He has a feeling that he's being watched by the police, and it's been unnerving. I told her to keep him from doing that. Anything he might tell Murphy or Cooney wouldn't advance the investigation at this point. Besides, when this all comes to a head, he might be able to make a case for acting in self-defense."

"And," Mickey warned, "put you in hot water for not arresting him in the first place. I think if I were you I'd keep that part of the equasion under wraps for now."

Adam agreed to do so.

PART THREE

"Honesty is the first chapter in the book of wisdom."
Thomas Jefferson

55/ QUESTIONS

Adam's eyes were slow to adjust to the change in light from the late afternoon sun outside to the shadowy tavern lighting he'd stepped into.

"Hey…over here." Murf slid out of the booth. Adam shook his clammy hand and sat across from the large man wearing a navy blazer and blue oxford shirt. An empty glass was on the table and a pitcher of beer centered on the polished oak. Murf spoke first, "So how you liking the west end beat? Heard you're working with Carl Rodland. I recommended that, you know…he's a good man. I helped him get his first job with the department."

Adam wondered if Murphy pulled everybody's strings. "So far so good. Me and Carl get along really well."

"You look awfully serious, Adam. Lighten up, for God's sake, are you just back from someone's funeral?"

Adam shook his head, trying to come up with some kind of ice-breaker, but failing to get a quick handle on one.

Murphy flashed his wide Irish smile, "By the way, do you know the difference between an Irish wedding and an Irish funeral?"

Adam puzzled, "Can't say that I do."

"One less drunk."

Adam smiled for the first time. Murphy's humor was engaging. The two men small talked for a few minutes about family and friends. "How's the new little boy doing…? Andrew, isn't it?" Murf inquired about Susan and Anna as well. It struck Adam how much his former partner knew about his life away from work, and the thousands of conversations that had passed between them over the past year.

Adam didn't want to be getting home too late, so he swallowed hard on what would be was likely to be an amateurish interrogation of his old friend. "Do you happen to know a girl, about eighteen or ninteen, named Holly?"

"No, should I?"

"How about a girl about the same age by the name Brandy?"

Adam sensed a squirm, then a narrowing of Murphy's eyes. "The only Brandy I can think of is a street girl…or used to be."

"That's the one…Hillside neighborhood?"

"Yeah, why? Where are you going with this? I think you damn well know that Brandy is missing. Let's shoot straight, Adam. If you know something, maybe you should be telling me."

Adam had been thinking about the sequence of his questions all afternoon. He continued. "Do you know if she was connected with this John James, or Jesse James, I should say?"

"Why, have you talked with her? Did she give you some information? If so, I'd like to know what it is. You've spent enough time in Hillside to know that everybody knew James, but you'd never know it by the number of people who went to his funeral. Sad…the kid's entire life was a tragedy."

Adam found Murphy's sentiment rather strange but didn't run with it.

He'd go to his next query, "Do you know a girl named Lucy?"

Murphy laughed, "You're baiting me, Adam. Yes, as you damn well

know. Keep going. A good looker with a bad attitude: 'Loosey Goosey' they call her. She's Brandy's running mate. And, as you probably know, she's disappeared too."

Murphy drained his glass and poured another, then locked eyes with Adam. Another deep swallow of beer, "You're playing games Adam, and I have to say you're not very good at it. Asking questions that you already know the answer to won't get you anywhere. Now, if you've got any leads on the James murder…just spit them out. Oh, who's this Holly? How does she fit into Brandy and Lucy's disappearance? We just might be looking at some foul play...like kidnapping...or worse."

"One more question, Murf. Something that I don't already know the answer to. Okay?"

Murphy sighed deeply, his face flushed: "Who's this Holly? You answer that or this conversation is over. Not only that...but I might have you arrested for withholding information. As you know, or ought to, that's some serious stuff."

Adam swallowed hard. If his friend only knew what he knew. As dangerous as it might prove to be, he was determined to keep John Belak out of their conversation. "Murf, answer one last question...then I'll tell you everything I know."

Murf drained his glass, glared his antagonism "...I'm running out of patience, but go ahead and shoot."

"The James autopsy report is missing. I've learned that you were the last person with access to the file."

Murphy laughed, "Who in hell told you that? That's privileged information, son. Don't go snooping where you don't belong."

"I'd rather not say who told me what, Murf. And, I'm not snooping." Adam checked his watch. He hadn't told Susan that he'd be late.

Murphy noticed, "Don't worry. I called Susan this afternoon and told her you had an important meeting after work. Quit nursing and have another beer," Murf didn't wait for an answer and filled Adam's glass. "You tell me two things and I'll fill you in on what you're sniffing around about: who is this Holly and who told you about the ME's report? And, you're not leaving this bar until I get the answers I need. Understood?"

"Okay, mostly from a former cop...name's Larry Symanski, he's the one who told me about the report." Adam waited for a reaction to the name of a former cop who had cast aspersions on Murphy's reputation. Murf smiled without comment. Adam followed a brief lull, "Now it's my turn; Holly is Holly Goeden, aka, 'Loosey Goosey'."

Murphy sat back in the booth, "That helps." He scratched his head and gave a crooked smile to Adam. "Of all people to get information from! I'm going to tell you something about Larry the Letch and a few other things that go no further than me and you...and Father Frank if you choose to confide in him about anything we're talking about. Frank's solid. I know you've talked to him, Adam, but he wouldn't say what that meeting was about.

"Let me start with something you told me shortly before your transfer," Murf said. "Do you remember telling me that you were looking for an old Buick with tinted glass that was prowling the Hillside? Anyhow, that's when I decided that you might be getting into something over your head. Then those notes to 'call me' from Lucy...Cooney told me about them. We thought it best to...can I say, keep you out of harm's way. Oh, I might add, Cooney's got the autopsy stuff buried away for now...for the moment it's priviledged information. Can you live with that, Adam?"

"Yes, sir." Adam felt humbled by his superior officer and almost wished he'd listened to Father Mickey's advice about waiting before having this confrontation. He offered a weak apology, "I didn't mean to get out of line, Murf. But this case is getting kind of close to me and my family. I've gotten to know Holly, or Lucy...almost too well. She's scared as hell."

56/ MURPHY'S STORY

Brenden Murphy would talk for nearly an hour almost without interruption. He began with an explanation about a call from Will Dusken, the Duluth Police Chief, back in the fall. Dusken was going to reactivate a vice squad that had not survived the budget cuts of years before. Prostitution arrests still occurred, but mostly the cops had been looking the other way; that, along with arrests for smoking pot; many citizens and taxpayers, he claimed, now considered prostitution to be a victimless crime. The proliferation of hard drugs, and their connection with other violent crimes, however, needed more attention. Murf knew Hillside, and Dusken believed he was the best man for the vice squad job and wanted him to head up a reinstituted task force. Murf's initial focus was on Jesse James and his corral of girls of underage girls. Jesse was a known dealer and a pimp who had done time, but whoever pulled Jesse's strings remained unknown. The tip on the mysterious Buick led Murphy up blind alleys, most of which were in west Duluth. The guy who spent his time on Raleigh Street and out in Fond du Lac remained a person of interest, but he and Cooney were only keeping tabs on his whereabouts. "We saw him visit the crime scene one afternoon. You know the old adage, the criminal always returns to the scene…" Murf refilled his glass. "But, we've been reluctant to pinch the guy without something a bit more substantial."

Adam learned that his recent transfer and his partnership with Carl Rodland (who was also on Murphy's task force), had been arranged by Cooney. Cooney was also on the task force. Murf rambled for a minute, "Then, with James out of the picture, Brandy…I'll call her Brandy Doe for now, went missing. That gave a new sense of urgency to everything. Now it was a hardball game, and we're still spinning our wheels," Murphy said—his expression grave.

"Going back a ways, it wasn't until you and Phil Symanski were browsing the ME's report on Cooney's desk that we made a connection that neither of us had given thought to. Enter Larry Symanski," Murf said. He explained that 'Larry the Letch' was caught with his hands in the cookie jar some years before. Larry was putting a squeeze on the Johns that his dancer friends at a gentlemen's club were sexually involved with. Very selectively,

Symanski extorted them…"Let's just say that you're an influential person, with money of course, and you're contacted by someone in the police department with a threat: 'We'll expose you if you don't cough up some cash'…classic case of extortion!"

Although enthralled by Murfs discourse, Adam's skepticism hadn't been allayed. Who was he supposed to believe? Murf continued, "Well, wouldn't you know, one of the Johns being extorted was a man (Murphy didn't give a name) with a relative on the police commission. That commissioner contacted me, and shortly afterwards, I found the bad apple. Larry still had some cards to play with, and the commission—to avoid a black eye over the corrupt activity—the police chief 'allowed' Symanski to resign the force and keep his pension elgibility. I guess we'll go to any lengths to avoid having one of our officers being disgraced and fired."

Adam was getting an altogether different picture of Symanski. Murf continued, "Remember, Symanski still had the commissioner over a barrel, and that gave him some residual influence to be taken into account. Regardless, it stunk up the department for months." Murphy fidgeted with a salt shaker as he considered what to say next. "That old bastard still pokes around where he doesn't belong. So we, Cooney and me, decided to give Symanski some misinformation and see where that might take us. We suspected that his son—your former partner—kept his father abreast of everything that was going on in Hillside. Including the James investigation."

"Not Phil, Murf. He's a straight-shooter…I should know. Jeeze, he's the godfather of my son!"

"I'm not accusing anybody Adam, I'm just saying that the kid thinks his dad was some kind of 'super cop' back in the day, and that I set him up. Lot's of negative vibes between us. I might add that if Larry tells his kid to buy some ocean front property in Utah, Phil's gonna bust his ass to go out and get some."

Adam nodded his understanding but stayed quiet. Murf went

on, "So, whenever his dad would ask him 'What's going on?' Phil would naturally want to impress his dad and do his father's bidding. Right?"

Adam couldn't disagree with that. "I know he always felt as if he had to live up to his dad's high expectations." Then a light went on. Adam realized that it was Phil who suggested that his father join the meeting with Father Mario the previous week. "I think I get it, Murf. We, our little group of amateur sleuths, brought him in on everything we knew."

Murf smiled, "We knew that, or most of it anyway. But there was nothing you could divulge that we weren't already aware of. We hoped that Larry Symanski might give your group some tidbit of information that we didn't have. That's why we asked Father Mario to suggest that your priest friend, Mickey, visit with Father Frank up at NERC. Is this making any sense to you, Adam?"

"It's pretty complicated…but I'm getting it" Adam said. "If Larry Symanski is the man you're trying to trip up, he's got an insider to keep him one step ahead of you."

Murphy nodded, "Let's get back to Father Frank for a minute. Frank is very guarded about what he says and does. And, very perceptive. That's why this girl Holly, who visited NERC with your priest friend, was a curve ball. His description of the young lady didn't register with me or anybody else at the time. Now I know. Thanks for that."

Adam let out a 'whew'…"Then you probably know that Symanski led us all to believe that you were the …s.o.b…. behind everything."

"Either me or Cooney, Symanski hates us both with a passion."

"We all got that."

"So…" Adam gave his next words long thought, "So, you think it's actually Symanski who killed the James kid. I'll be damned."

"Hold your horses, Adam. Larry Symanski was at the Black Bear Casino over by Cloquet all night when James went down…a perfect alibi. Being the obnoxious asshole that he naturally is, fifty people can attest to where he was that night. But, he might have arranged it—at best, he might be an assessory to the crime. That's where we are now…and where we've been for far too long."

"What's next, Murf?"

"Well…we've got to find Brandy. I've met with her family down in Forest Lake. That's not her 'real' name, you know."

"We figured that, I mean me and Holly. But even Holly doesn't know her real name."

"She's Olivia Larsen. Been missing for five days already. Tragic. But, at least now we know where Lucy is. And, it's probably not safe for her, or your family, to stay with you much longer."

"Do you know what happened to her apartment?"

Murphy laughed, "Haven't you been listening? Rodland keeps us informed on everything that goes on out in west Duluth."

"Duh!" Adam's face reddened, "I guess I'm still learning Murf."

The two men had been visiting for nearly two hours when Adam's cell rang. "Probably Susan…"

"I've gotta take a leak, back in a minute…" Murphy slid out of the booth.

"What are you up to, Adam?" It was Phil Symanski. "Haven't heard from you in a couple of days. My dad told me that Holly's living with you and Susan…how's that going?'

"So far so good. I'm talking with Murf right now; he thinks Holly should be somewhere else. So we'll…"

"Adam, sorry but I gotta run. Keep me posted."

When Murf returned from the men's room he tapped his watch, "It's nearly six. I told Susan you'd be home about now. Anything else for your prime suspect? I'm told that your little group thinks I'm involved in some shit. A little advise…be careful, Adam. Don't mess with me. Okay?"

Adam's jaw dropped an inch, "I know better that that, Murf. Thanks for clearing up some stuff that's been bothering me."

Murf offered a half smile, "I'll have Rodland pick up Holly in the morning. I've got a safe house in mind. Okay?"

"Do you really think she's in danger?"

"What do you think, Adam?"

Adam flushed, "Stupid question, huh?"

Murphy let it pass with half a nod. He offered his hand, "Let's keep each other posted…"

Adam laughed, "That's what Phil just said; 'keep him posted'…"

Murphy's expression became grave; "What are you talking about?"

Adam mentioned that Phil had recently called him.

"Probably best if you keep young Symanski out of the loop. He probably knows too much already." Murphy reconsidered, "Unless, that is, unless we want to use him to bait our hooks. Okay? I know the two of you are tight."

Adam, although surprised, promised he would. As the two men walked toward the door Adam commented, "I couldn't help but notice your watch. Is it a real *Rolex*?"

Murf put his thick hand on Adam's shoulder in an affectionate gesture, "Yes, it's authentic. A gift from my wife Barbara last Christmas. I've always wanted one and she can afford it. I think Frank told you about my wife…she's one wealthy lady. But, don't get the idea that that's why I married her." Murphy did not elaborate that his wife had had epilepsy since childhood. "I didn't know who her dad was until after I asked her to marry me. But, I'd be lying if

I told you that I wasn't delighted to find out that I didn't have to be a cop if I didn't really want to." He didn't have to tell Adam that he was about as uncorruptable as any public servant could be.

57/ MOTIVE

On the drive back to Riverside, Adam's cell rang. It was Phil again.

Adam didn't like talking while driving so let it ring off. If his family budget wasn't so strained, he'd have a *Blue Tooth* system installed in his car. As he reviewed the conversation he'd had with Murphy, something occurred to him. Something Holly had told him. He'd forgotten to ask about the note that Murf had allegedly passed to James one night.

"Damn, how would he have explained that?" Interrogation and conversation were apples and oranges. Adam had allowed Murf to control a situation that ought to have been his. Was it all a snow job? He wondered how long it might take for him to be in a league with the likes of Murf and Carl Rodland. It bummed him to realize that everyone seemed to be one step ahead of him on everything. When he got in the door, Anna rushed him and wrapped her little arms around his knee. He picked her up before hanging his jacket in the hall closet, "Daddy bery cold! Holly warm…" It was the first time he'd heard his daughter say Holly's name.

Susan was holding Andrew when she met him in the living room, "Do you know anybody with a sporty black Audi? It's not the kind of car we see in this neighborhood and I've seen it cruising by our house this afternoon." The Trygg's had a corner duplex on Sunnyside and Cato Streets in the Riverside neighborhood. "Once it slowed down…very conspicuously, almost as if he wanted me to see him. Anyhow, Holly's kinda spooked…wants to talk with you about moving on. She thinks she's a danger to us."

"She'll be gone tomorrow," Adam said. "Murphy's relocating her to a safe house. He didn't say where."

Susan puzzled, "Are you sure you trust…?"

Holly came into the living room, "Can we talk, Adam?" She gestured toward the room she shared with Anna. Adam nodded, followed Holly. He noticed that her few clothes were folded on her bed and Susan's travel bag rested on the floor. "Fill me in on Murphy," she said with a sharp edge to her words. "He's got a way of schmoozing people."

"What do you mean? Schmoozing? Is that like bullshitting?"

"Bullshitting with chocolate frosting."

Adam would be careful not to divulge anything he considered to be sensitive. He told her that he believed both Murphy and Cooney were clean. He didn't mention the vice task force, nor her friend Brandy. "He wasn't surprised that Larry Symanski had bad-mouthed him. There's some really bad blood between them." Adam went on to tell her that Murphy wanted to move her to some place safe. "Susan told me that someone's been cruising by the house."

Holly nodded, "I don't know if I want Murphy to know where I am. I still don't trust him. I'm losing faith in everybody…" She let the thought drop without naming names. "How about if I just take off somewhere? Get me a different car or some different license plates and head off into the sunset. Nobody would ever find me." Then she had a thought, "Maybe that's what Brandy did…just took off."

"Murf's worried about her, and you."

Holly went to the window, folded her arms across her chest, and took a deep breath. Without turning toward Adam she said, "I'm going to tell you something that you won't like…it's about you, and I hope you'll forgive me for saying it."

"Go ahead. I've got thick skin."

Holly turned, her face was streaked with tears. "Adam you're very naïve about some things...maybe you weren't cut out to be a cop."

If Adam winced, Holly didn't notice it. "Have you ever had a clear motive for someone killing Jesse? My dad beat him up because he was abusing me. Someone had a stronger motive than that. What might that have been? And...why would that someone resort to murder?"

Adam shrugged, "Maybe he knew something he shouldn't. Someone wanted to silence him...at least that's my best theory."

"You're too vague, Adam, but getting a little bit warm. I'll let you in on something I haven't told you. I knew Jesse pretty well. We'd partied together more than a few times. Him, along with Brandy and me. Anyhow, Jesse was a big mouth—it was like he wanted to impress people with what he knew. I've already told you that he and Brandy dated a few times...do you remember that?"

Adam did, "Okay. Go on..."

"Jesse knew the boss; the guy me and Brandy called 669. I think, and believe me...I don't know for certain. I think he told Brandy who the controller was. So, if 669 was worried about Jesse's big mouth, he'd have to do something about it. Right?"

"And, if this controller learned that Jesse had told any of his girls..."

"Now you're getting it, Adam. Then the girls would be in danger as well. Assume that this mystery man learned that Jesse told Brandy. Then what? Then, take it one step further..."

Adam nodded, "He, whoever this 669 is...he might think that, being you and Brandy were best of friends..."

"Seems to me that the motive isn't too difficult to figger out. Silence the 'rat' and then the rat's women."

"You're a reincarnation of Sherlock, Adam." Holly said.

Fighting back tears she said, "My gut is telling me that something bad has happened to Brandy." Then her tears flowed, "*Dear God...keep her safe.*"

Adam left the room wondering if Murphy knew all of this but hadn't said anything. And, he wondered if Holly was right...was his naivity something that would dissappear with experience, or was police work an art that he might never master? When he picked up his son from the playpen, he wondered something even more sobering...would he be around to see Andrew play hockey like his father had?

58/ FATHER AND SON

Michael decided that the Saturday afternoon was too nice to spend their time together wedged in a movie theater—even if his friends had already seen *American Sniper*. So what if he would feel out of the loop whenever Kris Kyle's name came up in teenager conversation. Instead, the two of them decided to spend the day at the beach. Michael brought along a Nerf football and forced Mickey into the low-sixty-degree water on his first pass. Mickey's conspicuously white body turned ten shades of blue. Spent from running in the heavy afternoon sun, they set up the beach umbrella that Tom had sent with them and relaxed. As they unwound from the activity, Mickey's eyes watched Michael's eyes as girls in skimpy bikinis passed in front of them along the shoreline. Amused, Mickey realized for the first time that his son was of an age when hormones were stirring and sexual thoughts ran rampantly through his thoughts. As a tease, Mickey commented, "Those girls seems to be about your age wouldn't you say?"

Michael flushed, "Who? I didn't notice."

Mickey suppressed the grin that was ready to crease his face.

"Do you have many kids my age in your parish?" Michael steered the conversation without tacking a 'Dad' or a 'Mickey' to his question. Mickey could tell that his son still struggled with what to call him.

"A few. Maybe ten or twelve who are fifteen. I see them every week during the school year for Confirmation classes. Why, son?"

"Just askin'. Do they ever…like confide stuff with you? I mean, do you get into their lives…school stuff, sports, you know?"

"Yeah, they do—but not too much. I get along with the kids pretty well, but some things—really personal things—get aired out when they go to confession. These days, I'd have to say, that doesn't happen very often." Mickey smiled at a fleeting memory. During his first parish assignment at Saint James he befriended two misfits from Denfeld High School: namely Randy Flynn and Jimmy Rossini. The boys had a grunge band and taught Mickey how to chord on an old Silvertone guitar they'd given him. Although that was ten years and twenty stories ago, he still kept in touch with both of them and reveled in the success that each had achieved. Mickey shared that story with his son.

"Pretty cool," Michael said. "Do you still play the guitar?"

"I do. I could teach you some of the basics if you'd like."

Michael smiled, "That would be really neat."

Mickey made a mental note. He'd seen a music shop on Tamiami Trail not far from Meg's house. If the shop was open this afternoon, he might stop by and see what they had in used instruments.

Mickey sensed that Michael was trying to get to something but wasn't quite able to get it out. "What I like about kids your age is that they've got so many things going on inside, but they don't quite know how to process them."

Michael nodded with a serious expression fixed on his face,

"...Or know who to talk to about them. Adults I mean. Parents, teachers, even priests...they're...what can I say?" He spent a long moment to contemplate how to follow up on what he wanted to say. "I think most adults are too removed from their kids' day to day stuff—like school. Friends...well, you just don't' want them to know when something's bothering you. Does that make any sense?"

Mickey smiled, "Perfect sense. I'd guess that one of the hardest things to talk about is girls. Am I right about that?"

Michael flushed, brushed away sand that rested on the corner of the beach towel he was sitting on. Without meeting Mickey's eyes, he mumbled: "Girls are a problem all right. Especially some of them."

"The ones you like are probably the most difficult to talk about wouldn't you say?"

"Exactly!" Michael finally looked up. "One girl I can talk to is my cousin...but she's only thirteen, so she doesn't know much about most things. But...she said that you might be someone to...like...talk to about something that's bothering me. And, she promised not to tell any of this to her brother."

For the second time in minutes, Mickey swallowed the urge to giggle. Michael's girl cousin was his niece, Katie, and her brother Mattie one of his son's best friends. "Well...I'd say that your cousin Katie is quite wise for a thirteen year-old...wouldn't you?"

Michael nodded. His voice tightened, "I kinda like this girl at school. She's taller than me and really smart. And pretty. Even some of the older guys, high school guys, flirt with her."

"She's kinda intimidating then?"

"Oh yeah!" He explained that next month was the Spring Fling—a dance at the school for ninth graders. It was, in Michael's words: 'A big deal'. "So...I wanna ask her...before someone else does...but I don't know if she likes me at all. She picked me first to be on her team when we had a geography contest in class last week…but that's probably because I'm the second smartest kid."

"What's the girl's name?"

"Janine. Janine Norris. Her family is in the furniture business so they are pretty well known down here."

Mickey was trying to contain his amusement with his son's torment. He knew how difficult this conversation must be…and felt special that he was the person being confided in. He could remember the same issues in his life at fifteen. Ironically, the girl he might have asked to a spring dance back then was also the smartest girl in his class—and that girl was Michael's mother; Mary Reagan.

"I suppose you tense up every time you see her, and when that happens, you lose every ounce of confidence that you needed to ask her to be your date for the dance?"

"Really tense up, Mickey. It's like I just know I'll say the wrong thing and look like an idiot." He laughed at himself. "You know how it is to be nervous…you get all tongue-tied…and red-faced; kinda like I am right now."

"What's the worst thing that could happen if you asked her, Michael?"

"She'd say no…or she'd laugh…that would be even worse."

"Or both."

"That would be a …" Michael couldn't find the right word to describe the devastation.

"Humiliation?"

"A super humiliation!"

Mickey considered making a suggestion with an easy escape clause for Michael. "Here's what I'd do, son. Imagine this; imagine that you've just hit a home run and won the game for your team. Okay? And Janine was watching from the front row. So…with that in the back of your mind, you've got a ton of confidence, you're feeling super-good about yourself...right?"

Michael laughed, "I suppose."

"Okay, so you've gotta imagine the self-confidence. That's the first step. Then...who's your best friend at school?"

"Mattie."

"Okay, maybe you tell Mattie what you're up to...maybe not; that's up to you." Mickey went on to imagine a perfect scenario for his son—an encounter with a perfect ending. "And there you have it...Janine was secretly hoping you'd ask her."

Michael's smile was priceless! "Really?" he mumbled as his eyes shifted away from Mickey's. The boy was still a little dubious.

* * *

On the way from the beach to Michael's house, Mickey found the shop he was looking for. As luck would have it, the guy they talked to had an old *Fender* acoustic guitar priced at seventy dollars—for another five an instruction book was included. After burgers and fries at *Five Guys*, the father and son returned to the Blanchard home just after six. Tom and Mary had eaten but saved dessert—a strawberry and rhubarb pie—for the guys. After that, Mickey spent a few minutes teaching Michael how to hold the guitar and how to finger the frets with his left hand. He demonstrated the three basic chords: C, G, and D; then allowed the boy to try some strumming on his own. Michael had long fingers and had little difficulty in slipping along the Fender's fretted neck. After an hour or so, Tom and Mary joined the musicians in the living room.

"Go ahead, Mickey," Mary encouraged. "Play us a song."

"Yeah..." Michael agreed with enthusiasm.

Mickey played an old favorite of his so that everybody could sing along with him. *"Michael rowed the boat ashore...halleluiah..."*

After a few songs, popcorn, and a game of Monopoly, Mickey said his goodnights and headed back to Meghan's house. As he drove Kenny's topless Jeep down Goodlette to Golden Gate, and then north on Highway 41 to Banyan Boulevard, Mickey breathed in the humid evening air as he said a prayer of thanks for his wonderful day. He felt a healing of sorts...a most welcome healing...Tom and Mary had a comfortable relationship; something he might never have been able to provide as a husband and father to Michael. And, Mickey smiled with an inner satisfaction; he and Michael had just had one of their very best days together. *"I am abundantly blessed with Your goodness and love,"* he spoke into the star sprinkled night.

59/ UNINVITED

Ash Wednesday and the Lenten season arrived in late February, Holly had been relocated to a place safe from her perceived demons, and March was settling in like a lamb. Mickey and Mario were having lunch at an *Olive Garden* located near the Miller Mall on the wide hilltop overlooking the city of Duluth and Lake Superior below. "So, it was a great visit...I'm happy for you Mick," Mario said. "I've prayed that one day you would get to a place where you realized that things have worked out in the way they were supposed to. The Maestro up there conducts some beautiful music if we take the time to listen. For the first time in a long while I truly believe that you are listening."

Mickey smiled, "You always make me feel better about myself, Mario. Thanks." He checked the time on his iPhone resting by his elbow on the booth tabletop: "Well, I'd better be off, Amigo. Oh, by the way, Adam told me to remind you that we're getting together on Thursday night at Jerry's Place." Jerry's place was a casual reference to Mickey's Saint Gerard's parish.

"A suit and tie occasion?"

"You don't own a tie. Casual is preferred, pizza will be provided, bring your own bottle." Mickey stood, "God bless you, Mario." The two men said their good-byes and headed out into the mild March afternoon. Snowflakes the size of nickels were dancing in the air; creating a fresh white blanket upon the bleak landscape. "Drive carefully," Mickey heard his friend call from the other side of the parking lot. "Say 'hi' to your mom."

Mickey had promised his sister that he'd visit their mother after his return from Florida. But, guilt was a much stronger reason for driving the seventy miles north to Hibbing than was his promise to Meg. He hadn't been a good son for quite some time. Before visiting his mother, Mickey had arranged a conference with Doctor Lorna Huber, Sadie's physician, at the Fairview Mesaba Clinic.

* * *

Father Frank Polich, who was proving to be a key person in the ad hoc group consisting of Adam, Fathers Mario and Mickey, was the first to arrive. He wore the same wrinkled khakis, scuffed boots, and black sweatshirt that he had worn every time the others had seen him. Brenden Murphy had agreed to join the group for their second meeting tonight. He and Frank were the two people who seemed to best know the backgrounds of those who were considered to be 'people of interest'. Holly was staying out of circulation and living in a safe house for now, and Larry Symanski hadn't been invited back after the his obnoxious rantings at the earlier meeting.

Adam was talking with Mario when his cell phone rang. He checked the caller ID…it was Phil Symanski. "Let me take this, Father," Adam said. "I'll join you at the table in a minute.

"What's up, Adam? I called your place and Susan said you were having a meeting at Saint Gerard's. She said your case group was getting together. You didn't tell me anything…"

Adam wished Susan hadn't said where he was, or why he wasn't home. "Yeah, we're just kicking some things around…that's all."

Phil wanted an explanation, "Why?" He wanted Adam to tell him the purpose of the meeting and who was there. "And, why wasn't my dad invited? Is it because Murphy and him don't get along? I still think you guys have allowed a fox to sneak into the henhouse."

Adam was beginning to regret confiding in his friend. He wasn't going to get into another argument; "I've told you many times that I disagree with you on this. I had Murf pegged wrong…so did your dad."

A long pause, "How about me, Adam? Can I join you guys tonight?"

"You're on duty tonight, Phil."

"I'll see if Cooney will give me a couple hours off…I want to see the James murder solved as much as anybody. He should understand that."

Adam didn't want to tell Phil that Murphy would be upset, or that he doubted that Phil would bring anything of importance to the table. "It's probably not a good idea right now. Anyhow, Frank said he wants to keep the group as small as possible."

"And secretive," Phil grumbled. "Do I know this Frank guy? "I don't think so."

"Is Holly going to be there?"

"No. Why do you ask?" Adam wondered what had given rise to his friend's questions, but didn't ask.

"What if I just showed up at the church where you're meeting, Adam? Without an invitation. Would you or this Frank guy just throw me out?"

Phil was weighing on Adam's patience. "I don't know. How about I just fill you in on things tomorrow?"

As Adam joined those seated at the table he wondered how Phil seemed to know so much…he had tried to be careful about what he shared with his his former partner, and he doubted that anybody else in the group had confided in him.

* * *

Obviously troubled, Brenden Murphy entered the basement meeting room a few minutes late. His 'I'm sorry' was followed by the sad news he was carrying. "Just heard from the State Crime Bureau that the body of a girl named Olivia Larsen was found in a swamp near Hugo; that's down near Forest Lake. Apparently murdered and then dumped." Murphy choked up, "I knew her as Brandy. She was a street girl that worked for James…and she was a close friend of Holly's. I've also just finished talking to Holly. She's devastated. She told me that Brandy had once dated Jesse and that she knew much more about what was going on than Holly ever did. Of course, she's scared as hell right now."

The room was quiet for a long moment before Mickey said the prayer for the deceased… *'Eternal rest grant onto Olivia, dear Lord, and may Your perpetual light shine upon her…"*

After a moment of silence, Murf spoke. "I want everybody in this room to know that I'm here as citizen Murphy. And, the same goes for Mr. Trygg. What we're doing is highly unusual…police investigations don't involve community imput.

Nods of understanding went around the table. Murphy continued, "So, now—with Brandy's death— we have another twist as well as an even greater sense of urgency. We've known all along that the James murder had some connection with prostitution and drugs. And we've believed that someone was getting worried that Jesse probably knew too much: on the streets the more you know the more you're at risk."

Frank inquired about the Larsen girl. "How was she killed? Do they know yet?"

Murphy nodded, "A single gunshot to the head; probably a .22 caliber handgun." Murf didn't have to suggest that it was probably the same perp and the same weapon. He had brought along the ME's secreted autopsy report to share with the group. "Our crime scene was badly compromised, hopefully the Hugo site will leave us with something to go on. We were unable to find either a bullet or shell casing. As I've mentioned before, our victim was brutalized, and the .22 caliber gunshot wound occurred some two or three hours afterwards. The initial person of interest, as you've already been told, has admitted to beating the deceased with a baseball bat and leaving him at the scene. John Belak, that's the guy's name, however, does not own a firearm of any kind. We've been through the firearm registration lists a hundred times. In Saint Louis County alone, there are nearly eighteen hundred .22 caliber handguns on the books. Half of the Duluth police force has one at home—myself included."

Frank Polich updated the group on his street work in Hillside and at NERCC. "A handful of people might have had a legitimate reason to kill John James, but none of them are saying much of anything. As you all know, there's a code on the streets: nobody rats…what happens on Hillside stays of Hillside. And, there's the fear factor. Whoever killed Jesse James is still out there, and anybody who talks is putting themself in harms way."

Mickey asked Murphy where the investigation stood right now, "There must be someone you are looking at. I think we've all got a handle on the motive…but…"

Murphy was about to answer when the door to the small basement meeting room opened, "What the hell…"

All heads turned as Phil Symanski entered the room. "Hey, guys…do you mind if I join you?" Without waiting for Murphy's answer he took a folding chair from the stack against the wall, and slid into a space next to Adam. "I'm Phil Symanski…my dad was with you when you first met." His eyes went to each person around the table. "Adam and me were partners when the murder went down…I still patrol the Hillside neighborhood; afternoon shift." Phil had been only a few minutes behind Murphy and had waited outside the door wondering if he should go inside. He'd promised his dad that he would.

Murphy looked to Adam, "Did you invite him?"

Adam shook his head, "No. Besides, he's supposed to be working tonight…aren't you, Phil."

Phil's expression was grave, "I felt I had to join you, buddy…I think I might have a lead." His assertion captured everybody's attention. He went on to say that he'd talked with a kid…"He'd only speak to me if his name was kept out of things…I promised." Symanski said that the John Doe he spoke with told him that James worked for a guy who lives on a farm outside of Esko—a rural community west of Duluth. He said that James had been skimming this guy's drug money—mostly meth."

Before he could finish Murphy interrupted, "You talking about Zukar?"

Symanski nodded, "Leonard Zukar."

"Shit, Symanski…" Murf glanced toward the two priests: "Sorry, Fathers. As I was starting to say, everybody in the department knows who Zukar is and what he does. We've busted him several times…"

Frank Polich spoke, "Zukar's got the best lawyers money can buy. Anyhow, what does this informant say about Zukar?"

"Only that he'd have a motive to rub out James. So…I checked out where he was on the night of the murder. He won't talk to anybody without a subpoena."

Symanski's information was laughable. "That's it?" Murphy blurted in unmasked disgust. "You dumped a shift to tell us that

Zukar pushes drugs and James was a distributor?"

"Jeeze, Murf, I didn't know you guys knew that."

"Let's get on with things," Frank suggested. "Where did we leave off..." he looked at his notepad. "Mickey, you had just asked where things were." Father Frank looked to Murphy for a response, "What say you, Murf?"

Murphy didn't have much to say, but he caught an idea from somewhere in the back of his mind; an old ploy from some old crime magazine he must have read. He offered a red herring: "We think there might be someone inside; inside the department I mean. This can go no further than among us, understand? It would cause a scandal if anyone knew that we were looking at one of our own. Worse yet if we're proven to be wrong."

Faces around the table were glued on the veteran cop. Adam noticed a few beads of perspiration on Phil's brow, saw his friend swallow deeply. Murf had his audience on the edge of their chairs and knew it. He looked from one to the other, "We've been going through all our files on hookers and johns and vice crimes of every shape and color. Believe me, it's a thorough search...going back ten years. Some things have come to our attention; some very dangerous stuff..." He paused to let his next words enjoy an added gravity. "I'm watching Charley Cooney very closely these past few days. He's the one who wanted the ME's report pulled from the file. And, there's some stuff about his daughter. Frank can fill you in on that if he thinks it's relevant."

Later, Murf would tell Cooney that he'd used him as bait for young Symanski. Cooney, he was certain, would get a big kick out of it.

60/ CONVERSATIONS

Mario hung around after the others had left. "Did you catch the wink, Mickey? I'd swear Murphy winked in Frank's direction when he mentioned Cooney's possible complicity."

"No, I missed it. I was watching Adam's friend, Phil. He was taking notes on everything Murphy was saying."

"I thought Adam looked annoyed," Mario said.

"Or, embarrassed," Mickey said. "It was clear that Symanski had no place in the discussion. The Zukar stuff floated like a lead balloon.

"I felt bad for him and told him so before he left."

"He was the first one out the door," Mario said.

Mickey, kicked an ice chunk from the back wheel well of Mario's car. "Adam has told me that the father and son are really tight. It might be that the son feels bad about what's been going on, and he wants to try and compensate for his father's obvious exclusion. Might just be something like that, anyhow," Mickey said. "Did you know that Phil is the Godfather of Adam and Susan's son Andrew? The Baptism was the first and only time I'd met him. Seemed nice enough. He told me that he's a registered member at Saint Matthew's parish."

Mario sipped from his can of Diet Coke, shuddering at the chill it made as it passed down his throat. "You haven't said anything about your mom. How's she doing? What did her doc have to say?" Mario had known the Moran family for a long time; since his first assignment as an associate pastor at the Blessed Sacrament Church nearly fifteen years before. "If it's none of my business just say so."

Mickey laughed, "My business is your business, Mario. You know that." He bit his lower lip nervously, "Her doc is candid…I like that, but I wasn't prepared for what he had to say."

"Don't tell me…"

"It's pretty far along, Mario. The tumors have spread..." Mickey choked on his emotion...tears escaped his downturned eyes. "Mom and I prayed together a lot. I haven't told Meg yet. But mom wants to go to Florida; 'just for a visit' she says. But I think she wants to pass away down there. Whatever time she has left she wants to use doting on her three grandkids." Mickey blew his nose, "She wants me to talk with John Dougherty at the funeral home in Hibbing. She told me that Amos had made arrangements for her long before he died."

* * *

Adam and Phil walked out of the church together. The mild afternoon had surrendered to a more typical chill that got to one's bones in seconds. Adam groaned a 'Brrrr' as he slipped on his wool gloves. "I thought I told you not to bother coming tonight, Phil."

"I know. You don't have to remind me; I made an ass of myself, didn't I?" Phil shook his head and continued, "You know...I still go back to our earlier conversations about this James murder. Remember how we both felt that Murphy had his hands in it? Now, he's become everybody's ace investigator...the light in the looming darkness! I wish I could say that I'm still not convinced that he's blameless."

Adam considered his response. "I think money motivates most people to go afoul of the law...and Murf has all the money he could possibly want. No, like I've said, I'm almost positive Murphy is clean."

"Almost? It's not just money, Adam. It's power and influence," he chuckled to himself..."and women. Women with a capital W!"

"A valid point, I guess." As best he could remember, Adam hadn't said anything about Murphy's having cheated on his wife to Phil. "But you know as well as I do...we usually go with our gut feelings; and my gut tells me we were wrong about Murf."

"Well, both my gut and my head still feel differently. Say, how about you and Susan and Linda and me go out to dinner or a movie one of these days?"

"Sounds good to me, Phil," he lied, "I'll pitch the idea to Susan."

* * *

Frank Polich and Brenden Murphy lit up a cigarette in the church parking lot. Polich laughed, "Did you ever hear about Father Mickey's parking sign? He had placed it by the entry to this lot, just over there..." he gestured. It said something like 'parking violators will be baptised'. It made the papers some time ago."

Murphy laughed, "That's clever. He's clever."

"The Bishop made him take it down. Yes, Mickey's quite a character: unorthodox, free-spirited...gets him in hot water with the bishop I've been told."

"I like him," Murphy said. "He didn't have much to say tonight, but neither did Mario. Those two go back quite a ways, don't they?"

Frank nodded, drew in a lungful of smoke. "I could tell Mickey was visibly upset when you started our meeting with the news of that Larsen girl. Did he know her?"

"Not to my knowledge. He knows the girl's friend, Holly. He told me that he would be calling Holly after the meeting," Murf said. "I wonder if he has her new Tracphone cell number?"

"I thought you provided the number to everybody at the table."

"No. I gave it to Adam, Adam passed it to Father Mickey. I was watching very closely. Just the three of us have it," Murf assured.

"Her life won't get back to anything resembling normal until we nail the people who..." Frank took his last drag, shook his head. He stepped on his cigaretee butt before completing his thought, "I'm convinced that it's more than one person we're looking for…"

Murf frowned, "What makes you think that, Frank?"

"Just a gut thing. Nothing more than a gut thing."

The two men parted with a handshake. Murphy started his car and allowed the engine to warm while he called Charlie Cooney. "Not much," he answered to his friend's first question on what happened at the meeting.

Cooney had read the wire on the Larsen girl. "Says that they put the time of death at somewhere between two and five Sunday morning; the twenty second."

Murf mentioned their uninvited visitor. "What he was thinking I have no idea. That took balls."

"Probably just doing what his dad told him to do. The kid's like a pawn for Larry the Letch," Cooney said. "Maybe I should give him a reprimand when he comes in tomorrow. He dumped half of his shift you know. And, he lied—kinda, anyhow. He told me there was a meeting at his church that he had to attend for an hour or two."

"Clever. Didn't you sign the permission slip?"

Cooney laughed at himself, "I guess I did at that."

"I'd say just let it go. I planted something that he'll probably pass along to his father." He explained the ruse.

As expected, Cooney was amused, "I don't trust you either, Murf," he laughed at his friend's witty red Herring. "Young Officer Symanski must think the two of us are in cahoots."

*　　　　*　　　　*

Adam already had Holly's new *tracfone* number in his cell directory. He texted rather than make a call: *'some bad news. I guess you already know about Brandy . Call me when you get my message.'* He put his cell in his pocket, started his car, and waved at Murf and Frank who were standing next to one another by their parked cars. As he headed out of Benton Park for Riverside, he tried to process what had taken place at the meeting. 'We're still just spinning our wheels' he mumbled to himself. Now there were two murders and others may be following. And, the only two people he could connect to both Jesse and Brandy were his 'Jeckle and Hyde' friend, Lucy—and Murphy. He no more than thought of Holly when his cell phone vibrated in his shirt pocket. It was Holly.

"So, what's up, Adam? Got your message just now. You're right, Murphy did call me a couple of hours ago." Holly's voice was strained as she talked about how devastated the news had been. "Hard as it is to admit, I wasn't surprised, Adam. We've talked about it. When I wasn't getting answers to my calls I knew something very bad was going down. But this," her voice left her for a moment…"this scares the hell out of me."

Adam consoled as best he could: "All I can say is that I'm sorry."

Holly was sniffling, wanting to change the topic: "So, it had to be Murf who gave you my secret number? I'm surprised. He doesn't want me to be in contact with anyone in the outside world. I've only been here three days and I'm already going stir crazy. It sucks! Big time!"

Adam listened to her complaints over how she had been shuffled around for a third time in the past week. "It's far better than some alternatives I can think of." He added, "You'd better make friends with being stir crazy…we've got a bad ass out there and we both have a feeling that you're on his list. You might spend your idle time racking your brains for anybody that had it in for you and Brandy and Jesse. We don't have much of anything to go on right now."

"Can you let my dad know what's been going on, Adam? I think it's safe to give him my phone number."

"Ask Murf the next time you talk to him. He knows what's best."

* * *

Mario said his good-bye just before nine, "Be safe, my friend." Sadie usually stayed up until ten, so Mickey gave his mother a call. He had resolved to be a better son and was determined to take the time to call his mother every day—even if only to say 'hello' and 'how are you?'

"My goodness! What on earth has gotten into you, Mickey? I think you've called me nearly every day for the past week. I told you not to worry about me. I'm doing just fine."

"Well, how about me, mom? Or, does everything always have to be about you?" Mickey teased. "Jeeze, I call to say hello and you blow me off with a 'leave me alone'...it breaks my tender heart."

"Oh, no, Mickey! Please...! You must know I didn't mean to..."

Mickey's humor was his mother's stress. "Just kidding, Mom. I didn't mean to upset you."

"Well, you did. I just meant to assure you that I'm feeling fine and looking forward to spending a month or two in Florida. I told Meghan to rent that condo on Third Street across from Saint Anne Church. I can walk to morning mass every day that way." The two of them talked about family stuff for another few minutes. Sadie finished by telling Mickey about Michael's call the day before. "What a wonderful boy you have, Mickey. And, how thoughtful of Mary to let him call his Nana whenever he wants to. Did you know that he's practicing the guitar you gave him every night?" Sadie laughed, "He even played *'He's Got The Whole World In His Hands'* for me. I can't wait to see my grandkids."

61/ INTRUDER

Martin Yahrmatter had been a custodian at the downtown Duluth precinct for thirty-one years. In all that time the short, stocky, man with a ruddy complexion, had never reported a suspicious activity to a supervisor. One January afternoon he stood at the desk of Sergeant Charles Cooney and waited for the officers Mr. Cooney was talking with to get on their way. Martin was very nervous when he introduced himself. Cooney could see the man's stress, "Yes…Martin isn't? I've seen you a thousand times…sorry I've never introduced myself to you. I'm told that you do a great job."

Martin smiled, relaxed slightly. "Thank you sir." Swallowing hard he got to the reason for his concern. "It may be nothing at all, sir…but someone was in the file room down the hall last night. About ten o'clock; that's when I take my cup of coffee…about ten or so. Millie, that's my wife's name…anyhow, she packed some apple pie in my lunch pail last night so I might have taken more than ten minutes."

Cooney nodded, "And you saw someone doing something?"

Martin didn't know. "I'm not quite sure. At first I thought it was one of the officers I've seen before on afternoon shift …but the man was wearing street clothes. And, I only saw him from behind. I was afraid that if I said something to him, then he might report me for taking too much break time. I've never had anything bad on my work record sir." He paused, and dropped his head, "So I kinda hid near that closet in the hallway, so he couldn't see me."

Cooney could see that Martin's face was drained of color and the hand on his broom was shaking, "We have a registry book at the desk over there. Whoever goes into the file room needs to sign up, and then get the room key from me." Cooney opened his middle desk drawer and found the key exactly where he always kept it. "I don't see any names in the registry. Can you describe the person you saw for me?"

By now Martin looked as if he might faint right there in front of him. Martin had trouble getting his next words out: "I'd hate to say somethin' and be wrong 'bout it. His head was taller than the file cabinets, I'd say that. And he was wearing a winter jacket. It was dark…or medium…like it could have been gray—light or dark?"

"Was he heavy-looking? Thin? Anything else you remember?

"I'm sorry, sir. Like I said…"

Cooney smiled, thanked the man, "If you can remember anything else, please let me know, Martin. I'll look into it; here's my card…I'll write my cell phone number on the back."

"Thank you so much, sir. Can I keep it? Or should I get it back to you when I can't remember anything?"

"You can keep it, Martin. Maybe put it under a magnet on your refrigerator at home."

Martin promised he would do just that.

* * *

Cooney had several matters to deal with, but followed up on Martin's report after clearing his desk of some priority matters. The surveillance camera for the hallway leading to Records had been lifted to alter its focus. The person that entered the department had probably come into the building through a supply door near the back. Upon entry, a broom might have been used to shift the camera angle away from where it should have been recording. "Clever," was Cooney's one-word description of what he surmised had happened.

"What's missing?" Murphy asked, as he found his colleague standing in the narrow doorway to Records. "I heard the janitor saw something."

"Don't know much yet. I've got Phyllis and Ginny are working on that right now. Someone should'a said something about the camera."

"Were the file cabinets locked?"

Cooney shook his head, "We've been kinda lax about that, too. No, they weren't, Murf. My bad." He didn't remind Murf that he had been one of the last people in the Records room when he retrieved the medical examiner's files the previous afternoon.

Murf was musing over what someone might have been looking for. "An arrest file of some kind? Something in the personnel files?" The 'why?' was the key to motive and Cooney had no idea what someone might have been looking for.

"It almost looks like an inside job to me," Murphy's eyes were scanning the room of cabinets. "No, it had to be an inside job. The supply door on the north side of the building is always locked, and you say the lock didn't appear to have been jimmied or tampered with. Furthermore, the perp would have had to use a key to the Records door. If he'd borrowed yours he'd have to have stolen it from your desk drawer…then he'd be caught on one of the other cameras. Speaking of cameras…have you checked the one outside the building?"

Cooney scratched his head. "Ten minutes ago. Nothing on the outside camera either. That camera's angle was turned as well— the one on the corner of the parking lot. So, I'm afraid there wouldn't have been enough sweep to cover the side door. That must have been done earlier in the day. The guy might have gotten on the grounds between the fence and the building, then edged himself along the north wall."

Murphy nodded, "That's very possible. Any ideas of who we might be looking for, Charlie?"

"My first thought was Larry Symanski. He turned in all his keys before leaving the force, but he might have had dupes made before that."

"Burns my ass to think that he's getting a pension." Murphy wanted to spit but swallowed the bad taste instead. "That's another story we both know all to well. Who else can you think of?"

"I got a feeling that it's the confidential personnel files that were compromised. The drawer wasn't completely closed. Don't think I haven't been racking my brains. Parker's been in a funk since ...since before Christmas. Louie Burns got written up for an off-duty bar fight in Cloquet a couple of months ago. Bailey was passed over for his promotion; he claims someone gave him a bad report."

"Shelby?" Murphy asked.

Cooney shook his head, "Could be almost anyone, Murf. I'll have Ginny go through every file, item by item." Ginny was Ginny Bonnicato, the department file clerk of nearly twenty years. "I'll ask her to drop whatever she's working on now and go from A to Z."

63/ ALBERT

Holly Goeden was losing her battle with stir-craziness. She had to get away from the 'safe house'—as far away as possible! If only there was someone she could trust to help her escape. If she had that someone, she could borrow some money and get to her car. With wheels she could lose herself somewhere. Anywhere. Maybe Father Mickey? He was storing her car in a garage at his church. He might be willing to bring the car to her...and, maybe he'd agree to borrow her a couple hundred dollars. Maybe Adam would help? No, it would jeopardize his position with the police department. Frank Polich? He helped kids in trouble. Then a name came from out of the blue. Albert! Albert Jorgenson, the wealthy widower, her favorite old John.

* * *

"I'm in a jam, Allie." Holly contrived a story about an old boyfriend who was giving her trouble. "He beat me up once. If I could just get away for a little while I'd be okay."

Albert was delighted to hear from pretty Lucy. He said that he could take her anywhere she wanted to go, just so long as he got back before Friday. On Fridays he played poker with his cronies. "Never miss my Friday afternoon poker, you know…" he said.

Holly gave him an address, "I'll meet you in the alley behind my aunt Sarah's house; in half an hour…okay?" There was no Aunt Sarah, but she'd have to tell a thousand lies in order to get away from where she was. She packed a few items of clothing and crawled out the bathroom window.

Albert, dressed as always wearing a suit and tie, and driving his spotless white BMW, was right on time. "Where we going pretty lady?" he greeted Lucy. He often thought of Lucy in the same way Richard Gere thought of Julia Roberts in '*Pretty Woman*'—one of his all-time favorite movies. "How about we find a place for some lunch and catch up on things? I skipped breakfast again this morning," Albert said as Holly slid into the passenger seat and buckled herself. "Lately I've lost my appetite. I get up and take my meds of course…" He went on to recite his list of cholesterol and blood pressure meds, along with several supplements. "I read somewhere that Saw Palmetto is good for the prostate and I always take an aspirin along with Vitamin D…" It took Albert two blocks to finish his list. "I was thinking that we might go to the police after lunch and report this old boyfriend of yours. We'll get a restraining order or something. Then I could take you anywhere you'd like to go."

Holly said that would only make him more angry. "Could you drive me to Forest Lake?"

"Down by the Cities?"

"Yes…north of Saint Paul. It's only two or three hours from here."

Albert seemed reluctant, "Kinda far. I didn't think you wanted to go that far away. How about going to Hinckley? They've got a casino there you know. We could play the slots."

Holly considered some options. From Hinckley she could catch a bus to almost anywhere. "You know, that sounds like a pretty good idea."

Albert was rethinking his suggestion: he shook his head and stroked his chin. "I have a better idea, Lucy. How about we have lunch somewhere and I let you borrow my car? You could just drop me off at my house after we eat. If I need to go somewhere, Eddie next door can take me. I won't need my car until Friday afternoon. That gives you two days to work things out. How does that sound?"

Holly brightened as she processed the unexpected opportunity. She could get to Forest Lake, and back to her place, in a few hours; but probably not without anyone knowing. It wouldn't be long before Murf would be having a bird. Then, he'd probably put her behind bars where he could keep tabs on her 24/7. Her 'escape' was probably already reported. "That would be great, Albert," she blurted without giving his offer any more thought. "But, let's just pick up something, maybe at a Burger King, on the way back to your place. I'm feeling a little rushed for time." When she suggested the alternative she saw the brooding frown on Albert's face. "Nah, a bad idea. If we did that then we wouldn't have much time to visit, would we?"

Albert smiled, "That's better. Someplace nice, maybe Italian. How about that restaurant we ate at back in...gosh, what was it, two months ago already?"

"Perfect. I remember it well. It was Valentini's wasn't it—out on London Road. That's not too far from here."

63/ BERNARD BOCCACIO

It was after two when Holly dropped off Albert at his home; a large three-storied brick building near Duluth East High School. She's asked him for a fifty-dollar loan and he gave her two hundred. "If you need more just ask when you bring back my car." He gave Holly a scheming smile, "and then we'll…you know what…after you get back. Okay?"

Holly gave him a peck on the cheek and headed toward I-35 south. She found her cell phone in her purse and called Murphy's number. She'd confess to Murphy that she was on a mission, but wouldn't say what or where, and she'd promise to be back at the safe house by tomorrow night at the latest.

Murphy was pissed! "You'd better have a damn good reason for this, Holly. Anything happens to you…" he dropped the thought. "Where are you anyhow? That I need to know. I can arrange a tail so you'll be safe."

Holly would feed him half-truths. "Just getting some fresh air. That place you put me is getting awfully stuffy for a free spirit."

"Funny! Tell me, are you in the neighborhood?"

"Yep, and I can take care of myself just fine."

"…Lucy…" Murf still had trouble using her real name. "Don't get cocky and forget that someone's out there looking for you."

"I know," she said. "I'll let you know when I get back," then she hung up.

* * *

Holly felt exhilarated as she pushed the BMW to speeds she'd never driven before; just to see what Albert's ultimate driving machine could do. The afternoon sun was brilliant and the radio station she found blasted the Eagles, CCR, and Three Dog Night…Holly sang along with '*Joy to the World*'… *"Jerimah was a bullfrog, was a good friend of mine..."* she bellowed as she sailed past Sandstone, Hinckley, and North Branch in the fast lane of I-35.

A part of Holly was tempted to just keep going. By evening she could be somewhere in Iowa, or Wisconsin, or one of the Dakotas…then what? Keep going south or east or west? At some point she could ditch Albert's car and catch a bus. Foolish thinking, she knew, but the thought of adventure pulsed in her veins. The interstate sign read that Forest Lake was twelve miles ahead. She would try to locate Brandy's parents and see if they had her book. Brandy's book was everything! Both she and Brandy had kept a secret diary of sorts. The dancer at the Saratoga Club had told them that keeping track of names and dates was their secret treasure. Although Holly didn't know exactly what she would be looking for at Brandy's, yet she felt positive that she'd find something. While there, she might visit the cemetery where her friend was buried.

* * *

Adam's cell phone sang it's familiar ditty. "Murf here. Your girl has flown the coop, Adam. My bad. Should have had the house watched more closely. She told me she's 'getting some fresh air' but I think she's on the run. No idea where."

"I'll call Mickey and see if she's been in contact with him. That's where her car is stored."

"Good idea. If you learn anything get in touch, okay?"

* * *

Mickey saw Adam's name on his caller ID but didn't pick it up. The priest was engaged in the strangest conversation he'd had in months. Just after one that afternoon, a large man wearing an expensive wool topcoat and an expensive suit was at his door. Mickey saw the Bentley parked out front before opening his rectory door. When the man introduced himself as Bernard Bocassio, Mickey recognized him from Bruno's funeral. After inviting the man into his living room and offering him coffee, Mr. Boccacio began explaining the reason for his visit. "It's been three months today, Father." He didn't have to remind Mickey of the occasion as Mickey had offered his morning mass for his friend Bruno.

"I guess I had to talk to someone and you were the one friend my son seemed to be closest to." Bernard went on to confess that he hadn't been a good father, "I'm an SOB in a lot of ways," he said without a thought about a more appropriate termonology. "A control freak in today's vernacular. I was bullied as a kid and hated myself because of it. But in college, I had a realization. I realized for the first time that I was smart—very smart. Being smart and creative could put me on the fast track to wealth—finance and investments was where the big money was there for the taking. I took what I knew to be the best road to wealth." Mr. Boccassio rambled for three boring self-consumed minutes. "Long story short, in the process, I became a bully myself—not in a physical way, but in insidious ways. I developed the notion that money and power gave me the right to push people around, and the more I used my influence, the more I discovered how true it was. That's the way the world works you know: with money you can buy anything you want, most notably people." He explained how he'd bought a trial judge's decision in a high-profile case only weeks before. "Nobody will ever be able to trace how I made it happen. That was the beauty of it."

Mickey's patience was waning as Bococcio's ego continued to manifest itself. His neck was tired from nodding at the man's power-point presentation. "When my wife died, and only days afterwards my son…" Bernard needed his handkerchief to dab at his eyes."

Mickey didn't believe the tears were heartfelt but he allowed the senior Boccacio to continue.

"I finally realized how wrong I've been all these years."

After ten heart-wrenching, and tearful minutes, Mickey's guest retrieved an envelope from his suit pocket. "Your bishop sent me all of Bruno's effects shortly after the funeral. For weeks I couldn't look at them. He, my son, was a good man, Father. A much better man than his father ever was. My wife often told me that Bruno liked to write and that one day he planned to pen a novel—something autobiographical she told me." Bernard fidgeted with the papers in his lap. "My wife knew our son, I didn't. He confided everything to her. Among his effects was a letter he'd sent to his mother last July. He told her that he had been diagnosed with a brain tumor. 'Don't tell him,' Bruno said. Him, of course, being me. So, his death was imminent and he lived with that prognosis." Mr. Boccacio needed a break from his narrative, "Is your offer of coffee still good?"

Mickey excused himself and went into his kitchen. In a minute he returned with two cups…"It's gonna be pretty thick, sir…it's been sitting since breakfast."

Bernard handed several pages of yellow legal pad paper to Mickey. "Bruno was very troubled about something that you might be able to explain to me. It concerns you, Father."

Mickey scanned the familiar handwriting. Bruno had recalled their last conversation about the *sacramental seal.* He swallowed the lump in his throat and came close to tears himself. After a painful moment he looked up and met Boccacio's eyes. "I remember it well, sir."

"Please, just Bernie, Father."

"Bernie. Anyhow, your son had heard a tormenting confession just before the conversation he mentions here." Mickey wondered if it was okay for him to divulge the nature of their conversation without violating the sanctity of the *seal* himself. He needed to make a quick judgment. "A man had confessed to committing a murder...here in Duluth. He wanted to tell me about what he knew, but was bound by our priestly vows not to divulge any detail of another person's confession. I'd guess that with his tumor, and his mother's death...the *seal* was strike three for your son."

Bernie knew that much. "So he couldn't tell you? Anything about the confession, I mean. Like names, dates...you know, details."

"He could not...and I dared not probe. I know it ate away at him for weeks afterward." Mickey could no longer restrain his tears, he sobbed..."and I didn't know what to do to help him with his burden. I wasn't the friend I should have been to Brew. I bear some of the blame...I loved your son." Mickey couldn't continue.

"But now, since my son is gone, you can talk about it without violating what you term his confessional *seal*?"

"Perhaps. I'm not really sure, though." Mickey could not reveal that he had heard the confession of the man who had confessed to Bruno that Saturday afternoon. "What do you want to know, sir?"

Bernard Boccacio cleared his throat, "If Bruno died in order to preserve his oath to his church...I mean, if that was the defining reason that he took his life...would God forgive him? He was an honest and decent man in every way, and he served his God without reservation for twenty years...truly he could not face condemnation...could he?"

Mickey was certain that Bruno was in heaven and assured the man's troubled father that that was what he believed. Nevertheless, he would choose his words carefully. "God's forgiveness knows no boundaries. He chose Bruno to serve Him and he most certainly took Bruno home to be with Him. I can not, and I will not, believe otherwise."

Bernard looked out the picture window to break his eye contact with Mickey and collect his thoughts. For the longest minutes of his visit, he stared at something beyond the room; maybe it was the pine tree in front of the rectory, or the bird perched on the power line above the sidewalk, or maybe…maybe nothing at all. Finally, he met Mickey's eyes once again. "Thank you, Father…Mickey. As I said, I wasn't a good father to my son or a decent husband to my dear wife…" He took a long and deep breath: may God rest their souls. It's been years since my last confession, Father. Would you please…?"

Mickey held the man's large hands and listened to the most sincere confession he'd heard in years. The two men cried together and felt an enormous relief when their conversation ended. Bernard stood from the sofa, "For the first time in years I think I can live with myself, Father. I'll have to believe that there is hope for the hopeless."

64/ BRANDY'S MOTHER

Holly found what she believed might be the Larsen's address in a phone directory at a convenience store. When she found the neat rambler in a quiet neighborhood she parked her car across the narrow street. To her left was the playground, and beyond an elementary school that she remembered Brandy reminisce about. She pictured her friend playing there as a child with all the hopes and dreams and invincibility we bring into adulthood. Looking back toward the house, she saw a woman in the picture window staring out at her expensive BMW. She swallowed hard, put on a smile, and walked up the narrow sidewalk wishing she had given more thought to what she might say to her friend's mother. She said a quick prayer and rang the doorbell.

Mrs. Larsen was a petite woman dressed in a fifties house dress and wearing spotless white Nike shoes. Her expression was worried when she met Holly's eyes—the same eyes that Holly remembered so well. "Mrs. Larsen, my name is Lucy…I was a friend of your daughter."

Mrs. Larson sniffled, "yes…oh, please do come in." Holly was certain that the woman had no idea who she was.

The living room was meticulous and neatly furnished. A radio was playing an old Sinatra tune in the kitchen. Holly saw an ironing board draped with a man's partly pressed shirt through the doorway. "Do you have a few minutes, Mrs. Larsen…or am I…?"

She smiled and said she'd unplug the iron and get her visitor a cup of coffee, "It's decaf if that's okay. Or, I have some tea."

"Decaf would be just great."

While Brandy's mother was out of the room Holly regarded photos of her friend as a baby, as a teenager, as a high school graduate. How sad the lingering memories must be.

Holly told a story of her relationship with Brandy. It was deliberately, and mostly, fabricated. "We both liked to write. On weekends we'd get together and share some of the highlights of our week…our jobs, and friends, and boys we'd like to meet…you know, girl talk." She embellished the story with fond times shared together. Then, after nearly fifteen minutes, she got to the essentials: "Brandy had many friends in Duluth…good friends. We'd all like to do a memorial of some kind for your daughter and I'd like to write up something…a kind of eulogy. It would be a great help if…" she paused to get the right words, "… if I could borrow her diary for a few days. I drove down from Duluth this afternoon with the hope that you might know of where Brandy's …"

"The book with all the names and dates and numbers? That's the only one me and her father found. Didn't make much sense to either one of us. I think Vernon, my husband…he's getting his ice house off the lake today, anyhow, I think he threw it away with lots of other things."

Holly shook her head, "Oh my…that would be her directory of friends. It would have helped me a great deal in contacting her friends for our little memorial."

"I could look in her bedroom if you'd like…or call Vernon?"

"Would you please, Mrs. Larsen?"

"Please…just Elise, my dear. Mrs. Larsen sounds too…you know, too formal for my daughter's friend."

Holly nodded, "Elice it will be."

Elise excused herself and retreated to the back of the house; two minutes became five…then she returned to the living room with a notebook in her hand. "Is this what you wanted…was it Lucy? I always get mixed up with names."

Holly nodded, smiled, then opened to a random page, "Yes…exactly. Our friends from Duluth; may I borrow it for a while?"

"My goodness, Lucy dear, you can have it. It doesn't mean anything to us." Then she paused, "Will Vernon and me be invited to your…what did you call it…tribute, memorial?"

Holly assured the woman that she would let her know the date and time and particulars. At the door, Mrs. Larsen said…"It means so much to me that our daughter had such good friends. Vernon and I worried so that she was going around with a bad crowd in Duluth. But she was a good girl, wasn't she, Lucy…?"

*　　　*　　　*

Adam and Carl Rodland were cruising by the former Stowe Elementary School west of Benton Park, and talking about a rash of broken car windows in the neighborhood. "We'll have a ton of reports to file this afternoon," Carl said. "Why is it that we always suspect kids are responsible?"

Adam smiled, "Probably because kids are usually the ones who get a kick out of making trouble. Too often, though, we get the mistaken mindset that the bad ones define their whole generation."

One of the vehicles they had received a call on was a Dodge Caravan with a ski rack on the roof. Carl commented, "Have you heard from your friend Phil lately?" Adam hadn't. "Nothing since our meeting a few days ago—the one at Saint Gerard's. I still feel bad about that. The only one who seemed to be friendly with him was Mickey." Adam, like most who knew the priest, was becoming comfortable with the casual nickname. "I think Phil was only trying to help us out. Murf made him feel like an asshole."

"Murf doesn't see Phil the same way you do, Adam. And, there's lots of bad blood between him and Phil's dad. Did you know that it was Murf that had him canned…or, maybe I should say that Murf made him file for an early retirement?" Carl laughed to himself at the memory.

The two talked about their mutual friend, "I had Murf pegged wrong," Adam admitted. "Thought he was a person of interest until we had a long talk not too long ago. He's an interesting guy…" Adam's phone vibrated in his uniform pocket, "Speak of the devil…"

Adam listened more than talked, then put his phone away. "That was Murf who just called." Adam told his partner that Holly had taken off somewhere. "He's worried that she might have left town."

Carl was privy to all that had been going on in the James murder case.

"Is there anything he wants us to do?"

"Yes. He asked if we would head over to Father Mickey's place and see if he's heard anything…he said to check the garage and see if Holly's car is still there."

As they were approaching Saint Gerard's they saw the white

Bentley pulling away from the curb. "Wow, don't see many of those up here— especially in Benton Park. Mickey must have some wealthy friends I don't know about," Adam said.

"Nothing about Father Mickey would surprise me," Carl said.

Mickey met the two officers at the rectory door. His face was drawn and cheerless, his eyes red. "That was a tough one," the priest said as he let them in. "The father of an old friend," was all he said. Adam filled Mickey in on Murphy's call. "Have you heard anything from her, Father?" Mickey hadn't. "We can check the garage if you'd like." The three walked behind the rectory and found that Holly's car was where he'd parked it. The three small-talked for a few minutes before the officers left.

"Oh," Carl said to Adam as they drove off, "Before Murf's call, I was going to tell you about your old partner. I heard this morning that Phil has taken a vacation. I guess he told Cooney he was going to spend a week out in Colorado, I guess."

Adam said, "I know Phil likes to ski…and, I seem to remember him telling me that his mother lives out somewhere near Denver." Adam shared the story Phil had told him some time before. "I got the impression that his family was kinda dysfuntional. I wonder if he'd be going out to visit her?"

65/ FOLLOWING UP

On the drive back to Duluth Holly called Murphy. "I thought I'd find Brandy's diary, but I think her father trashed it. But I found something else that might help us out anyway. She had a directory of sorts with names and phone numbers."

Murphy's first question however, was the obvious, "Where in the hell have you been, and where are you now?"

"I've just visited with Brandy's mother down in Forest Lake. A sweet old woman."

"Then you're on your way back as we speak?"

Holly smiled to herself, "Yes daddy! Don't worry, I'm fine. The road trip was just what I needed."

Murphy insisted that she meet him at the diner in west Duluth where she had worked until a few weeks ago. "I'm in the neighborhood, Cooney's with me." He added: "Don't worry, I've spoken with a Mister Boles and he's holding your job for you; that's if and when we get this case resolved."

Holly said she had to return Albert's car, and agreed to go back to the safe house on the condition that she be given some latitude to get out and about from time to time. She'd negotiate something with Murf when they talked: she might even try to offer the book in exchange for some freedom.

"We ain't got all night. Come here before you return the car."

* * *

On the drive back to Duluth, Holly teared as she thought about Brandy's mother. Elise's grief was contagious. Holly's sole purpose with the surprise visit was tainted and she felt it more deeply now than when she was sitting in the Larsen's living room. She wanted something and she got it...mission accomplished! Now the remorse was settling in. The memorial she had promised Mrs. Larsen had to be arranged. She owed that to her friend, the Larsons, and herself. If she didn't go through with it, Holly would not be able to live with herself.

Murphy and Cooney were already seated when Holly arrived at the diner nearly an hour later. Boles usually closed at seven, and it was a few minutes after seven when she knocked on the heavy back entrance door. The owner unlocked the door and, without so much as a greeting, gave his favorite waitress a puzzled look. "Why didn't you tell me about this mess you're in? I'd have helped you out in any way I could; I hope you know that. Oh," he said as an afterthought, "I've got something for you before you leave."

The only lights still on in the small restaurant were in the kitchen, and a table lamp toward the back, where the two cops were having coffee. Holly sat next to Murphy, passed him the book. "I haven't even looked through it," she said as she placed it on the formica tabletop and sipped the glass of ice water that rested next to a sweating pitcher off to the side.

Murf moved to the other side of the booth so he could read along with Cooney. "Oh, my god…Clancy's name's here." Clancy was a county commissioner. There were a few other familiar names, including Jesse James' with a small heart beside it. "You're listed, Murf," Cooney said as he pointed his finger to a page with a few other M names. "Most of it looks to be alphabetized."

"I'd imagine that most of the guys used phoney names. I know I would." As Cooney turned to the S's he commented, "We could make a small fortune if we did what Larry the Letch did a few years back. I've seen four or five people here that would pay big time if we wanted to blackmail them."

Holly puzzled at the comment, "What am I missing here? Larry the Letch?"

Murf met her eyes, "You've met him. Remember Larry Symanski from your meeting with Adam and the padres? I wasn't there, but I've been told all about it."

"Yeah, he was a creep…Adam's friend's dad, I mean—shifty eyes, arrogant bastard…bad vibes from all of us, not just me."

When the two men finished scanning the names Murphy shrugged, "I don't see much of anything here. Do you think we ought to start making some calls? This is a homicide case and we've gotta touch all the bases PDQ. The case is freezing to death!"

"Right, we've gotta run all these names, even if we'll be stirring up a hornet's nest in the process. Maybe you and I should do the calling. And, Judy Forbes...she'd be good at this." Judy was the only woman on the newly established vice squad and a veteran with the utmost respect of all that knew her. "Let's get Trygg involved, too. Adam's been on this case from the start," Cooney suggested.

Murphy smiled at Holly, "I saw you pull in. I'm not even going to ask you where you got that BMW you're driving. I just hope it isn't stolen."

Holly returned his smile, "I'll have you know that I've got friends that aren't cops or priests."

The two cops laughed, "Let's return the car and get you back where you're supposed to be, Holly."

"Just a minute," Holly protested as she took the book that rested under Cooney's hands. "Let's make a deal. You cut me some slack and I help you with the investigation. I know some of the names that you don't. Don't forget, I was a street girl. Note, I said *was*! Past tense...and I mean it." On the drive back from Forest Lake Holly had done some serious thinking about where she had been and where she wanted to go. If she were ever going to have a BMW of her own, she'd better get her butt off to college.

Murphy looked to Cooney, "I have no objection to that...what say you?"

"I think Holly and Judy might make a damn good team. Let's do it."

* * *

As Holly was about to leave, her boss caught her elbow. "Just a minute, I've got something for you on my desk. Com'on back with me." Holly followed Boles to his closet-sized office. "Here it is," he found a small business card in the top drawer. "Guy asked me to give it to you when I saw you. He'd been in a couple of times. I could tell he was lookin' for someone…had a cup of coffee and left. Must'a been you he was lookin' for." He handed Holly the card.

Trevor Windsong

Pro Shop Manager

Golf lessons by appointment

218-878-BEAR

"A tall guy with his long hair in a ponytail. Looked like a linebacker."

Holly didn't know what to think or say. "Thanks," was all that came to mind. She gave Boles a quick hug and walked briskly to Albert's BMW in the lot outside. On the drive back to Albert's, she put her memory into overdrive. "Trevor Windsong," she said. Her dad's friend apparently wanted her to know something. Was it case related? Or personal? On the back of his card was a scribbled note, 'My cell is 218-442-8020'. Some feeling inside told her 'it's personal'…if so…something to think about.

* * *

Holly and Adam met Judy Forbes at ten the following morning. Judy was a full-sized African-American woman with a keen sense of humor. "Twenty years with the department got me this closet in the back of the building…but I demanded a space with a window, and I damn well got it." She pointed at the two by two window with an outside cage. With the bright morning sun, the protective cage cast a pattern of squares across the wall across from her desk. "It was a detention room before I claimed it," Judy said. She offered coffee from a decanter on the small table where they were sitting and pointed to an ice bucket stocked with several bottles of water. "That's all I got, help yourselves. I think some cookies will be arriving soon if Cooney keeps his promise."

Judy had already spent an hour reviewing the thirty pages that Brandy had written on. "I've already checked the names of people I can contact. Not exactly a 'Who's Who in Duluth'; but there are some interesting names our girl Brandy met along the way. I still don't understand why a John would ever use his actual name. I'm sure we'll find some bogus entries on this list." Judy had made copies of the pages for both Holly and Adam so they could peruse together. "Let's start with the A's…"

Holly almost gasped when she saw the second name on the list. After Bradley Allen was the name Albert Allquist—her Albert! "I'll take Allquist," she offered, almost too enthusiastically. "I know him."

Judy's eyes narrowed but she said nothing. She said she would take Allen and moved their attention to the B's.

Between Holly and Judy nearly a third of the names were familiar, but Adam was drawing blanks as he followed Judy's review. "Aside from Murf and the county commissioner, I don't know a soul," Adam shrugged, and wondered to himself: Why was Murf's name always popping up?

"That's okay Adam. It might be a lot easier to call folks you don't know, than what Holly and I have to do," Judy assured. "I think we've got about…let me see…thirteen people to check with before we go to the remainder on the list. I'll take the sensitive ones…and maybe you could take the three with Twin Cities area codes," she suggested to Adam. "Holly, you've said that there are five people here that you're willing to contact."

All agreed that a followup personal contact with some of the people on the list would be best. Appointments could be made over the phone. Despite her mild protest, Cooney insisted that Holly would have a police escort whenever she left the safe house. "It's really delicate stuff and we're sure to get some resistance. So, we've got to be discrete" Judy said. "When we tell them that this is a homicide investigation they'll cooperate. Or, more than likely, they'll freak out. Nobody wants to have a subpoena delivered to their front door or to their workplace."

Adam took another look at his copy of the names. He puzzled over a name in the J's…it was strangely familiar but he couldn't place it. He wished he had his wife Susan's memory. She never forgot a name or date. Maybe it would come to him later.

Holly hadn't talked with her dancer friend, Margo, in months. The name Margo Laine, on her list of names, had to be the same one that Brandy had introduced her to at the Saratoga Club. That would have been shortly after the two girls had first met back in 2012. She called the number from the table Judy had set up in the narrow hallway outside her office. When she introduced herself as Holly, Margo didn't have a clue who she was, and was about to hang up her phone. "Oh, sorry, I forgot, you knew me as Lucy…Brandy's friend." Margo relaxed but was wary about what she would disclose. The two girls caught up on recent happenings. "Tragic," was the word Margo used several times. "She was a sweet kid. I know that she was planning to go to college some day."

"I know. We often talked about that. I think we were a lot alike, Brandy and me."

Margo had another call coming in and had to end the conversation, "Maybe we can have a drink or something later." Then she dropped the 'F' bomb: "Lost the call." She wouldn't say whether or not the caller might have been a customer of hers.

Earlier, Holly had told Murphy about the story she had given to Mrs. Larsen about a memorial service. Murf agreed that it might be a good idea to go ahead with what she was planning.

After Holly had asked a few pointed questions that went nowhere; Margo began sounding impatient. The dancer couldn't believe anybody would do such a thing: "Jesse, well…I hate to say it, but the bigmouth had it coming." Holly brought up the idea of a memorial service for Brandy. "Her mom said the funeral was small and only a few of Brandy's former friends from Forest Lake had been there. I have a priest friend who, I'm sure, would put together something really nice." Holly would call Father Mickey as soon as she finished her conversation with Margo.

"The only thing that might help with what you're doing," Margo said almost in passing, "there's a guy named Pratt…Darrin Pratt, I think. He used to run with that James guy. See if the police have already checked him out. I think I heard that he was the one who inherited Jesse's little business—girls and drugs—up on hillside."

Holly had heard the name before and had seen it on Brandy's notebook list. "If we haven't already checked him out, we surely will. Thanks, Margo. I'll let you know about the memorial as soon as we've got a date." After putting her phone down, Holly tried to place the name Pratt. Like Adam, sitting across from her at the card table, she struggled to place where she'd heard the name. When she asked, "Not a clue," is what Adam said. Sooner or later it would come to her. Margo promised to let Holly know if she heard anything that might help get Brandy's murderer.

When Adam and Judy suggested the three of them have lunch at a restaurant down the street, Holly declined, "You guys go ahead. I've got a call or two I want to make."

Adam offered to bring her back a sandwich. "Sure," Holly said, "Chicken salad if they've got it."

When her project partners left, she went into her purse and found the gold-edged business card. She wondered if she should call the casino or his cell number. She chose the cell number.

Suprisingly, the voice was familiar. How could she remember the voice of someone who'd only spoken a few words during a very casual conversation some time ago? After Trevor's 'hello' there was a long pause at her end…what to say?

"Hello?'

"Oh, I'm sorry…is this Trevor?

"Yes, ma'am." Then a pause on his end. "Am I in some kind of trouble?"

Holly puzzled for a moment, then realized her mistake. She had used the Duluth Police Department phone…not her cell! Holly apologized and explained that she was doing a 'research project' at the police department.

Trevor's laugh was softer than than she might have imagined. "Your dad told me that you were working with some Adam guy on a project, but he didn't elaborate." Trevor took a deep breath before asking, "Is this Adam guy a steady of yours? I mean, do the two of you date?"

Holly laughed, "Just a married friend of mine."

The two of them talked easily for another five minutes about, of all things, golf! Holly didn't know much about the game, but realized that golf was a comfort zone for Trevor. "Sure…I'd enjoy learning after…"

Trevor finished the thought for her, "I understand, after things settle down in this case you're on." The longest pause in their conversation was followed by Trevor's invitation. "Can I have your phone number, I mean, maybe we could have dinner or something?"

"Trevor…I can't right now. Please…"

"I understand," Trevor said.

Holly knew he didn't understand. "Trevor, I'll call you; can you be okay with that? I'd truly enjoy going to dinner some time."

Both offered expectant goodbyes.

61/ CALLER ID

The name Tommy Jordaine from the 'J' page wasn't on anybody's preliminary followup list, but Adam had heard the Jordaine name somewhere before. He wondered if a cold call would accomplish much of anything. Maybe he'd give it a try later. He had three other names from the Twin Cities to contact first. "Adam…" Holly got his attention. "I'm gonna call Father Mickey." She explained her promise to Mrs. Larsen about a memorial service for Brandy. "Can you believe I never knew that my best friends real first name was Olivia?"

"Great idea. I'm sure Mickey would be willing to help." Then it occurred to him, "Say, maybe we could invite all these people on our list to the memorial service. Obviously they knew Brandy one way or another. We might be able to find out some interesting information that way. Let's run the idea by Judy…"

"And Murf," Holly added.

Judy agreed with her two project partners. "Go ahead, Holly. Why not find out what your priest friend has on his calendar for next week?"

"Will do. If he's willing, then we can set things in motion right now." Judy agreed. "I'll let Murf know what we're up to."

Judy punched in button for Murf's extention: "Say, Murf, when you finally drag your butt down to where we're meeting why don't you bring some cookies with you…wait, make that donuts. I know you guys are hoarding a box full of those cream-filled ones in Cooney's office. I saw them."

* * *

Mickey was reading the *Duluth News Tribune's* morning paper when Holly called. The headline story was bad news for the Mesabi Iron Range where he'd grown up. *Keetac*, a large taconite plant in

Keewatin had announced a shutdown and layoffs. More than 400 workers would be affected. To Mickey, the unfortunate story was a familiar one to the locals. The Range economy had always been cyclic, and almost totally dependent on the steel markets out east. Apparently, demand was soft these days, and stockpiles of the taconite pellets that would be converted into steel were sufficient to warrant a shutdown. If *Keetac* was being idled, Mickey wondered if maybe the other neighboring plants would be making the same announcements before summer. Mickey had several friends and former Hibbing High School classmates that worked in the mines—from Keewatin on the west to Babbitt and Hoyt Lakes on the east Range.

He picked up his cell and greeted Holly. "Are you back in Duluth? I got your 'road trip' account from Adam and his partner yesterday…" Holly explained her brief runaway and then her idea of a memorial service for Brandy. "Better yet," Mickey told Holly, "how about if we have the service at the Newman Chapel on the UMD campus? It's perfect. I'm sure Mario would be open to the idea. I'll call him and get back to you in five minutes."

*   *   *

"I haven't done anything like that in quite some time, Mick. But, yes, of course I'd be more than happy to help out. I can make arrangements for a small reception, coffee, soup and sandwiches…we could use the faculty cafeteria. I know the kitchen ladies; they think I'm the coolest priest on campus."

Mickey didn't offer his friend the obvious retort he was looking for. He got back to Holly. "We're set. How about a week from today at the Newman Center on campus?" Holly liked the idea and gave Mickey the phone number of the Larsens in Forest Lake. "It might be a nice touch if you called her. They are Catholic and it would be comforting for them to hear about the memorial from a priest."

Adam was getting nowhere with his three names. His first, a man named Beckers, was answered by a woman who said nobody by that name lived there. His second rang fifteen times without an answer and no 'leave a message'. The third, a man named Nierengarten, was eighty and hadn't been up to Duluth in years. "You might be looking for my son, Daryl, he's got one of those smart-alec phones." He gave Adam a number that got him a: 'We're sorry, the number you are trying to reach is no longer in service.'

Adam looked again at the list and his attention went back to Tommy Jordaine. Jordaine had a 218 area code, so he lived somewhere in the Duluth area. Adam punched in the numbers. A woman answered, "Tommy's at work…who's calling." Adam could only come up with an "I'm just an old friend of Tommy's."

"What's your name…? I can tell him you called and he can get back to you when he gets home later this afternoon."

"Adam Trygg, maybe I'll just try again later."

"Okay. I'll tell him." Her voice betrayed her suspicions.

When he hung up the phone, Adam realized that if the woman had Caller ID, she might have seen that his call came from Duluth police headquarters. He stepped away from his table and peeked into Judy's office, "Say Judy…does the phone I'm using register as the police department to whomever I'm calling?"

"It does…why?"

* * *

By late afternoon the three had contacted or left messages for every traceable name on the list. Of thirty-nine calls they had made, only eleven offered any scant measure of information. Guilty men, six of whom were married, and promised to do anything just to keep from having their names revealed. Four of them agreed to attend a memorial service if :'we can just keep this matter to ourselves'; one promised he would send a check to help with any of the costs that might be incurred.

Holly called Darrin Pratt, the man that Margo, Brandy's friend from the Saratoga Club, had given her. Thinking outside the box, she identified herself as 'Bonnie James', a sister of Jesse's from Gary, Indiana. She was surprised that Pratt didn't hang up on her despite the fact that he might have seen where her call came from.

"I see yer workin' with cops. Wha'cha want with me?"

"Following up on my brother's murder, Darrin. Remember Brandy?"

Darrin was surly, "Yer shitten me, Jesse din't have no sister." Darrin wasn't the sharpest knife in the drawer, but he'd play dumb anyhow, "Sorry, I ain't never known nobody named Brandy. Anything else?"

"Not now," she said. After hanging up, she circled the name and made a note: 'Follow up necessary.'

67/ MORE QUESTIONS

As Mickey contemplated planning a memorial service for someone he'd never met, he realized how consumed he had become with an investigation that seemed to have landed in his lap. How had it all happened? Did it start months ago with a conversation he had with Bruno? Or, was it with Holly Goeden's confession not too long afterwards? Or, was it Adam who had drawn him in? He considered the cast of characters who had become a part of his every waking hour. Looking at the blank legal pad resting on his desk, he began to make a list of names. Adam Trygg was a registered Saint Gerard's parishioner, albeit not a regular attender at mass; and an officer with the Duluth police. Holly was a troubled girl with a checkered past in the disreputable Hillside neighborhood. Brenden Murphy was a fallen away Catholic and veteran police officer. Charlie Cooney was another cop, but someone whom he'd never met. John Belak was Holly's father, and still a 'person of interest' in the murder investigation—though he knew better. The Symanski's—father and son, were two men he'd only met briefly but didn't have a favorable impression of. And, then there was Father Frank Polich...along with his closest friend, Mario. He drew a line through the last two names, both priests like himself who had been caught in the same web that he was in. Adam was, Mickey believed, above reproach.

The one common denominator with the other five names was obvious: aside from Holly and her father, all were law enforcement people. Who was telling the truth? Murphy, for example, had led everyone to believe that he was a clean cop with a very wealthy wife. Yet, at the same time, when he had asked Adam if he'd ever met the woman—Mrs. (Montgomery) Murphy, Adam said he hadn't. "Nobody I know has ever met her," Adam had acknowledged. To Mickey, that fact was disturbing. How easy would it be for two 'respected' cops to coverup everything? And...to build a believable case against Larry Symanski, a man whom everybody had come to despise?

Mickey went back and forth as he tried to get his head around the network of characters: Cooney and Murphy were as tight as clams and privy to all the inside scoop. The Symanskis...especially Larry, was the perfect 'fall guy'—obnoxious and unlikeable—with a sexual misconduct past. Adam had shared with him the extortion scheme that had forced Symanski to resign, and that the former cop had a serious grudge with Murphy. A hatred that was mutual. Phil, like Adam, a young cop, was probably in over his head in the invistigation of two related homicides. Mickey stared at the name Holly Goeden. Of all of them, she might have had the best motive for killing the pimp John 'Jesse' James...and maybe the opportunity. He found himself thinking like a TV detective, 'motive' and 'opportunity'—the two keys. Yet, his eyes kept returning to the affable

Murphy. He recalled Adam's initial mistrust and suspicions about his former partner, and how those feelings had taken an about face after having a few beers in a local tavern. Again he went back to his earlier premise: If Murphy and Cooney were in something together they could effectively steer the others in whatever direction they wanted. And, it seemed to an amateur like Mickey, they wanted to finger Larry Symanski. "If anybody is out of their league, it's me!" he admitted to himself as he folded the paper and went to the fridge. He shook his head as he looked inside at dated cottage cheese, sour milk, a jar of pickles, and a bottle of ketchup. In the freezer was a carton of Moose Tracks ice cream that he had purchased last July. "Why doesn't anybody buy any groceries around here?" He answered his own question: "Because you're too lazy, Father!"

It was a Saturday mid-morning when he called Adam to inquire about what the 'Brandy List' he'd been working on had revealed. He wondered if both he, along with Mario and Frank, knew half of Duluth's population in one manner or another. If that was so, maybe the threesome should be given an opportunity to review the list. After all, he and Mario were planning the memorial service.

Mickey called Adam: "Sure, Father, I've got it with me. I can't see anything wrong with letting you three look it over. If you'd like I can swing by the rectory on my way to the drug store. Anna's picked up some kind of crud at day care. How about fifteen minutes?"

Of the names the two of them reviewed, Mickey wasn't much better than Adam at recognition; he did know a Jim Johnson from his days at Saint James parish years before. "Half of all Duluthians are Johnsons or Carlsons or Andersons." Both laughed at the reality. He noticed that the name Tom Jordaine had been circled on Adam's copy, but didn't inquire. "I think I know this Silva," and later, "Jeeze…I wonder if this is the Torrence that works for the bishop over in Superior? I sure hope not. But, the phone number has the Superior area code. Let me get my phone book, Adam." The number, however, checked out. Mickey cursed under his breath before saying he'd follow up on Torrence himself.

The two men discussed the memorial service for a few minutes. "Ask Holly if she has a photograph of Brandy that we can borrow. I have a good friend with a flower shop downtown, and Mario is connected to every bakery in Duluth. He's addicted to those custard filled éclairs you know. They're as dangerous as tobacco and liquor."

Adam noticed his name on a short list scribbled on the legal pad Mickey was making notes on. "Are you starting a list of people to send invitations to? I see the names of our core group written down," He pointed to the priest's short list.

"Kinda. Truth be told, Adam, along with considering invitees, I've been trying to put the pieces of our puzzle together. Like everybody else, it seems that I'm getting absolutely nowhere."

Adam puzzled, "the murders?"

"Yes, the murders," Mickey acknowledged. "I'm raising more questions than I'm finding any answers. Can I ask you something that's been bothering me? It's about Murphy."

Adam nodded, "Sure."

"Well, he's gone from our villain to our sage, and frankly, I'm puzzled by it. Can you explain to me what he's said or done to convert you? Beyond buying you a few beers one afternoon?"

Adam explained as best he could remember, but found himself wondering what Murf had disclosed that made them fast friends again. Probably, more than anything, Muff's explanation of his wife and all the money they had. "Why would he mess with drugs or hookers if he was already financially well off?"

Mickey had to ask, "Has anybody ever checked that out? I mean, you once told me that Mrs. Murphy remained somewhat of a mystery…that nobody you know has ever even met her. And then there's Cooney. What do you know about his background?"

Adam puzzled, "Shouldn't be too hard to find out about Murf's wife. I have the impression that she's not in good health. But...we all know that the Montgomery's were millionaires. And, I'm sure I've told you that Barbara Montgomery Murphy and her sister inherited their father's wealth. Cooney? Well...what can I tell you? He's divorced...his daughter has had some troubles in her past...he's been on the force for more than twenty years. He's kinda private about himself."

Mickey scratched his head, "Nobody's bothered to check out your fellow officers have they? Like, how many cops are there in Duluth anyway? And, as far as investigating goes, there are probably quite a few Montgomerys in the Cities where Murphy's wife grew up, too. How do we know that Mrs. Barbara Murphy is actually one of Leland Montgomery's daughters?"

Adam gave Mickey a questioning look, "Are you thinking...?"

"I'm not thinking anything, Adam. I'm just curious. None of us have much that's tangible to go on. If they, Cooney and Murphy, were in cahoots somehow and we're being manipulated...?" Mickey let the thought drop. "Lot's of if's, Adam. I can't help wondering if the list you guys are working on is actually the list that needs the most attention. Maybe someone ought to look more closely at your two leaders."

Adam looked uncomfortable, "Maybe...?"

"And another thing, Adam. Somehow I remember someone saying that they saw Murphy giving John James some kind of note. What's that all about?'

Adam smiled for the first time in minutes, "I did ask Murf about that. It was actually the day after we met that time at the bar in west Duluth. He told me that James had skipped his last two meetings with his probation officer. Cooney asked Murf to pass on a reminder, and to tell him to get his ass, sorry Father, to get himself in and take care of the matter. That's all."

Mickey offered a dubious smile, "And you believed him? To me, that's something that could be checked out as well."

After leaving the rectory, Adam was more confused than he had been in some time. How would he go about investigating his fellow officers without getting himself in deep trouble? Who could he trust to help him? His first thought was Phil Symanski. Phil shared Adam's early suspicions about Murf…and what about talking with Phil's dad? No, that would only rile Murf and Cooney. Besides, Phil's dad, Adam believed, was a slimeball. Then…he realized that Murf's story about the guy he called 'Larry the Letch' hadn't even been checked out. What if that was a fabrication? What if Larry wasn't what Murf had portrayed him to be? He thought of his new partner, Carl Rodland. Carl had partnered with Murphy and knew him well. Slowly, the issues that Mickey had raised were settling in Adam's thoughts like a bank of fog from the big lake that gave Duluth its gateway to the world.

68/ THE BROTHER

Brenden Murphy studied the file clerk's report at his desk. He scanned the personnel files, stopping at the S's where he noted that Larry Symanski's didmissal report was not checked off. That could only mean that the file was not missing. He cussed to himself; another theory slid down the drain. Three general files could not be located from the master inventory list. The file for Lisa Cooney, his friends's troubled daughter, was not located, but Murf knew that Charlie had taken it out some months before. Not a problem to Murphy. Also missing was a file for Michael Dooley…Dooley's file, Murphy remembered, had been sent to Saint Paul, as Dooley was facing other charges down in Ramsey County. The third was a man named Thomas Jordaine. Murphy couldn't place the name. He'd follow up on that later. Cooney walked by Murphy's desk, "Say, Charlie, does the name Jordaine ring a bell?"

"Don't think so. What are you working on?"

Murphy explained. The second step would be tedious: every file would be reviewed for it's entire contents. Murf knew that a few pages in his own file had been extracted and destroyed. He'd deal with explaining that later. On a hunch, he called the Jordaine number. A woman answered, "I'm sorry, Tommy's not home at the moment."

Murphy heard a man's voice in the background. "Who am I speaking to?"

"Muriel, his wife. Why? And who am I talking to?"

Murphy identified himself as a Duluth police officer, but did not divulge the reason for his call.

A long pause followed, "You're the second cop that's asked for my husband. I want to know what's going on, officer. This is beginning to sound an awfully lot like harassment to me."

"We're conducting a homicide investigation, Mrs. Jordaine. Only routine stuff, you understand. Your husband's name came up on a list of people who knew the deceased. Probably nothing for you or your husband to be concerned about."

"Nothing to be concerned about! A homicide investigation! Are you kidding?...should I contact a lawyer? I mean, what does this mean? Is Tommy a suspect in somebody's murder for God's sake?"

"Not at all, ma'am. We're just trying to get in touch with all of the victim's friends."

"What victim? Someone me and Tommy should know about?"

Murf would be careful not to divulge that the first victim was a pimp, and the second a prostitute. "I think it's best for all concerned that I talk with your husband about this. Would you please ask him to call me at this number?"

* * *

Later that evening, as he and Susan were putting the kids to bed, Adam's phone rang. He smiled when he saw the name on his caller ID, "Well, how's the skiing out there in Colorado?" he asked. "You didn't tell me you were taking a vacation...I had to learn it second hand from Carl Rodland."

Phil Symanski's voice had an edge, "I haven't done any skiing yet. I just needed to get away for a few days."

Adam wondered if Phil and Linda were struggling with their relationship or...? "Did you go out to visit with your mother?" Then it struck him like a belly punch; Phil's stepmother was a Jordaine!

Phil didn't answer Adam's question. "Say...Adam." A long and painful pause followed the two words: "I understand Murf called my brother—what's that all about? His wife told me that she's being harassed by you guys and might need a lawyer—something about a homicide investigation that's going on." He didn't mention that he'd also been told that Adam had called his brother's wife only the day before Murphy.

"What are you talking about, Phil? We aren't harassing her in any way." Adam couldn't lie to his friend. "Let me bring you up to speed on what's been happening since you left." He explained the events that started with Holly's trip to Forest Lake and the list of names that Brandy had in her diary/directory. "I didn't remember that you had a brother, or half-brother, I should say. So I couldn't place Tommy's name when I called. If I had, you know that I would have talked to you before I tried to contact Tom.

A long silence ensued. "So, what's the big deal if my brother had a little fling? Is it worth ruining his marriage over?" His tone was sharp and defensive. Phil was obviously very agitated. "I'm cutting my vacation short and catching a morning flight back to Duluth. You can probably tell I'm a little pissed. Let's the two of us talk when I get back."

Adam hadn't known about Murphy's call to Mrs. Jordaine a short time before Phil's call to him. He apologized. "Phil...please don't be angry with me. You know I wouldn't do anything intentionally..." He'd no more than apologized when he realized how naïve he must seem to Phil. Yet, these days, even Phil was becoming an enigma to him. He had been keeping his friend in the loop...while Phil was narrowing his loop to him. Friendships need to be elastic in order to grow.

Phil's last words were strained, "Like I just said, I *need* to talk with you, Adam." The word, *need,* had the weight of a cement truck. "Will you have some time tomorrow afternoon?"

For long minutes Adam puzzled over his friends appeal. Susan found her husband sitting at the kitchen table with the strangest expression on his face. "What's the matter, hon? You look like you've seen a ghost. Something about the case...?"

"I don't know; I honestly don't know. Maybe you can help me figure this out." Adam and Susan talked for nearly an hour before going to bed. Maybe Holly had been right when she told him that he probably wasn't cut out to be a cop.

69/ TOM JORDAINE

Brenden Murphy called the Two Harbors police chief, a man named Avery Ross, whom he had met on occasion over the years. "Avery, Murphy from Duluth PD here." The two men rehashed a case they had worked together on a few years back. "Gartner's still doing time at Stillwater last I heard," Murf said of the felon they had busted in a series of high profile burglaries along the North Shore. Murphy moved the conversation to the case at hand. "We've got a couple of homicides, one here in Duluth and another down in Forest Lake.

We've been spinning our wheels for months on one of them, the other is only two weeks old—down in Forest Lake." Avery was familiar with the James murder, but knew only a few details of a girl Murf knew as Brandy. "Her real real name is Olivia Larsen, she spent some time here in Duluth." Murf informed.

"Yeah, hell yes, I know Tommy Jordaine. Manages the Holiday gas station down the street. What's with Tommy?"

Murphy explained the routine follow-up on the names in Olivia Larsen's book. "Probably nothing more than some guy getting horny and cheating on his wife, but..."

"Not Tommy, Murf. Jeeze, he goes to our church. Very active, distributes communion. Three great kids, his oldest a pretty good hockey player for our Agates; his youngest daughter Cindy, babysits for us on occasion. I think you're shaking the wrong tree here. I'll talk to him if you'd like. He lives a block from me on Pine Street."

"Thanks, Avery, but I'd rather talk to him myself. I can fill you in later...how about coffee sometime this afternoon?"

* * *

After filling his tank at the Holiday station Murphy went inside to pay. Since working with the vice squad, he wore casual clothing; today it was khakis and a windbreaker with a *PGA* golf logo, and a well-worn Twins cap. Stocking a shelf toward the back of the store was a tall man with his back to him. "Looking for Mr. Jordaine," Murf said to the clerk at the till as he ran his credit card through the scanner. The clerk, a petite woman wearing a name plate that read Jill Verant, gestured to Murphy's right, "That's him over there, sir."

As Murf turned toward the back of the store, the clerk couldn't help but notice the shoulder holster behind his thin windbreaker. Her voice quivered,"Would you like me to get him for you, sir?"

"Not necessary. Thanks." Murf wandered back to the aisle were the man was bending over to finish a bottom row of *STP* cans. He stood over the man until he'd unpacked the case and stood. "Tom Jordaine?" Murphy asked. He'd no more than uttered his question when he nearly gasped his surprise. The tall man was a mirror image of a much younger Larry Symanski. The likeness was stunning: same narrow face, protruding ears — even the narrow mustache.

"Can I help you?" the man said with an easy smile.

For a moment Murf was at a loss for words. He apologized, "I'm sorry if I look surprised, but you are the spitting image of a cop in Duluth that I once knew…Larry Symanski."

"Oh yeah, that's my dad. I've been mistaken a hundred times; getting used to it by now. What can I do for you? Motor oil or an additive?"

"No, my car's been running smoothly. Say, Tom, do you have a place where we can talk for a few minutes? Privately?" He flashed his badge discretely. "I'm officer Murphy, Duluth police."

Jordaine frowned, "You the guy that's been calling my wife?"

Murphy nodded. "Hope I haven't upset her too much. She seemed kinda irritated."

"Come with me, my office is back there," he pointed toward the back of the store. "Jill," he called to the front counter, "I'll be in my office."

Inside the small, overheated space, Jordaine offered Murphy a folding chair and seated himself behind a cluttered desk. "First off," he said. "My wife said that she suggested getting a lawyer. I'm as frustrated as she is about this. Am I under suspicion for something? Something serious?"

Murf could sense the man's nervousness. "Let me explain what I'm working on and then you can decide if you'd like to have an attorney…is that okay with you?" Just to be safe, he recited the Miranda rights "*…to remain silent and have an attorney with you.*

Do you understand?"

Jordaine nodded, then said "I do. God, this is beginning to sound like I'm in big trouble—rights and all, like on TV. My attorney is Mr. Phillips, Mark Phillips. Should I call him before I say anything?"

"That's entirely up to you, Mr. Jordaine."

Murf could sense a tension that went from his face to his shoulders. He was licking his lips and trying to clear a dry throat.

"First tell me what all this is about, then I'll decide what to do," his voice had settled into a grave tone.

Murphy explained the homicides and the book that included his name. "Do you know…or, I should say, did you know a young woman named Brandy? A prostitute that hung out in Duluth?"

Jordaine's answer was quick and decisive, "Never heard of her, sir. And, I've never had any …how can I say this?…any dealings with a prostitute. Never! This is crazy."

Murphy believed him but had some gut reservations. Jordaine was getting more agitated by the minute. He was certain that if he pressed harder something would come out. A line of perspiration crossed Jordaine's brow, his hands fidgeted with a ballpoint pen, his eyes lost contact. "Are you okay?" Murphy asked. "Something you want to tell me about?"

"No…I'm not okay, Mr. Murphy," Jordaine began to tear. "I've done something terrible…but, not anything with prostitutes…I swear to God."

Tom Jordaine's detailed story took nearly five minutes to explain and involved a dominating father. What he divulged was as outrageous as it was revealing. When he finished, he dabbed at his swollen eyes. "I suppose you're going to arrest me…aren't you? All I ask is that you don't do anything to embarrass me in front of my employees…and, please let me explain things to my wife before…"

Murphy smiled, "No problem with either, Tom. Will you come in tomorrow? I'll be at the Duluth station. We'll need a formal statement. If you want your attorney to come along, that will be just fine with me."

Jordaine nodded, "What's going to happen to me, sir? I mean, am I going to be booked? Maybe even go to prison?"

"We'll see what we can do. But...I'll need your word not to talk with your father about any of this. As you can certainly understand, you're dad is in big trouble. Can you promise me that?"

"You have my word on that, Mr. Murphy."

70/ ONE O'CLOCK

Phil Symanski's flight arrived in Duluth at 11:30 in the morning. Upon retrieving his car from the lot, he called his brother Tommy. The two talked for several minutes. Although Tommy was irate with his half-brother, he would be careful not to reveal too much about his meeting with Murphy. "Why haven't you told me about what your cop friends have been doing? Damn it anyhow, Phil! You had to know all this stuff, but kept me out of the loop. Muriel's beside herself and I'm tempted to tell her everything; even about the girls dad messes with. Let me tell you, I'm not going down for this, Phil—no friggin way! You and dad better come up with something...and damn soon. I told this cop, Murphy, I'd be in to see him. I've been read my rights...and I'm going to see him tomorrow."

Phil tried to placate his angry brother to no avail. "Don't get all heated up over this. Be careful about anything you say to Murphy—he's got it in for dad. We'll come up with something."

"What? Tell me what, genius. Muriel's had another call from this Murphy jerk. Wanted to know where I was on certain dates and times. She can't keep making excuses for me. Next thing I know he'll be knocking on my friggin' door with handcuffs. Then what?"

Phil had no answer to the 'then what'. "Have you talked with dad?"

"Hell no. Have you?"

"No. But…I'll do that after I talk with Trygg. He trusts me, and I think he'll tell me what Murphy is up to…and then I'll know what they all know. I'm betting that they don't have shit to go on."

"I'm betting they do." A silence passed between the brothers. Tommy continued, "When I turn myself in, I'll tell the cops everything I did. And, I sure as hell don't know anything about any murders. I've already told Murphy about my stealing some files— but I haven't told him why. I'll give them a full confession and suffer the consequences for my part. Only thing is, there's a lot of stuff I don't know about." Tom had to pause and catch his breath. "If dad knows anything about the murders, that's between him and the Duluth police. I still don't have a clue about what that's got to do with me. Two friggin' people are dead, for Christ sake."

"None of that has anything to do with you, don't sweat it." Phil Symanski could feel the sky dropping down on him. "Don't do anything stupid. I'll call you tonight, after I've got more info"

"Just a minute! Info on what? Murders? Have you and dad been up to something— some kind of withholding evidence?"

"No. Don't get heated up."

Phil had four hours to kill before getting together with Adam. He thought about calling Linda and telling her that he was back in town a few days early, but dismissed the idea. He needed time to think…to come up with something, anything that might alleviate the stress he was feeling at the moment. He was resolved not to talk with his father until after he'd talked with Adam. He drove up to the

Skyline drive, a narrow roadway across the rim of the city, offering spectacular overlooks of the sprawling city below. The past few days had been mild and the snowmelt was obvious everywhere. What little remained of the snowbanks along the winding highway were a crusty brown, the dormant grass on the south side of the hill yellow, birch trees stood like white ghouls among the dull green pines. He pulled over to a rest stop and got out of his car. When the breeze off the lake touched his face he felt the icy chill of tears he hadn't realized were streaked across his unshaven cheeks. As he stood at the railing and peered down at the city hugging the river below, he let his emotions overwhelm him. Sniffling, he said to himself, "*My Lord...what have I done? Can you ever forgive me*?" He cried unabashedly. "*What can I do? Please, I beg of You, help me*."

Phil hadn't prayed in years. But, the feeling of helplessness was overwhelming. "I can't go on like this...I just can't." He thought of Father Mickey as he looked far toward the western edges of the city, and wondered if the priest would be home this afternoon. Mickey had always treated him kindly. He wondered if he had the courage to let go of the terrible guilt that was eating at his insides. He wondered even more about the consequences. Yet, someone out there had to be able to help him and it probably wasn't his friend Adam...nor was it his father. "Damn you, dad!", his curse was swept into the wind.

* * *

Mickey had just returned from a hospice visit and was making a peanut butter and honey sandwich while listening to a *KDAL* talk program when his office phone rang. In his haste, he spilled honey on his knuckles and onto the countertop; then rubbed the back of his hand on a paper towel as he put down what he was doing and rushed to his office. "Yes, Phil...I'm free until three or so. What's up?"

Phil answered, "Just want to talk about some things…some personal stuff that's been bothering me," he was careful not to show the stress that was choking him.

"Just stop by. I'll be in my office." He licked his sticky knuckles as he spoke. He checked the time; it was just before one. "If you haven't eaten I'm making sandwiches."

Phil tried to smile at the invitation but realized his face was too tight to lift his cheeks. "Thanks, Father…I'm not really hungry right now."

*　　　　*　　　　*

At one o'clock Murphy was brushing breadcrumbs from his bologna and mayo sandwich off his desktop. He had talked briefly with Holly that morning and with Judy Forbes. So far the names from Brandy's list hadn't revealed anything promising; all agreed that a followup was important. He had briefed Cooney on his meeting with Jordaine at his workplace. Cooney thought Murf should have brought the man in. "Are you certain he'll show up tomorrow? Murphy was. "Gut instinct, Charlie. I'd like for you to join us. I'd like to have a witness to what he tells us. I wouldn't be surprised if he had his attorney with him. He's scared as hell, but I don't think he knows anything more than what he's already told me about the breakin and theft of some files. I told him to return what was stolen but he claimed he'd given them to his dad."

Cooney fingered his chin; "I wonder if we should bring in Larry Symanski right now…or…give him more rope to hang himself with?"

Murf thought it best to wait.

*　　　　*　　　　*

At one o'clock Holly was supposed to be meeting with a man

named Albert something from Brandy's list. Murf was curious as to why she seemed so enthusiastic about what should have been a touchy matter. He hadn't connected the name with Holly's borrowed BMW escapade of a few days before. All that Holly had revealed was that she thought she knew the man 'from somewhere'. She could tell that Murphy didn't believe her.

* * *

At one o'clock Adam and Carl Rodland were finishing their burgers at a *Wendy's* on Grand Avenue. Both men being avid sports fans, their conversation moved from spring training in Florida, the Twins new manager Paul Molitor, and the disappointing Gopher basketball season, before returning to people in their investigtion: from the Symanskis, to Murphy, and then to Holly Goeden. "She's really a looker," Carl said. "And smart," Adam added. "I hope she gets her life together once all this is over."

Carl, like Adam, was a happily married father of two kids; a teenage daughter and an eleven year-old son. "I worry about my Michelle," Carl admitted. "She's as pretty as her mother was at sixteen, but far more worldly. I mean, these days aren't anything like when the two of us grew up. Computers, smart phones, and—more than anything—their values…me and Michelle talk about that a lot. She finds it hard to imagine life without a cellphone and iTunes. Right now she's dating a kid that's on Denfeld's basketball team. A tall drink of water, gotta be five inches taller than I am and I'm six feet. What worries me and my wife the most is that he's in a band that plays in bars on weekends."

Adam wondered about what the world would be like when his soon-to-be three year-old Anna was a teenager. "I guess I've got all that ahead of me, don't I? It boggles my mind to try and think about the world in…2029; that's when Anna will be sixteen."

"Enjoy one year at a time, Adam. Say, I'm looking forward to

Anna's birthday party. Wife's picked up a kid's cell phone that talks back. Might as well get her acquainted with today's technology young—so she won't be lost by the time they're five."

As they were about to slide out of their booth, Carl asked what time Adam was meeting with Phil. "I wonder what's going on with him. Must be something important if he'd cut his vacation short to get back here. I have a feeling that it might have something to do with his half-brother."

"I thought you told me once that he and his brother weren't very close; that he hardly ever mentioned him in all the time you two spent together."

"That's true. Honestly, I don't know what to expect. As I said, Phil seemed anxious to talk to me. Could be something to do with their father." Adam had another thought, "Or Linda. I have a feeling that their relationship might be in the tank."

Carl gave Adam a pat on the back as they got up from their booth and headed toward the door, "Their father is quite a piece of work. I would't be at all surprised if Larry Symanski knows more than either one of us about the murders. Not surprised at all. Murf sees it that way, too."

71/ PLANNING A MEMORIAL

Indecision. Mother Nature couldn't decide on what kind of afternoon to provide: rain or snow? Compromise. In her wisdom she sent down a blanket of windblown sleet upon the Port City of Duluth.

Mario peered out at the hunched-over students, heads bent against the sleet, half-running from the parking lot to the classroom buildings beyond his front yard. He was glad that he didn't have any business outside. He wandered back to his desk and paperwork.

He was a masterful organizer and the memorial service was coming nicely together. The priest had been on the phone with the Larsens in Forest Lake earlier this morning. Although he and Mickey had agreed to create a fictitious history of Brandy's life in Duluth, it bothered him to be blatently dishonest. "Yes, she had many friends here on campus." "No, not quite every Sunday…but quite regularly." "Always had a smile for everyone." Mrs. Larsen's heart was warmed by Mario's depiction of Olivia's world. She would send him several photographs of her daughter, "But none of them are recent, Father," she admitted. "To be honest, Vernon and I haven't seen much of our daughter these past two or three years. We worried a lot about what she was doing up there. It sure helps to know she was happy."

Sitting at his desk, Mario called Father Frank at NERC. Frank had agreed to provide some 'friends' for the deceased girl so the memorial service would validate Brandy's popularity. "Actually, there are three or four kids that knew her, Mario. They said she was well-liked, and kinda quiet…always seemed to blend into the background. They knew she was prostituting herself, but the kids I deal with these days are very permissive."

Frank laughed, "One of my kids, Barry Glavan, agreed to leave all of his ear, lip, and nose rings behind for the occasion. Even said he'd wear a long-sleeved shirt. You wouldn't believe all the art work that young man has crawling up his arms."

Mario laughed, "You're a good man, Frank. We all appreciate what you do for those kids."

"They do a lot for me as well. I can't describe the feelings when one of them gets his or her act together…and there have been several. Some of them keep in touch with me. Great feelings when it happens."

"It always works both ways, Frank. I mean, I get the same satisfaction from the kids I work with. We're on the same page. Oh, by-the- way, thanks for getting a group together; that will make our little event even more special."

"I think I could fill a bus to watch a chess match if it would get them outside our little facility. There are still a few that I can't trust to get back on the bus when the service is over. Vigilance...always, vigilance!"

72/ THE TRUTH SHALL SET YOU FREE

It had been nearly an hour since Phil Symanski's visit and the torment in Mickey's soul was unbearable. He tried to pray for guidance, some divine intersession, some ray of insight. He called upon his friend Bruno, *"my dear brother in Christ...now I know what your burden was like. Help me to be strong, to do the right thing...I am as lost as you were."* When stressed, Mickey was a pacer. He strode from the couch where he had been kneeling in his attempt at prayer, then through the kitchen, and back into the shadowed office where he'd heard the young man's confession. Then he turned back once again and retraced his steps. The pain of what he now knew had moved up his spine and into his head with a spiltting fury. Still he paced. The irony struck him like a bolt from heaven, almost as if Bruno was reminding him of that morning's Gospel. John's Gospel. His Bible was still resting on his desk where he had prepared his homily for the morning mass; the story of the woman caught in adultery and about to be stoned. Jesus bent down and made markings in the dirt before telling the gathered crowd *'let those of you without sin cast the first stone.'* How profound those few words! How powerful! Mickey, still searching for something Scriptural, read further...Jesus was saying to those Jews who believed Him, *'if you continue in My word then you are truly disciples of Mine; and the truth will set you free."*

The truth will set you free!

Mickey looked out at the late afternoon drizzle before reaching for his jacket slung on the back of the swivel chair he had been sitting on. He needed to walk, needed fresh air, needed some escape from his office confessional—the place where Phillip Symanski had unloaded the burden of his sins only an hour before. The north-western wind was biting. The drizzle had frozen into a buckshot-sized hail, stinging his face, and crunching under his footsteps on the pavement. He walked down the avenue toward the park. The 'truth will set you free' rang through his head, as if it were trapped inside of a giant bell that tolled those few words over and over again. If he didn't clear his head the torment would drive him crazy—crazy like Bruno must have been.

Phil's words reverberated: 'I'm sorry, I'm sorry…' he must have said a hundred times. Despite Mickey's pleadings, all Phil would say was that somehow he would make things right. Then he repeated, 'Pray for me, Father…pray for me, Father…' over and over. Mickey had been so dumbfounded that he couldn't remember how the lenthy confession ended. He remembered giving his absolution then bits and pieces of conversation afterwards but…how had he left it? What was Phil intending to do? He didn't say how could he possibly 'make things right. Even more puzzling was the reason behind the man's transformation. Phillip Symanski, it seemed to Mickey, was a time bomb ready to explode.

Mickey found himself nearly a mile from the rectory when the hail yielded to a thick, wet snow—a wet snow that stuck to him like Phil Symanski's sin. His feet were cold as the slush had penetrated the leather of his loafers, his ungloved fingers tingled. Despite the discomfort, Mickey felt as if he wanted to walk forever and never turn back.

* * *

Returning to the rectory he noticed that he had missed several calls:

two from Mario, another from Frank, and a text from Adam. The young officer had promised to keep Mickey abreast of of the investigation on a day-to-day basis. 'Nothing happening. We're still clueless. I'll keep in touch. Don't forget Anna's birthday!'

The calls from parishioners would have to wait until his thoughts had sufficiently cleared and he could speak and think coherently. *'God, how I need to talk with Mario. He's the only one who can help me with this."* His eyes began to tear at the reality of his circumstance: nobody on earth could help him with his new burden. The *sacred seal* was a shackle on his body, mind, and soul. Sobbing he realized...the truth had set Phil Symanski free and that same truth would be Mickey's eternal Elba— his exile on an isolated island prison where no one might ever learn the truth.

Monday, March 30: 2015

73/ MICK AND MURF

The beginning of *Holy Week* is an intense time for any priest, but especially so for Father Mickey Moran. Despite the burden of the recent confession, he had managed to rejoice with his parisioners on Palm Sunday. Later in the day he lunched with Mario—as he usually did on what had become football-starved Sunday afternoons—and, despite the weight of his burden, he had a reasonably good time in the company of his closest friend. Every fiber of Mickey's being wanted to divulge his painful secret; even if only to tell Mario how badly he was tormented inside and why; much as Father Bruno had attempted to do with him only four months before. As he knew only too well, when the forces of desire and demand are in conflict, stress is the inevitable outcome. Instead of the soul-to soul conversation, Mickey would have to settle on conversation between the two sports junkies. The two priests watched Michigan State beat a stubborn Louisville basketball team in the 'Elite Eight' of the NCAA hoops tournament. Talking basketball, and later, the Twins spring training roster cuts, took some of the edge off Mickey's misery.

The Monday morning Gospel was from *John 12*; the apostle that Jesus so loved was also Mickey's favorite. While going over the schedule for the coming week the night before, he recalled a homily he had used several years ago, while at Saint James parish. He jotted some notes and left them on his desk to look over again the following morning.

Mickey read the Gospel, "*Six days before Passover Jesus came to Bethany...*" It was the day before Jesus would be entering Jerusalem and Jesus was visiting the home of Lazarus and his sisters, where a banquet in His honor had been prepared. Martha served the meal while Mary doted on Jesus. Mary had brought a costly perfume into the room where the men were sitting, she anointed Jesus' feet, then dried them with her hair. The loving gesture brought protest from Judas Iscariot, who believed the oil could have been sold and the money given to the poor. In his reprimand of the soon to be traitorous disciple Jesus admonished; *"The poor you always have with you, but Me you will not always have."*

Mickey's brief homily held the theme of mercy. He told his congregation: "Somewhere I remember reading a definition of mercy. Whomever it was that said it was someone who had a most interesting perspective. He, or she, claimed that mercy was *'joining into the chaos of another's life'*. He claimed that Mary might have been gifted with a premonition of what was to come and chose to become involved in the only way she could. "The room was filled with men," Mickey described, "no place for a woman to be in those days, and furthermore, she touched the feet of the honored guest—another taboo. Her's was an act of divine mercy as she chose to become involved in the chaos of what Jesus knew was preordained for Him."

After mass Jillian Abbot stopped by the sacristy to tell Mickey that his sermon had struck a chord with her. "Thanks to your words I am going to get involved in the chaos that is my son's life." Mickey knew that her youngest son had been convicted of the heinous, and widely publiced, crime of battering his own child: the boy later died. "I will shut him out no longer, Father. I will show him a mercy that I might not have found had I not come to mass this morning. Maybe the Lord brought me here…and, maybe the Lord inspired you to share your perspective on mercy."

It was moments like this, although all too rare, that made Mickey appreciate his calling to be a priest. "What you have told me, Jillian, has struck me in much the same way as it has you. Quite often I'm called to practice what I preach myself. Thanks and may God, in His own infinite mercy, bless you and your son."

* * *

Two people knew essential parts of the unraveling story, while Adam Trygg remained in the relative dark. One of the two, however, could say nothing about his part of the story. Father Mickey, searching in vain for a way to impart some lead without violating his vow of secrecy, called Brenden Murphy on Monday afternoon. Mickey would be careful…very careful! "Father Mickey here, Murf…Happy Easter…" he greeted.

"And the same to you, Father. How have you been?" Mickey took the lead, "Had a wonderful visit with my son in Florida since we last talked, he's nearly as tall as I am, and I'd have to admit, much better looking," Mickey said. He went on to detail episodes of his late March visit in Naples.

Murphy had no children of his own, but always indulged those who did with a genuine interest in their families. Mickey had taken Michael to a spring training baseball game; "Are you a Twins fan, Murf?"

"Only mildly," Murf admitted, "But the Vikings…that's entirely another matter!" Murf had played football while in college at Bemidji and loved the game. The two talked briefly about the new Viking's stadium under construction on the former Metrodome site in Minneapolis.

"Say, the reason I called was to see if our group was planning another get-together…it's been a few weeks and I'm wondering…?"

"Matter of fact, Father, I've been thinking the same thing. We've had a couple of breaks since last week and…" Murphy paused, wondering how much information he should share. He continued with a brief description of the Thomas Jordaine connection to the investigation. As Murf explained, Mickey wished that he could have provided the missing pieces of the puzzle Murphy was working on. "So, Phil has a brother with a different surname; that's news to me." Mickey, careful not to divulge what he already knew, felt forced to play dumb—even worse, to blatantly lie to a man he had come to respect. "Where is the Jordaine information taking you, Murf?"

"Not far enough, I'm afraid. We know he's the guy that rifled the police files and why he did so. We also know that Larry Symanski was behind the theft of files …" Murf paused for long seconds. "And it appears as if Jordaine's father had something going on with Brandy… but that's as close as we are right now." Further, Murf explained that the senior Symanski had used his son's name while seeing the young prostitute, which explained Thomas' name in Brandy's book. And, that it was Tom who stole the police files to protect his father from any further embarrassment regarding his past indescretions. It was obvioius that Larry Symanski had strings attached to his two sons and that they, for whatever reasons, "the boys do pretty much whatever their father demands of them. We're sitting on any action for now…we've got two homicides to focus on and that's a handful." Murf said. "The files have been recovered and both father and son will be facing formal charges when the time is right," Murf said. "More than likely, they will plea-bargain and end up with misdemeanors and a year or two of probation."

Mickey saw an opening of sorts, "So…how is Phil taking all of this?"

"I don't know if he knows anything yet. He's been out of town, you know, and we've hush-hushed things here as best we can. If Phil knows anything it didn't come from his brother…Tom is shittin' bullets these days. Sorry, Father, I forgot myself."

Mickey swallowed hard, "Phil's back in town; I saw him the other day."

"Oh, I didn't know that. I put the case to bed over the weekend. Took the wife to the Mall of America so she could catch up on her wardrobe replacement project. Cost me a bundle. She said she saved me over two hundred dollars with all the sales. Go figger!"

Mickey laughed, "That paid for the gas and an overnight then."

"That's exactly how she sees it, Father."

Mickey could hear that Murf had another call coming in, "Well, let me know when we have the next meeting, Murf."

"Maybe later this week. I'll get back to you, Father."

*   *   *

And then there was one: One person who had put all of the pieces of the sordid story together. That solitary person, however, had both hands tied behind his back and a gag in his mouth. Mickey was struck with clarity by something Murphy had said; the father had always had strings tied to his two sons! Larry was not only a manipulator but a psychopath as well.

74/ MISSSING PERSON

How awkward will this be? Mickey wondered to himself as he spoke with Adam Trygg while eating burnt toast at his kitchen table and a Greek yogurt. "Absolutely! I can't stay very long but…sure, I'll be there." Adam had invited Mickey to stop by later that evening for birthday cake. Anna would be turning three year's old and the Trigs were having a few people over to celebrate the occasion. Included among the invitees were Phil Symanski and his girlfriend Linda, the Rodlands and, of course, Anna's favorite—Holly. "No gifts, please, Father. Anna's already got a toybox full of things to play with."

Murphy's text message came just after noon. "Call me ASAP."

Mickey called but had to leave a message. He tried Murphy's police station number…Charlie Cooney answered. "Murf's not in, Father. I can fill you in on what's just developed."

Cooney told the priest that Larry Symanski was missing. On Monday mornings Larry always had an early breakfast with his chums at a local Kenwood restaurant. He was usually back home before eight. His wife had a dentist appointment at ten but her husband hadn't returned, so she called the restaurant and learned that Larry hadn't been in that morning. Next, she called his buddies and they confirmed that Larry hadn't shown up. Finally, she called the police.

"Does Tom Jordaine know what's going on?" Mickey asked. "He seems to have been in-the-know all along."

"No. Murphy's talked with him already. Just a minute, Father…

Murf's just arrived. I'll pass the phone."

Murphy was frazzled. "I screwed up," he said. "We should have had Larry in for questioning right after we talked with his son Tom first thing this morning but…damn…I got into something else and then we got this report from the Two Harbors police. We've got an APB out on Symanski's car. He couldn't have gone too far yet. We've checked the Amtrak station and the airport. Nothing either place."

Mickey's gut turned at the news. He wanted in the worst way to spill what he knew…before anything terrible happened.

"No, Tom's been contacted by the local cops. He told them he hadn't talked with his father in days. I believe he's telling the truth. He said he would help in any way he could. He's already confessed that his dad put him up to the breakin here at headquarters. He doesn't seem to know much of anything else. The word 'confessed' struck a sharp nerve with Mickey. "Have you been in touch with Phil?"

A long pause from Murphy's end, "I'm not going there yet. I've alerted Adam; he'll be talking with Phil at his daughter's birthday party later today. We'll go from there. This Symanski family is fuckin' dysfunctional." He'd no more than said it when he wished he had chosen a better word—his recovery was weak, "Awfully messed up I mean".

What family isn't? Mickey thought but didn't say. "I'll probably be seeing Phil tonight." He explained Anna Trygg's having a birthday party.

Murphy thought a moment; "If you see him, just try to read what Phil is like, Father—his demeanor and such. See if you can read what's going on with him. I have this gut feeling…you know? That something isn't right with him either."

"Will do," Mickey understood and ached, with every fiber of his being, that he could tell Murphy what the cop needed to know.

* * *

The only people from the group that Mickey hadn't talked with this morning were Holly, Mario, and Frank Polich. He wondered if they were up to speed on the new developments. The memorial service was set for the following evening at the UMD Newman Center. Ironically, the three of them were planning to meet at Mario's place in two hours.

He called Mario. As Mario picked up the phone, Frank Polich, who had just arrived, walked into his office. "Coffee's on, Frank. Be with you in a minute. I'm talking to Mickey right now."

"The service is shaping up nicely," Mario assured Mickey. "The Larsens will be in town this evening, and Holly is taking them out to dinner at the Pickwick. You're welcome to join them if you're free, I'm committed and Frank has bowling league."

"I'll have to pass, Amigo. Adam's daughter has a birthday party tonight. Say, have either of you guys talked with Murphy lately?"

Mario posed the question to Frank, "Nope…neither of us. What's going on these days? Holly's been through her list of names without discovering anything helpful. Haven't talked with Adam in over a week."

Having nothing more to say about the ongoing investigation, Mario switched to the topic of his friend's recent Florida trip. "Say, I loved the photo you sent; the one of you and Michael with T.C. at the Twins game." TC was the popular Twins mascot. "Looks like Michael is nearly as tall as his dad, but much better looking…and, I'm sure, quite a bit smarter."

Mickey had heard that comparison before but agreed, "We had a blast. I even enjoyed my sister Meg on this trip. I must be mellowing with age."

The two small-talked another minute or two and Mickey decided it might be best to allow the conversation to drift back to the memorial that Mario and Frank were putting the finishing touches on.

Before hanging up, Mario asked Mickey to greet the Tryggs for him. "Holly told me the other day that she's been invited, too. She hasn't seen little Anna in two weeks and wants to see her and little Andrew in the worst way. She's found a *Dora the Explorer* doll for Anna—one that talks. I'm thinking of getting you one for your birthday. That way you'll have someone to talk to when you're bored."

"Good idea. Then I wouldn't have to listen to you and become even more bored."

"That'll do, Amigo. See you tomorrow. Frank says 'hi'."

75/ DEAD MAN WALKING

On the previous Friday morning Larry Symanski had followed Murphy to Two Harbors and parked down the street from the Holiday station where he could watch what was going on. He cursed the reality that his nemesis was onto something. How had that dull-witted cop found his son, he wondered? Someone…most likely one of his sons, must have blown a whistle. His sons had always been as weak as their mothers—two women that had abandoned him years before. What was Murphy hoping to get out of Tommy? Larry was confused and obsessed in equal measure. His son, Tommy, knew enough to implicate him in the breakin—which was a minor felony at best. Phil, however, knew enough to put him behind bars for the rest of his life. His thoughts went from Tommy to Phil. His younger son was the weaker of the two, and was much more easily manipulated. Phil also liked money and Larry had plenty of that. His last call to Phil's cell wasn't answered; nor was a call to his land line. Larry's second and third calls were likewise ignored. Unusual, highly unusual! Phil always returned his calls—always! Larry Symanski stewed as he kept his eyes focused on the Holiday station, across and down the busy street, from where he was parked.

What's been taking them so long, Larry Symanski wondered. The longer Murphy was in his son's shop, the worse it seemed. He lit a cigarette, took two drags, and tossed it out onto the street. He tried Phil's phone number again. This time his son answered: "Where in hell have you been?" Larry said. "I've been trying to get ahold of you for hours."

Rather than answer his father's question, Phil asked: "Have you talked with Tommy lately?"

"I'm planning to do so in a few minutes." Larry wouldn't say any more until he learned what Phil knew. "Why?"

"Why. He's being harassed by the police. Murphy's on to something."

"Have you talked to your buddy, Trygg, lately?"

"Like I've already told you, I'll be seeing him tonight. You sound nervous, dad."

"No…I'm fine," He lied. "We'll get together after I've talked with your brother…and you talked to this Trygg guy."

"Sounds good. You sure you're okay?"

* * *

After more than half an hour, Larry Symanski observed Murphy leave the station and get into his car. Surely, if Tommy had spilled his guts, Murf would have arrested him on the spot. Maybe, just maybe, he had things figgered all wrong. Maybe Tommy had kept his mouth shut. Tommy, after all, had too much to lose—family and reputation and all. He had done well for himself. No, on second thought, he was certain, the despised Murphy was putting the screws on his son. Things were going badly…this wasn't simply a little bump in the road. For a long moment, Larry Symanski felt like a dead man walking. As Murphy's car was moving out of sight he was about to get out of his car. "Shit," he saw a Two Harbors police squad drive slowly by. Maybe it was too risky…maybe the local cops were on some kind of alert. He'd better get his ass out of Dodge. Tom could wait.

The elder Symanski had some serious problems and he knew it—a noose seemed to be hanging above his head.

As he drove back toward Duluth he considered his shrinking options. He laughed to himself at his first thought. He'd read about people in trouble staging their own death…an overturned boat in a remote lake that would appear to be a tragic accident was a popular scenario. Larry had a cabin and small boat on Island Lake north of the city…but the lake was still iced over. He also had a *Skidoo*. There might be a patch of open water under the bridge on Highway 4…he could…No, that idea wouldn't work any better than the first. Larry needed to come up with something much better— a disappearance of some kind? He forced himself to think outside the box: a new identity in a new place far from Minnesota, maybe even Mexico…or someplace in South America where they didn't have any extradition agreements with the US? Yet, the more he processed the ideas that passed through his troubled mind, the more he realized that he was over-scheming. The bottom line, he realized, the best escape was the most simple one…just drive away and keep going. Get another car as soon as possible. He was smart enough to realize that he'd probably get caught at some point, but every elusive day would be a blessing of sorts. He thought of the stuff he'd need: money, his computer, maybe even some items he might use for a disguise. Too many details, too little time—he dismissed all of the above as he might the junk mail that was delivered every day.

No he couldn't do that. Haste makes waste…he'd need cash as his credit cards could be easily traced, his computer had too much of his illicit dealings on it's harddrive. That would have to be buried somewhere far from Duluth. By the time he reached London Road, a tree-lined street that ran parallel to the Lake Superior shoreline in east Duluth, he seemed certain of one thing…he would be making a run—PDQ!

76/ BIRTHDAY PARTY

As Mickey parked his car on Cato Street in Riverside, an old blue-collar neighborhood in far western Duluth, he counted six cars; one of them an expensive looking Audi. Among the Trygg's invited friends; one of them was obviously quite well to do. He was greeted at the door with a warm smile from Susan Trygg, "Thank you so much for coming, Father. It makes Anna's special day even more special."

Susan introcuced Mickey to the Rodlands, "Carl is Adam's partner on the police force…and this is Sally Rodland." Mickey recognized them from his church…they were not regular mass attendees. Something to work on he noted. "And, you know Phil of course, this is his friend, Linda Miller."

Phil smiled widely, "Good to see you, Father. Adam tells me that you were down to spring training recently. What do you think about the Twins' chances this year?"

Mickey's mouth went suddenly dry. Phil's greeting was almost too familiar, too folksy, too rehearsed: as inappropriate as it was bizarre. Worse, there wasn't the slightest trace of tension or remorse behind his words. "Better…I mean, the Twins," he managed to say. "Better than the last few years anyhow." So blown away by the young cop's charade, Mickey's response came from a place he wasn't sure of…he almost stuttered as he repeated, "Hopefully a lot better I'd like to think."

Adam, carrying baby Andrew, was a step behind Phil Symanski; his warm greeting was as genuine as the man himself. "Good to see you, Father. Loved the photo you emailed from Florida. Both Susan and me thought Michael was a spitting image of his dad." Adam offered his son to Mickey, "Take the little guy and come over and say hello to our little princess." Adam's eyes moved toward the kitchen entryway of the small duplex unit. "And meet her little friends, Cheryl and Robby from next door." Mickey loved the smell of babies and relished the opportunity to have Andrew in his arms. He gave the boy a small kiss on the forehead, endured the boy's deep frown, and turned toward the kitchen along side of Adam.

Before he reached the kitchen to greet Anna, Holly caught his elbow.

"Well, well…so happy to see you, Mickey. And, you too, Andrew," she sofly touched Andrew's chin and the boy sent a sharp cry into Mickey's ear.

"Thanks, I needed that, Holly. Andrew was just warming up to

me," he laughed. "Good to see you, too." Holly had arrived just behind Mickey and was walking toward the birthday girl in the kitchen.

"How about a hug?" Mickey's face reddened as Holly, wearing a lowcut white blouse, embraced him with enthusiasm. "I'll talk with you later about Brandy's memorial service," Holly said. "Your priest buddies are awesome guys." She winked, I'm thinking of switching to Mario's parish, he's so smart…and so spiritual."

Before Mickey could argue her contention, Phil was standing behind them like a shadow. "Say, Holly, how you doing? I thought you might be willing to join me outside for a smoke. Fill me in on this Brandy thing…I'm feeling out of the loop these days."

Holly puzzled, "…I just got here, Phil." Feeling awkward about the invitation, she nodded that she would. "Will you excuse us for a few, Father?"

"Yes, I've got to visit with Anna and her friends for a bit." He jostled Andrew who was quiet at the moment and feeling more comfortable in the arms of a stranger. "We can catch up later, Holly."

"Let me, Father…" It was Phil's friend Linda Miller offering to take the boy. "I'll bring him to Susan. I'd guess it's Andrew's nursing time." Mickey had another awkward moment when Linda took Andrew from him, the boy's little hands were gripping Mickey's shirt collar. As he allowed Linda to remove Andrew from his arms, the boy started to bawl. Andrew went from Linda to Susan standing nearby. Susan hushed her son and excusing herself, left the living room. For a moment Mickey stood by himself as Adam had already joined the kids in the kitchen. One of Anna's little friends had taken a handful of unattended birthday cake and Adam was trying to calm his daughter while making repairs to the cake at the same time. As chaotic as the birthday scene appeared to be, Mickey felt a sudden pang of regret over all the birthdays with his son that he had missed—fourteen of them! He approached Adam who was making a mess of his repair job at the kitchen counter. "You might try a spatula," he offered, "the knife you're using doesn't seem to be doing the job."

Mildly frustrated by the mess he was making, Adam turned to Mickey. "If you'll entertain the kids a minute, I'll go find Susan."

When Adam returned, Mickey was on the floor helping the children make a lego castle. As he was linking the top pieces, little Robby took a swipe at the structure; sending fifty blocks across the kitchen floor. Anna let out a shriek, threw a handful of Legos at her little friend, and ran to her mother. "Make Robby go home," she cried. Adam couldn't suppress a smile, "Looks like you started something, Father, maybe we need a spatula for something else."

A few minutes later Holly had returned, smelling of rancid cigarette smoke. "I think Phil's as whacky as his father, Mickey. And, I feel like I've just been through an interrogation. He wanted to know everything Murphy knew…and, would you believe…he wanted my address and phone number—so we can keep in touch!"

Mickey's blood pressure escalated, "What did you tell him?"

"Not much of anything. He seemed frustrated. Said he'd have to talk more with Adam…'get back in the loop' was the way he put it."

* * *

On the short drive back to the rectory, Mickey replayed the two hours of birthday party in the muddle of his mind. The Tryggs were happy, wonderful people. The Rodlands seemed to be much like Adam and Susan—young and hopeful. Holly never looked better. It almost seemed as if the past weeks or months had matured her beyond her years…given her a peace that had been missing from her life. Gone was the sultry look of the streets, born was a natural beauty and a glimmer of confidence in a positive future. In their brief conversation, Holly had confided that she had already registered for the fall semester at UMD (Mario had helped get through all the hoops) and that she had a wealthy benefactor. "I think you'd love Albert, Mickey," she said. "He's an old widower with no kids. He's kinda adopted me, I guess. Anyhow, he's promised to pay my tuition so long as I keep good grades."

And…he contemplated Phil Symanski's demeanor. Mickey had noticed how Linda seemed to tell him what to do and when to do it. At one time she said to Susan, "No thanks. Phil doesn't need ice cream with his cake…" before cutting him a small slice. Mickey could see that the cake sans ice cream wasn't what Phil had hoped for. Later, when Phil was talking with Carl Rodland, she came to his elbow and announced, "We're going now. Get my coat, Phil." Phil did. The most perplexing part of the evening was the confounding 'Old Buddy' behavior of the man who's grave confession Mickey had heard only days before. What had he expected of Phil? Avoidance? Guilt? Contrition? None of these were even remotely apparent. It was almost as though the confession hadn't actually happened and the clocks had been turned back a month. Phil Symanski's presence in the room had deeply troubled him. But, how could he possibly followup and further engage the mysterious and dangerous son of Larry Symanski? And, what about the father, obviously the man who pulled the strings of his two marionette sons?

77/ THE MEMORIAL

The week before, the memorial service for Olivia Larsen had been moved from the early Thursday evening to mid-afternoon. The two priests were committed to Holy Thursday obligations at their respective churches. The memorial service was, at first somber, then celebratory. Father Mario provided a remarkable eulogy for the deceased girl, using ideas provided by Holly and Frank and the Larsen family. Mario's intent was to create a much better post-Forest Lake life for Brandy than she had actually lived during her years in Duluth. Several offered extemporary comments: Frank spoke, (followed by a select few of his NERC wards), Mickey added a touch of levity, and lastly Holly came to the front of the room. Vivacious, insightful, and with humor, Holly stole the show. "My friend Brandy talked often and with deep affection of her parents…Elise and Vernon, and how they had always been there for her." The Larsen's beamed, then teared, when Holly asked them to come forward and say a few words.

After the ceremony, Holly visited with her father, John Belak, who had surprised her with his presence at the service. "How did you know about this, dad? I was almost blown away to see you come in the door."

"Your dad keeps up on the affairs of his daughter far more than you realize. You know you're all I've got in this world…and I love you very much."

Holly's eyes misted, "I wish I could honestly say I love you too, dad. I wish I could get over you're leaving me and mom. I wish a lot of things, I guess. But…thanks. It means more than you can realize having you come and support me tonight." A tear escaped the corner of her eye.

John fought back tears of his own, "We've got time to repair things, sweetheart. I want that to happen…okay?":

Holly gave her father a hug. "I'm willing to try," she said through the tight emotion caught in her throat. "Say, have you talked with Mickey yet? He might be the only person other than me that you've ever met. And, he will be leaving for some church things at Saint Gerard's in a few minutes."

Belak said, "I intend to. But, I'd like to speak to that man named Murphy first. Is he here?"

"Right over there," she pointed toward the large man speaking with the Larsens. "He's the guy with red hair in the navy suit."

"Will you introduce me, Holly? I'd like to ask him about some things."

Holly caught Murf's eye and waved for him to come over. "Murf, this is my dad, John Belak. He'd like to meet you."

Murf took John's hand in his vice-like grip. "My pleasure, Mr. Belak." He squinted, "I know I've heard the name, but can't make a connection at the moment," he lied.

"I'm the guy that beat up the James guy…before he was murdered. I've given statements to a Mr. Cooney about that." Murphy's expression became serious. "I guess I knew that. I did read Cooney's report on your testimony." Murphy didn't mention that the pending aggravated battery charges against the man that were still pending.

John Belak seemed surprised, expecting more than the man's casual recall of what should have been a significant piece of the investigation he was covering. "Where do I stand right now?"

Looking confused, Murf blurted: "You'll probably get notification of a trial date one of these days soon. You're out on bail right now, aren't you?"

Belak nodded at the obvious. His impression of Murphy was one of an officer's incompetence. "Should be soon, don't you think?"

Now it was Murphy's turn to nod, "I suppose. Say, John, I've got to talk with that guy over there," he pointed toward Adam Trygg. "Nice meeting you."

John's eyes narrowed, his disappointment written like an unexpected belly punch across his troubled expression. Holly, standing at his elbow, was equally disturbed by Murphy's uncharacteristic nonchalance. Feeling her father's disappointment, but not apologizing for her cop friend's behavior, she excused herself. "I've got to mingle, guys. I'd like you to meet Adam and Susan Trygg before you leave, dad. Okay? I'll talk to you later, Murf."

Later was less than five minutes. Murf came over to where Holly was talking with Mario. "Say, sorry I brushed you guys off. Frank was collecting his kids and I wanted to say hello to a couple of them. Two of them, Ronny and Skids, were kids I sent Frank's way a year ago. They're coming around. Both will be back on the street in another month or so."

"You might have told my dad that."

"Holly...please don't lecture me on bad behavior."

Holly felt put down by a man she, like Adam, had come to respect. "Okay, no lectures, Murf," was all she could say.

78/ INSIDE JOB

John stayed in the background for several minutes watching the interactions of people he didn't know. When Holly left Murphy standing by himself, he approached: "Can we go outside, Mr. Murphy, talk with some privacy? Some things I believe you ought to know about." Murphy seemed like a different person, "Be happy to…John, wasn't it? Holly's father?"

Outside, the pre-dusk skies were leaden and the hilltop wind brisk. The two men found a nook behind the building where John could light up a cigarette. "Do you know a man named Darrin Pratt?" Belak asked.

"Quite well…may I call you John?"

Belak nodded, blew his exhale away from Murphy, coughed. "What do you know about him?"

"A friend of James', he's been arrested for possession, vandalism …a host of things. We've interrogated him on at least three occasions and learned nothing about James' murder. Why do you bring up his name?"

"He's scum, you know; as well as a pathological liar. We've talked, Pratt and me, a few times. He knows more about Hillside than probably anybody in your department. He's the one that led me to James in the first place—told me where he liked to hang out and watch his girls. And, he's the one I went to once I heard about James being murdered. We both went to the murder scene a few days after the yellow tape was removed. I found the exact location where I encountered James—and, if you've seen Cooney's report, you already know what I did there. Anyhow, I don't think any of your team located the spot. There were blood traces in the dead grass where I first encountered him that night—probably twenty yards awy from where James' body was later discovered. So, James must have dragged himself some distance before the murderer found him. Not that what we found would be of any use that late after it happened.

But, I've taken some pictures of the site where I beat him up."

All Murphy said was 'okay', and asked him to bring them in.

John knew that his information wouldn't change anything that was going on in the investigation, but hoped to get Murphy's attention with it. "Right now, Pratt's scared shitless: afraid of you guys, but even more, so is the man who called the shots; or managed the James pimp for this girl Brandy and my daughter. He's the guy behind half the shit going on under your noses. No offense to you, but he says that he thinks there's a cop on the take. Claims that the murders gotta be an inside job. Have you contacted some stripper at the Saratoga Club? Pratt seems to think that someone there could put a finger on the ringleader."

Murf hadn't, but didn't say as much. John knew more than Murf would have guessed, the well-built and street-savvy man had spent his share of time cruising Hillside, and talking it up with some of the bad asses there. He would let the man talk. "Where are you going with all this, John? Any other names than Pratt you've heard about? I'm all ears."

John Belak's story had been borderline believable up until now. "So what about the man inside the department?"

"Pratt says he thinks he has—says that he might be able to finger your rotten apple. But he's afraid of what might happen to him. He thinks that the cop knows who I am, too…and that both me and my daughter are in danger. I haven't been able to get any more than that out of him. That's pretty much all I know. If it's a cop that Pratt says is 'one damn dangerous dude'…you probably work with him—maybe he's someone you see every day." John shoved his hands deeply inside his pants, "anyhow, I have a feeling that this Pratt guy could be squeezed."

Murphy would remain noncommittal. "To be perfectly honest, John, what you're saying is a lot of conjecture. 'He thinks', and 'he believes', along with 'I think and I believe', along with a dollar bill, will get me a cup of coffee on Superior Street."

John put out his cigarette, pulled up the collar on his light jacket, "You might be right. Anyhow, I didn't want to say anything to Holly about any of this because I think she might know these guys. Another 'I think'—but I thought you should know just the same."

"Does the name Symanski ring a bell with you, John?"

"Can't say that it does. But whoever murdered James was driving a fancy car…Pratt thinks it was a Lexus or a BMW. He saw it only a brief second after he heard the single gunshot. Then he got the hell away as fast as he could."

79/ PHIL'S FANCY WHEELS

Larry Symanski spent less than ten minutes getting what he needed from his house. All he could find was thirty-four dollars in loose bills. He grabbed his laptop, some toiletry items, and a change of clothes before saying goodbye to his home of thirty years. He had a feeling that he might never have the opportunity to be here again.

On his way out of town he found an ATM and withdrew $200, filled his gas tank, and headed south on I-35. In less than four hours he made a second stop and stole some expired license plates from an unattended used car lot in Richfield, an inner ring suburb of Minneapolis. He'd had enough time to come up with a plan: continue south toward DesMoines where he might be able to spend a few days with an old army buddy. He still wasn't certain where he was going to end up, but he was feeling a heat that he couldn't see…yet knew was out there somewhere ahead or behind him. Going west toward Omaha, where the Symanski's had some shirttail relatives, would be an obvious guess for anyone pursuing him. He had another army buddy in Kansas City but, for some reason, was reluctant to continue on the interstate. All the money he had with him was less than 300 dollars and using a credit card, or another ATM would be too risky. For a man who always had a plan…he found himself woefully unprepared for his flight.

Benny Wheaton wasn't too happy about having unexpected company—especially from a Nam vet he never liked. The two men caught up on things in less than an hour. "You can spend the night but, I'm going to be out of town tomorrow," he lied. "You'll hav'ta be on your way in the morning." Larry left before Wheaton was up the next morning, without offering so much as a goodby or a thanks. And, he left without a clue as where it might be safe to go next.

Larry Symanski had never felt more alone as he pulled into a small park in Pleasant Hill east of the Iowa capital. The mid-morning was sunny and warm for early April. Kids were out in t-shirts playing on the monkey bars, slides, and swingsets; their mothers nearby. A scene that made him think of his own two grandkids—Tom's children. He felt a sudden and overwhelming remorse about leaving them behind, and for Tom and Muriel who would suffer the consequenses of his mistakes. Tommy, he knew, had already been contacted by the police…Phillip would probably be next. It was Phil who worried him the most. Tommy didn't know everything, but Phil did. And, Phil was the weaker of his two weak sons. He didn't dare to try calling either of them; didn't dare use his cell phone for any calls.

A police car cruised slowly down the street behind Pine Valley Drive where he was parked. He wished he had stolen Iowa plates; his Minnesota plates would be conspicuous and easily traced. He watched the squad car pass, waited five minutes, then drove east to Highway 65 and found a cheap motel. He parked behind the building and out of sight from the highway, then checked in. It wasn't even noon yet, but he needed to get off the road and do some serious thinking. He paid fifty-two dollars in cash for the single bed room. In his duffle bad were his computer, the few clothes he brought along, and next to his shaving kit—his .22 caliber pistol. He wondered if using his computer would give authorities a reading as to his location. Best not to risk it. He sat and stared at a framed picture of an outdoor scene; thick woods, a pristine lake, and a wide-antlered moose wading in the weeds. The painting reminded him of home…the endless prarie of cornrows was an alien landscape. Perhaps this was as good a place as any to be over with it all. Larry Symanski felt like crying but no tears would come.

* * *

Adam's curiosity had been troubling him since Anna's birthday party. When the guests were leaving his house, Adam walked his friend out to the curb where his car was parked. "Nice wheels," he commented as Phil opened the door to his Audi SS coupe. "How in hell could you afford something like this on a cop's salary."

Phil laughed, "I couldn't. It's just a rental, Adam" he lied. "I've always wanted try out something quick and sporty," was Phil's rejoinder. The posh leather interior had a scent that Adam could only envy. The other appointments were as stylish and luxuriant as one might expect from a new sports car.

"Be careful not to pick up any dents or scratches. You'd be in debt for years." As he waved goodbye to Phil he couldn't help wondering if his friend had been telling the truth.

Back inside he commented on the car to Susan. "That's not the Phil I know, she said. "Quick and sporty?"

* * *

The following morning, when Adam reported to the west Duluth precinct office, he was surprised to be greeted by Brenden Murphy. "Let's catch up on things, Adam." Murf gestured toward a small office off to the side of the front desk. "Rodland has taken your squad in for servicing so we've got an hour or so to talk."

After explaining Larry Symanski's sudden disappearance the previous day, Murphy shared his conversation with Holly's father, John Belak. "I'll tell you, the guy's got some street smarts. We talked for nearly an hour after the memorial service—by the way, it was a nice event you folks put on. Anyhow, both Cooney and me are convinced there's a Symanski connection to the James murder...and, probably Brandy Larsen's as well. I don't know if you're aware that I've talked with Tom Jordaine. If he knows more than he's already told me, I'm gonna get it out of him one way or another. And, believe me, I know how to squeeze a guy."

Adam nodded, "You said 'a Symanski' Murf. Does that include Phil?"

"There are three of them, Adam. Yes, that includes Phil, doesn't it?"

"You know...there's something I've been meaning to ask you. Can we check bank records, I mean, find out how much someone's got in their savings and checking accounts?"

"Not a problem. Why?"

Adam mentioned Phil Symanski's new car. "Must have set him back fifty grand, maybe more. It's got every bell and whistle imaginable."

"Do you have any idea where he banks?" Murphy queried. "Wait, let me call downtown; maybe he's on direct deposit. If so we'll have an easy trace." Murphy pulled his cell from his jacket pocket, "Charlie, I want you to check something for me."

Within fifteen minutes Murf's notebook was filled with numbers and dates. "Bingo!" he said. Four days after the James murder—back in September— our friend Phillip Symanski made a twenty thousand deposit, then on the third of October, another ten grand. Then on the seventh, a check to Bloomington Audi in the Cities for fifty seven thousand, eight hundred and seventy dollars: Not too bad for a cop with his salary."

"So…what's next, Murf? I wonder if Phil knows anything about his dad. He was cool and collected last night at Anna's party."

"We've got an APB out on Larry. So far, we've come up empty—like we have for much too long."

"Should we call Phil in…for questioning, I mean? We've got enough with the bank records don't we?"

"Maybe. We'll give it a few more days. We've got both Phil and his brother under surveillance already.

80/ CHIRPING LIKE A CHICKADEE

Larry Symanski looked around the dingy motel room. Five empty bottles of Budweiser rested on the bedstand; one remained from the sixpack he'd purchased the previous afternoon. Opening the heavy drapes his eyes stung at the bright morning. His only memory of the night before was watching the local news on TV. Nothing was reported about a missing Duluth man. His head ached, but he felt more rested than he had in days. He drank the last beer before showering and brushing his teeth. What to do next: continue east? Or, head south toward Missouri. What difference did it really make, he wondered? He flipped a coin as he stepped outside…heads he'd go south; tails he'd continue east. Tails. He decided to avoid heavily traveled I-80 on his way from just outside Des Moines toward Illinois. The headache from the night before was still pounding and causing his eyes to water and blur. He pulled off onto a gravel side road off of Highway 6, somewhere between Newton and Grinnell in west-central Iowa .

For the first time in a long while, he felt a stirring of his conscience. Remorse had always been a stranger to Larry Symanski. In a TLC program he'd seen on TV years before, he'd learned that his behavior closely fit two primary criteria of a psychopathic personality: he was manipulative and hurting others never seemed to bother him. How, then, had he made his life such a living hell? The crimes he had committed were just part of what he did for a living, and the victims simply people who were in his way, he had little regret about any of that. But…the idea of having to pay the price had never seemed a reality that he might have to cope with. Concerns of the moment were as perplexing as were his feelings of being alone and estranged. His two sons would figure things out for themselves—pay the consequences of their weaknesses. If they had only said 'no' he'd have found someone else to do the dirty work that had to be done. Both Phil and Tommy had learned one thing very well in their formative years: 'obey your father'!

No, he realized as he sat behind the wheel of his car, it wasn't his sons that mattered anymore…it was his two grandkids that troubled his thoughts more than anything. But…why? Why the sudden and almost overwheming worry about what they would they think of their grampa; a fugitive who was being hunted like a dog. He eyed his duffle bag resting on the passenger seat beside him and swallowed hard. Then, after a long thought, he unzipped the duffle and removed his .22 caliber pistol. When he contemplated suicide, he realized that taking his life might be even worse for his grandkids to deal with. Tears came to his eyes. Did he have the guts? Or was he, like his sons, a pathetically weak and cowardly man?

Still in tears, he laughed at himself—how stupid he was. A reality struck him like a face slap; he couldn't do what he coerced his son to do. He couldn't kill—not even his pathetic self. Prison would be bad, for sure, but having someone find him dead with his head blown apart…sitting in his car, or somewhere out in the endless rows of corn, woud be much worse. How can one possibly measure a degree of disgrace, he wondered as he gazed absently at the abandoned farmhouse framed in the mid-morning sun? You can't.

You can only hope to have the courage to live with it—and pay the penalties a just society requires. His sons would get what they deserved...but those grandkids...what would they have to suffer through? Kids their age could be very cruel. He could only conclude that each and every Symanski would have to suck it up and live with what had been done.

On a gravel road out in an Iowa cornfield, Larry Symanski made his final decision. It would be better to turn himself in to the police down here, than to risk being arrested while driving back to Duluth. He'd have to face the music back in Duluth where his crimes had been committed...but the circumstances might be less humiliating. And, there was always the possibility that he'd be able to beat the system one more time. After all, he knew some damn good attorneys...some real sharks. He backed out onto Highway 6 and headed west to where his Monday had started. For the first time in days, Larry Symanski had a smile on his face. He imagined a headline banner in the Duluth paper: 'Larry Symanski Exonerated'.

*　　　*　　　*

Highway 6 became Hubbell Ave as Larry passed into Pleasant View, a suburb with a large campus, in northeast Des Moines. He pulled off Hubbell and asked a stranger for directions to the nearest police station. The young woman asked if he needed help, "Too late for help," Larry said, "but thanks anyhow." The directions were simple. Five minutes later he parked his car, took a deep breath, and took the narrow sidewalk up to the low-roofed modern brick building.

"My name is Larry Symanski...I'd like to speak with the chief or any police officer that's on duty this morning," he said in a pleasant tone.

The secretary said, "that would be Bill Wordy. He's the man in there," she pointed to a room with the door ajar."

*   *   *

When Adam and Murphy arrived at Phil's apartment later that morning, they found their fellow cop in plaid boxer shorts, preparing a breakfast of bacon and eggs in his small kitchen with a sun-splashed Lake Superior view. Somehow, Phil knew their arrival wasn't for a social visit. "I'd offer you guys some breakfast…but I have a feeling that you're here to take me downtown. I'm guessing that you've probably found my dad."

"We have Phil, but how about I invite myself to breakfast first?" Murf brought his humor to a difficult situation. Everything was nearly prepared and the eggs looked like Murphy would have ordered them at a local Perkins. "Maybe I'll just indulge myself, Phil. I'm always hungry you know, and bacon is a major weakness of mine. After that, the three of us can go downtown. Why not put some clothes on—then we'll talk a bit."

While Phil was getting dressed, and Murphy had finished the last of Phil's bacon, Adam's cell phone rang. "Is Murf with you?" The voice was Cooney's. "I've been trying to get ahold of him for half an hour." Murphy had a habit of turning his cell off whenever he was 'thinking' as he put it. Adam passed his phone to Murf.

"Well, I'll be damned!" were his first four words. He listened another minute before returning Adam's phone, and walked to the kitchen window without speaking. "I'll be damned!" he repeated as Phil entered the kitchen in jeans and a Grandma's Marathon t-shirt.

"Just got the latest update, Phil. Take a chair and have the last cup of coffee—I think Adam left some in the pot." Perched on an outside balcony railing, beyond the condo kitchen, was a black-capped Chickadee. Murf turned to Phil, "Looks like the gig is over," he said in a somber tone. "Your dad's having lunch in Des Moines as we speak: a PB&J sandwich with a guy by the name of Bill Wordy."

Phil gave Murphy a strange expression, "Who's this Wordy guy?"

Murf took his cuffs off the back of his belt. "Wordy's a local cop in a nice little college town south of here. Wordy just called Cooney and told him that your dad has been chirping like..." he pointed to the balcony railing, and allowed a small smile to crease his face. "Chirping like that little chickadee out there." He then proceeded to read Phil his Miranda rights.

Friday, July 3, 2015

81/ RETIREMENT PARTY

The Friday afternoon was splendidly sun-splashed: an ideal day for northern Minnesotan's to begin their holiday celebration of America's Independence. In addition to the 4th, a gathering of friends would celebrate another special occasion—the early retirement of a Duluth police officer. In Brenden Murphy's invitation card to his closest friends he wrote a personal note. 'Sorry I couldn't quite make it twenty-five years. Rather than just put in my time I'm going out on the top of the game! ! !'

When Adam pulled into the secluded 'Montgomery Pines' property, Susan and he were greeted by Murf, and his wife Barbara. Both were wearing casual shorts (Murf's a gaudy shamrock print) and tees along with their wide welcoming smiles. "Congrats, old man," Adam offered as the two men shook hands, and walked together up a pine-shrowded trail toward the spacious lake home beyond.

At the end of the following week, Brenden Anthony Murphy would be officially discharged; calling it quits after twenty-four years. His wife Barbara had invited an intimate group of friends to mark the occasion. The Murphy's had a lovely summer place on four acres of Island Lake shoreline just miles north of Duluth (an inheritence from her wealthy father) and they wanted to share in the occasion. She had invited the Cooneys, the Tryggs, the Rodlands, Holly and her handsome date, three priests—Mickey, Mario, and Frank Polich—along with a few fellow officers that Murf had enjoyed working with over his years on the force.

At most parties, it's quite predictable that the men will congregate to discuss guy things, while the women do much the same apart from their husbands. And, this occasion played out in that fashion; by mid-afternoon it was like two separate parties in close proximity. Barbara, a marvelous hostess, had hired a chef to put on a pig roast, with every imaginable trimming, so that everybody could be free from having to assist with any of the preparations. Being a demure woman by nature, her role was that of a facilitator. One of the officer's wives was a fashion designer, and Barbara invited her to show the ladies what was coming out in the fall.

Murf, for his part, manned the beer keg, and a well-stocked bar, that were situated on the wide patio-deck overlooking the pristine lake. Unlike his spouse, Murf was a natural at being in center stage. His first of many stories that afternoon was designed to poke fun, and—he hoped—somewhat embarass his young colleague. "I'll never forget the first time I worked with Adam," he told the guys. "We got a call on a domestic disturbance: 'shots were fired' the dispatcher warned before we arrived on the scene. After discovering the wife had shot her husband for walking across her freshly mopped floor, I called Sarge Cooney at headquarters…'looks like we have a homicide here,' I reported to Charlie."

Murf winked before looking toward Cooney for confirmation…Cooney nodded as if he remembered the event well. Murf picked up his story, "Cooney wanted to know exactly what happened, so I passed Adam my phone to explain things. Adam told Cooney about the wife's killing her husband for tracking up her wet kitchen floor. Cooney, knowing Adam was a young officer dealing with his first homicide asked: 'Have you placed her under arrest, Trygg?'" Murf paused…"Adam said, 'no sir'. The floor is still wet."

Adam flushed at the laughter surrounding him, but played the straight man perfectly. "I remember it as well as you do, Murf. I did exactly what you, my hardened veteran mentor, had taught me to do in situations like that."

Murf gave Adam a hardy laugh along with a slap on the back. "Well spoken, son." After a long swallow of beer, Murf's expression became more serious…"This guy is gonna be a great cop one day. How can he possibly fail…? He's had my expert training…and he's got three padres to help him out whenever things get too hairy for one cop to handle."

* * *

After a pontoon ride around the lake, all the pork everyone could eat, and the early evening settling in, those remaining at the party came together around a large campfire. Before heading back to St. Gerards, Mickey had to raise a question about the case that had brought so many of them together months before: "What was it that led you guys to Phil Symanski in the first place? I mean, even before the father made his confession down in Iowa?" Mickey had felt like a gorilla had been lifted off his back when the news of the two arrests had made the news months before.

Murf took the question, "First, I think it was mostly Adam's doing. The sports car Phil was driving puzzled him enough to suggest that we check his friend's bank account transactions. From there we found a trail to follow—always follow the money, they say. After that, the two of us began examining Larry Symanski's finances as well as Phils," Murf explained. "That search took us to a stripper at the Saratoga Club, and that eventually led us to a motorcycle shop where drug and hooker money was being laundered by Larry and his associate—a CPA and, believe it or not—a member of the police commission. Larry was connected to a multi-state trafficking ring out of the Cities suburbs—Spring Lake Park, if I remember correctly. He also had some links to a guy on the Red Lake Rex."

Murf left his story hanging, "I'm leaving all that to Charlie, here."

Murf raised his glass in a mock toast to Cooney, "Sorry to be jumping the shit on you my friend."

Adam took a cue from Murf to continue with the story. "But we both hit a wall with Phil's father having the perfect alibi, along with a hundred witnesses, for the night James was murdered. At the time, we thought Larry must have hired a hit man…but that road wasn't taking us anywhere," Adam explained.

Curious, Mickey met Adam's eyes: "Did Phil actually confess to killing James? And, what about the Larsen girl several months later?"

"Not in so many words—Phil's smart enough to avoid saying too much too soon," Murf picked up the question sent to Adam. "He wouldn't believe that his dad had actually fingered him to the cops down in Iowa. After we cuffed him that morning at his place, he sat in the back of the squad next to me on the ride to the station downtown. After a quiet few minutes, Phil started crying his eyes out, 'I'm sorry Adam', he kept telling Adam who was up front and driving. Then he looked out the window for the longest time before asking: 'Will you visit me in prison if I go there?' When Adam didn't give him an answer, Phil shut up big time. Later that afternoon, me and Charlie grilled him. The interrogation lasted nearly three hours, but didn't get us anywhere."

"How did Phil take your refusal, Adam?" Carl Rodland, who had joined the others in the circle, wanted to know. "Adam's never said much to me, and we work together every day."

Adam's voice tightened, "At the station, before I headed back to west Duluth, I promised him that I would keep in touch with him."

"Have you?"

"No…not yet, anyhow," Adam answered.

"Will you? I mean…he's Andrew's…" Carl let it drop.

"I don't know. I left all the contact with Phil to Murf. Now I guess the ball's in Charlie's court. None of us have been saying much about the case for quite a while. The DA and the Symanski lawyers are doing their thing."

Murf nodded without speaking.

"Can you tell us where things are right now?" Susan, who snuggled against her husband's shoulder, asked Murf who had been unusually pensive for the past few minutes. "Adam mentioned to me a while ago that Phil has pleaded 'not guilty'. Is that actually true?"

"Afraid that's where it's sitting right now," Cooney answered for Murf, who didn't look up from his deep contemplation. "His dad claims that his son did the two killings, while the son continues insisting that his crazy dad is framing him. He says that everybody who knows his father knows that he's a pathological liar. It's still pretty convoluted, and the animosity between the father and son isn't helping things get resolved. Now, Phil's girlfriend has come forward with sworn testimony that the two of them were together on each of the dates in question."

"You guys still have a mess to deal with, don't you?" Carl said. "Are you totally off the case, Murf?"

Barbara Murphy answered for her husband, " I certainly hope he's done with it. We've got plans ahead. That's a big part of the reason why I've wanted Murf to hang it up for good—and right now is none too soon. I would like for the two of us to enjoy the years we have left to the fullest. Lots of places we both want to see and things we want to do."

Murphy nodded absently, still self-absorbed.

"Both trials won't be coming up until some time early next year," the yawning Sergeant Cooney added as he stood from his chair and stretched. "So, it's looking like your hubby might not be entirely off the hook yet. I'll do my best to pinch hit for him wherever I can."

82/ 'MAYBES'

The fire crackled and the stars sparkled as the quiet night enveloped the last two couples remaining. The Murphys and the Tryggs were enjoying a last glass of wine while sitting contentedly in the screened gazebo, protected from the aggravation of hordes of mosquitos. "I'm glad we didn't get too wrapped up explaining where the Symanski crap is sitting right now," Adam said to his heavy-lidded mentor. "Did you notice how quiet Father Mickey became when Cooney mentioned that Phil wasn't admitting to anything? He's a compassionate guy…*maybe* all this chaos we've gotten him hooked into bothers him more than we realize. I've been wondering if he's planning to visit Phil between now and the trial."

None of the three listening to Adam's thought offered a conjecture.

* * *

Adam had been waiting all day for Murf to tell him something: "Something that maybe you should know about," is the way Murf had put it when they last talked weeks ago. Before leaving he wanted to venture that question. He was holding Susan's hand when he asked: "Something you wanted to tell me, Murf? I mean…wasn't it something Larry Symanski told you when you first interrogated him at the county jail?"

Murf was slow to answer, "Can't remember what that might

have been," he lied. "Must not have been anything very important. *Maybe* it will come to me later."

"Sounds good to me. Wasn't it you who always told me that it's best to just let sleeping dogs lie?"

"Yep, that I did. No need to wake'em when you don't need to."

Adam stood and helped Susan to her feet. "It's late, we told the Susan's mom we'd be home before ten—it's well after that already. I've, I mean we both have, had a wonderful time today." He felt a lump in his throat that was hard to swallow. Clasping Murf's large hand, he got out a few words that seemed almost stuck in his throat: "Good luck, my friend. I want you to know how much I have appreciated all you've done for me. I'll never be able to…"

"Don't get all choked-up kid," Murf said through a cloud of cigar smoke. He smiled the smile of an insightful veteran: "You'll do the same for some rookie down the road. By the way, something just came to me: Cooney and I have recommended you for a distinguished service citation. *Maybe* that's what it was that I forgot to mention. Anyhow, *maybe* one of these days you'll see a few extra bucks in your paycheck."

"If that what you wanted to tell me, that's great news."

"Yep, that's gotta be it." Murf put his hand on Adam's shoulders, "I'm getting old…need all the beauty sleep I can get these days, you know." Seldom at a loss for words, all Murf could come up with was; "Great seeing the two of you again. Drive safely…and give those two kids of yours a hug for me and Barb." As difficult as it might have been for Adam to compliment the veteran, it was equally difficult for Murphy to accept the heart-felt compliment.

* * *

After leaving the Murphy's party, Holly was thinking some *maybes* of her own. She had never felt better about herself and the future she dreamed of creating. She remembered when Adam first told her that she could be anything she wanted to be. The two of them were having coffee in the diner where she worked at the time. *Maybe* the wheels of that lengthy process were beginning to turn. Looking across at her date, her smile came from a warm place inside. Trevor was quiet and deep—both qualities that she needed in her life. *Maybe* he was the one…the man that she might be sharing her awakenings with. "You promised that you'd teach me to golf one of these days," she said.

Trevor took her hand in his, "*Maybe* tomorrow morning…if you'd like," was all he said. What he didn't say, but wanted to, was "*maybe* we could spend tonight together…and get an early start."

Holly let the invitation hang for a long moment, "It might be nice if I could stay at your place tonight. Then we could…"

* * *

After the Tryggs had left, Barbara Murphy asked her husband, "Why didn't you tell Adam what you said you were planning to? I think you weren't being entirely honest about the pay raise that might come along. I know that's not what you really wanted to tell him. So, what was it, hon? You know I hate secrets."

Murf placed his arm around Barbars's shoulders: "I think I told the truth when I agreed with Adam—'let sleeping dogs lie'. After seeing the love between he and Susan…I just had a feeling that it was best to keep whatever it was to myself. What we don't know won't hurt us, my dear. That's doubly so for my friend Adam."

Murf kissed his wife's forehead and said good night. There were parts of Larry Symanski's confession that only he and Cooney were aware of. No good could possibly come from Adam's knowing what his friend Phil Symanski might have done if things hadn't worked out as they had. The father had told Cooney that his son was planning to start a duplex in Riverside on fire one night while the family was asleep. Why Phil would even consider something so horrific was still a mystery. Murf could only hope against hope that none of those sordid details would be revealed once the trials began.

Lying next to his sleeping wife, Murphy frowned. It was best that Barbara, and all the others, be spared the other threats that had recently come to light…things like he himself being a target in a devious murder spree that included Holly as well. Like always, Murf wouldn't sleep well that night. *Maybe* once he was able to leave all these troubling things behind him…*maybe* then…*maybe* when he turned in his badge next week…

* * *

Phil Symanski smiled after his visit with the well-known Twin City attorney who had agreed to take his case. *Maybe* he could beat the murder wrap with his girlfriend's solid testimony and her father's money. *Maybe* then he'd finally break the manipulative strings of a father he had come to despise. As he looked around the crowded county cellblock at all the losers—mostly druggies and thugs—he felt a swell of indignation…he wasn't of the same cut as they were; he was a sworn officer of the law and thus a tier above the riffraff. Then, from that dark place inside, it struck him…maybe he was a bigger fool than any of them were.

* * *

On his drive from the lake party to the St. Gerard's rectory, Father Mickey pondered the dilemma that may never completely go away. He, along with the two Symanskis, were probably the only three people who knew exactly what had been happening—and why—over these past months. And he was bound by the *seal of the confessional* to never divulge that truth: a truth very much like the one that had tormented his friend Bruno for the remainder of his short life. Bruno had chosen an eternal sleep…*maybe*, Mickey thought, *maybe* he'd find the elusive peace that might allow him to cope with a burden that his late friend could not. He yawned as he pulled off of Grand into Benton Park. And, *maybe* he'd be able to sleep tonight...and wake up refreshed in the morning. He remembered something he'd said one Sunday morning not long ago...mercy he believed was 'joining in the chaos of another's life'. *Maybe* his Lord was telling him to practice what he preached. *Maybe* he would visit the two imprisoned men. '*Maybe*', for Father Mickey, was an enigma...but also a word bursting with unseen expectations. And, *maybe* tomorrow would be his own independence day.

THE END

OTHER WORKS BY THE AUTHOR...

'The Mesabi Trilogy'

To Bless or to Blame (ISBN: 978-0-9724209-0-7)

An historical drama, romance, set on the early Mesabi Iron Range.

Ruthless and driven, entrepreneur Peter Moran is bigger than life in the rowdy mining hub of Hibbing in the early 1900's. A "compelling debut novel" and NEMBA award finalist.

Trade paperback (2002). $18.95

A Blessing or a Curse 978-0-9724209-1-4)

Sequel. Ambition runs in the Moran bloodlines. Obsessed to achieve what his unscrupulous father never could, Kevin Moran plunges into a political battle against the established Iron Range power structure. An historical drama, romance.

Trade paperback (2003) $19.95

Blest Those Who Sorrow (ISBN: 978-0-9724209-2-4)

Sequel. A psychological thriller completes the Mesabi Trilogy. Kevin and Angela Moran are swept far from their familiar Hibbing roots in a page-turner of deceptions and delusions. "A deftly crafted drama!"

Trade paperback (2004) $16.95

Other novels

The Hibbing Hurt (ISBN: 978-0-9724209-3-8)

Murder mystery set in Hibbing, 1956. A racial abduction/homicide stirs the conscience of the ethnically rich Iron Range community. Pack Moran is hard-nosed cop who unravels the complex conspiracy.

"There are no heroes in this tragedy."

Trade paperback: (2005) $14.95

Flag' (ISBN: 987-0-9724209-4-0)

Angry and conflicted, 18 year-old Amos Moran is a runaway who ends up in Flagstaff, Arizona. Connected to earlier novels, this forth generation Moran is a compelling character. Amos witnesses a murder, falls in love with a spirited coed, and risks his own life to save that of an innocent Navajo man. "Action packed!"
Trade paperback. (2006) $13.95

Saint Alban's Day (ISBN: 987-0-9724209-5-2)

The consummate political thriller with a wide Minnesota scope. Amos Moran accepts a controversial political appointment while coping with a psychopath from his past. The prison escapee had threatened his family. Drama builds in McGauley's most provocative story.
Trade paperback. (2007) $14.95

A Passage of Redemption (ISBN: 978-0-9724209-7-6)

Mickey Moran is a misunderstood and disillusioned priest in search of the passion that once inspired his calling. Brian Slade is a destitute young man searching for any thread of hope. The two men aare a contrast in every conceivable way except in their appearance—they have a doppelganger link! What happens to both is a creative masterpiece.
Trade paperback: (2012) $14.95

The Sons of Marella Windsong: (ISBN: 978-1-62890-103-0)

Marella Windsong is a single mother raising fraternal twin sons who are as opposite as night and day. Trevor is night—a brooding teenager and a driven athlete with a vein of recklessness and sudden rage. Travis is day—a sociable, easy-going, academically inclined young man with a fondness for computer gaming. A near-death tragedy results in a reconstructive surgery that will change Trevor's life in ways that will reorder the lives of those closest to him. His surgery turns out to be a 'blessing in disguise' as his raw athletic talent comes to the attention of the Minnesota Twins. Father Mickey Moran once more is the orchestrator of an exciting drama.

Trade paperback: $14.95

The Last Moran (ISBN: 978-1-4951-2557-7)

Sometimes what seems to be an innocent lie can mushroom into something with distressing consequences. Yet, at times, that very same lie can inspire a series of events that will transform the lives of many people in positive ways. When the hidden truth of Mary's deception comes to light, her son and the boy's real father will open their souls with all the emotion that makes us human. Another of Father Mickey Moran's rollercoaster life.

Trade paperback: $14.95

Children's books

Mazral and Derisa: An Easter Story (ISBN:987-0-9724209-9-0)

A spiritually uplifting Easter fantasy involving a mouse and a dove in ancient Jerusalem. A Resurrection miracle occurs in a cave on a Calvary hillside. Trade paper. (2004) $12.95

Santa the King (ISBN: 987-0-9724209-8-3)

An incredible fantasy in which one of the Wise Men is spiritually led to the North Pole where he becomes Santa Claus. The story combines the 'real' Christmas with the delights of Santa. "A delightful story for young and old alike." Hardcover. (2005) $13.95

The Midnight Hour (ISBN: 987-0-9724209-6-9)
A mischievous elf named Nathan almost ruins Christmas for all of the children of the world when he puts a sleeping potion in Santa's hot chocolate. A story that provides a positive message of redemption, and a story that will not be easily forgotten. Hardcover. (2011) $14.95

Minnesota author Pat McGauley is a former Hibbing High School teacher. Born in Duluth, Minnesota, McGauley grew up in Hoyt Lakes. He graduated from Winona State University (BS: '64) and the University of Minnesota (MA). A former political candidate, iron mineworker, regional historian, and state agency commissioner under Governor Albert Quie, McGauley resides in Hibbing, MN and Naples, FL.